EVER MY LOVE

LYNN KURLAND

JOVE
New York

A JOVE BOOK
Published by Berkley
An imprint of Penguin Random House LLC
375 Hudson Street, New York, New York 10014

Copyright © 2017 by Kurland Book Productions, Inc.
Penguin Random House supports copyright. Copyright fuels creativity, encourages
diverse voices, promotes free speech, and creates a vibrant culture. Thank you for buying
an authorized edition of this book and for complying with copyright laws by not
reproducing, scanning, or distributing any part of it in any form without permission.
You are supporting writers and allowing Penguin Random House to continue to
publish books for every reader.

A JOVE BOOK and BERKLEY are registered trademarks and the B colophon is a
trademark of Penguin Random House LLC.

ISBN: 9780515156164

First Edition: April 2017

Printed in the United States of America
1 3 5 7 9 10 8 6 4 2

Cover design by Katie Anderson

To Kara, for always being on my side of the table

Acknowledgments

To Kara B., again, and Amanda O. for all things legal; Tricia B., for weighing the pros and cons of Seattle neighborhoods; and, last but not least, Brandon C., stalwart friend and all-around great guy who gives venture capitalists a good name.

Thank you all for being in the right places at the right times.

As for anything else, I am, to the relief of many, no doubt, neither a lawyer nor an investor, so any mistakes in legal or investing details are entirely mine.

Prologue

*T*he freshly laid wood crackled and popped in the hearth, a fitting accompaniment to the rain falling softly against the roof. A heavy black cauldron hung on a hook over the flame, full of something that steamed as it simmered. A woman leaned close, sniffed, then cautiously tasted what she'd tossed into the pot earlier that morning. She considered, then nodded. It would do well enough for supper. If nothing else, there was plenty of it.

When one wore the title of MacLeod witch, one learned to be prepared for any number of unexpected guests.

Moraig MacLeod continued to stir her stew, happy at the thought of something hot on a chilly fall evening. She imagined her visitor who had yet to arrive might feel the same way. She had no idea who that soul would turn out to be, but she'd felt a shift in the world earlier in the day. She'd had enough experience with that sort of thing to know what it usually meant.

She hadn't always lived in the little house she occupied at present, and she hadn't always had a gift for knowing what was coming her way. Time had taught her many things and led her in paths she never would have anticipated in her youth. Then again, her youth, whilst tolerable enough, was something she tended to leave in the past, where it belonged.

She reached out and pushed a hearthstone back into a spot it seemed determined to liberate itself from and gave thought to the events of the past pair of days.

She didn't often have any sort of commerce with the souls

in the village—they were happy enough to leave her alone with her thoughts in the forest—but she'd had occasion to encounter a handsome young man at the grocer's shop the McCreedys had just opened. He wasn't a local, which had perhaps worked in her favor. He'd been a polite lad and apparently unafraid to carry a sack full of tinned goods home for her. His courtesy had extended to chopping a decent amount of wood as well before he'd joined her for a bit of last week's stew.

She'd been thoroughly delighted to listen to tales of his life in the Colonies, including his recent eluding of his father's clutches long enough to come to Scotland for a few months. And who could blame the boy? Whilst she had heard tales of New York and its glittering finery, who with any romance in his soul wouldn't want to spend as much time as possible where dreams and forests and heather were reflected on the surfaces of still lochs?

The lad had promised to return in a pair of days with materials to shore up a few things in her home, and she hadn't refused the offer. Her skills lay with midwifery and herbs, not hammer and nails. Any help with a bit of repair work on her ancient abode was very welcome indeed.

She gave her supper a final stir, then straightened and walked over to her front door. There had been no knock, but there had been no need for one. The shift in the air had been enough. She opened that door to find a young woman standing there on her front stoop, soaked to the skin and looking profoundly terrified.

Moraig understood that, more clearly than she supposed she would ever admit.

"Sanctuary," the girl pled hoarsely.

Moraig studied her visitor for a moment or two. The gel couldn't have been more than ten-and-five, though it was clear those green eyes had seen more than they should have for one so young. "Who are ye, lass?"

"Ceana Fergusson."

Moraig lifted her eyebrows briefly. If that one was a Fergusson, then she was a McKinnon. She opened her door widely. "Come in."

The girl didn't move. "I tried the keep," she said, looking

as if she had just paid a visit to hell instead. "The stones . . . and the walls . . . the roof—"

"Bit of a storm," Moraig said, because that was a simpler tale for the time being than the truth. "Took the roof right off."

"That was a mighty storm then."

"So it was, lass."

The girl looked at her. "Are you the MacLeod witch?"

Moraig smiled. "I am."

The gel paused. "Would it offend you if I made a sign of ward against you? Just to be safe?"

Moraig laughed before she could stop herself. "Of course not. Do what you must."

Ceana Fergusson did so, then whispered a prayer as she stepped over the threshold. Moraig shut the door behind her, then walked across the rough stone floor toward her sleeping nook. She rummaged about in a trunk for something suitable, then handed it to her guest.

"There you are, lass. Perhaps not stylish, but dry."

Ceana's hands were trembling badly as she took the simple dress. Moraig might have felt justified in suspecting that the cold had gotten to the girl, but she was who she was and she knew better. With the way the child was examining the fineness of the cloth, Moraig suspected questions would come sooner rather than later.

She went back to tending her stew whilst Ceana changed into dry clothing, then she saw the girl seated by the fire before she scooped out a bowl of something strengthening. If Ceana looked at her spoon as if she'd never seen anything so fine in her life, well, what was to be done?

Moraig understood.

She made herself at home on her own stool and waited until her guest had finished her first bowl before she offered more. She added the accompaniment of a large mug of ale because it looked as though Ceana could use the same. It was a pewter mug, as it happened, because Moraig had learned from the former MacLeod witch not to hand guests anything made of pottery. Too fragile for the sorts of conversations that were inevitably had near that stone hearth.

Ceana finished her additional supper with the enthusiasm of one who had apparently not eaten recently. She gulped the remainder of her ale, then set everything down on the floor at her feet. She glanced carefully at her surroundings, shivered, then looked at Moraig.

"I must repay you."

"No need," Moraig said easily. "Highland hospitality, my gel."

Ceana shook her head. "I cannot, mistress. I cannot take charity."

Moraig suppressed a smile at the *and because you're a witch* that had been added not entirely under Ceana's breath. She understood that as well. She considered for a bit, then nodded, as if she'd just hit upon the perfect solution. "I have some mending that needs seeing to, if you can do that."

Ceana closed her eyes briefly. "Witchly items?"

"Even a witch must have warm things for winter," Moraig said mildly. She paused for a moment or two, then smiled. "There is a lad coming from the village in another day or so to help with my roof if that won't trouble you. Perhaps you two can discuss pleasant things whilst you're working."

Ceana wrapped her arms around herself. "I don't think I can take advantage of your hospitality that long."

"Winter is hard upon us, my gel. No need to rush off until you've your feet under you. Your future will wait for a bit longer until you have. Perhaps you might see what the village holds for you in the spring."

Ceana looked at her with large, haunted eyes. "The village is gone, mistress."

"The one near the keep is," Moraig agreed, "but another has taken its place a bit farther down the way." She smiled. "And then there is the wide world beyond that to explore. I'll show you, when you've rested."

"I feel as if I'm dreaming."

" 'Tis Scotland, lass. What else can you expect?"

Ceana closed her eyes, let out her breath slowly, then looked at Moraig. "I think I might do well not to expect anything at the moment." She hesitated. "Who is the lad, if I can ask?"

"Just one with a good heart," Moraig said. "Fleeing an oppressive father, or so I gather, and in need of something to do. Archie is his name, if I remember it correctly. Perhaps you might understand what drives him."

"I imagine I might," Ceana said with a yawn.

Moraig smiled to herself as she rose. She gathered Ceana's supper things up and took them into the kitchen, supposing that room was also something the poor thing didn't need to investigate at the moment.

She soon saw her guest settled on a pallet in front of the fire, then settled herself in her own chair with a fine candle and a good book. If Ceana stared at both as if she'd never seen their like before, well, that was something for the gel to think about later as well.

She looked up from her book eventually to find the girl at her feet sound asleep. There were still lines of tension on her face, but perhaps that was to be expected. One didn't travel as far as Ceana Fergusson had obviously come without having the journey take its toll.

In time, though, those lines faded. Sleep was the great healer. With enough time and good fortune, it could also give one dreams, which was perhaps the most healing thing of all.

Moraig MacLeod, witch for a clan that had once been and would be again, closed her book, and leaned her head back against her chair. She would seek her bed eventually, but for the moment she was content to simply sit in front of her fire, listen to the rain on her roof, and allow herself the pleasure of wondering what the future would hold for that dreaming lass at her feet. She would do whatever she could to nudge things along, of course, but time would do the rest.

It certainly had in the past.

Chapter 1

Scotland in my dreams.

Emmaline Baxter took a firmer grip on the key to her rental car, looked around at the rain-drenched everything, and congratulated herself on successfully getting herself to her present location with her luggage, her sanity, and her person intact. It had been a long journey, in more ways than one, but as anyone with any romance in her soul knew, when you were taking charge of your life and running full tilt into your perfect future, you ran to Scotland.

She stood still, lifted her face to the sky, and savored. It wasn't that she hadn't been rained on enough over the course of her life, but this was Scottish rain. It felt different somehow, as if it were the sort of stuff that had fallen on centuries of history and bagpipers and guys wearing kilts and carrying swords.

It was magical.

That was actually a fairly accurate word to describe her trip so far. She hadn't had any trouble flying from Seattle to London, the train north had been on time, and her reserved car had been waiting for her in Inverness as promised. Getting from Inverness to the village of Benmore had been a bit of an adventure, but she supposed that was due more to weariness than it was to being set free with keys to a car designed to be driven on the wrong side of the road. She hadn't encountered anything more dangerous than the sight of fluffy sheep grazing on hillsides as she'd wended her way north. The day had been a success so far.

She was, however, starting to see the smallest of clouds on the horizon, and it had everything to do with the hotel she was looking at presently.

She put her hand on the wrought iron gate in front of her and studied the place that would be her home for at least the next week. It boasted a grim sort of austerity, a look that would have been right at home in a BBC adaptation of a Gothic novel. It was tempting to speculate on how few amenities she might find inside, but she forbore. As long as she encountered only ghosts in formal dress instead of Norman Bates in a kilt, she would be fine.

Besides, it was November, it was rainy, and it was Scotland. What else did she need? It was tempting to burst into song right there in the street, but perhaps later when she was better rested and more able to convince any potential constabulary that she was just happy, not punch-drunk.

She adjusted her backpack over her shoulder, took a no-nonsense grip on her suitcase handle, and let herself inside the gates. She shut them behind her, then suppressed a yawn on her way up the path to the front door. She ached with weariness, but promised herself somewhere flat to lie down very soon.

The inside of the place was no more welcoming than the outside, but she wasn't there to live, she was there to sleep at night after spending her days dreaming her way through the Scottish countryside. As long as she had a bed, a bathroom, and a place to stash her stuff, she would survive.

She greeted the owners who manned the desk as if it were the last thing that stood between them and inevitable destruction, signed what was necessary, then happily accepted her key and directions to her room. The climb up the narrow staircase was an adventure, and there was more Victorian austerity waiting for her inside her bedroom, but she ignored it. She had ignored all the one-star reviews the inn had earned, so she probably deserved exactly what she was getting. None of that mattered at the moment. She had a turret room, she had rain, and she had Scotland.

Life was very good indeed.

She shoved her suitcase into a corner, dumped her backpack on the bed, then left her room to look for the bathroom. The floorboards creaked badly enough that she wasn't entirely sure she wouldn't go right through them, but fortunately her mission was accomplished without trouble and she was soon back in her room, wondering if anyone would notice if she just took a minute or two to sit on her bed and rest.

That was a mistake, she decided a couple of hours later as she woke with her face plastered against her backpack. She'd thought that taking a sleeper north would have given her a chance to sleep off a bit of her jet lag, but apparently that hadn't been the case. Freezing her backside off earlier that morning while waiting for the rental car place to open hadn't done the job, either.

She sat up, waited until her head cleared, then decided the best thing she could do was just power through the mental fog. She could sleep later.

She staggered back downstairs, considered asking for suggestions from her hosts, then thought better of it. There wasn't anyone at the desk, and those were either pot lids or swords being used in the dining room. She had absolutely no desire to investigate which it might be. She had a phone and knew how to use it. That would just have to do.

She pulled up a travelers' guide to the village of Benmore and its surrounding environs, scrolled through the possibilities, then looked out the front-door window at the rain. That she suspected the blurriness of the scene wasn't entirely due to the rain led her to believe that maybe she would be better off limiting herself to the village for the afternoon. She could leave anything farther afield for the next day, when she would actually be awake enough to get to it safely. For the moment, a good walk was probably the most sensible choice. She left the inn and its *Great Expectations* vibe behind her and went off to explore.

She walked through the village and enjoyed the illusion of being a local simply out for a leisurely stroll. She passed a post office, a touristy kitsch seller or two, and a shop that proudly proclaimed itself Fergusson's Herbs and Sundries. She was an over-the-counter sort of gal when it came to medicine, and she wasn't sure she needed any sundries, so she decided to give the place a miss and keep going. She yawned her way past places she supposed she wouldn't remember in the morning, but made a mental note about the location of the two pubs she'd seen on opposite ends of the main street. No sense in not knowing where to get dinner, if she could stay awake long enough to eat it.

All in all, the village was a very charming place with people seemingly going about their lives in an ordinary, unremarkable way in spite of their spectacular surroundings.

She thought she might envy them.

She noticed a little grocery store tucked into one corner of a weathered building and decided a quick boosting of her blood sugar might be a good idea. She made sure she knew which direction to turn once she left the shop, then went inside.

She wandered up and down the aisles, not exactly sure where to start or what she wanted. It would have been easier to shop if she hadn't felt as if she were walking through thick fog, but there wasn't much she could do about that. Jet lag was, no matter how much willpower a person had, absolute hell.

She picked up a couple of things with wrappers she thought she might successfully remove without undue fuss, then staggered over to the checkout line. She was unfortunately behind a trio of well-dressed women who seemed less interested in paying for their groceries than they were in pestering the cashier. She looked around herself, hoping rather desperately for a chair she could use until they had finished. There was no chair to be found, so she settled for the sturdy support of a steel post. She leaned, closed her eyes, and hoped she could stay awake long enough to get herself back to bed.

"What are you lassies about?" a weathered voice asked.

"We're hunting, aren't we, girls?"

"Grouse season is over," that same well-worn voice said tartly, "which perhaps ye don't ken."

Emma opened her eyes at that. The last thing she wanted was to get downwind of something that sounded very much like a shooting party at Pemberley. She looked at the three women standing in front of her, facing off with the no-nonsense granny manning the cash register, and considered the players there. She couldn't say she knew much about hunting past what she'd seen on TV, but she suspected that heels that high, skirts that short, and jackets that flimsy were definitely not on the *What to Wear* list of any person worthy of being trusted with a shotgun.

The woman behind the counter was dressed very sensibly

in a sweater and a stern look, and she had to have been every day of eighty. If anyone would know about the local grouse season, Emma suspected it would be her.

"Make haste, gels," the granny said. "There's another customer behind you. Come up from the south, too, did you?"

Emma realized she was the one being spoken to. "Ah, actually no," she managed. "I'm here from the States."

"Are you here for the hunt?" one of the girls demanded.

Emma looked at her blankly. "The hunt?"

"She doesn't know what we're talking about," one of the trio said, "though I'd be suspicious of her reasons for coming this far into the woods, no matter what she says."

"I'm just here for the scenery," Emma protested.

"Well, there's scenery enough in the area," one of the other women said shortly, "but keep your eyes off the prize."

The proprietress made a sound of impatience. "He's not a prize, and I don't think he fancies being hunted. Leave him to his peace in the forest."

Emma listened to the trio discuss why an apparently eligible bachelor shouldn't be hiding in the woods and had to admit she was tempted to suggest that those girls perhaps rethink their plans. Guys who holed up in the boonies generally seemed to have good reasons for the same. She envisioned their quarry being an old man, grizzled and lacking critical grooming implements like a razor and shampoo. A bit like Bigfoot, only in a kilt.

"But he's rich," one of the women said.

"Gorgeous," said another.

"Rich."

"You already said that, idiot."

"Is he American?" the third one said, looking slightly confused. "Or British?"

"He's Scottish," the first one stated firmly.

"No," said the second woman just as firmly, "he's—"

"A Sasquatch?" Emma asked.

The huntresses in heels turned three almost identical scowls on her, then gathered up their purchases and started toward the door in a huff. They hadn't gotten outside before they were back in deep discussion about a new strategy for obtaining a sight of the very rich and elusive recluse in the forest.

Emma looked at the woman manning the register and attempted a smile. "Sorry. Couldn't help myself."

The woman smiled. "I've no argument with what you said. Those gels that come up from the south—" She shook her head again. "Not sure they know what they want."

Emma knew exactly what *she* wanted, and that wasn't some guy who had ditched hygiene for too much time alone with nature. She put her things on the counter, then looked casually at the woman ringing them up.

"Is there really a guy hiding in the forest around here?" she asked. "I'm not interested in him—just interested in not getting mugged by him."

"These woods are full of all manner of strange things," the woman began, then she looked over at the door when the little bell jingled. She glared at the man standing half inside the shop. "We're closed, ye wee fiend."

"But Mrs. McCreedy, the sign says you're still open."

Emma had to admit the guy had a point. He also had on some sort of official jacket. Maybe he would know how many innocent tourists the hermit in the woods had scared the hell out of so she would know what number not to find herself added to.

Mrs. McCreedy, apparently the shop owner, pointed a bony finger at him. "I've decided to close up early, Hamish Fergusson, just for you. And so you don't have to ask, aye, 'tis because you fair frightened the life from me last week."

The man named Hamish stuck out his chin. "You were speeding."

"I was on my bloody bicycle!"

"Speeding—"

The woman might have been every day of eighty but she could certainly fling a water bottle like a major league pitcher. Hamish Fergusson ducked back out of the shop and pulled the door shut to protect himself. Emma managed to stop gaping long enough to retrieve Mrs. McCreedy's weapon of choice and return it to her. Who knew when she might need it again.

"Thank you, lass. Very kind." Mrs. McCreedy smoothed her hand over her hair. "That lad is annoying, but what can you do?"

"Run him over with your bicycle next time?"

Mrs. McCreedy laughed, a happy sound tinged with what Emma was fairly certain was potential delight over one Hamish Fergusson lying in a ditch. "Aye, I think I just might. You're staying at Southerton's inn, I understand."

Emma blinked. "News travels fast."

"Small village," Mrs. McCreedy said pleasantly. "From America, did you say?"

"Seattle," Emma agreed.

Mrs. McCreedy nodded. "Lovely place, that. You're here on holiday, then?"

"Yes," Emma said, "mostly. I needed a change of scenery."

"I understand that," Mrs. McCreedy said with a nod. "Plenty of scenery here for the viewing, especially if you've a strong stomach for things of a more . . . magical nature."

"Really," Emma said dryly before she realized Mrs. McCreedy wasn't kidding. She blinked. "You're serious."

"Highland magic saturates these hills, lass. Now, if you'll have my advice on where 'tis to be found, I think I can point you in the right direction."

"I think I might like to know where it is so I can avoid it," Emma said honestly. "I'm not much of a believer in supernatural things." Actually, she wasn't any kind of believer in anything that smacked of anything remotely paranormal.

She paused. All right, so she had occasionally pondered the problem of socks losing their mates, but that was most likely a dryer issue, not ghosts in her laundry. As for anything odd happening in her current locale, Scotland was drenched in history, not things that went bump in the night.

Surely.

"I wouldn't wander overmuch on MacLeod soil," Mrs. McCreedy said, obviously not offended by any inadvertent expressions of doubt.

Emma pulled herself back to the conversation at hand. "MacLeods," she repeated, wondering if she needed to be writing that down. "Are those local landholders?"

"Aye," Mrs. McCreedy said. "The laird James and his brother—his cousin as well—own most of the land in the area." She looked off into the distance for a moment or two, then seemed to come back from wherever she'd been mentally— no doubt wandering over that MacLeod soil—and looked Emma full in the face. "I think I won't say anything else."

Emma wanted to point out that she hadn't said anything at all, but decided that wouldn't be polite. "I don't suppose you would have a map that might tell me which paths I should avoid, would you?"

Mrs. McCreedy looked a bit startled, if such a thing were possible for a woman that seasoned. She continued to look at Emma as if she'd just seen a ghost, then reached under her counter and produced a single sheet of paper. She looked at it for a moment or two in silence, then folded it up and held it out with a hand that shook just the slightest bit.

"This will be what you need," Mrs. McCreedy said. "No charge."

Emma took the map and forced herself not to unfold it and have a look at it right there in the store. The terrible nature of not knowing surprised her with its intensity. Just what did her new map show? Treasure? Haunted castles?

Reclusive millionaires?

The possibilities were endless and past tempting to contemplate, but she didn't want to look like the gawking tourist she most definitely was. She smiled instead and tucked the map into her jacket pocket.

"I'll return it," she promised. "Thanks so much."

Mrs. McCreedy nodded, but said nothing else. Emma wasn't one to endure uncomfortable social situations any longer than necessary, so she escaped the store before anything else weird happened, pulled the door shut behind her, and started back up the street toward her hotel.

She only made it half a block before she couldn't take the suspense any longer. She looked around her in her most surreptitious fashion to make sure she wasn't going to be interrupted, leaned casually against the corner of a building to get out of the wet, and unfolded the map.

Well, that looked a bit like the village, a determination that was made quite a bit easier by the label of *Village* placed on the appropriate spot. That was, however, the only thing about the map that made any sense at all. She didn't want to concede anything that might make her sound crazy, but she had to admit that what she was holding in her hands looked remarkably like a treasure map. She saw a handful of things that could have represented castles or large houses, but the rest was a smattering of Xs, as if some crazy teenager had spent the past year digging around in his father's backyard, looking for loot.

The map wasn't an original, though it looked as if the original had been hand drawn. It was a photocopy, and obviously not fresh off the copier. In fact, she supposed that if Mrs. McCreedy had charged her for it, she might have been tempted to return it and ask for a refund. It was so creased she could hardly see what lay in the folds, and unfortunately those folds seemed to be obscuring the exact location of some of the more prominent Xs. She stared off into the distance for a bit, wondering what she might find there with a bit of effort, then she realized she was doing exactly what Mrs. McCreedy had been doing in her shop while talking about those MacLeod landholders—

She decided quite suddenly that maybe she'd just had enough for the day. A Gothic inn, bounty hunters in short skirts and heels, and now a treasure map delivered by the local green grocer. All of that would have seemed nothing terribly out of the ordinary if she hadn't been wandering around in a fog. All she needed was a good night's sleep and things would look much better in the morning.

She turned and walked back to her hotel. She didn't believe in omens or portents or things of a paranormal nature. She had come to Scotland because there was sky and heather and mountains that reflected on the waters of still lochs. She had more photographs of the same than she wanted to admit to buying, but pictures had been all she'd been able to manage at the time.

Now, though, she had the real thing within reach. What she wanted was to take her view of those raw Scottish elements and hammer them into gold and silver, to immortalize them somehow. She hadn't decided exactly how that was going to happen, never mind how she might use it to salvage her business, but perhaps that was something better left to think about in the morning as well.

She paused and looked up at the gray sky for a moment or two. It was odd that she'd chosen the village of Benmore to land in. The name of the place had come to her a few months earlier, almost as if she'd dreamed it. She knew that wasn't the case, but maybe it didn't matter how she'd wound up where she was. She was there and she was going to make the best possible use of her time.

She got back inside the inn, then managed to get to her

room without trouble. She kicked off her shoes, brushed her teeth, then dug around for pajamas before deciding that was just too much trouble. She shucked off her jeans and felt her way into bed. She realized that she still had on her coat and she hadn't managed to get any dinner, but she was too far gone to care.

She pulled her coat up to her ears, snuggled down in spite of the springs that poked her in the back, and surrendered to the pull of sleep. Her conversation with Mrs. McCreedy echoed in her mind, but she didn't have the energy to even shake her head over it. Maps, recluses, and warnings about magic? Those were all probably things the villagers trotted out simply to keep the tourists happy.

She didn't believe in ghosts, magic, or treasure maps. She liked mysteries that were solved with common sense and good old-fashioned detective work. Anything else was too out there for her.

She would get up in the morning, make a very sensible list of things to do, and leave anything else in the realm of dreams, where it belonged.

Just being in Scotland was magic enough for her.

Chapter 2

A fire crackled and popped in a well-used hearth in an equally well-used pub, reflecting off the faces of three women who lingered north of Hadrian's Wall in search of an elusive and reputedly quite exclusive quarry.

"I reminded us all before in the shop that he's rich," said the first.

"And gorgeous," said the second. "Remember gorgeous."

"Available," purred the third. She looked narrowly at her mates. "If I find him, I get him."

"You don't know where to start looking," scoffed the first. She paused and frowned. "I'm not sure any of us knows that, and that shopkeeper wasn't keen on giving us directions earlier, was she?"

The third young woman waved away the concern. "She probably didn't want to look daft. They swear he lives in this part of the Highlands, near this village, so what else is there to know?"

The first seemed to be unconvinced. "But there are many rich men here. Hard to decide which one he might be, wouldn't you say?"

"But those rich men are married," the second pointed out. "The lairds, that is. But he isn't a laird, is he?"

"Does it matter?" asked the third. "If he cared to, he could likely buy himself a title." She paused. "As we decided earlier, he's a Scot."

"And gorgeous," the second said. "Still."

"I think we're forgetting the difficulty," the first said with a sigh. "He is, as we know, reclusive."

A hush fell over all three as they no doubt considered the difficulties that presented.

The recluse in question sat in the shadows, sipped his whisky, and tried not to draw attention to himself by rolling his eyes too loudly. By now he should have been used to all the scheming and plotting that had dogged his poor self for the past handful of years. There were more sightings of himself than Nessie. As time had passed and the steady stream of fortune hunters hadn't abated, he'd begun to feel a kinship with the waterlogged beast. If he'd been able, he might have asked its advice on how to remain elusive on a long-term basis.

It was surely better than the alternative.

"But he has a lovely name," said the second girl. "Nathan MacLeod—"

"Oh, you're an idiot," the first one said. She seemed to be something of an authority on their current subject. "His name is *Nathaniel* MacLeod."

"His middle name is Fergusson," the third said, "but that likely isn't anything we should say too loudly here. I understand they're not a popular clan in this area."

"A Fergusson," the second said breathlessly. "My granny was a Fergusson. I can use that to bond with him right from the start."

Nathaniel set his whisky aside and decided he'd heard enough. Nay, the Fergussons weren't a popular lot in the area, but that likely had more to do with the local constabulary than anything that lay in the past. Sadly enough, he'd become something of an expert in what had gone on in the past with those lads.

He was also an expert in his own genealogy, which allowed him to state with a fair degree of certainty that his mother had indeed been a Fergusson, his father a MacLeod, and it had been a love match from their first exchanged glance over the threshold of a little cottage in the woods up the way. He had spent three decades enjoying their obvious love for each other before—

Well, before his life had taken a radical detour from what he'd had planned, which was something he did his damndest not to think about any more than he had to. He rose, nodded to the barkeep, and made his way without dawdling from the pub. He heard quick footsteps behind him and cursed himself for not being swift enough to make his escape.

"Nat, you forgot your change."

He stopped on the street and looked back to find Fiona MacLeod standing there. She was, thankfully, just the tavern keeper's daughter, not one of the trio of lassies on the hunt for his reputedly handsome and filthy rich self. "Change?" he echoed.

"Da said you forgotten it. Thirteen pound eight-seven." She smiled. "Likely don't want to forget that much, aye?"

"Definitely not," he said, holding out his hand. If that hand shook, well, perhaps it was dark enough that only he would notice. He gave Fiona a hefty tip, but that didn't erase what she'd said.

1387, if one were to remove critical punctuation.

"You off on another adventure?" Fiona asked.

He wondered absently if he would ever manage to hide his surprise when things caught him off guard. With all the practice he'd had over the course of his very long thirty-five years, he should have been better at it. Unfortunately, he imagined he looked as if Fiona had just planted her foot in his gut, but there you had it. His life was not one fit for lengthy scrutiny.

"Adventure?" he wheezed.

"You know," she said, "all that moneymaking Da says you do. Jetting off to London or New York."

"Paris," he said thickly. " 'Tis Paris this week."

"I wish I could jet off," she said wistfully. "It sounds exciting."

If she only knew. "You have time yet," he said.

"I'm sixteen. Old enough for jetting off."

He managed a smile. "Not with me, lass, but I'll bring you something back from my next trip and let your father inspect it for propriety."

"Oh, would you really?"

He started to assure her that he would, but he was distracted by the feel of something unseen figuratively tapping him on the shoulder. Fate, no doubt, or perhaps one of her more ironic cohorts such as Father Time. He didn't bother to investigate who it might be. He simply advised Fiona MacLeod to get herself back inside, then walked away before he thought he might need to be running.

1387. Those were numbers that didn't care to be ignored for too long.

He jumped inside his decrepit Range Rover, apparently the vehicle of choice for any self-respecting recluse, and wasted no time in getting himself home. If he drove a bit more quickly than he might have otherwise, who could blame him? He had a schedule to meet, a schedule that certainly wasn't one he set for himself. He knew better than to argue when he began to feel the pull of something that, if someone else had been describing it to him, he would have considered completely barking. There were times he almost wondered if he might be losing his mind.

He put his car behind his house in its accustomed spot and let himself in the back door. The only benefit to his current life, he supposed, was finally feeling as though he had a home. Perhaps five years of being rained on and eaten alive by midges was enough to claim his rightful place amongst the ranks of proper Scots.

That last bit he cherished, if he were to be a bit maudlin about it all.

He dropped his keys on the table and went to fetch his gear. The only trouble was, when he felt called on one of these, ah, *journeys*, he never knew how long they would last or what he would find whilst on them. He could only hope the present summons to a time definitely not his own would entail a brief stay. He had emails to check and business to see accomplished in the current day.

The current day. Even thinking it made him sound daft.

He strapped his sword to his back, then pulled it free of the scabbard, just in case. Truly, he had to do something about his current straits. He was definitely the one living his life, but it was beginning to feel a little surreal. Heaven help him if anyone became entangled in his madness.

He helped himself to a couple of chocolate digestives, checked to make sure the fire in his stove was properly banked and the kettle wasn't left on the stove, then walked over to the door. He took a deep breath, opened the door, then stepped outside.

The whistle of a blade coming his way had him ducking before he even thought about what he needed to do to save his own sweet neck.

And the game, as the saying went, was on.

It was noon the next day before he had the chance to truly catch his breath. He stood with a pair of companions inside the safety of the MacLeod keep and was grateful to be out of the rain.

"'Tis unusual that you're back," Angus MacLeod said suspiciously. "A miracle, one might say."

"Ach, leave off, ye fool," Lachlan MacLeod said with a gusty sigh. "He comes and goes as he pleases, as he's been doing for years now."

"If I didn't ken better," Angus continued stubbornly, "I'd say he were a witch."

Nathaniel didn't care for the tone of Angus's voice, as it happened, and generally did his best to do whatever it took to dispel anything that might cause it. When one loitered in a time and place not one's own, it was best to fit in as thoroughly as possible. He shot the laird's son a skeptical look. "Are ye that daft in truth, Angus?"

"He is," Lachlan MacLeod said with a snort. He reached over and slapped Angus on the back of the head. "He's a lad, ye fool, not a witch."

"A ghostie, then," Angus insisted.

"Angus, stop being daft," Lachlan said, sending Angus a look that said he'd do well to shut his mouth very soon indeed. "Never know when he'll come home, but I'm always relieved to see him. Ye might share that feeling when ye think about how he saved yer sorry arse last evening."

Angus mumbled his thanks, which Nathaniel accepted loudly and with an equal amount of praise heaped on the head of Malcolm MacLeod's son, because when one found himself standing in a keep full of medieval clansmen, one also tended to want to be as pleasant and accommodating as possible. Angus had his reasons for not particularly liking Nathaniel, but those were reasons Nathaniel couldn't change for him, so he tended to let them lie.

He accepted a cup of ale from a rather handsome serving

wench, toasted his backside against the fire in the middle of the hall floor, and draped the persona of laird's bastard son around his shoulders like a well-loved plaid. He was happy enough for something warm to drink and someplace safe to linger for the moment. Getting to the keep had been a dodgy business the night before, only because when he'd walked out of his house, he'd walked right into a bit of a disagreement between raiding parties from neighboring clans. He supposed he was fortunate to be alive to even enjoy the memory of those heart-stopping moments.

But since he was alive and warm, he sipped at his strengthening brew and considered the absolute improbability of his life.

He was, as fate would have it, the middle son of a simple Scottish girl and a dyed-in-the-wool Anglophile, grandson of extremely old New York money, and founder of a very successful venture capital group. He owned a couple of cars, played too much golf, and was never equal to resisting the lure of coffee in a Parisian sidewalk cafe. His life wasn't without its complications, but he had good attorneys and a decently large bank account.

That was in the present day.

Or, rather, in the future. He suppressed the urge to scratch his head over what was when. There were times he honestly had trouble keeping his location straight.

His location at present—in the past, of course—was Scotland during the glorious Year of Our Lord's Grace 1387, and his persona was medieval bastard. He was extremely thankful that Malcolm MacLeod had been so indiscreet about his liaisons, for it provided him with a perfect cover story. That he needed a cover story was something that left him wanting to find something very strong to drink if he thought about it too long.

Then again, the situation on a fundamental level was absolutely barking. It was certainly nothing he'd ever expected to have happen to him, partly because he had never considered the possibility of the same. Time travel? Medieval clansmen with his death on their minds?

Ridiculous.

Yet there he'd been one pleasant afternoon, enjoying a round of golf with his father and his sire's younger brother at a small, private tournament, wagering substantial sums of money in an effort to distract his relatives and himself from his own mother's untimely death, when a spot of inclement weather had sent him and his uncle scampering for cover in a handy bit of forest.

That was when things had gone awry.

He didn't like to think about the handful of days that had followed. Apparently one did not present himself at the keep of the laird of the clan MacLeod in 1382 without a damned good reason as to why he found himself there. He'd thought his subsequent capture and deposit into the dungeon had been a practical joke at first, but that had only lasted a few hours before he'd realized that he had fallen down some sort of rabbit hole to another world entirely. He'd seen his share of dungeons, true, having indulged his curiosity for medieval things fairly regularly over the course of his life, but he'd never seen one that had been as full of vermin and muck as the place he and his uncle had been tossed.

He'd honestly thought he would never see daylight again.

He and his uncle John had been hauled out of that hellhole eventually, though, and he had immediately trotted out a tale that would have made his most despised medieval literature tutor weep with joy. He had styled himself a lesser of the bastards sired by the laird himself, and identified his companion, Master John, as a very pious priest who had been so overcome by the opulence of the castle's dungeon that he had been rendered mute. He supposed he had been extremely fortunate that Laird Malcolm's roaming habits had unwittingly furnished him with details for a tale that had satisfied most everyone within earshot.

His escape from that alternate, medieval reality had been as abrupt as his entrance and just as inexplicable. He'd eventually staggered out of that Highland forest without his uncle because he hadn't been able to talk the fool into coming with him. That was perhaps a tale better thought on at a different time.

He'd run all the way back to his rental cottage, found himself proper clothes, then checked his phone only to find that his father had been taken to hospital in Inverness. He'd arrived there in time to watch his father clutch his chest a final time, then shuffle off this mortal coil.

He'd been devastated.

He'd gone through the motions of grieving, burying, and settling affairs. He'd thought his inadvertent trip to the past had been an aberration, something he could chalk up to bad luck and too much whisky.

He had quickly discovered how wrong he'd been.

That had been five years ago. He was currently older, wiser, and thoroughly and unwillingly fluent in medieval Gaelic. He had absolutely no idea how that improved his life in modern-day Scotland, but he supposed it might come in handy at some point. It certainly came in useful in the past, which was currently his present.

He had another long drink of ale. It seemed the very least he could do.

He looked around the hall at present for any stray, inebriated priests, but his uncle was nowhere to be found. John was a mystery. He had indeed flirted with the idea of being a vicar in the twenty-first century, but he had also been a compulsive gambler, an obsessive golfer, and a lover of all sorts of drink. His wife was gone and his children off and grown. Perhaps in the end it didn't matter to the man where he found himself, though Nathaniel suspected his uncle missed the links. No amount of trying to convince him to come back to the future had swayed him, so Nathaniel had left him where he was and watched over him as often as time permitted.

As for himself, the traveling back and forth at the whims of a pocket watch–clutching worker of destiny—perhaps it was Father Time with his hand on the wheel, as it were—was starting to wear on his patience, but he was still trying to work that out. When he spent at least half of his life with a sword in his hands, trying to keep his head on his shoulders and his belly unpierced by medieval steel, he tended to look at the viscidities of modern life with a bit more who-gives-a-damn than he might have otherwise.

It was a bit like a chess game, he had decided. He wasn't unaccustomed to games of strategy when it came to his business so he understood the principles well enough, but he didn't necessarily care for them in his private life. His time in the past, he had come to believe, was governed by the accomplishment of something that only he could see to. Once that deed had been done for that particular foray into a time not his own, he was always free to go home until called for again. Why there wasn't another bloody MacLeod clansman capable of doing what he did, he couldn't have said.

It was just so damned gratifying to be needed.

"Weel, let's be about it then," Lachlan said, setting his cup on the floor and stretching his hands over his head. He grinned evilly at Nathaniel. "Best blend into the forest as usual, aye?"

"As you say," Nathaniel agreed.

If there was anything he was a master at, it was blending in. He supposed he'd learned the art early on thanks to his parents, both of whom had perfected the skill of being whatever they'd needed to be at the time to appease family and friends, then carrying on with their own lives when alone. He had honestly never thought the skill would be so useful to him, but life was, as he tended to admit after a pint or two, extremely strange.

After all, it wasn't every day that a man could find himself worrying about where his most volatile stocks would land before market close in the morning, then find himself using a medieval broadsword to defend an equally medieval keep later on that afternoon.

"Those bloody Fergussons," Angus complained. "Why are there always so many of them?"

"'Tis a good thing," Lachlan said, slapping his cousin on his back. "What would we do else?"

"Wench ourselves to death?" Angus suggested.

Nathaniel refrained from comment lest Angus think following in his sire's thoroughly indiscreet footsteps was a good idea. He left the keep with the rest of the rabble, but had to admit Angus had a point. It was amazing how those damned Fergussons could lose so many men yet still have so many more to bring to any given skirmish. He had begun to suspect they abducted unwary travelers on a regular basis and gangpressed them into service.

If the battle began with a prayer offered by Nathaniel's uncle, well, he wasn't going to argue. He didn't consider himself particularly religious, but he wasn't opposed to a few prayers offered on his behalf. The truth was, as much as he had grown fond of the men he now called cousins, he didn't fancy himself dying on a medieval battlefield whilst defending them.

The morning wore on in a way that wasn't particularly pleasant, but he hadn't expected anything else. The Ferguss-sons were determined and the MacLeods weary from not just the current skirmish. He'd already had a full report of what had gone on earlier in the week whilst he'd been off seeing to other business. If that business included more keeping his investments in the twenty-first century in good shape and less roaming through medieval forests, scouting for Malcolm, well, who was to know—

"Nat, duck!"

He did without thinking, thanked his cousin—however many generations removed he might or might not have been—for saving his life for the second time that day, then turned his mind back to the battle at hand. It looked like it might go on for quite some time.

At least the future, as he knew very well, would keep for a bit longer.

Chapter 3

There were, Emma had to admit as she examined her current location, several benefits to driving on the left. The first one that came to mind was that when she got distracted by scenery, she apparently naturally fell off the left side of the road into a bit of gravel instead of to the right into a bit of a long, winding river.

That was definitely a glass-half-full kind of moment.

She turned the engine off, then indulged in some restorative deep breathing. The morning had gone fairly well, all things considered. Hot shower, clean clothes, and an almost edible breakfast had gotten her off to a good start. She hadn't hit anything in the village and she'd found her way out into the countryside without any trouble. Of course, her very recent brush with plunging her car into a river had been a thrill—and not a good one—but if that was the worst that happened to her, she wasn't going to complain.

She took a final deep breath, then peered out her windshield at the forest that loomed up in front of her. The road leading into it didn't have any no trespassing signs posted, but she wondered if it might be wise to figure out where she was before she wandered onto someone's private property, found herself mistaken for a grouse, and shot on sight.

She checked her phone but had no signal. Inconvenient, true, but nothing that couldn't be solved by using a good, old-fashioned physical map. At least that way she could very reasonably claim ignorance if she wandered where she shouldn't have. She pulled out the map she had bought earlier that morning at the local gas station and unfolded it until it took up most of the front seat. It was easier that way to ignore Mrs. McCreedy's map that she hadn't gotten around to taking back to the generous, if not slightly misguided in matters of magic and its ilk, shopkeeper.

The damned thing was almost burning a hole in the passenger seat, truth be told. She could smell the metaphorical smoke from where she was sitting.

She forced herself to focus on the map in front of her. She realized very quickly that it wasn't going to be of much use except on more substantial journeys. The village was there, true, but that was about as detailed as it got.

She looked without much hope for some sort of exploded view of where she was, but found nothing. She sighed, folded the map back up into approximately its original configuration, then looked over at what she really didn't want to become too familiar with. Unfortunately, she knew she had no choice but to concede the battle. She took the treasure map and carefully flattened it against the steering wheel, trying not to get too involved in wondering what in the hell the mapmaker had been thinking when he'd whipped out quill and ink. Maybe Mrs. McCreedy's great-grandson had made it for her and those were things he'd buried for future use. She wasn't opposed to running into a decent cache of either snacks or doubloons, so she threw caution to the wind and gave the thing a serious look.

She identified the village, then traced her route north and a bit east until she thought she might be looking at where she was. She didn't see any Xs crowding around her, so she supposed she was safe from whatever those indicated. A little wander in the forest couldn't go too wrong. She was comfortably far away from the MacLeod family castle and not anywhere close to Cameron Hall, so maybe she could avoid any encounters with angry lairds as well.

She folded the map up carefully and put it back on the passenger seat. The world didn't end, so she took that as a good sign, then climbed out of her car and locked it behind her. She put her phone in her pocket, realized there was no hope of getting her bearings from the sun, then set off in what she hoped was the right direction.

The forest, once she entered it, was a bit spookier than she'd expected it to be, but she supposed that had more to do with the cloudiness of the day than it did the shadows in the trees. She zipped her slicker up and continued on, undaunted. No self-respecting Seattleite would have paid any attention to what was falling through the branches, and she was nothing if not seasoned when it came to rain.

Stillness descended until all she could hear was her footsteps against the earth. Peaceful, true, but having nothing to do but walk gave her far more time to think than she wanted. She'd put on a good face as she'd been bolting from her life, but she was quickly coming to the realization that she had to face where she was.

The truth was, she was at a crossroads. She was a year or so away from being thirty, recently broken up with her boyfriend, and staring at the ruins of a business she'd built from scratch. What of her savings she hadn't been forced to give to an unscrupulous business partner, she had used to buy a ticket to Scotland and pay in advance for the first week of her stay. She had six months' worth of income stashed in an account she had managed to keep separate from any business entanglements, but once that was gone, she was out of money and out of options. She had to come up with a solution, and fast.

The solutions she didn't consider were insolvency, piracy, and moving back in with her highbrow parents who would sigh lightly every time they saw her. Where that left her, she just didn't know.

She had to pause and take several deep, strengthening breaths. She would manage it. All she had to do was put one foot in front of the other. She had come to Scotland for inspiration, and she fully intended to find it. She just needed some peace and quiet to get her head together and start a new chapter in her life.

Things definitely could have been much worse. She could have been living eight hundred years earlier and been on her way to the Tower of London. She could have been missing her shoes. She could have had a lifetime of the same sort of truly awful tea and stale cookies she'd made a pre-breakfast meal of back in her room. When she looked at it that way, her life was looking pretty good.

Besides, in the end, where she found herself was her choice. She had chosen to take a step out into the darkness without knowing whether her foot would find solid ground or thin air.

She really wanted it to be the former.

At least that seemed to be the case at the moment. The ground was solid if not a little damp, the air was clean and crisp, and she had on warm clothes. She couldn't complain.

She continued to wander through woods that seemed more like a church than just trees and sky and rain and felt the peace of her surroundings sink into her soul. She paused at one point only because she found herself standing on the edge of a lake. She watched the water for quite some time, hoping she wasn't trespassing. The tracks she had begun to follow were definitely something she remembered from Mrs. McCreedy's treasure map, but that wasn't much help because she couldn't remember where they'd led to. Even more unsettling was realizing she should have made a better mental note about the location of those mysterious Xs.

She looked around herself casually, but didn't see any pirates peeking out from behind the trees, primed to attack if she got too close to their hiding places. She did, however, see a house sitting on the shore, actually not far from where she stood. It didn't look all that inhabited, so maybe it was a holiday rental. For some odd reason, the thought of that made her heart leap a bit. Maybe she would ask around in the village and see if it was for rent. She could think of much more uncomfortable places to pass the winter.

She let that thought settle around her for a bit, enjoyed it probably more than she should have dared to, then turned away with at least something of a plan in place. Peace, quiet, and water in front of her for a couple of months. Who knew where that might lead her?

She walked through the forest in the opposite direction from the lake. It was cold, but she had shoes and a decent jacket. With any luck, one of those pubs in the village would have a fireplace with an empty spot next to it. She would have her ramble, then go have lunch and get warm. The thought was appealing enough to leave her walking more quickly than she realized until she had to stop and catch her breath.

She frowned. Was that ringing?

It wasn't her phone; it was more a metal on metal sort of

sound. She pulled her phone out of her pocket and checked it just to be sure, but that wasn't what she was hearing. She looked around herself and considered. She couldn't see anyone nearby, but what did she know? Actually, for all she knew, it was that rumored recluse hiding in the trees in front of her, sharpening his knife and fork before he grabbed her and plopped her into a boiling pot of water to cook her up for supper.

She rolled her eyes at herself. Admittedly, there was something about the woods she was standing in that was, well, *unusual*, but it was the sort of unusual that no doubt accompanied anywhere that found itself in Scotland. She took hold of her inclination to have a peek at things she should probably have left alone and started to give it a stern talking-to, then she blew out her breath. She knew she was going to have a friendly little look at what was going on, so there was no reason to tell herself otherwise. If she found something odd, she would just turn and run like hell. That useful plan made, she continued on silently, then came to a halt at the edge of a clearing with far less grace than she might have hoped for on another day.

No, it hadn't been her phone making that ringing noise.

It had been the guys with swords in front of her making that ringing noise.

She had to reach out and put her hand on a tree, not necessarily because she wanted to lean on something, but because she was having a difficult time trying to decide what she was looking at and she needed something real to hold on to. She couldn't say for certain, but it was reasonable to suppose the guys in front of her could have been either actors on a movie set or a reenactment group taking things way too far.

Or they could have been hallucinations.

It was tempting to really give that idea the nod of approval it deserved. There was even a mist surrounding the men fighting there, as if they were truly part of some of group that existed only in her dreams.

Scotland in my dreams. She'd actually thought that, hadn't she? Maybe she needed to be more careful in the future with what went on inside her head.

The battle, if a battle it was, was like nothing she'd ever seen before. Actually, that wasn't completely accurate. The filthy clansmen shouting, the men dying, and the metal swords

clanging were everything she'd ever seen in movies, only this
was a hundred times more intense—

A dark-haired man stumbled suddenly out of the fog. He
caught sight of her, then stopped so suddenly, he almost lost
his footing on the slick forest floor. He was covered in what
looked like blood, but surely it was just some sort of stage
stuff, or something he'd bought down at the local costume
shop.

It looked real, though, and so did he.

If she was hallucinating, she found she didn't want to disturb it. She stood, frozen in place, and tried not to breathe too
loudly. If she kept very still, she might get a decent look at her
companion before he disappeared.

He was beautiful, and she could say that as someone who
had spent her share of time dispassionately judging the models
she'd drawn in numerous art classes. His face was planes and
angles, but in such perfect symmetry that she almost took her
phone out and grabbed a picture so she could do his features
justice once she had a pencil to hand. He was much taller than
she was, likely a trio of inches over six feet, and looked as
though he spent a fair amount of time working out—though
she supposed that came less from time spent at the gym and
more from time spent with, well, a sword.

Good heavens, she was losing her mind.

His eyes were green. She could see that from where she
stood.

He looked as if he'd just run into a wall, but perhaps that
expression of surprise was what most hallucinations wore
when they found themselves facing a human. It was the only
explanation she could come up with on short notice, and it
seemed reasonable enough to her.

"Damn it to hell," he blurted out.

She listened to him add several other things she didn't quite
catch, though she had to admit he had a very lovely accent.

Yes, she was indeed losing her mind. It was the only thing
that made sense.

He stepped backward, then ducked. She knew why, because
she'd heard the whistle of sword coming his way as well. She
clapped her hands over her eyes because, really, the last thing
she wanted to see that morning was some guy meeting his end
on the end of a sword. She waited for the sound of a sword

whistling through the air, or a scream, or yet another crisply enunciated curse.

But she heard nothing.

She took her hands away from her eyes, then blinked a time or two.

The glade was empty. Well, it was empty except for a bit of mist and the sound of rain falling lightly against the last of fall's leaves. What she should have said was that it was missing every last one of the men she had just been looking at not a handful of moments before.

She felt something slide down her spine that wasn't quite terror but really couldn't have been called anything else. She stood there, frozen in place, her fingers digging into the bark of that tree, hearing that man's voice ringing in her ears.

Then she turned and ran.

It was certainly the most sensible thing she'd done all year. She ran until she burst out of the forest, then she kept running until she had flung herself inside her car. She locked the doors, turned the car around, and drove like a madwoman back to the village.

Her teeth were chattering and her hands on the wheel were extremely shaky, but that was just because she was cold. She hadn't just seen anything odd. Perhaps she'd had a waking dream brought on by truly the worst cup of breakfast tea she'd ever had in her life. And those things that she'd found to accompany that tea? Awful. She wasn't sure what to call them, but she suspected that not even smothering them in chocolate would have redeemed them from their resemblance to sawdust. The hot breakfast downstairs hadn't done anything for her except convince her that she wouldn't be signing up for it again.

She reached the village without getting lost, no mean feat considering her state of mind but perhaps less impressive than it might have been if there had been more than one road leading into and out of the most substantial nod to modern civilization in the area. She parked, locked her car, then wasted absolutely no time in going straight up to the turret room in her hotel. She locked the door, crossed over to stand in the middle of that room, and shook.

She shook until she thought maybe her trembles came less from terror and more from a serious dip in her blood sugar level. She reached for her phone to see what time it was, only to realize she didn't have her phone. She looked around her frantically, then looked out her window to see if she'd dropped it in the front garden. Her case was royal blue and white so it surely should have stood out against the grass—

She forced herself to think about where she'd been so far that day. She'd had it on her way into the forest, but she'd had it in her hand, not in her coat pocket. She remembered reaching for that tree, but couldn't remember if she'd been holding on to her phone as well or not. It was possible she'd dropped it on the floor of her rental. Heaven knew she'd been concentrating on other things besides setting it carefully down somewhere safe.

She forced herself to leave her room and retrace her steps back to her car. She searched the whole thing thoroughly, but found nothing but those damned maps that had caused her so much trouble already. She straightened, stood next to her car, and let out a deep, shuddering breath. There was absolutely no way in hell she was going to go back to that haunted forest and look for it at the moment. Not when it was cloudy and gloomy and probably going to get dark at the most inopportune moment possible.

Highland magic.

Well, if that was what they wanted to call it, more power to them. She thought *hallucination* was a better term for whatever was going on up the way, but she didn't imagine she was going to want to argue the point with anyone any time soon.

She thought, though, that she might need to make some adjustments to Mrs. McCreedy's map.

She pulled her coat more closely around herself, but that didn't help matters much. She was starving, cold, and more than a little freaked out.

The first could be solved easily enough. She locked her car, then headed for the pub farthest away from her hotel, hoping the walk would do her some good. At least there she might find the company of real, live people.

Fifteen minutes later she had ordered herself a decent meal, avoided another encounter with the Terrible Three from Mrs. McCreedy's store, and was settling into a corner near the fireplace, a comforting cup of tea on the table in front of her.

She leaned her head back against the worn bench, closed her eyes, and tried to forget what she'd seen.

"I won't speak ill of them, but you do what you like."

"'Tisn't ill-speaking to speculate," said another voice stubbornly. "And you must admit, odd things go on up in those woods."

"Aye, and goodly amounts of money come flowing down from them into the village to benefit the likes of you, so don't blether on about what you think you know."

Emma wondered if the present was the proper time to get up and ask if she could have her lunch to go, but unfortunately she was just too tired to move. If that lack of enthusiasm led to hearing a few things that might explain a few other things, well, she wasn't going to protest. Fortunately for her, the old man prone to blethering seemed perfectly happy to dish with the rest of his buddies, which worked for her because she was perfectly happy to eavesdrop.

Though after a few minutes, she wondered why.

Highland magic was apparently just the beginning of the odd things that went on in the area. Ghosts, bogles, an influx of gold diggers from down south: those were all discussed at length, with judgments passed accordingly.

But then their voices lowered and the juicy stuff was brought out and presented for examination.

Emma listened through a lovely lunch of chicken and veg, though she had to admit after a few bites that she was only chewing out of habit. What she really wanted to be doing was using her energy to make noises of disbelief over the things she was hearing.

Time-traveling lairds? Money dug up from gardens? Murder and mayhem that stretched through the centuries and found itself solved in times and places not her own and with medieval implements of death?

She had to have another gulp of tea. All that was starting to sound more plausible than she would have wanted to believe, especially that last part about swords.

She was actually rather glad she'd already finished her meal because she had certainly lost her appetite. She grabbed her coat and made her way as inconspicuously as possible to the front door. She paused outside on the sidewalk and wondered if she might really be losing her mind. That seemed like the most reasonable thing she'd thought all day, which probably should have given her pause.

She pulled her slicker more closely around herself, gave herself a good mental shake, then walked off back toward her hotel. She wasn't losing it, she was just tired. She would go back to her temporary home, pretend it was bedtime not noon, and pull her covers over her head.

She would consign her day's events to the receptacle entitled *Jet Lag Hallucinations*. Then she would take hold of the reins of her life and get back to her very sensible way of doing business. Maybe she would find out who owned that cottage on the loch and see if they wouldn't rent it to her for a month or so. It would make a perfect home base to use while she put some miles on her rental car and explored the nooks and crannies of the Highlands.

The one thing she was sure of was that she wasn't about to go near that very strange part of the forest again. Her phone could rot there for all she cared—

Well, she couldn't survive without her phone, which meant she would have to go back and look for it. She looked up at the sky, which was, unsurprisingly, obscured by clouds. That was comforting, actually, but didn't do anything for helping her know how much more daylight she might have. The very last thing she wanted was to get lost in the forest because she'd gone looking for her phone when she should have waited until morning. Besides, if she waited until morning, perhaps anything spooky might still be sleeping off a long night spent doing what it did to inspire the locals to greater heights of tall-tale telling.

She paused on the steps leading up to the inn's doorway and looked back over her shoulder at the garden there. It was a rain-soaked delight with plenty of places where shadows lingered even in daylight. She shook her head, primarily at her own silliness. Her encounter earlier had been nothing but her imagination running away with her. She had worked herself up over the thought of running into a recluse, added to it the odd nature of Mrs. McCreedy's map, then had a close brush with a river while she'd been driving. It couldn't reasonably have been anything else. Not Highland magic.

Definitely not the sight of a green-eyed man in a ratty

kilt that she suspected she would have a very hard time forgetting.

She turned her back on the garden and walked inside the inn. A restorative nap, a decent supper later, and absolutely no more unnecessary venturing into the forest. She would have another look at Mrs. McCreedy's map and mark the whole area it illustrated as off-limits.

Then she would get to the business she had come to Scotland for without any more undue and unsettling distractions.

She studiously ignored the fact that what she had come to Scotland for were dreams.

Chapter 4

Nathaniel stood in the kitchen of his house that overlooked the loch and stared at what lay there so innocently on his table. Well, his sword was there as well, which
was perhaps not such an innocent thing, but at least it was
cleaned up and awaiting its usual trip into the back of his closet
for safekeeping. What he was looking at next to his sword was
what gave him pause.

It was a mobile phone.

It wasn't just any mobile phone. It was a relatively
unscathed, Scottish-flag-encased mobile phone that someone
had quite possibly dropped in the forest earlier that morning
before she had made a hasty trip back to wherever she'd come
from. He'd already spent part of the afternoon trying to unlock
it with no success whatsoever. Frustrating, but hopefully not a
portent of things to come.

He had to assume the phone belonged to that dark-haired
gel he'd seen in the forest—though perhaps saying that he had
seen her didn't quite describe the encounter. He had been in
the past when he'd almost run bodily into her standing in the
future.

Or at least he hoped she'd been in the future.

He'd almost lost his head as a result of his surprise, but he'd
managed to save his sweet self and pull back into his proper
time period. Or, rather, the time period where he'd been loitering. At the time.

He sighed deeply. His life was, he had to admit, extremely
odd.

At least he was safely tucked into the modern part of his life for the moment. He picked his sword up and carried it back to the bedroom, then hid it behind a trio of hand-tailored suits he only wore when forced. He looked at them for a moment or two, then decided it wasn't a good use of his time to think about when he might need to wear one of them next. He shut his closet door and went back into his kitchen. He considered what to do about that phone lying there on the table, then decided perhaps it wasn't unreasonable to venture into the village to see if he couldn't find its owner.

There was an added benefit to that piece of altruism, and that was potentially eliminating the possibility of someone lurking in the woods nearby, looking for her phone and perhaps seeing things she shouldn't. Heaven only knew he encountered enough of those sorts of women as it was. Why the rumors that went around the pub about him weren't enough to frighten them off, he surely didn't know.

He put the phone in his pocket and made sure his house was put to bed for the moment. No sense in giving anyone reason to execute a rescue of his stove, again perhaps seeing things they shouldn't have.

Besides, he needed dinner and a stiff drink. He didn't keep anything in his own house save a few bottles of wine that were too expensive to casually open, simply because he'd had his own brush with drinking too much and he knew better. But a pint down at the pub or a glass of whisky at someone else's table? That he could do.

He looked at his mobile, then cursed the lack of reception in his house. It was almost as if he lived in some sort of time warp where modern conveniences just didn't exist.

He didn't allow himself to start down that well-worn mental path. The irony of it was just too much.

He would obviously have to head to Inverness soon if he wanted to see what those of the legal profession were combining. He tended to think that no news was good news when it came to lawyers and their business, but for all he knew, he would be on a flight to JFK to deal with them sooner rather than later. At least in New York, he didn't have medieval clansmen trying to kill him.

Unfortunately, that respite never lasted very long.

Half an hour later, he was walking into McCreedy's for the

barest of necessities, grateful he'd caught her before she closed up for the evening. Mrs. McCreedy was busy tending a pair of well-seasoned widows, so he nodded politely to the three of them and went about his own business. If he lingered a bit until the shop was empty, well, who could blame him? He didn't trust very many, but that woman behind the counter was one of them. She'd gotten him out of more than one tight spot with a nod toward the back exit.

He made polite chitchat with her whilst she was ringing up his tins of nonperishables, then leaned casually against her counter and laid the phone down.

"Any ideas?" he asked.

"Ah, a proper Scottish tribute right there," she said approvingly.

"Unfortunately not mine."

"Did you pinch it from some southerner who vexed you?" she asked sternly. "Not sure I'm in the market for stolen mobiles, lad."

He smiled. "Nothing as nefarious as that, I assure you. I found it in the woods near my house."

"And you didn't try to unlock it?"

"Would you expect anything else?"

"You're a canny one, Nathaniel, to be sure." She picked the phone up, studied it, then looked at him. "You didn't see the owner?"

He wasn't sure he dared admit that he might have, but he supposed there were reasons enough why he might have seen a gel in the woods.

"I think I may have seen her in the area," he conceded. "Tall, dark-haired, a bit too thin."

Mrs. McCreedy nodded knowingly. "I've seen her. She's here for a week at Southerton's inn, though I don't know how she'll manage that long there, things being what they are in that house. I think she came from the States to take in the scenery."

"Brilliant," he muttered. "They're coming across the Pond to look for me now."

"And aren't you a fine catch," Mrs. McCreedy said with a laugh. She raised her eyebrow and shot him a look. "If I were fifty years younger, don't think I wouldn't be fishing for you.

As for the other, her you're wanting is at the pub, or so I heard a bit ago. Her name's Emma, if you're interested."

"Your spy network, Mrs. McCreedy, is no doubt the envy of Her Maj's secret service."

"If you only knew, my lad," she said sagely. "If you only knew."

He didn't imagine he wanted to know more than he already suspected, so he simply wished her a good evening and escaped whilst he still could. He carried his sustenance out to his car, then walked up the street to the pub.

There were two pubs to choose from in the village, though he supposed the ever-increasing tourist trade would have supported more. He chose Keith MacLeod's place because it was the more touristy of the two, and he favored it precisely because of that. It put him more often than not in the way of those who came to try to flush him out of the forest, but it kept him out of the way of most of the locals. He definitely had good reasons for that, and those reasons were, put simply, the laird from up the way, the laird's brother, and that same laird's cousin. Those lads tended to frequent the tavern down the street.

He had done a flawless job of never encountering any of them over the past five years, and he thought it was best that it stay that way. Having more than a passing acquaintance with James MacLeod's fourteenth-century progenitor was odd enough. That he was actually doing any, er, *time traveling* was likely something that would have seen him safely installed in the local insane asylum if anyone knew, and that was something he wanted to avoid. The very last thing he wanted was to be answering any questions from James, Patrick, or Ian MacLeod about his own activities.

He'd heard the rumors about them, absolutely barking speculation about why those three looked as if they had simply up and stepped out of a medieval battle scene.

It was absolute rubbish, of course. James MacLeod and his kin were just men with a terrible fondness for the past who had made themselves a little kingdom there near the forest. He wasn't about to tell them about any of his own adventures, no matter if they might or might not have been kin. He was a MacLeod, true, but there were MacLeods aplenty in Scotland.

For all anyone knew, he was related to that lad over on Skye. His own sire had traced his lineage to yet another branch of the family, but Nathaniel supposed no one he knew would be interested in that.

He realized with a start that he was fair to finding himself in true peril a heartbeat before he walked into that trio of London lassies he'd seen several days before. He spared a moment to marvel at their tenacity before he ducked into a darkened alleyway. He slipped around the back of the pub and ventured inside the kitchen. It certainly wasn't his first time using that entrance, and he suspected it wouldn't be his last. He almost ran bodily into Fiona's father.

"Keith," he said, relieved. "Good to see you."

Keith MacLeod, yet another of the innumerable MacLeods in the area, pursed his lips. "Hiding, Nat?"

"You know me," Nathaniel said, giving the kitchen a cursory glance to make certain there were no huntresses, stray medieval clansmen, or American gels with long, dark hair hiding amongst the veg.

"I do," Keith said, "and I trust you, which is likely more important, aye?"

Nathaniel looked at him then. "Sorry?"

Keith blew out his breath. "You, having a care with Fiona. She's young and apparently mad for you."

"I can't imagine why," Nathaniel said, "and I'm old enough to be her father."

"So I keep telling her," Keith said seriously. "Complain about your knees a bit more and perhaps she'll believe you. Now, what do you need?"

"Besides a safe haven and a whisky?" Nathaniel asked. "Information, mostly. Have you seen a woman with long hair, maybe a Yank?"

"She's up at Southerton's, but Mrs. McCreedy likely already told you as much. She just left here a few minutes ago, so you might catch her if you run. I'll have supper waiting when you get back, if you like. Takeaway or not?"

Nathaniel opened his mouth, then realized he didn't know. He'd been dealing in the currencies of life and death for the pair of days so deciding what he wanted to eat, never mind where he wanted to eat it, was simply beyond him. He looked at his host helplessly. "I have no idea."

Keith nodded toward the back door. "Be off with ye then, laddie. I'll have something waiting for you after you've found your prize."

Nathaniel rolled his eyes with what he hoped passed for a dismissive laugh, then slipped out the door and made his way to Southerton's. He saw one alleyway blocked by an SUV, so he continued on to the far side of the garden and rounded the house to the front.

He wondered when it was he would stop running into things that potentially spelled his end. He hid behind a trellis and peered at the little tableau standing there in the light spilling down from over the front door.

Damn it, what next?

He had the distinct feeling his anonymity was about to become a fond memory, and that had everything to do with those three women standing there.

He recognized his American quarry right off and realized he had grossly misjudged the fairness of her face. Quietly beautiful, if her looks could be thus qualified. What he wanted to do was sit down and paint her. A pity he had absolutely no skill with paintbrush or pencil. He wondered absently if she would sit still long enough for him to learn how to use either.

There was, he noticed with a certainty that surprised him, something slightly fragile about her, something that said she'd had just about all she could take that day. He realized he was reaching for the dirk down the side of his boot only after he realized that he was neither in a time where he could rush out and defend her nor carrying a dirk.

He set aside the alarm he felt over those realizations and forced himself to turn his attentions to the other two women standing there. Unfortunately, he didn't have any problem identifying either of them.

The wench on his Yank's right was none other than Sunshine Cameron, countess of Assynt. He didn't know much about her past what she looked like, but she seemed to keep that ferociously competitive Robert Cameron in check, so Nathaniel supposed she must be fairly strong-willed herself. But that wasn't what gave him trouble. It was that she was standing across from her sister, Madelyn, the lady of Benmore, wife to one Patrick MacLeod.

The same Patrick MacLeod who happened to be brother to

the laird up the way, a man Nathaniel absolutely didn't want to visit with over a pint down at the pub.

Perhaps he should have added *genealogy expert* to his résumé. Just trying to keep straight all the people he had to avoid was becoming a part-time job.

"I don't know how he found me."

Nathaniel listened to the sisters comfort the woman he could only assume they knew, then it occurred to him what she'd said. Who had found her, and why was that so upsetting? He could certainly understand being stalked, but his reaction was generally annoyance, not fear.

He eavesdropped shamelessly and gathered that she had been discovered by someone she had left behind quite happily in the States, and she was unhappy enough about the turn of events that she was considering changing lodgings. She seemed highly uncomfortable about that as well. Money worries, perhaps, or simply an unwillingness to pack her gear. Who knew?

He pulled away from the temptation to trot out and hoist a sword in her defense—again, something he realized uneasily that he'd already been tempted to do. She was a mystery and one he had no interest in investigating further. He had enough of them in his own life without adding another to the mix.

"And I've lost my phone. I think events are conspiring against me."

It's Fate, he wanted to call out, but decided it might be best to just keep that thought to himself. No sense in drawing attention to himself unnecessarily.

"Let's go borrow a flashlight and we'll come look around the garden one more time," Sunshine said. "I'm sure it's around here somewhere."

Nathaniel wondered if it might be wisest just to drop the phone and run. If he were especially clever, he might manage to just set the damned thing on the front step and bolt before anyone was the wiser—

"We'll fix the other, too," Madelyn MacLeod offered as they made their way back inside. "Patrick can make that happen."

Nathaniel suspected Patrick MacLeod could make all sorts of things happen. He stood there and contemplated what the lord of Benmore might need to be fixing for longer than he should have. He realized what he was doing when he saw three lassies with torches returning to the outside.

There was no time like the present to get the hell out of Dodge, as his American cousins might have said.

He supposed, as he sprinted past the front door, that his direction had been ill-advised, but he wasn't at his best. He didn't want to look and see if he'd been spotted, but damn his curiosity if it didn't get the better of him. He cast a quick glance at the trio of women standing just inside the doorway.

They were looking at him as if they'd just seen a ghost.

He decided it was best not to try to sort that for them. He vaulted over a hedge of roses, cursing the rip in his jeans and the cuts on his hands that he earned as a result, then ran bodily into a black Range Rover. He should have remembered it was there given that he'd seen it not a quarter of an hour before, but he was, as he'd noted before, not at his best.

The window was down, which he didn't think was a particularly good thing. He was fortunate he hadn't landed in the lap of—

Well, hell. That was Patrick MacLeod's Range Rover, and that was the young Himself sitting behind the wheel. Nathaniel pulled himself back from where he'd been plastered half inside the man's car, grasped the roof to hold himself upright, and tried to catch his breath.

"Need help, mate?" Patrick MacLeod asked politely.

"Oh . . . ah—"

Nathaniel thought he might best serve His Lordship by reaching out and helping him retrieve his jaw from where it had suddenly fallen to his chest. He had the feeling that Lord Patrick's condition had less to do with the potential damage to the car than it did the fact that he might as well have been looking in a mirror.

Patrick's mouth moved, but no sound came out.

Nathaniel supposed he had an unfair advantage, having given the potential for the current encounter a great amount of thought beforehand, but he wasn't above using that advantage ruthlessly. He smiled pleasantly.

"Lost my cat, what?" he said in his best Etonian accent. "Must continue the search, sorry."

Then he did the wisest thing he'd done all day: he turned right and fled.

The man's headlamps went on, but Nathaniel didn't linger in their light. He bolted back up the way to the pub, met Keith at the back door, and tossed him twenty quid.

"Your change—"

"Please, nay," Nathaniel said, with feeling. If he had to hear any numbers he didn't want to hear, he would simply sit down on the ground and weep. He took his supper and jogged back to his car, praying he wouldn't see anything else he didn't want to see. The Yank's phone burned a hole in his pocket, but he ignored that as well.

Altruism? What absolute rot it was. Never again.

He would have to get her damned phone back to her, but it would have to be done without kicking up a fuss. He should have just dropped it in the garden and let her find it, but the grass had been damp. He would just have to wait until the next day, then take it and leave it somewhere she could find it—perhaps at Mrs. McCreedy's.

He got himself out of the village without encountering any stray noblemen in black SUVs, then continued on his way home without pausing to check his email or do any of the business he should have been doing. It would keep, and so would the phone in his pocket.

He would worry about the rest in the morning.

Chapter 5

E*mma* stood on the front steps of the inn she had just checked out of and wondered if she would spend the rest of her time in Scotland seeing handsome men popping out of shadows while never getting to actually meet them.

There was something about the guy she'd just watched run past her, though, that was uncomfortably familiar. She wasn't ready to swear to it, but she suspected he was the one she had seen earlier in the day, in the forest. The obvious difference was that he was darting across front gardens and leaping over hedges instead of stumbling out of medieval battle scenes, but it was hard to deny how much he looked like that guy with the sword. She was almost tempted to ask Sunny and her sister if they'd seen him before, but then she would have had to explain where she had seen him before and she thought that might just make her sound more crazy than she already felt.

"Let's go grab dinner at my house," Madelyn MacLeod said, "then we'll get you settled."

Emma dragged herself back to the matter at hand and looked at Sunny's sister. "You know, on second thought—"

"Oh, no," Sunny said cheerfully, "you don't want any of those. Come on, this will be fun."

Emma held on to the handle of the suitcase she shouldn't have packed in such a rush. "I'll be okay," she said firmly. "I'm already paid through the week here and—" She had to take a deep breath, because she simply couldn't bring herself to finish that sentence.

She was paid through the week, damn it, and she didn't

want to spend the money to double book herself into another place, especially since she hadn't asked for a refund at her current spot. She hadn't dared. Mrs. Southerton had checked her out, then tapped her *No refunds, no matter the reason* sign meaningfully. Emma had realized there was no point in arguing.

That she'd even had to contemplate arguing was, in short, devastating. One of her less savory reasons for having come to Scotland had been to get away from a rather messy past—more particularly her ex-boyfriend, who had contributed so heavily to that messy past. That he should be continuing to make life miserable for her shouldn't have surprised her. That he had tried to get her kicked out of her accommodations surprised her even less. What baffled her was how he'd known where she was, but that was maybe something she could think about later.

She took a deep breath and looked at her companions in turn. "I honestly do appreciate the rescue, but I can handle this. I had a moment of weakness there, but I'm fine now."

Madelyn touched her arm briefly. "Emma, let us help you, just this once. Sunny and I have both been where you are." She paused. "Well, Sunny might not have been, because she's had the good sense to date great guys, but I understand completely what it's like to be involved with someone who turns out to be the world's biggest jerk." She smiled. "When I came to Scotland to take my dream vacation, my ex-fiancé got here first and just about ruined my life."

"Oh, I don't think that'll happen," Emma protested, in a last-ditch effort not to impose. "Sheldon's annoying, but I can handle him."

Madelyn looked at her in surprise. "Sheldon? Sheldon Cook?"

Emma knew she was wearing the same look. "Yes, actually," she said in astonishment. "Do you know him?"

Madelyn reached over and took Emma's suitcase from her. "I've had a few legal dramas with him. Please, let me have the chance to make his life miserable." She shook her head. "How in the world did you ever get mixed up with him?"

"It's a long story," Emma began.

"Fabulous," Sunny said, taking her backpack away from her. "We have plenty of time. My husband's in London, so I'm camping out with Maddy. You can fill us both in over dinner."

"Then we'll deal with finding you somewhere else to stay." Madelyn looked at Sunny. "Jamie has that little place not far from the lake that he bought last year. Wouldn't that be perfect?"

"It would be," Sunny agreed. "Great location."

Madelyn looked at her sister blankly, then she smiled faintly. "Well, I understand the view is excellent."

"That's what I've heard, too," Sunny said with an answering smile.

Emma suspected something was going on, but she didn't bother to pry. Her own sisters were famous for inside jokes between themselves, so she understood how that went.

"I know my brother-in-law has been looking for someone to stay in the place and air it out," Madelyn said. "I'd honestly be very surprised if he didn't pay you to do him the favor."

"But you don't even know me," Emma said. She looked at Sunny. "I only took your class for a few months—"

"And wasn't that a fortuitous crossing of our paths?" Sunny said with a smile. "You need a place to crash, Jamie needs a property manager, and Maddy wants to give grief to some scumbag lawyer I'm guessing annoyed her back in Seattle." She slung the backpack over her shoulder. "Everyone wins."

Emma attempted a smile, but failed. "I don't know what to say."

"No need to say anything," Madelyn said cheerfully. "We're thrilled to have company. Oh, there's Pat parked over there. Let's get home and get dinner started."

Emma would have attempted a last protest that their help was just too much for her to accept, but she found herself too busy trailing after the Phillips sisters across the garden and over to the side gate. Emma guessed that was indeed Madelyn's husband getting out of that SUV parked there. He opened the back up, then turned to look at them.

She almost had to sit down.

He looked so much like the guy she'd seen before in the medieval costume, she could have sworn they were brothers.

"Pat, this is Emma Baxter," Madelyn said. "Emma, my husband, Patrick."

Emma shook his hand and babbled something she hoped

didn't sound completely unhinged. It took her a moment or two to rein in her surprise.

"Do you have a brother?" she asked, because that sounded more reasonable than asking him if he himself routinely dressed in a kilt and faded in and out of mist in the woods. She wasn't sure how wondering the same about a potential brother was any different, but she was really reaching for anything that sounded remotely normal.

Patrick MacLeod looked slightly startled. "One, aye. Do you know him?"

She realized she was in too far to escape without sounding crazy, so she decided she would just keep going and look confident. "He didn't go running through the garden just now, did he?"

Patrick took her bags from his wife and sister-in-law, put them in the car, then shut the hatch. He turned and looked at her. "That lad I think you saw is a local, but I've never met him. I understand he owns the cottage on the loch."

"We were just thinking about him earlier," Madelyn said with a smile. "Nathaniel MacLeod, isn't it?"

"The very same, I believe," Patrick said. "He came vaulting over the hedge just now and left a dent in my car."

"What was left of *him*?" Sunny asked with a laugh.

"He ran off before I could find out," Patrick said. He looked at his wife and lifted his eyebrows briefly. "Odd happenings in Scotland, aye?"

"Very," Madelyn agreed. "Maybe we should have made the effort to go visit him before now, all isolated and alone like he is out there without neighbors."

"Or we could continue to just let him have his privacy," Patrick said wryly. "If he's hiding, he probably just wants to be left alone."

"I don't know how he manages that," Sunny said with a snort. "I think there isn't a socialite in London who hasn't pinned me at a party to ask me about him."

"What do you tell them?" Madelyn asked.

"I say that I understand he's molded from all the rain, he's extremely ugly, and that all those rumors of his staggering wealth are grossly inflated." Sunny looked at Emma. "I guess you'll know better than the rest of us how much of a recluse he is, given that you'll be living next to him."

Emma smiled weakly. So that was the guy everyone seemed to be hunting. That was obviously how he'd perfected that sprint he'd demonstrated for them earlier.

"Well, as long as he's not dangerous," she managed.

"Meek as a lamb, I'm sure," Sunny said cheerfully. "I think he travels a lot, actually."

Emma didn't want to speculate, so she simply got into Patrick's SUV where invited to, then realized what she was missing. She turned and looked at Sunny, who was sitting next to her. "I'm forgetting my car," she said, "and really, this is too generous—"

Patrick handed his keys to his wife, then hopped out of the car. He opened her door and held out his hand. "I'll bring it along for you."

"I couldn't—"

"You could," he said easily.

She dug reluctantly in her purse and found her keys, then handed them over slowly. "It's the gray Ford in the back."

"I'll find it," he assured her. "See you gels at home."

Madelyn got into the driver's seat and looked over her shoulder. "Feel like you're being kidnapped?"

Emma smiled in spite of herself. "A little, but I'd rather think of it as a very welcome rescue."

"Ulterior motive," Madelyn said airily. "We're counting on you to dig up dirt on that reclusive Nathaniel MacLeod. Sunny and I have been trying to figure him out for the past couple of years with absolutely no success. No one seems to know anything about him."

"That they're willing to tell," Sunny corrected. "I think Mrs. McCreedy knows a lot more than she's willing to divulge."

"Do you think he's dangerous?" Emma asked casually. "Really?"

"Mrs. McCreedy says he's delicious," Sunny said, "which is her highest level of praise, so I would say reclusive? Yes. Dangerous? No." She shrugged. "People come to Scotland for various reasons, I suppose, and privacy is definitely one of them. The rumor is that he was born here, so maybe he just feels like it's home."

"Or he doesn't want to deal with the London social scene, which you apparently love so much you can't seem to stay away from it," Madelyn said sweetly.

Sunny hit her sister, Madelyn laughed, and Emma supposed they wouldn't mind if she let them have at each other. She was suddenly finding it difficult to breathe in and out without wheezing. She'd had her own reasons for coming to Scotland, and privacy had been very high on her own list, damn it anyway.

She wasn't at all comfortable with how easily Sheldon had tracked her down.

She made the occasional bit of polite chitchat with the sisters as they drove to Madelyn's house, tried not to gape at what was less a house and more a small castle, then followed the sisters inside. The first room she saw was apparently the great hall, though it was relatively cozy in spite of its size. She would have asked for details, but she was suddenly distracted by the sight of a large, thuggish-looking guy walking into the room with a kindergarten-age girl on his hip and a pair of squirming toddlers corralled under his other arm.

"Mum, Uncle Bobby isn't going now, is he?" asked the older child.

Uncle Bobby looked like he might need to get to the nearest brawl sooner rather than later, but Emma supposed it wouldn't be polite to say as much.

"He's got things to do, Hope," Madelyn said as Uncle Bobby swung her down and promised her he would be around whenever she needed him but he was definitely not wearing pink nail polish no matter how much she whinged about it.

Sunny took one of the other toddlers, snuggled it close, then leaned closer to Emma. "One of Patrick's bodyguards, not a relative," she murmured. "Terrifying, isn't he?"

"Very," Emma managed. Bodyguards? Who had bodyguards up in the wilds of Scotland?

She wasn't sure she wanted to know.

"The kids adore him," Sunny continued. "He's sort of like a huggable pit bull."

Emma could understand how that might be a desirable thing in a babysitter. She would have felt perfectly safe walking through the roughest part of town if Uncle Bobby had been babysitting her.

"I'm going to try to get my little one here down for bed in the guest room," Sunny said, "but I'll be back in a bit."

Emma looked at her seriously. "Honestly, Sunny, this is too much," she began. "I don't even know where I would begin to repay any of you—"

"If you knew what others had done for me over the past handful of years, you wouldn't think this is much at all," Sunny said seriously. "You'll pay it forward, I'm sure, and you really would be doing Jamie a favor by staying in that cottage. I imagine Patrick's already called him to work out details." She shrugged. "You could offer him money, I guess, but he wouldn't take it. When you meet him, you'll see why. He's laird of the glen, and you've stepped inside his borders."

"Very, ah, monarchical."

"And that, my friend, is the understatement of the year. I'll give you my number before you go. We can get together for lunch in a few days and you can fill me in on what Seattle gossip we don't get to tonight. Maddy will want to come, too, since she knows your ex. I'll be back in a minute."

Emma nodded, then found herself standing alone in the great room of a house belonging to people she didn't know, in a country she didn't belong to, without really a place to stay that felt secure.

Just what in the hell had she gotten herself into?

Patrick peeked around a corner suddenly. "Dinner?"

She'd had an early dinner at the pub, but she thought she could manage something else. It would give her something to do besides wring her hands. "Wonderful," she croaked. "How can I help?"

"Come chop veg, if you like."

It seemed like the least she could do.

A couple of hours later, she found herself sitting at the table enjoying coffee and dessert. Madelyn and Sunny both had gone to see to more family bedtime routines and she was left with the good lord of Benmore. She had already been assured of a place to stay for as long as she wanted it, though she honestly wasn't sure she could accept it.

"So, a spot of trouble?" Patrick asked mildly. He looked at her. "Madelyn didn't gossip; she just thought I should know a few details so I didn't make a hash of supper conversation."

Emma managed a nod. "Ex-boyfriend," she said.

"Madelyn says she knows him. One of those vile lawyer types, I understand."

"Isn't your wife a lawyer?"

He smiled. "Indeed she is, and a very good one. But this lad of yours, does he not want to be your former boyfriend?"

She put her fork down because that seemed to remove the possibility that she might drop it at an untoward moment. "He didn't like getting dumped," she agreed, "but it's less about wanting me back than it is about wanting me destroyed." That was understating it, she supposed, but maybe that was all Patrick needed to hear.

"Some people have a very hard time letting go of things," Patrick said philosophically, "especially when their pride has been wounded." He leaned back in his chair. "Did your former boyfriend know you were coming overseas?"

She shook her head. "I didn't think it was any of his business any longer where I went or what I did." She didn't add that she had left the States in part to get away from him, though she supposed Patrick would figure that out on his own.

He frowned thoughtfully. "So you discovered late this afternoon that your Sheldon had called," he said.

"My *former* Sheldon."

Patrick smiled. "Of course. What did Adara say he'd wanted? I'm assuming she was manning the front desk."

She felt a little queasy. "The village is that small?"

"It is," he agreed, "and yet still there are places where a body might have, shall we say, a bit of anonymity."

She could only hope. "She said that someone had called, wanting to know when I'd checked in and how long I was staying. Apparently she'd tried to stall him, but he was very aggressive. He told her he was my fiancé and I'd forgotten to give him money for our wedding before I'd left, so he needed to get in touch with me right away."

"Clever," Patrick said with a sigh. "And, again, you hadn't told him anything about your plans."

"I haven't talked to him in months. I can't imagine how he knows I'm even in Scotland, never mind that I was there at the inn." She sipped her coffee to give herself time to think for a moment or two. "The only people who know are my parents, but I made them promise to keep their mouths shut."

"Did they fancy him?"

"You could say that."

He smiled. "Family can be . . . opinionated."

"I'm suspecting you would know."

"My older brother has a hard time believing I can drag myself from one end of the day to the other without his aid," Patrick said dryly. "My fists have no trouble telling him when I've had enough, but I don't imagine you can sort things that way."

"That and poisoning Sheldon's bourbon aren't options," she agreed. "So here I am, left with the only option being to run."

"It has its place," he said, "and I've done it often enough myself in the past." He considered. "I think if you've a mind to allow the trail to stop at the inn, I can help you. Your hire car could be returned and you can stay at the cottage. We have a little runabout you can also use as long as you like."

"Oh, I couldn't," she said without hesitation. "Renting your cottage—"

"Rent?" he echoed with a smile. "Nay, lass, you're working there for the winter, didn't you know? Caretaking and all that. You'll surely need a car. I'm doing this strictly for my benefit, of course. I don't want to find my lane cluttered up with your rubbish ex-boyfriends."

She couldn't even bring herself to smile. "Lord Patrick—"

"Patrick," he corrected, "and you should know I'm accustomed to always getting my way. I can't get to Inverness for another pair of days—I'm assuming that's where you hired your wee runabout—but we'll go then, if that suits. I'll see you out to the cottage now, then I'll go have a word with Adara and throw the Southertons off the scent. I can slander a Yank barrister as well as the next lad."

"Hey, careful," Madelyn said, walking back into the kitchen. "Mind your manners."

"National pride," Patrick said archly.

"Oh, I know all about your national pride," Madelyn said sweetly. "It's why I never want to go see sights with you, remember?"

Emma watched them as they discussed briefly the difficulties of an American trying to see English sights with a Scottish husband and had to admit that she envied them their obvious happiness. She had no idea how long they'd been married, but it looked as if it had been a blissful union for decades.

Time was a funny thing.

"Emma, you must still be exhausted," Madelyn said, putting her hands on Patrick's shoulders. "I imagine Patrick can let you follow him there, then show you how to start the fire. Just call me in the morning if you have trouble. Those old stoves can be tricky." She smiled. "It took me a bit not to feel like I was about to burn the house down, but I'm sure you won't have that problem."

Emma could only hope. She couldn't believe she was accepting help from almost perfect strangers, but at least for the night, she couldn't see any other alternative.

She thanked Sunny and Madelyn for a lovely evening, then followed Patrick outside to her waiting car. She didn't remember as much of the drive to the cottage as she should have, and she definitely struggled to memorize directions for starting the stove up the next morning, but she didn't think anyone would blame her.

An hour later, she was snug and warm in a cottage that she was certain no one would simply discover on a whim. Sheldon would have no idea where she was, neither would her parents. For all she knew, not even that privacy-lover Nathaniel MacLeod would run into her unless she put herself in his path.

She considered the small bedroom, then settled for a couch that found itself fairly close to the stove. She pulled the blanket up to her ears, snuggled down, and felt safe for the first time in longer than she wanted to think about.

No wonder that reclusive Nathaniel MacLeod hid in the woods.

She thought she might understand.

Chapter 6

Nathaniel decided that if he didn't get hold of himself soon, he was going to be missing critical parts of himself because some fourteenth-century clansman was going to cut him to ribbons before he realized there was a sword coming his way. He was so befuddled that he was starting to run into things in both the past and the future without paying them any heed.

His present situation was proof enough of that. It should have been so innocent, the current morning where he found himself in his proper century with nary a medieval clansman in sight. A little run along a path he'd been down countless times, a bit of peace for thinking, and an ear cocked for the sound of rental cars carrying women on the hunt for the recluse up the hill. His light exercise should have been accomplished with no trouble and no fanfare.

Instead, he'd practically run into trouble before he'd seen it coming. In his defense, he'd never before seen anyone inhabiting that little cottage James MacLeod apparently owned. He had no idea who had owned it before—he thought it might have been Ryan Fergusson—but the point was, he'd never had to look out for any lodgers on his morning exercise.

This was also the first time he'd ever paused to watch smoke coming out the front door. He stood there and watched the doorway belch out a coughing woman as well. He noted, with an emotion he couldn't quite identify right off, that it was his Yank.

A more romantic lad than he might have suspected there was something akin to Fate at work.

He realized once he was on her front stoop and pulling her away from the smoke that she was staring at him as if she'd seen a ghost. He didn't suppose he was all that much to look at, though the lassies who came hunting him seemed to feel differently. At least he'd left his sword at home, a happy decision he generally made differently. One never knew when one was going to be called on to investigate some happening or other in the past.

He suppressed the urge to sigh. His neighbor obviously recognized him from his ill-advised dash across Southerton's garden. Best to help her concentrate on something else as quickly as possible.

"The Aga?" he asked.

She nodded, wide-eyed.

"Trying to burn the house down, are you?"

"That hadn't been my plan," she said, "but I'm afraid I'm about to."

He moved past her and peered inside the kitchen. It looked to be less an out-of-control fire than a fire that had been fed damp wood. He had experience enough with that. "I'll see to it. Just wait here."

"Thank you."

He walked into the house and grabbed the first thing he laid his hands on to hold over his mouth and nose—it was unfortunately something of hers that smelled lovely enough that he paused to appreciate it before he thought better of it—then set to saving James MacLeod the trouble of building himself a new guest cottage.

He threw open a few windows, brought the night's fire back to life properly, and set the kettle on for tea. He brought in a goodly stack of wood to dry out thoroughly, then supposed that was the best he could do short of taking up residence on her sofa and tending the stove constantly. It took less than half an hour, long enough to decide that perhaps he should invite himself to breakfast.

He turned, leaned back against the sink, and looked at his new neighbor, who was standing just inside the door, watching him. He returned the favor, now that he was at his leisure to give her a proper examination.

It was as he'd decided the night before. She wasn't beautiful in the fashion magazine way that most of the gels who came hunting him seemed to be, but lovely in a quiet sort of way that left him wanting to sit down and study her a bit longer. She was fair skinned, pale eyed, and possessing a waterfall of dark, straight hair flowing down her back. He wondered why she was in Scotland, though perhaps the question of why she was half a mile from his house was more pressing.

He answered the latter easily enough. Madelyn and Patrick had obviously offered her refuge in James MacLeod's cottage. It also occurred to him that he'd heard her say something about someone having tracked her down in Scotland. He could understand how she might not like that, given his own experiences with the same.

"Breakfast?" he asked, reaching for a reasonable distraction from his unhelpful thoughts.

She pushed away from the doorway. "Of course. I'll see what I can put together."

"Nay," he said, "I mean, would you like breakfast?"

She stopped and looked at him in surprise. "You want to buy me breakfast?"

"Not anywhere in the village at this hour that you would want to try," he said wryly. "I'll dig around in your fridge and see what's available."

She gestured toward a basket on the counter. "I don't have anything in the fridge, but Patrick left me that." She paused. "You know, Patrick MacLeod. He's the lord of Benmore Castle."

"Aye," Nathaniel managed, "so I've heard."

"I haven't put anything away yet."

"Too busy trying to burn the house down?"

She wrapped her arms around herself. "Apparently so. This isn't exactly how I wanted to repay them for their kindness."

"I'm vexing you for sport," he said. "Don't give it another thought. A bit of air and the place'll be good as new. In the meantime, we'll put our feet up and stay warm whilst we're eating the five-star meal I'm about to prepare. Any ideas what the young Himself sent along?"

"None," she said. "I was too tired to look last night."

"Then have a seat, lass, and I'll see what his tastes run to."

She sat and watched him. He was far too old and jaded to

find himself made nervous by a woman, but it had been a very long fortnight. That was surely the only reason his hands were less steady than he would have liked them to have been.

Patrick MacLeod had gifted her enough food to last a week, which spoke well of his generosity. It was odd to be the unwitting beneficiary of that, but there was nothing to be done about it. It was also odd to be preparing to sit down to breakfast with someone he didn't know whilst that someone was wearing nightclothes and wrapped in a shawl, but perhaps she didn't realize what she was wearing. Perhaps she didn't care.

Perhaps he was just a comfortable sort of lad who put all around him at ease with his delightful self.

He eventually set down two plates of eggs, sausage, and fried tomatoes in as much of a nod to traditional English fare as he could make, then sat down across from her with the intention of making polite conversation.

"You're wearing pajamas," was what came out instead.

Truly, he needed to make a change in his life. Too much time in medieval Scotland had obviously done his table manners a disservice.

"I thought you might make off with my cheese if I left you in here unsupervised long enough to change."

He almost smiled. "I cooked you breakfast," he pointed out.

"And eyed that cheese with undisguised admiration." She looked at him knowingly. "You can't deny it."

He wondered if it were possible to fall in love at first sight. "Caught," he said, then he smiled and applied himself to a decently fashioned breakfast made from ingredients provided by a man he hoped he would never encounter at the local greengrocer.

His life was complicated.

But what he'd had to work with had led to a decent meal, even if he did say so himself, and he was pleased to see that his companion wasn't above tucking in with a decent amount of gusto. He wasn't above it, either, which led to more eating and not a great amount of conversation.

"You are a very good cook," she said finally. She sat back and sipped her tea. "Thank you."

"You're welcome." It was on the tip of his tongue to say that he imagined anything would have been better than what that poor Southerton woman could produce whilst having to live under the same roof with her husband, but he stopped himself just in time. He shouldn't have known anything about where his breakfast companion had been staying, because he shouldn't have been loitering in the garden of her inn.

Never mind anywhere else she'd apparently recently been.

He looked at his hostess and supposed there was no time like the present to trot out decent manners.

"I suppose introductions are in order," he said. He held out his hand. "Nathaniel MacLeod."

"Emmaline Baxter," she said, shaking his hand briefly, "but don't call me that. There are lots of you MacLeods in the area, aren't there?"

"It would seem so," he agreed. "Either happy marriages or not enough to do during long winters; I never can decide which it is." He helped himself to his own tea. "Here for vacation?"

"In this cottage or in Scotland?"

"Take your pick."

She pulled her shawl more closely around herself. "I'm running away," she said. "Well, maybe less running away from something than running to something better. Scotland seemed like a good destination."

He could understand that well enough, given how much running he'd done over the course of his life.

"What about you?" she asked.

"Ah," he said, grasping for something undemanding and mostly honest to say, "I was born here." It was a bit more complicated than that, but he wasn't sure how much detail she would care for.

He'd been born in Inverness, in hospital, though his ma hadn't been at all keen on the idea. She put her foot down with his younger sister and had her in a medieval crofter's hut, to his father's dismay. His older brother had been born in the States, something he still complained about.

As he said: complicated.

"I've been a bit of a gypsy," he said, settling for fewer details than more, "but I've been here in the Highlands for the past few years. Needed somewhere to land, and this seemed as good a place as any."

"Not to criticize or anything," she said slowly, "but it's pretty remote up here."

"Privacy is vastly underrated." He shrugged. "A good satellite connection and nowhere's too remote, is it?"

"No, not anymore," she agreed. She studied him for a few minutes in silence, then smiled faintly. "You know what they say about you in the village, don't you?"

He could only imagine. "I'm the recluse up the hill?" he asked politely.

"The filthy rich, eminently desirable, and irresistibly attractive recluse up the hill," she corrected. "And that was just what I heard in the checkout line at McCreedy's."

"Irresistibly attractive?" he repeated.

"Or so I heard."

He laughed in spite of himself. "I fear to pursue that lest you find me other than self-effacing, but feel free to tell me more if you like."

She shrugged. "I don't know any more than that. Just wanted to see what you thought." She looked at him seriously. "I wanted to make sure I'm not living next to a serial killer."

He would have made light of that, but there was something about the tone of her voice that resembled what he'd heard the night before at the inn, so he kept his damned mouth shut. She was running, and obviously from something she didn't like. If she wanted to assure herself her neighbors were safe, there was a reason for it.

He wondered what that reason was.

He shook his head. "I'm just a starving poet trying to write the occasional bit of verse whilst fighting off scores of women who can't read first form." Among other things, of course, but those other things he fought off were just not all that important at the moment.

"First form?"

"Seventh grade in America."

She studied him. "I get the feeling most women don't want you for your iambic pentameter."

"Sad, but true. Unfortunately, rumors of my wealth and irresistibility are, I must admit, grossly exaggerated. But what of you? What mischief do you combine in order to feed yourself?"

She sighed and toyed with her teaspoon. "I'm not sure at the moment. I used to make jewelry."

"Used to?"

"Lost it all in a bad business deal," she said lightly, "which I'm trying not to think about very often." She set her spoon down. "You know, I'd better get to the dishes. I have no idea what time it is, but it feels late. I lost my phone yesterday and apparently lost track of time right along with it."

And then she very purposefully didn't look at him.

He hadn't made a bloody fortune at the negotiating table, never mind keeping himself alive on various medieval battle-fields, by not being able to read his opponents. He scrambled for something to say, because he suspected she expected it.

He also had the feeling she had seen him stumble out of the past, damn it to hell.

At least he'd had his hair hanging around his face and down to his shoulders. He'd had the good sense to put it in a ponytail that morning.

"You know, that's odd," he said, congratulating himself on spewing out intelligible words instead of frantic stammers. "I had some Yank bang on my door this morning and tell me about a phone he found somewhere in his wanderings," he said, lying with abandon to save his own sweet neck. "I wonder if it might be yours?"

She looked at him in surprise. "Another American?"

"A balding lad with a Hawaiian-print shirt. Know him?"

"Thankfully not." She seemed to relax a bit. "What did the phone case look like?"

"Hello Kitty?"

She blinked, then looked at him narrowly. "You're not funny."

"I'm damned clever," he corrected. "As well as a bit of an acquired taste, or so I hear. Want to go for a walk? You can see the sights along the way to my house, then decide if the phone is yours."

"Is this like inviting me up to see your etchings?"

"Would you come if that were the case?"

She laughed a little in a way that he wasn't quite sure how to take and seemed to think that was answer enough. He helped her clear the table, then saw to her dishes quickly whilst she went into the loo and changed into something that looked quite a bit less like nightclothes.

"Thank you," she said. "Cooking and cleaning up? I'm not

sure those girls down in the village know what they're missing."

He smiled. "Don't noise it about or I'll never know a moment's peace."

"Probably not." She considered, then looked at him. "Any suggestions on the fire?"

"Use the wood I brought in," he advised, "and don't be shy with those starters in the crock by the sink. One ought to do it—just tuck it under the wood in the morning, then light it if it won't catch all on its own." He shrugged. "I'll leave you my number. Ring me if you need aid."

"That's very nice of you," she said slowly.

"I'm just hoping for more of His Lordship's very fine preserves. Don't eat them all before I can get back this way, aye?"

She pointed to her door. "Out."

He smiled and went to hold the door open for her. He waited for her to lock up, then started off with her up the path toward his house and the loch. Not many people used it, which he supposed pleased him well enough. As he'd said, he liked his privacy. He also was happy to enjoy the rain and the addition of good company on his journey.

They reached his house sooner than he wanted, but there was nothing to be done about it. He wasn't sure she'd had enough time to forget what she no doubt thought she had seen, but he wasn't sure he could solve that at the moment, either.

"Want to come in?" he asked as they stood at his door, partly because he was in the Highlands and he wasn't about to let her stand outside in the rain and partly because he found himself surprisingly unwilling to let her simply walk off.

"Oh, I'm fine here," she said, hovering at his threshold. "I'm sure you have things to be doing."

Catching up on one of my lives would have been the first thing out of his mouth, but he didn't suppose that was all that useful. He didn't press her, but rather simply nodded and went to fetch her phone off the table. It began to ring before he reached it, which surprised him. The bloody thing hadn't made a peep before.

He picked it up, then carried it back to the door. "Yours?"

"Yes."

"It looks like someone is ringing you," he said, handing it over.

She frowned as she took it. "That's odd. I got a new number before I left the States and haven't given it out."

He didn't want to point out that whoever had stalked her all the way to the village might very well be capable of finding her phone number, mostly because, again, he wasn't supposed to know anything about her situation.

"I think it might be a local number," she said. She held it out to him. "Recognize this?"

He saw all the numbers, truly, but the only ones that had any meaning for him were the last four.

1387.

He had spent all the years when he might have been considered an adult masking his reactions, which was the only reason he didn't shove her bodily off his front stoop. He took a deep breath.

"I've just remembered an appointment," he said. He didn't like the edge to his tone, but there was nothing to be done about it. If he didn't get her very far away from him immediately . . . well, the truth was, he had no idea what might happen to her. The last thing he wanted was to drag someone else into his madness.

"Sure," she said slowly. She smiled politely. "Thank you—"

"I have to hurry."

She lifted her eyebrows briefly, and he didn't blame her a damned bit for it. He was being intolerably rude, but he had no choice. He practically shoved her off his deck and escorted her off his property.

"Another time," he suggested.

"Maybe," she said. "Thanks for my phone."

She turned and walked away. She didn't dawdle, which he would have regretted at a different time. At the moment, he just wanted her safely away.

He could feel time nipping at his heels. Nay, not just that. He could feel that bloody time portal closing, and he had to get through it before it did. He didn't like to think about what had happened in the past the first and only time he had purposely refused to step through the gate that opened for him.

At least he could think about it. The MacLeod clansman he later learned he could have saved if he'd been in the right place certainly couldn't.

He ran back to his house, slammed his door shut, then bolted back to his bedroom to don his medieval gear. He could only hope, as he generally did, that no one was watching him. Restraints would be in his future otherwise, he was sure of it.

He pulled his sword out of the closet, made sure his house was put to bed as best it could be, then took a deep breath.

He opened the door and walked back into the past.

Chapter 7

Emma walked along the village main street and wondered if the time had come for her to start looking under planters and around corners for leprechauns and wood sprites. There was something very strange going on in the surrounding environs, and it wasn't limited to everyone driving on the wrong side of the road.

Her nose for that sort of thing was definitely giving her trouble, in spite of her demanding that it cease and desist. She blamed her childhood for her unwholesome skills. She might have been a regular kid by day, but by night, she had been a world-class snoop. Being able to scout out the terrain ahead of time, along with having an ear cocked for any plans and schemes that might have been brewing, had saved her endless amounts of grief with her parents and siblings.

That begged the question of why she hadn't done a better job of taking note of all the red flags waving frantically when she'd first started dating Sheldon Cook, but that was probably something better left unexamined. She had plenty of mysteries demanding her attention at the moment without adding ruminations over her past decisions to the mix.

Take the day before, for instance. She'd spent the afternoon in James MacLeod's little cottage, feeding her fire as she'd been taught earlier that morning and trying not to think about the inexplicably weird behavior of her extremely good-looking neighbor. Her efforts had been halfhearted at best, which had left her succumbing to the temptation to put on her deerstalker and examine the facts.

He had cooked her a fabulous breakfast, which had definitely gotten their relationship off on the right foot. He'd followed that up with a nonthreatening invitation to walk to his house, which had been equally pleasant. She'd almost begun to think that she could let her guard down a bit when he'd abruptly changed gears and practically shoved her off his porch. It was as if he'd suddenly discovered she carried the plague.

Crazy came in all varieties, apparently.

It was a pity, mostly because she'd hardly been able to look at that guy without having to remind herself to keep breathing. But she had turned over a new leaf on her way across that big, blue ocean, and that leaf-turning had as one of its components the solemn vow to avoid nuttiness in any and all varieties. Nutty but handsome was just not going to cut it.

Apparently sitting in a cottage with nothing to do with her hands besides wring them wasn't going to cut it, either, which was why she'd decided it was time she pulled herself together and got down to business. She would find pencils and paper and at least start experimenting with design ideas. She would breathe in Scotland, set it down on paper as best she could, then hammer it into permanent metals when she had the chance. The very thought of that new direction and the opportunity to perhaps breathe life into a former business made her pulse race a bit with an enthusiasm she hadn't felt in far too long.

She also had to admit, if she were going to be entirely honest, that she had come into town in search of cell phone reception, since it was something she definitely didn't have at her house. It was important to have that sort of thing when one wanted to see if there might be any art supply stores in the area or find out where to get the best batch of fish and chips.

If one happened to type a neighbor's name into a handy search engine to see what sorts of details could be unearthed about that neighbor, who could blame one?

That was, she had to admit, the very first thing she'd done once she'd parked in the first public parking lot she'd come to. She'd seen nothing about art supply stores, hadn't really cared what she'd unearthed about local restaurants, and been somehow unsurprised to find that there was absolutely nothing about a Nathaniel MacLeod in Benmore, Scotland.

There was plenty, however, about a Nathaniel MacLeod in both London and Manhattan.

She would have considered that nothing more than someone having the same name as her neighbor if there hadn't been a picture of her breakfast buddy in a suit. She'd scrolled through his details, frowned thoughtfully over the oddly familiar name of his grandfather's company that he had apparently been a part of for several years, then killed the page before she discovered anything else. Snooping was useful, but sometimes that little warning voice that shouted *Here be dragons* was a voice best listened to right away.

She had put her phone in her pocket, then crawled out of her car and decided on Mrs. McCreedy's store as a good first stop, mostly because she'd wanted junk food to distract her from things she didn't want to think about. She'd found sugary things slathered in chocolate, but she'd also had a text show up as she'd been leaving the store.

Him you're wanting to avoid is following your credit card tracks. Let me know when you want to go to Inverness to dump your rental.

She had read that text from Patrick MacLeod several times, but it still said the same thing. She was tempted to wonder how Patrick had learned what Sheldon was up to, but quickly decided maybe she just didn't want to know. She'd had a sufficient eyeful of Uncle Bobby. For all she knew, that was just the beginning of the odd things about Patrick MacLeod's friends.

She didn't doubt that a person's credit card trail could be readily traced, she just couldn't believe that Sheldon had managed to do the same. He offended everyone he met and the only people who continued to talk to him after that offending were ones who couldn't avoid it. If he'd gotten someone to help him, it had been because he'd paid them—

"Emma?"

She jumped. Her phone jumped as well, then decided to swan-dive onto the sidewalk. Facedown, of course. She looked over to find none other than Nathaniel MacLeod himself hopping out of his dusty SUV to come execute another rescue. He picked up her phone and turned it over. Emma looked at the shattered screen and was more relieved than she should have been that she hadn't left a search for his possible criminal record open in her browser. It was bad enough that she hadn't cleared that text from Patrick.

Nathaniel ran his finger over the screen, then went very still. He'd obviously read Patrick's text, but since he didn't know anything about her life, his careful expression was probably due to Patrick's enigmatic language. She pulled the phone out of his hands and put on a smile.

"Just some residual stuff from home," she said cheerfully. "No worries."

He studied her for a moment or two. "You know," he said, then he cleared his throat. "Sorry. Too much shouting recently."

"Soccer fan?"

"Something like that. Anyway, I'm driving to Inverness this morning on business. If you'd like, I can help you leave your car there, as was suggested. I'm assuming that is Lord Patrick texting you."

She nodded. "It is, though I have to say I really don't like accepting favors from them."

"Favors?"

Why not spill her guts right there on the sidewalk? That wasn't her usual modus operandi, but she was out of her depth at the moment. "He and his brother are insisting that I stay at the cottage for free. I shouldn't have accepted, but I was off-balance before. I've got to change that today."

"I'm sure they can afford it," he said without hesitation. "Do them both a world of good."

She wasn't sure how to judge that. Who knew how much it cost to keep a historical property like Benmore Castle running? She'd only seen the main MacLeod castle as an X on a map, so she could only speculate on its size. She didn't want to think about the expense—

She realized her hand was shaking, but there was nothing to be done about that. It was cold and raining, and she was suddenly quite chilled over a text that should have had her scoffing.

"Being backed into a corner is never a pleasant thing," Nathaniel offered cautiously. "In regard to both cars and life. Your car, though, can be sorted easily enough. My fault on your phone as well. I'll replace it."

She shook her head. "It was old—"

"I don't think it was, so let me see to it. Do you need to run back to your cottage, or shall we just go from here?"

She let out her breath slowly. "I can go as is."

"Then let's be off. Where did your hire car come from? The place by the station?"

"I hate to admit this," she said, wincing, "but I honestly can't remember."

He did smile then. "Jet lag is hell. Where's your car now?"

"Up the street."

"Can you drive?"

She shot him a look that he apparently found amusing.

"I take it that's an aye," he said. "I'll wait for you then, shall I?"

She paused, then looked at him. "I have unhealthy food from McCreedy's in this bag. I can share on the way back, if you'd like."

"And so I am repaid tenfold for my prodigious generosity."

She smiled, then looked at him. "Finish your business from yesterday?"

He hesitated. "I'm not sure that business is ever finished, but aye, 'twas done very quickly and hopefully for a few days at least. Let's flee the scene before that catches up to me."

She supposed the enigmatic nature of that should have had her perking up her ears, but maybe it was indicative of how her day was going that it didn't. She simply nodded and walked off to get her car.

The drive south was substantially less stressful than her initial drive north had been, but this time she wasn't half asleep and it definitely helped to have someone to follow. She couldn't deny, though, that she was relieved when she pulled into a rental place behind Nathaniel and turned the car off. Realizing she was indeed in the right place was a bonus.

She wasn't all that surprised to learn they wouldn't give her a refund on even what would be unused days. She was fully prepared to just walk away, but Nathaniel shot her a brief look and took her place. He leaned on the counter and smiled at the girl working there. Emma had to admit that if she'd been on the other side of that Formica slab, she would have given him anything he wanted. Whatever his faults and potential nefarious life activities might have been, the man was absolutely charming. No wonder he had so many women hunting him.

"Surely we can work something out," he said smoothly. "If not a refund, then an extension or a trade, aye?"

Emma realized she was nodding in agreement, then rolled her eyes and stopped. The girl across the counter unbent, but only far enough to agree to put the rental contract on hold until Emma could perhaps get to another city in the south and pick up a different car. She wasn't going to argue. She also didn't think it was the right time to mention that she hadn't planned to be in any other cities, never mind somewhere as far south as London. She took the deal, signed what was necessary, then slung her backpack over her shoulder and walked outside with Nathaniel.

"I'm not sure how soon I can get to London," she admitted. She looked up at him and resisted the urge to feel a bit faint. "I really hadn't planned to go that far south."

"I hadn't imagined you had," he said, "but it seemed wise to throw whoever's troubling you off the scent. Renting a car there might be a good piece of misdirection."

She considered. "I suppose I could try to get one of your fans to pick the car up for me."

He pursed his lips. "Don't think that idea hadn't already crossed my mind, but I don't think you'll need to fall on your sword quite yet. I'll have my attorney send one of his errand boys to do your dirty work for you."

She smiled in spite of herself. "Very kind. And very expensive-sounding."

"Considering the vast sums of money I pay him for his services, I think the man can splash out himself for this. Let's find a place to sit for a bit and I'll make a couple of calls."

"Is there an art supply store nearby, do you suppose?"

"I imagine so." He paused and looked at her backpack. "No purse?"

She was tempted to avoid the question, then decided there was no reason not to be honest. "It's my go bag."

His mouth fell open a bit. "Your go bag?"

"Yes," she said simply. "Just in case."

"I don't suppose you have chocolate and packets of crisps stashed in there, do you?"

"No, just money, a copy of my passport, and survival rations. I have junk food in this other bag."

"Interesting."

She wasn't about to tell him about Bertie Wordsworth, spy-turned-chauffeur, who had instilled in her the compulsive need to have that kind of thing always ready. It was better to let the identities of her father's rather eclectic staff remain safely unmentioned.

She let Nathaniel put her backpack in his car with her things from Mrs. McCreedy's, then didn't argue when he stopped a quarter hour later in front of a shop that looked as if it might have just what she needed.

"Need cash?" he asked.

She stopped with her hand on the door handle and looked at him. "Thank you," she said quietly. "I have plenty."

"Exercising my rusty chivalry."

"It doesn't seem all that rusty to me, but thank you, still."

He smiled. "I'll settle the car nearby. Find me when you've finished."

She nodded, then got out before she could think too much about his offer and weight it with more importance than she should have.

Rusty chivalry. She wasn't sure she'd ever experienced even that. She wasn't quite sure what to do with it, which perhaps said more about the sort of guys she'd been dating than she cared for it to. It was time to make a change, definitely.

She browsed inside the shop for a bit, picked up a few things to use in keeping herself busy, then paid with cash. That she was having to do that was less frightening than it was annoying—and most likely unnecessary. The only people who had any idea what she was planning were unfortunately her parents. The only thing in her favor was that she hadn't left them with an itinerary past where she intended to stay for the first week. Throwing them off the scent would be easy enough.

She stepped outside and took a deep breath before she started thinking about that too much. She saw Nathaniel's SUV down the street a bit and started toward it. It was only as she got closer that she realized he was on the phone and he didn't look at all happy. He caught sight of her, smiled, then opened the door for her. She tossed her stuff in the front seat, then decided that giving him a bit of privacy was probably the chivalrous thing for her to do.

She grabbed the smaller of the sketch pads she'd bought, liberated a pencil from a pack, then went to look for a bench to sit on. That was one thing she thought she might come to truly appreciate about Scotland. It might have been cloudy and threatening rain, but there were benches set in strategic places in spite of that. She took a plastic shopping bag and plopped it down on the bench, then sat and considered what might hold her attention long enough to sketch it.

The first thing she saw was Nathaniel MacLeod, leaning against the side of his damp Range Rover, scowling into his phone. He would certainly do for the moment. She opened up her book, took pencil in hand, and let her imagination run away with her. The beautiful thing about sitting on a damp bench in a place where it currently threatened rain was that she didn't have too many expectations for her art.

She'd been drawing for as long as she could remember. She had branched out as time went on, feeling a definite pull toward creating things with more than just pen and paper, which had likely been what had led her to jewelry. There was something about the riotous colors the earth could produce, aided and abetted now and again by technology, that had sent her careening down paths she hadn't intended to take.

She paused. All right, so she'd started off her jewelry career maybe a bit earlier than she wanted to admit courtesy of an unhealthy fascination with Friendly Plastic, but that had pointed her in the direction of seeing what she could heat up, which had left her with countless tiny pinpoint scars on her hands and forearms from her adventures in metalsmithing.

Where that left her at the moment, she couldn't have said. She just knew that there was something extremely healing about getting back to her artistic roots with the simplest of tools. And it had to be said that Nathaniel MacLeod was a stunning model, even if he moved so much that she was tempted to call out for him to stop.

He finally got off his phone, cursed quite enthusiastically for a moment or two, then shoved his phone into his pocket. She looked down to see what had come of her attempts to put him on paper, then froze.

She wasn't sure why she hadn't been paying attention to what she'd been drawing, but there before her was the man she had seen coming out of the mist, the one who had appeared, then disappeared.

Nathaniel MacLeod.

"Find interesting things?"

She shut her book so quickly that she dropped her pencil. He picked it up and handed it to her, then looked at her with a faint frown.

"Something wrong?"

"Nothing," she croaked. "Jet lag."

"Hmmm," he said, studying her. "That does take some time to get over."

"Do you travel much?" she asked, pushing herself to her feet.

"I have family in the States," he said slowly, "so aye. More than I like."

In New York? was almost out of her mouth before she had the good sense to keep her mouth shut.

"That's a long trip," she offered. She picked up the shopping bag, shook the rain off it, then tossed it in the trash. She looked at Nathaniel. "I'm ready if you are," she said.

He hesitated. "If you want to take in a tourist sight, I daresay we have time."

"That would be wonderful," she said, grateful for any sort of distraction. "What do you suggest?"

He studied her thoughtfully. "If you haven't seen the battlefield at Culloden, you should, but perhaps not today. Cawdor Castle is close. It's been in the same family for centuries, so I understand."

"That sounds unusual."

"Some canny lads in that lot," he said. "One of them desired a bit more room, then apparently convinced a few recalcitrant relations to sell him their land by burning a house belonging to one of them to the ground. And 'tis said the Scottish play is based on events that happened there."

"*Macbeth*?" she asked.

"The very same, though I think that's made up for the tourist value." He lifted his eyebrows briefly. "We could go investigate."

She looked at him seriously. "This is very kind of you."

"'Tis Scotland, lass," he said with a smile. "Hard not to be a wee bit fond of my native land."

Well, there was definitely reason for him to be fond of it, so she nodded, then walked with him back to his Range Rover. She was happy to let him shut the door for her so she could take a couple of deep breaths before they got on the road.

Her trail was now cold for anyone who might or might not have been looking, she was headed toward a real, live castle, and she didn't have to look at what she'd sketched until she was safely back in the house James MacLeod was loaning her.

Things were definitely looking up.

Chapter 8

H*e* needed to get out of town more often.

Nathaniel nodded to himself at the thought as he drove through the outskirts of Inverness and headed toward Cawdor Castle. He had never been, as it happened, only because he'd never taken the time. First he'd had his hands full of school, then he'd been embroiled in business in Manhattan, then he'd been caught up in his ridiculous life in the Benmore forest. The thought of simply taking an afternoon and strolling about a castle and its gardens, even though those gardens had no doubt already been put to bed for the year, was a pleasant departure from his normal routine.

He soon realized that perhaps a pleasant departure from anything but the castle's quite empty car park wasn't going to be possible.

"It's closed," Emma said in surprise. "I didn't think to check."

"Well, the family does live here," he offered, "so I can't say I blame them. They likely need some time off from all the rabble tromping through and gaping at their rooms."

"Too bad we don't have any connections," Emma said. "Apparently they do book private tours."

Nathaniel started to suggest that perhaps they could book one of those for a different day when he saw what looked to him to be something of a private tour heading toward the front gates.

"Let's see if we can fit in with that lot," he suggested.

"Do we dare?"

Considering what he usually dealt with, the thought of merely muscling his way into a group of well-dressed tourists seemed like nothing at all.

"Absolutely," he said confidently. "We'll see how far flattery gets us."

Emma didn't seem to be opposed to the idea, so he locked up his car and hurried with her to the front gates. He didn't recognize anything about the collection of souls there except their accents, which he supposed he might be able to imitate with enough effort.

He engaged the most senior-looking man of the group, expressed his disappointment at having arrived to find Macbeth's reputed home to be closed for the winter, and wasn't it the damndest thing when one didn't check one's phone often enough, what?

"Oh, too true," the man said. He paused. "Don't suppose you'd want to join us, would you?"

"Brilliant of you, of course," Nathaniel said, putting a saddle on his best Etonian accent and taking it out for a bit of a trot. If that accent contained a touch of lesser royal, well, what could he say? He was a damned fine mimic, if he did say so himself. "I can reimburse you now or perhaps later over drinks at the pub—"

"Dear boy, of course you won't. What did you say your name was again?"

"Nathaniel MacLeod," he said.

The man studied him. "Born and bred here in the north, or do I detect other flavors?"

"Eton," Nathaniel said with a deprecating smile, "as well as a bit of a slog through the familial firm in New York—"

"Your grandfather is Dexter MacLeod," the man said, looking stunned. "I know him. Well, not well, of course, but I've crossed paths with him at the occasional soiree. You resemble him greatly."

"I could only wish to," Nathaniel said as humbly as possible. "I wish he were here to walk these halls with us, but he's comfortable across the Pond." Actually, he wished Poindexter MacLeod would walk *into* the Pond and drown, but perhaps that was a bit too blunt for present company.

He and his grandfather had a complicated relationship.

"You'll take good notes for him, then," the man said cheerfully. "And your girlfriend here?"

"Emma," Nathaniel said, reaching for Emma's hand. "She hasn't met the old boy yet. We're saving that for Christmas."

"You'll come to tea next time you're in London," the man said. "I insist. I'll make sure you have my card before we part ways—oh, Helen, you won't believe who we have joining our little outing today."

Nathaniel made polite chitchat with Helen and her husband, Richard, then hung back with Emma as their hosts went ahead. Emma watched them go, then leaned in.

"Thank you," she whispered. "This is pretty fortunate, isn't it?"

Nathaniel had a different opinion, but that was because he felt something breathing down his neck. A draft, perhaps—or perhaps Fate. If it was the latter, he wasn't going to pay it any heed. He was safely away from his usual time-traveling haunts and had no intention of being thrust back into a spot not at all his own. He didn't even have a bloody penknife on his person. It was a little unnerving, he supposed, how proficient he'd become at surviving with his bare hands alone, but that was a skill he didn't particularly want to have to use at the moment. He would be content to simply tag along after his wide-eyed Yank.

"I have to add that I can hardly believe what I just heard," she added. "You sound like you should be working for the BBC. Do I want to know where you learned that upper-crust accent?"

"Probably not," he said with a smile. He squeezed her hand. "You're a good sport."

"And you're getting me into a closed castle, so I'll ignore the fact that you didn't answer. I wonder if they have a guidebook."

Apparently they did. It was provided without her having to ask, along with a personal guide as well. Nathaniel might have felt slightly guilty at how ruthlessly he'd used his connections, but he had indeed put in several years in his grandfather's firm where his working conditions had been only slightly above Dickensian. He tended to think of his grandfather as less Ebenezer Scrooge and more Scrooge McDuck, but running his grandfather's Upper East Side accent through a Scottish dialect filter in his brain had been one of his tricks to keep himself sane. If he could leverage some of that suffering to a more pleasant purpose at the moment, so be it.

As he walked through the rooms, he wondered why he hadn't come before. Cawdor was a lovely house, full of history and comfort and things arranged to suit the needs of a family.

The company they had tagged along with didn't seem to find it as luxurious as he did, but they were Londoners. He wasn't a snob, if that was the word he was looking for, but he definitely had a fair amount of national pride. If he began to hang back a bit from the group to better appreciate a local treasure without their running commentary, who could blame him?

Emma was apparently torn between watching their surroundings and watching him try not to grumble. He shrugged and attempted a weak smile. She only smiled wryly and continued on.

He tried to concentrate, truly he did, but his phone was buzzing incessantly, and he suspected that might be for reasons he shouldn't ignore. He looked at Emma.

"I need to deal with this," he said. "Do you mind?"

"Of course not," she said. She hesitated. "Think they'll notice if I just stay back here with you?" She smiled. "I won't listen."

"It won't be worth hearing," he said grimly. He caught the eye of their host and made a production of pointing at his phone. The man nodded expansively and had a word with one of their escorts, who stationed herself a discreet distance away. Obviously that was the best attempt at privacy he was going to manage.

It was, as he could have predicted without having to look at his texts, one of his lawyers trying to get hold of him. He didn't even have to assign anyone a specific ring tone to know which barracuda happened to be contacting him to give him more bad news. He'd already talked to his solicitors in London that morning about his own business. That he wasn't able to get through the day without something winging its way from Manhattan shouldn't have surprised him.

He dialed, sighing as he did so. His attorney's assistant

picked up immediately, which he supposed should have been gratifying. "Suzie, it's Nathaniel."

"I'll put you right through, Nat."

Well, he couldn't say he didn't appreciate that. He closed his eyes and steeled himself for whatever madness he could just imagine was coming his way.

"Nat," Peter diSalvio said cheerfully. "You're hard to get ahold of."

"Don't remind me," Nathaniel said with a sigh. "What now?"

"Granddaddy's making noise about those same bones he's been gnawing on forever. You know, all that money you have control over that he wants back."

"That was my father's money, not Grandfather's—" He rolled his eyes. "Stop that."

Peter laughed. "I just love to listen to you repeat yourself endlessly. You know nothing's changed. He wants you out and himself installed in your place. How's that bull's-eye on your back feel?"

Nathaniel didn't suppose he was equal to describing it. He sighed. "I can't deal with this right now."

"You never have time to deal with this."

"That's because it's total bollocks," Nathaniel said shortly, "which we've also discussed forever. It's my father's money, I'm the trustee, and Ebenezer will never prove that I've mismanaged the trust."

"He's added a new wrinkle," Peter said carefully. "He wants to challenge your father's will now."

Nathaniel dragged his hand through his hair. "Five years after the fact?"

"I didn't say he had a chance, I just said he was doing it. You can't not at least respond."

"He can challenge my father's will until he's dead but nothing will change."

"This conversation feels very familiar."

"That's because it is, you punter. What's it going to take?"

"I'm working on it," Peter said easily. "I wouldn't want to reveal any strategies on the off chance our conversation isn't as private as I would like it to be."

Nathaniel could hardly believe that he might again have to meet Peter diSalvio on a bench in Central Park with his attorney's former intelligence service bodyguards keeping an eye on things at a discreet distance, but he had the feeling he was going to be hopping across the Pond sooner than he cared to.

"I'm only calling to get you to book me into your schedule," Peter continued. "Lord Poindexter has his usual conference room set aside for a mediation session next month."

"Lord Poindexter," Nathaniel echoed with a snort. That was the one thing his grandfather didn't have that he wanted with his entire soul. He'd spent the past thirty years trying to marry himself some sort of English heiress, but all he seemed to come up with were New York socialites. The man was, Nathaniel had to admit, not worth the price anyone would have to pay to live with him.

"I might pop over next week, just to see your place."

That sounded serious. "If you like."

"I think I should," Peter said. "Besides, where's that famous Highland hospitality?"

Nathaniel sighed. "I'll dredge some up for you. Give me a couple days' notice and I'll come fetch you at the airport."

"Take care of yourself, Nat."

"You, too," Nathaniel said, and he meant it. He couldn't say he had many things to be grateful for when it came to the business with his grandfather, but having Peter on his side of the table was one of them.

He disconnected the call, put the phone back in his pocket, and took a minute to remind himself where he was and what he was doing. The castle wasn't exactly grounded in present day, which was a little disconcerting, but the woman standing halfway down the passageway gaping at a tapestry certainly was. He pushed away from the wall he'd been leaning against and walked over to join her.

"They keep this here downstairs," she said in awe. "Can you believe it?"

He looked at the hunting scene depicted there, then shrugged. "I suppose when you have all this history collected, you have to hang it somewhere."

She smiled at him and he felt it a bit like a fist in the gut. He didn't know her, which made it absolutely ridiculous to continue to have the feeling that he'd met her before.

He was going to have to get some control over his life before the utter improbability of it overwhelmed him.

"I think we're getting a tour of the tree now," she said reverently.

He frowned. "The tree?"

"The hawthorn, which I've just learned isn't so much a hawthorn as it is a holly tree. They built the castle around it. Cool, isn't it?"

He agreed it was and allowed himself to be collected right along with her by their guide, who was as full of as much hearty trivia as he could have wished for. A Scottish historian in her element? There wasn't much he appreciated more.

He walked with Emma down more stairs and into what might have been mistaken for a cellar in times past. In the midst of the floor, surrounded by a railing, was a tree.

"The donkey lay down beneath this very tree," the guide was saying, "and that was enough to assure the Thane he had fulfilled the inspiration of his dream."

Nathaniel realized he'd been gaping at the tree in much the same way Emma had been at that tapestry. It also occurred to him that he had missed quite a bit of the tale the guide had been telling them. He looked at her in consternation.

"Dream?"

She smiled. "The first Thane of Cawdor was looking for a spot to build a new home. Legend has it that he strapped a chest of gold to a donkey, the donkey wandered to this tree and lay down, and the perfect spot was thus selected."

Emma looked at her in surprise. "But this tree isn't still alive, is it?"

"Sadly, no. Building the castle around it, I believe, was too much for it. I'm not sure we can say with accuracy how long it lived, but they have run tests to verify when they think it was planted."

"Really?" Emma said. "When was that?"

"I believe the carbon dating puts it about 1372."

Nathaniel took a breath.

He let that breath out.

Then he felt his world cleave in two.

He clutched the railing, because his alternative was to fall into the pit surrounding that dead tree. He almost went down to his knees, truth be told. It was nothing but sheer willpower that kept him on his feet. That and Emma suddenly standing next to him with her arm around his waist.

He realized the tour guide was peering into his face, but he couldn't find the words to tell her to stop.

"Are you unwell, sir? Is he unwell, miss?"

"I'm fine," he rasped, heartily alarmed by how difficult it was to get the words out. "Fine."

He thought he might be ill. Those numbers weren't his usual ones, to be sure; those numbers were a thousand times worse. It was as if the whole world had shuddered.

"I'll go find you some water," the guide said. "Miss, if you want to come and sit on these stairs with him, he might be more comfortable."

"Nay, we should go," Nathaniel ground out. It was honestly all he could do not to fling himself over the railing and hope he knocked himself unconscious. It would have been the kindest thing he could have done for himself.

"I'll run fetch help, then," the woman said, sounding profoundly alarmed. "Sir, you look very unwell."

He felt very unwell. He simply closed his eyes, because he didn't have the energy to argue with her. He put his hand over his eyes as well and left it there until he thought he could pull it away without the faint lights in the cellar blinding him.

That took substantially longer than he thought it might.

"Nathaniel?"

He forced himself to pry his eyelids apart and look at Emma. He focused on her until there was only one of her standing there.

"Did she say something upsetting?" she asked, her face full of concern.

"History is full of startling things," he said, grasping for the first thing that came to mind. "I think I might be getting a migraine. Nothing more dire than that, I promise."

"Want me to ask them if there's somewhere you can lie down?"

"I'd rather get home as quickly as possible, if it's all the same to you," he said thickly. "We'll return."

She didn't press him. She did, however, pull his arm over her shoulders and nod toward the stairs.

"I can't carry you, but I'll make excuses to get us out of here if you can walk on your own."

"I can do that," he managed. "Thank you."

She didn't say anything else, but she did give him another look of concern. He smiled, sickly no doubt, and didn't even attempt a nod. He was fairly sure where that would get him.

1372. It should have meant nothing, but the terrible shudder in the world that had accompanied hearing that year had been undeniable.

What in the hell was going on?

"Sorry to ruin the day," he managed at one point.

"You didn't, of course," she said with a smile. "Just keep going before we run into anyone who's going to want details. I can't fake your posh accent which means we'll be completely busted."

She said nothing else, but he didn't miss how loudly she was thinking. He didn't want to imagine what those thoughts might be. For all he knew, she was wondering if the lads down at the pub should have added *nutter* to the list of things they called him.

He managed to get up the stairs and back through the castle before they unfortunately encountered their benefactors. He would have tried to bluff his way out the front door, but he found it was all he could do to stand there and breathe.

He was fairly sure Emma had blamed his sudden paleness on bad eggs, but he wouldn't have been able to swear to it in court. He managed a garbled *Thank you*, then listened to Emma extricate them from any displays of concern by accepting a business card. He realized only then that her accent was as crisp as that of any London socialite he'd ever been scolded by. He tucked that away to chide her about later, then listened to her promise to absolutely get their host's card to Nathaniel's grandfather. Her thanks were just the right amount of effusive.

The next thing he knew, he was standing in front of the passenger side of his car.

"Keys?"

He managed to get them to her, half surprised he'd been successful in keeping them on his person during the previous hour. He didn't protest when she tucked him into the seat and leaned in to buckle him in safely.

"That accent," he wheezed.

"I watch lots of British television."

He laughed a little, but it was a fairly miserable sound. He managed to uncross his eyes long enough to look at her. Avoiding sicking up his breakfast all over her was yet another success for the day.

"Not a trace of identifying markers in that accent," he said hoarsely. "And that can't possibly come from too much telly."

"I think you're too sick for details."

"Distract me."

She shut him in, then walked around to climb into the driver's seat. She started his fairly abused Range Rover up, pulled out of the car park, then paused to set the navigation system.

"Let me know if you need help," he said faintly.

"I think what I need is for you to close your eyes before you barf all over me."

He leaned his head back very carefully against the seat. "Can you drive this?"

"I can drive anything."

He smiled. "Can you indeed? Where did you learn?"

"Same place I picked up the accent."

"Are you going to tell me where that was?" he asked.

"When you stop moaning every time you breathe, sure," she said easily. "Wouldn't want to give you any reason to express surprise and admiration when you can't give it your best effort."

He smiled in spite of himself and was extremely grateful when she drove carefully enough not to cause him any added distress. It only took him a few minutes before he realized that she was indeed as competent a driver as she'd claimed. His poor head agreed thoroughly.

It did, however, take him until they were well past Inverness before he managed to stop wheezing, but that seemed to be enough for her.

"One of my father's under-chauffeurs is former MI6."

He opened his eyes and hazarded a glance at her. "You're not serious."

"Oh, I am," she said with a brief smile.

"I'm not sure if I'm more surprised by the lad's former employer or that your father has an under-chauffeur."

"Life is strange."

He started to shake his head, but suspected that wouldn't go all that well for him. He reached for her hand instead and squeezed it briefly.

"I want the details," he managed, "but you're right about my potentially not enjoying them properly right now. You could give them to me tomorrow perhaps, after I've recovered enough to cook you breakfast with things Patrick MacLeod will no doubt continue to provide."

She glanced at him. "You sound terrible."

"I feel worse. Thank you for the hasty exit."

"No problem." She paused. "That tree was odd."

"Aye," was all he could manage.

That tree had been odd, but odder still had been his reaction to that date. He swallowed with more difficulty than he would have liked, but he felt as if his body were utterly deserting him. He had never swum through molasses, but he thought he might be able to describe the sensation well enough just the same.

1372. He had never been so far back in time, never had any but his usual numbers come up and tap him on the shoulder. It had begun with 1382, of course, a number he'd seen on a receipt for a pub tab his uncle had stuffed into his golf bag. At the time he'd been rummaging through those clubs for clues, he'd been appalled to realize his father's brother had spent well over a thousand pounds on one bottle of whisky in one afternoon. It hadn't occurred to him until later that he and his uncle had been holding on to that bag together as they'd bolted for cover.

He'd discovered eventually that time had marched on in the past apace with how it proceeded in the future. What 1372 boded for him, he absolutely couldn't say.

All he knew was that he had to get home, and quickly. Or, rather, he had to get Emma home, then himself back to his house before things spun out of control. He had never, not once in his five years of the madness that was his current time-traveling life, felt anything akin to how the world had just shifted.

Just what in the hell had he done?

Or had time taken note of Emma?

He wasn't sure he wanted to know the truth of it. He just knew he needed to solve it, and quickly.

Chapter 9

Emma had thought there were strange things happening just on MacLeod soil. After her midday stroll through Cawdor Castle, she was starting to think the whole of Scotland was a hotbed of paranormal activity. Maybe it was time to meet the whole thing head-on and go on a ghost walk, just to see what the country really had to offer. A guided walk, though. She wasn't about to just venture off into the wilds and see what sort of paranormal activity she ran into on her own.

She suspected she might be sitting next to enough of it as it was.

She put that thought on hold for a moment or two as she negotiated the road through a small village. Nathaniel's SUV wasn't new, but it drove well and boasted a first-rate navigation system. All she had to do was follow directions and remember what side of the road to drive on.

But once they were again on a road that wasn't quite so congested, she realized that her passenger was asleep and she had nothing else to do but use all that free time for what it was designed for, namely poking her nose into mysteries that definitely weren't her own.

Something was Definitely Up. She didn't believe in paranormal kinds of things, but she had to admit there had been something extremely odd going on back there in the castle. She would have taken the time to examine just exactly how odd that something had been, but it had been immediately clear that she'd needed to get Nathaniel out of there before he fainted.

What had he seen that had set him off that badly?

She glanced at the man whose car she was driving. It was a bit hard to look at him, actually. He looked like he should have been on the cover of some magazine for Scottish gorgeousness, but he was so oblivious to the looks women gave him that she suspected if he knew what he looked like, he just didn't care.

At the moment, he looked like he was about to lose his lunch.

"Eyes on the road," he said, not opening his eyes.

She pursed her lips. "I wasn't looking at you. I was looking *past* you to admire the scenery over there."

He groaned. "Of course you were. I suspect the truth is that you wanted to make sure I wasn't on the verge of sicking up lunch in your lap."

"That thought had crossed my mind." She watched the road for a bit, then stole another look at him. "You look awful."

"Thank you."

Too bad it didn't detract all that much from his appallingly good-looking self. She drove for a bit longer, then glanced at him. "Do you ever look in the mirror?"

"Every morning, darling."

She smiled. "Do you frighten yourself?"

"A better question is, do I frighten you?"

"I am unintimidated by you or your pretty face," she said archly. "I didn't mention this before, but my undergrad is in art. I'm used to drawing perfect specimens while ignoring their accompanying egos."

He wheezed, but it sounded a bit like a laugh. "I will model for you any time you like if it means I can stare at you soulfully whilst you're about rendering my spectacular features on paper."

She couldn't help but smile. "You aren't really that conceited, are you?"

"If I am, I'm paying a heavy price for it at the moment." He shifted, then groaned again. "Thank you for driving."

"My pleasure." She paused. "Migraine or food poisoning?"

"Take your pick," he said grimly. "At the moment, it feels a bit like both. Are you all right to drive home?"

"Absolutely. At the very least, I'll just follow your

navigation's calm, soothing voice and ignore you while you're heaving your guts out the window."

"Very kind." He shifted, then sighed. "I feel approximately eighty years old."

"Well, you don't look a day over fifty."

"Don't mind me, then, if I succumb to my years and snooze again in this glorious bit of sunshine."

She suspected he would, and she wasn't surprised when he did. She stole the occasional glance at him, but that only left her shaking her head. He was hard to look at, but she supposed she could make the effort in order to draw him properly. Taking one for the team, as usual.

She was altruistic like that.

The trip back to Benmore was easy driving, and while Nathaniel's Range Rover was definitely bigger than what she'd gotten used to, it drove like a dream. She glanced at her passenger occasionally, but he didn't stir. She supposed that was enough of a stamp of approval for her.

He woke as she was turning onto the road that led to both their houses.

"I'll drop you at your place," he said, his voice hoarse. "I'm sorry for this. I'm not usually so enfeebled."

"I can walk," she said. "It isn't that far."

"But 'tis pouring with rain and you'll catch your death," he said, rubbing his hands over his face. He smiled faintly. "Thank you, Emma. I'm not sure what came over me."

"Bad eggs?"

"Well, if they were, they weren't yours," he said with a sigh.

She turned for her house, then stopped in front of it and turned off the car. She looked at him. "Thanks for the help with my rental."

He looked at her quickly, then put his hand briefly over his eyes. "Sorry," he managed, "I completely forgot about it. I should have had you stop at Patrick's to pick up what you said he's loaning you."

"I don't need a car for the next couple of days," she said with a shrug. "If I do, I'll walk." She paused. "I don't think I can actually take him up on the offer, but I'm not sure what else to do. I don't think there's any way Sheldon would have my credit card number, actually, but who knows?"

"Is your father's under-chauffeur tossing in his lot with your ex, do you think?"

"Not a chance in hell," Emma said without hesitation. Bertie lifted his eyebrows over her other boyfriends often enough in the past. That his eyebrows had disappeared under his cap the first time he'd met the illustrious Master Cook should have told her all she needed to know. "No, Bertie wouldn't be aiding and abetting him. There's something else going on."

"Your former lad must have interesting friends."

She smiled without humor. "He doesn't have friends; he has acquaintances who put up with him. I imagine he stormed down to the bank and talked the manager to death until the poor guy told him what he wanted to know just to get him to shut up."

"Not exactly legal, that."

"That's never stopped him before," she said, "though he doesn't usually find much success with that tactic." She smiled briefly. "He's a lawyer, you know."

"I am utterly unsurprised," he said, "knowing quite a few of those sorts myself. The good ones are worth their price."

"Like your friend in London?"

He nodded. "He's eye-wateringly expensive, but worth every pound—and believe me, he only deals in pounds, not pence." His phone beeped at him and he swore faintly. "Please tell me this isn't a text from him telling me I'm being assaulted from the south as well. I don't think I can bring myself to read it."

"Want me to read it for you?"

"My life is an open book."

She took his phone and looked for his message icon. She checked for the most recent message.

"It's from Geoff Segrave and says, *Call me*."

"Wonderful," he muttered. "Is that it?"

"Nope," she said cheerfully. "You apparently owe him money for what it cost him to send a flunky over to the car place."

"How much?"

"Ah, thirteen pounds and eighty-seven, well, what do you call them? Pence?"

He caught his breath. "Aye."

"Maybe you can just chuck a twenty at him?"

He unbuckled himself and took his phone back. "Let's sort it later, shall we? I think I need to get home."

"Sure," she said in surprise, but he wasn't there to hear it. He had already gotten out of the car, grabbed her stuff from the back, and was depositing it on her porch.

She got out of the car and walked up to her porch slowly, somewhat surprised by how eager he seemed to get her keys out of her hand and into her door lock. He opened the door, flicked on the lights, then set her stuff just inside. He smiled, though she imagined he didn't know how cross-eyed with headache pain he looked. His hands were shaking.

"I need to get home," he said quickly.

"I think you do," she agreed. "You still don't look so good. Are you sure—"

"I'm sure," he said. "Let me ring you when I feel more myself, then I can run you to Patrick's."

"Oh, there's no need, really," she said, facing off with the Aga and wondering if she might manage to win the battle this time—

"Emma."

She realized she was only half paying attention to him, but the seriousness of his tone surprised her. "What?"

"I think it's going to pour with rain," he said. "Stay in the house, aye?"

She looked at him in surprise. "What?"

"Stay in the house," he repeated carefully. "Please."

All right, so Definitely Up had morphed suddenly into Past Weird. Nathaniel MacLeod had gone from someone who looked absolutely green to someone who looked almost frantic. It was possible, she supposed, that that was his usual reaction to his lawyer's phone calls.

Or maybe it was something else entirely.

"Okay," she said. She nodded, because he was obviously taking great pains to nod at her. "Are you sure you don't want me to make you some tea before you go?"

"I need to deal with this, ah, lawyer thing right away," he said, looking as if what he really needed to deal with was a straight path right to bed. "Stay inside where it's warm."

She lifted her eyebrows, but couldn't bring herself to commit to anything else, not that it would have mattered because he was no longer there to see it. She leaned against the door-frame and watched him hurry to his car, hop in, and drive off. She stood there, motionless, until she heard the noise fade into the distance.

There were some extremely strange things going on in Benmore Forest.

She went inside her little cottage and shut the door thought-fully. She locked it for good measure, because she wasn't quite sure what she was thinking at the moment. She brought her stove back to life, congratulated herself on at least that small victory, then made herself some tea. She went to sit by the window that looked into the forest and tried to relax.

That was a strange place, that forest.

She stared at it until it seemed less strange than it did unsettling. She rose and paced around her house restlessly until she finally gave up trying to walk herself into serenity and instead unearthed the yarn and needles she'd also bought earlier that morning.

She only succeeded in eventually realizing—after several rows, of course—that she hadn't cast on enough stitches to make a hat for anyone who was older than three. She ripped everything out, then looked at the sketch pad she'd left sitting on the kitchen table. She opened it and looked at the portrait she'd done of Nathaniel as he'd stood next to his car.

Odd that she'd dressed him in a rather rustic-looking kilt with a sword by his side.

She opened her front door and looked out into the late-afternoon gloom. She imagined it would be fully dark in an hour, so maybe if she wanted to get out, she should do it sooner rather than later.

Stay in the house . . .

She frowned. Those numbers, 1387. Those were the same numbers she'd seen on her phone in his house on that morning when he'd thrown her out with as much enthusiasm as he'd just used in dropping her off at her house. What was that all about? Was his bookie calling him with what he owed? Was £1,387 the minimum balance his bank account could fall to and see-ing it freaked him out? Was someone in the village telling him how many seconds he had until a socialite from London came hunting him?

She took her coat off the hook by the door, grabbed her keys off a different hook, then stepped out onto the porch before she allowed herself to think about what she was doing. She pulled the door shut behind her and locked it, then looked out into the darkening forest.

The rain had let up a bit, which she supposed was a fairly useful thing. Surely there was no harm in a walk. It wasn't like she was going to catch pneumonia from a little rain. Besides, she wasn't planning on going far and she wasn't going to venture into the forest.

Well, at least not too far.

She shoved her keys in her coat pocket, made sure her phone was in her back pocket, and stepped off her porch.

There was something about walking that cleared her head and left her wondering why she didn't do it more often. She tended to get caught up in her thoughts probably more often than was good for her. She spent so much time working with her hands, even when she was drawing something in particular, that it generally left her with a great amount of mental space to speculate on all kinds of things she might not have normally. But at the moment, she had a limited amount of things to wonder about, so she indulged before she could talk herself out of it.

So Scotland felt magical. It was a spectacular country. Even the most jaded and cynical of tourists would probably have to admit that. She'd been expecting quite a bit thanks to Bertie the under-chauffeur who had filled her very impressionable mind with all kinds of historical tales about swords and heroes and battles. Add to that Mrs. McCreedy's odd little map, her own rampant speculations about the unusual recluse in the woods, and that hallucination she'd had of someone stepping from the mist . . .

Well, it was no wonder she had begun to think Highland magic was a real thing. Her imagination had run away with her to a paranormal sort of place where all kinds of unusual things probably felt most comfortable—

Or so she told herself until she heard the shouts and ringing of swords.

She didn't think, she acted. She bolted to her left, because her natural instinct was to go to her right and Bertie the former super spy had suggested to her more than once that if she were faced with a dangerous situation she should do what she wouldn't be expected to do.

She supposed she should have taken five seconds to think that through, but by the time that thought occurred to her, she was already twenty feet into the woods, and that was apparently twenty feet past the line where reality ended and hallucination began.

And then she saw him.

Him.

She froze in place and gaped, because she couldn't do anything else. That couldn't possibly be Nathaniel, surely, but it couldn't have looked any more like him if it *had* been him. The only difference between that man standing there and the guy who had been standing on her porch not half an hour ago was that the guy in front of her was dressed in medieval gear, his hair was hanging around his face, and he had a sword in his hands.

He swung his sword suddenly, right at her, and she ducked out of instinct. That was bad enough, but feeling something fall against her back was far worse.

That something was a man.

The Nathaniel who couldn't possibly be her neighbor pulled her away before the attacker she hadn't seen coming crushed her under his falling self. She clapped her hand over her mouth when she realized her attacker was falling because he was dead. Her rescuer, whoever he was, pulled her behind him, fought off another guy with a sword and very bad teeth, then took her by the hand and ran with her. She didn't argue. She couldn't argue. She was too busy trying to keep from completely losing it.

He pulled her back to a halt at the edge of the forest. The mist obscured her sight of what she knew should have been a faint track leading to her safe and cozy cottage. She couldn't see it very well at all—

"Go haime, gel."

She would have told him she couldn't, but he gave her a fairly healthy shove in the right direction. She stumbled forward, tripped, then went down on her hands and knees. She didn't stop to assess the damage; she simply heaved herself to her feet and fled.

She ran until she left the mist behind and she was somehow

standing on her own front porch. She knew it was her front
porch because the house looked the same and those were the
lights she'd left on spilling out of her windows.

But she was alone.

Oh, and she was also apparently losing her mind.

She dropped her keys a handful of times before she managed to get the right one in the lock and open her door. She
realized she was hyperventilating only after she'd gotten herself inside her cottage and locked the door shut behind her.
She pushed a chair in front of the doorknob, made sure she
had her phone, then rechecked all the windows. Everything
was locked up, but she still couldn't catch her breath.

She was too panicked to even cry.

She ran to the bathroom and locked herself inside there as
well. She looked at herself in the mirror and decided it was
best to ignore the smudge on her shoulder. It was mud, not
drying blood, and she was going to lose it if she didn't get hold
of herself very soon.

She stripped and stood in the shower until she simply
couldn't stand any longer, then she put herself into her pajamas and considered going to bed.

She was fairly sure she would never sleep again.

Just what in the hell was going on?

She took refuge in her kitchen and wondered if she had the
presence of mind to even make tea. A knock at her door startled her so badly, she shrieked. She grabbed a knife out of a
kitchen drawer, took a deep breath, then fumbled with the
chair wedged against the doorknob. It took a moment or two
before she could bring herself to open the door, but she managed it.

Patrick MacLeod stood there. He looked at her, looked at
the knife in her hands, then held up his hands slowly.

"Friend, not foe," he said.

The knife fell from her fingers, but Patrick had the quickest
hands she had ever seen. He caught it before it landed point-
down on the top of her foot. He straightened, then held it out
to her haft-first.

"I'll make tea," he said simply.

She let out a breath that didn't feel at all steady, then
attempted a smile. "Sorry. Long day."

He said something in return, but she didn't catch what it

was. She was too busy looking at him and seeing something . . . well, there was something about him that was different. He looked so much like Nathaniel that they easily could have been brothers, but that wasn't it. There was something about him that seemed a bit raw somehow and that wasn't just his rugged Highlander persona.

If she hadn't known better, she would have said that he absolutely would have been comfortable in that little battle scene she'd just imagined.

But that was impossible.

She had a very active imagination, that was it. Her imagination had years ago sent her in the direction of art and kept her from becoming a corporate attorney. It would, she was sure, provide a decent living when she took that imagination and used it to fashion wearable pieces of art that reflected sea and sky and heather on the hills—

"Emma, are you unwell?"

Was she unwell? She scoffed at the very idea. She wasn't unwell, she was . . .

She was completely freaked out, that's what she was. She was looking at a guy in front of her who she could easily imagine using a sword. She was living next to a guy she was starting to believe actually *did* use a sword. Unwell? She wasn't unwell, she was losing her mind. The worst thing about it was, she thought she just might find some company for that activity if she looked hard enough.

"Emma?"

"I'm fine," she managed, realizing that she was croaking as badly as Nathaniel had been that morning in the village.

That morning. Was it possible that it was only that morning when she'd dropped her phone and broken it?

Patrick was looking at her thoughtfully. "It can get a little—" He paused and seemed to be looking for the right word. He frowned again. "Solitude can be good," he said slowly, "but it can get a little—"

"Freaky?"

He smiled briefly and Emma wanted to close her eyes. She wasn't sure how he and Nathaniel could look so much alike without being related, but, as she'd pointed out to herself more than once already that morning, Scotland was a strange place.

"I was going to say *trying*, but perhaps that isn't the right word, either," Patrick continued. "I should have brought the runabout. I could have walked back home."

"Oh, I wouldn't have asked that," Emma said in surprise.

"I know," he said simply. "I'll bring it round tomorrow." He picked up a basket. "We thought you might want a few things to liven up the old place. Why don't I set it on the counter for you?"

Emma stood aside to let him in and tried not to weep. She was tired, that was it. It had nothing to do with the kindness of strangers. She shut the door, then sat down at the table, watching Patrick MacLeod make tea. He set her up with a cute little brown pot and a china cup on the table, then leaned back against the sink.

"I take it the very elusive and reputedly very desirable Nathaniel MacLeod ran you into Inverness?" he asked mildly.

She nodded. "He was headed there anyway, apparently. Hopefully that will throw Sheldon off the scent."

Patrick smiled. "I imagine it will."

"You and Nathaniel could be brothers, you know." She wondered if it might be ill-advised to point that out, but she couldn't help herself. The resemblance was uncanny.

"Funny, that," he said thoughtfully. "I don't think we're related, but who knows? We're a little foggy on our genealogy in my family, so for all I know, we're cousins. Tell me if he becomes a pest, though, and I'll have my brother exert a little lairdly authority over him."

"I appreciate it," she said. "And I don't know how to thank you for what you've already done."

He shrugged with another faint smile. "Highland hospitality. It all comes back round in the end, so no need to fash yourself over it." He pushed away from the counter and walked to the door. He paused, then looked at her. "Be careful in the woods," he said seriously. "The weather can turn very suddenly."

She wanted to say that wasn't all that could turn, but she didn't suppose pointing out that her stomach tended to turn when dead guys landed on her back was very useful at the moment.

"I'll keep that in mind," she managed.

He let himself out and pulled the door shut behind him. Emma locked the door, then decided it wouldn't do to leave things out to rot. She filled the fridge with what needed to go there, then looked at the little black nylon bag in the bottom of the basket.

She took it out, unzipped it, and realized it contained the barest essentials for a survival kit. There was a note there as well.

Might want to keep this to hand, just in case.

It was signed by the good lord Patrick himself, and somehow the words sent a shiver down her spine. In case what? In case she found herself locked out of the house and the thought of catching a fish and frying it up was more appealing than using her phone to text someone for help? In case she found herself facing Bigfoot and needed to use a fixed blade she was fairly sure wasn't legal to carry in the UK?

In case she found herself trapped in the midst of a reenactment battle and needed to make do with that little bag and nothing else?

She put it in her backpack just the same, because it seemed like a good accompaniment to her daily necessities. One never knew when being prepared might mean life over death.

She just didn't want to think about under what circumstances that might be necessary.

She forced herself to sit in front of her stove and drink her tea, then she checked her phone for any stray messages from her neighbor who couldn't possibly be anywhere besides at home nursing his migraine, then washed up and put the Aga to bed.

By the time she put herself to bed, she was starting to get back to that place where she thought she might be able to believe she was just having hallucinations. She was tired and she wasn't sleeping well. All kinds of things were possible when that was combined with tall tales from the local greengrocer and jet lag.

Surely.

Chapter 10

Nathaniel stopped in front of Emma's house and turned his car off. Perhaps coming to see her so soon after having encountered her in a compromising situation might be considered ill-advised, but it had occurred to him as he was washing medieval grime off himself earlier that morning that it would behoove him to keep Emma's focus on him confined to the present day.

He thought if he told himself that often enough, he might just manage to believe it.

There were odd things afoot, he would be the first to admit that. First that madness at Cawdor, then the journey back to 1387 whilst suffering a colossal headache, then seeing Emma standing in a place she most certainly shouldn't have been able to get to—

Oh, and realizing that someone was watching him.

It wasn't the usual gaggle of hens in high heels and short skirts. This was something entirely different. He couldn't say exactly what led him specifically to that conclusion—perhaps too many years in a different, more dangerous century—but he couldn't deny what he knew:

That someone was sinister.

He knew he should have set aside everything else in his life to investigate that, but he honestly had nothing left in reserve to even attempt it. What he needed was a day or two to simply sit with the events of the past week to see if something significant came to mind. Even if all he did was breathe without wondering what was going to send him careening into a time period not his own, that might be enough.

The truth was, if he didn't find a solution to his situation soon, he was going to go mad. He couldn't spend the rest of his life feeling as though his life belonged to someone—or, more to the point, some*thing*—else.

He wanted a handful of days where he didn't have to encounter any numbers that he knew would indicate a journey to a time not his own. He wanted more than a handful of days where he could simply live the same sort of life a normal bloke got to live. He'd never taken the trouble to determine exactly how far away from his house he had to get before the past stopped calling him, though he'd thought about it on the way over to Emma's cottage. New York was far enough, as was London.

Inverness was apparently not.

But Edinburgh might be. He was willing to give it a try. Daft as it might have sounded, he wanted to give it a try with Emma.

He knocked on her front door, then waited. He'd seen lights on, but that might have meant nothing more than she'd left them on behind her before she'd gotten lost again in the past. He had hardly dared believe his eyes when he'd seen her run into the midst of a battle earlier, but there'd been no denying it. He'd done the first thing that had come to mind, which was to shove her back into the future and hope she went.

The door opened suddenly and he jumped in spite of himself. He jammed his hands in his pockets, damned grateful that he was in a time period with pockets, and wondered how it was he could be so full of his thirty-five years yet feel as if he were approximately fourteen years old, looking at his first pretty girl and daring to think she might be willing to go have a coffee with him.

"Good morning," he said politely.

She looked fairly shattered. "Same to you," she said quietly.

"I was thinking to make a journey to Edinburgh," he said carefully, "if you're interested in coming with me. Separate rooms, of course."

She was watching him—too closely, if anyone was curious

about his opinion. He tried to look as respectable and modern as possible.

"Of course," she murmured. "I wouldn't think anything else."

Well, he would have suggested quite a few other things if he'd been in his right mind, but he was trying to be on his best behavior.

"Just a pair of days," he said with as casual a shrug as he could manage. "Just to get away."

"I'm just on a tight budget," she added slowly, "so I have to be careful. I've already imposed too much on Lord Patrick—"

"Lord Patrick will survive," Nathaniel said without hesitation. "Rich as Croesus, so I understand." He leaned against her doorframe, partly because he was exhausted and partly because there was something about her that he thought he might like to sit down and study whilst at his leisure. "I think I can afford a pair of rooms in the big city."

"Oh, but I couldn't let you do that," she demurred.

He looked at her earnestly. "I need a change of scenery and don't want to go alone. Edinburgh is a lovely place. There's a whacking great castle there, you know. There might be other interesting things as well. Can't remember at the moment—"

"There's the Camera Obscura," she said without hesitation. "And Holyrood, the Tolbooth—oh, and ghost tours. That'd be interesting, don't you think?"

With the number of things he had seen over the past five years—corporeal and not-so-corporeal—he thought he just might have an opinion on that.

"I could be persuaded to go on a ghost walk," he said.

She looked terribly torn. "I can't tell you how much I want to say yes."

He couldn't bear to tell her just how much his heart hurt at her enthusiasm. Bloody hell, the woman was going to be the death of him.

"You shall be my tour guide, then," he said. "Very necessary for the success of the venture."

"But that's the thing, isn't it?" she said slowly. "You're Scottish. How much tour guiding can you possibly need?"

He straightened and nodded toward the inside of her house. "You might be surprised. Besides, I'm always interested in someone else's perspective of my native land. Pack your gear and come to Edinburgh with me. It'll do you a world of good to get away from the grind at home. Feeding that damned Aga is enough to drive a lass to drink."

She didn't move. "I know what you're doing."

He experienced a moment of panic, but he was altogether too accustomed to moving right past that sort of thing. He fixed what he hoped was an innocent look on his face. "Mind reading now?"

"You're not very subtle."

"I make a living at being subtle. You simply leave me off-balanced."

"Me?" she said, looking very surprised. "Why?"

"I don't know where to even start," he said honestly. "And aye, I'm trying to keep you distracted." He hoped she wouldn't ask him why, because he was too off-balanced to come up with a decent answer for that sort of thing at the moment. "If nothing else, you can drive when I feel the need for a nap. We've already seen how that works, haven't we? Now, shall I put your stove to bed whilst you gather your gear?"

"Where did you go to school?"

"Eton," he said, breezing past her. "Stuffy old place, as you might imagine."

"I can imagine many things," she said, "and I wasn't talking about that. Where did you go to university?"

He paused at her stove, sighed, then turned and looked at her. He knew what she was doing and didn't want to give her any fuel for her fire. "I don't want to answer that."

Her eyes narrowed. "Where?"

He considered his alternatives. "If I tell you, will you come south with me?"

"Maybe."

"Very well," he said, dragging his hand through his hair. "St. Andrews."

"And you want me to be *your* tour guide?" she asked incredulously.

"I want you to let me enjoy your company for a couple of days," he said. "I'll find us a vile little hotel, we'll make a few visits to the worst chippy in the city, and we'll take in a few tourist attractions. I can afford that, I imagine."

"I suppose I could be your bodyguard and fight off the socialites who've probably put a tracking bug on your car just to see where you go," she conceded. She met his eyes. "You could consider that my doing my part for the cause."

"Perfect," he said. "Shall I see to your fire?"

"Patrick would probably appreciate it."

He supposed the man might, and whatever he could do to keep the lads from over the hill remaining over the hill where they belonged seemed a reasonable price to pay for his efforts with the cottage's stove.

"I probably should leave a note as well," she said. "So they don't worry."

"Or pop off a text," he said. "You could tell him you're rehabilitating one of the locals. I'm sure he'll be impressed."

She fussed with her mobile for a moment or two, but he didn't dare ask her what she'd sent. Better not to know, surely. He settled her house as he'd done his own, then waited outside for her. She was quick about her business, but somehow that didn't surprise him. There was a wench who seemed to find it necessary to be able to bolt at a moment's notice.

He understood.

She locked her door, paused for a minute with her back to him, then turned and took a deep breath. "I'm ready."

He smiled briefly. "You sound as if you're headed to the Tower."

"I don't like relying on anyone else." She looked at him seriously. "I can pay my way in Edinburgh if I take out cash. I think this sounds a little crazy, but it's probably better if I don't leave a paper trail."

"I have a thought," he said, reaching for her bag. "I'll cover things, then when the statement comes at the end of the month, you write me a check for the amount and I'll run it through half a dozen attorneys to hide the origin. How does that sound?"

"Slick."

"It will be." He would also watch hell freeze over before he let her pay off anything with his name on it, but perhaps that was something they could fight over later. He walked with her to his car and saw her inside, stowed her gear, then got them on the road before anything untoward happened.

His life was exhausting.

He watched her out of the corner of his eye as he drove, but she seemed content to watch the scenery. If he stopped once to give her the chance to hop out and pick a bit of heather, well, who could blame him? The woman wasn't just content to watch the scenery; she was breathing it in.

"Happy?" he asked at one point.

"I would live here forever, if I could."

He had been all over the world, seen wonders and monuments and priceless treasures, and he had to agree with her. Even if his life hadn't been so inextricably linked to Scotland, he would have lived there because he loved it. He had the feeling the time would eventually come when he had to do something besides be at the mercy of whatever it was that continued to make an absolute hash of his life, in any number of centuries, but perhaps he could put that off for another pair of days.

He took a little detour in Inverness, pulling to a stop outside where he garaged one of his indulgences. He looked at her.

"I thought we might want to drive something else from here."

"Something that gets better gas mileage?" she asked, frowning slightly.

"Ah, nay," he said. "Something that goes a bit faster. You know, for a long journey." He supposed there was nothing else to be said. He liked good food, expensive wine, and fast cars.

He was such a cliché.

He opened his door, opened hers, then unlocked his garage and rolled up the door. He looked at Emma to see her reaction. She looked at the car, then at him.

"Seriously?"

He smiled sheepishly. "I have no self-control."

"That's a Lamborghini."

"Indeed it is."

"Is this the extent of your problem?" she asked sternly.

He shifted slightly. "I might or might not have an Aston Martin garaged in London."

"I'm not paying off your credit card at the end of the month," she said darkly.

He smiled. "I wouldn't have let you."

"You're as rich as they claim you are, aren't you?"

"Richer, assuredly."

She looked at him, then laughed. "Humble about it, apparently."

"'Tis part of my charm." He held out the keys. "You can pull it out into the street, if you'd like."

"And drive it to Edinburgh?"

He hesitated, then ignored her smile. "My altruism extends only slightly past the curb."

"How far?"

He considered her. "What's the fastest thing you've ever driven?"

"My father's Bugatti."

He looked at her in surprise. "Is that so?"

"I'm not a fan," she said. "Too showy. But I have driven it more than he realizes." She held out her hand for the keys. "I'll pull your Range Rover inside and not tweak you about this one."

Which was exactly why he might well hand her the keys at some point. He pulled his car out, waited for her to pull his Rover into the same spot, then transferred their gear. He locked the garage up, half wondering why he bothered, then got them out of Inverness with as little fuss as possible. He glanced at Emma to find that she was watching him.

"Should I be nervous?" he asked.

"I'm just wondering about you."

"I'm not sure I want to know why, so let's talk about you instead. But let me find us a hovel to stay in first. I have a mate who has some connections that might suit us."

That was a gross mischaracterization of the reality, but that was probably something he would be better off not telling her at the moment. Brian did, after all, have a handful of little boutique places where Emma might be willing to stay if she didn't know their price. He spared a kind thought for whomever had decided a satellite phone was a good thing to put in his car, then waded through a pair of assistants to get to his end goal.

"Nat," the disembodied voice said with a laugh. "You lazy sod, where have you been? Slumming in some Caribbean resort?"

"My pasty-arsed self says nay," Nathaniel said dryly. "Brian, I have a friend with me who is listening to every vile thing you say, so watch your mouth."

"Ah, a *woman* friend?"

"Aye, and I'm trying to impress her with my good taste in mates, so, again, mind your manners. I need a pair of rooms in the city and a place for my car."

Brian laughed. "Of course you do. Don't you have a secretary for this sort of thing?"

"I don't, which you already know, and you owe me, which is why I called you personally," Nathaniel said. "Pay your assistant a bonus to find me something close to the castle, will you?"

"Done. I'll text you details. I'll meet you for drinks if you have an hour or two free whilst you're here."

"Absolutely," Nathaniel said. "Cheers." He hung up, then looked at Emma to find her watching him. He smiled. "Business mate."

"What do you do? I'm guessing you're not making payments on this thing."

"I invest," he admitted. He started to elaborate, then realized she had gone a bit still. "Not a fan of that sort of thing?"

"It's what my father does," she said with a shrug. "Big money behind the scenes. He's a bit abrasive, though, which is why others do his talking for him."

"I know the type," he said. Actually, he was related to that type in the person of his illustrious paternal grandfather. He didn't particularly fancy talking about that grandfather, who he'd fairly recently made a second career out of avoiding, so he pushed on to other things. "I am not a scorched-earth sort, if that eases your mind any."

"Your friend seemed to like you."

"He has no taste," Nathaniel said, "so I'm not sure I would take his opinion very seriously." He blew past a trio of lorries cluttering up the road, then settled in for a long drive made with reasonable adherence to the speed limit. "Your father sounds like he's made enough to buy himself a nice little runabout. Along with the lads to polish it up, no doubt." He shot her a look. "You needn't give me details if you don't care to."

"Oh, I'll complain about him all day," she said with a faint smile. "Tell me if you get bored."

"Not any time soon. Press on, lass, and pray let him have dealt out just deserts to someone who deserved it."

She snorted. "I'm not sure he's deep enough to factor that into anything he does, but I'll be happy to share some of the juicier details."

He had to admit after listening to her for a good part of the journey south that her father sounded like a first-rate—well, perhaps there wasn't even any point in calling the man uncomplimentary names. He was someone, Nathaniel decided, who he wouldn't want to share a meal with. He might, however, want to see if there were something of his grandfather's that Emma's father might want. Watching those two scrap over a choice piece of property might be worth the effort of setting the meeting up. Something to tick off his to-do list at some point, definitely.

"So let me understand this," he said slowly. "Your da paid for law school and had the keys to your Jaguar—"

"A perfectly restored '67," she interrupted. "And he hadn't paid for school, *I* had paid for school with an inheritance from my grandmother. The car was my prize for passing the bar." She sighed deeply. "It was a beautiful car."

"Of course," he said. "So, you had passed the bar, he was holding out your keys, and then tell me again what you did? I'm sure my ears failed me at that point in your story."

"I told him I didn't want to be a lawyer," she said. She paused. "I might have told him to go to hell as well. I'm a bit foggy on that part."

He glanced at her. "Foggy?"

"A bit."

He suspected she wasn't. "He disowned you?"

"Yes. After that, he drove my car onto his dock and pushed it into the lake. Then he billed me for the big, fat ticket he got for polluting."

He considered. "I'm not sure what bothers you more, but I'm starting to suspect it wasn't being disinherited."

"Nah, I didn't care." She shrugged. "My father's complicated. He has an MBA from Harvard, but what he really wanted was a law degree. None of my siblings wanted to go that route, so I was his last hope." She smiled briefly. "He wasn't pleased with my career path change."

"So if you didn't want to be a lawyer, what did you want to do?"

"I wanted to make jewelry," she said. She shot him a quick

look. "I'm not sure how serious that sounds, but I do have my undergrad in art. I wanted to make art in a way that it would change whoever was wearing it, if I can put it that way without sounding too far out there. I was on the verge of really having things take off when I met Sheldon."

"I'm getting the feeling that wasn't a good thing."

She sighed deeply. "Unfortunately, no, it wasn't. I decided that making peace with my father was worth a shot, Sheldon was exactly his sort of potential son-in-law, so I ignored the red flags and got involved with him. When he offered to broker some semi-serious investment money for me, I took him up on it so my father would stop complaining about my choice of occupations." She shrugged. "I leaped when I should have looked."

"Semi-serious money?" he asked, because that was what he always asked. He smiled briefly at her. "Sorry, I'm nosy."

She smiled briefly. "I am, too. Let's just say it was more than I had in my savings account but less than I could have sold that Jag for."

He nodded. "Understood. So, you had seed money, you had your business, and your father was happy with your choice of boyfriends. What then?"

"I woke up," she said simply. "I dumped Sheldon and he called the loan. It was nothing more than I deserved for not reading the fine print, I guess. Sometimes people do stupid things when they want things to work out."

"Sometimes people take a chance on trusting," he countered.

"I'm an almost-attorney. I should have known better." She sighed deeply. "It was either just pay him outright or forever have him looking over my shoulder to see what my business was doing. I wanted to be free, so I paid him." She looked out the window. "It's a funny thing, though. If I hadn't chosen that path to walk down, I wouldn't be here right now."

He knew all about innocent paths that led to places one couldn't have imagined, but he supposed the present was not the proper time to be offering that observation.

She looked back at him and smiled. "I will say, for the record, that my path has led to my riding in a Lamborghini while Sheldon's most definitely has not."

"Silver linings all around," he noted. He imagined there

was more to the story and he suspected that a decent amount of money had left Emma's account to go into the unpleasantly persuasive Sheldon's, but perhaps the specifics of that were better left unexamined.

"It's too bad I can't just shove him into some sort of phone booth and have that transport him to another location," she said. She was silent for a moment or two. "Or maybe another time."

He was enormously grateful for the necessity of concentrating suddenly on the road. It gave him something to do besides face the way those words hung in the air between them.

The saints preserve him, as Angus MacLeod tended to blurt out when faced with a feisty Fergusson.

"Oh, look," he said suddenly, "a village. I'm starved, how about you? We're not far from Edinburgh, but I don't think my poor tum will last that long. Also, I think I might spy a building of historical significance over there on the hill. Shall we?"

"That'd be great."

He hazarded a glance at her because he was terrible at not knowing. He'd never had a present as a child that he hadn't unwrapped days ahead of time, never read the beginning of a book without having read the final five pages, never not known exactly what he was walking into before he took the first step.

Unless it came to the past. That, he supposed, was the one thing in his life that came as a continual surprise.

He imagined he could add Emma Baxter to that list.

She wasn't looking at him, but he was aware of how hard she was ignoring the proverbial elephant in the room. If she didn't know what his other life looked like, she suspected. He would have staked his fortune on it.

Which left him back exactly where he'd started the morning: looking for anything to do to keep her mind off the past and on the present. A bit of lunch and a quick trip to that manor house over the way were going to likely be all that saved him.

He didn't want to think about the explanations he would be offering if they didn't.

Chapter 11

Go haime, gel.

Emma stood at the window of her hotel room and looked down at the people walking along the street below her. It was such a normal thing to be doing, that walking, yet all she could think about was what she'd seen in a forest two hundred miles away.

She had come to pull sea and sky and water into her soul so she could then pour them into metal. She had absolutely not counted on encountering any sort of metal that would be sharp enough to save her life.

She had felt the weight of a dying enemy against her back. There just weren't too many ways to spin that to make it seem like something else besides the truth.

And the truth was what she needed to find out before she went crazy from thinking it was all in her head.

She had watched Nathaniel's hand the afternoon before as he'd been fiddling with his keys at the reception desk and wondered if that hand was the same one that had wielded the sword that had saved her life. She'd listened to him discussing accommodations with the lad behind the counter and tried to imagine that voice gasping out a plea for her to get the hell home. It was too bad she hadn't paid better attention to both while she'd been in the forest.

As it was, the best she could do was replay the sound of that voice and the touch of that hand in her mind and soul until she thought she would go crazy.

She had distracted herself well enough the day before by

driving with Nathaniel to Edinburgh in a car that had to have cost him a cool half million dollars if it had cost him a dime. She wasn't unaccustomed to her father's ridiculously expensive cars, but it had been a pleasure to watch a man drive a car he was obviously half in love with.

Hard not to like him for that.

She had balked at the price of her room, but he'd casually set his keys down in front of her without looking at her. She had assumed it wasn't so she would take them and make off with his car—though she'd been tempted—but instead so she would remember that he could afford to put her up for a couple of nights. Having him also scribble *No strings attached* on the front of a brochure about the castle and slide it her way had pretty much sealed the deal.

"You can buy me breakfast," he'd said as he'd handed her the key to her room.

She hadn't argued. She had quite happily taken a gloriously decadent nap, enjoyed a lovely dinner, then shivered through a ghost tour conducted in temperatures that left her feeling extremely glad she was safely locked in the twenty-first century instead of freezing in a different, less-well-heated century.

She had woken that morning with plans to make very good use of her phone. If there was something unusual going on in Nathaniel's neck of the woods, she was going to figure it out sooner rather than later. Bertie the spy would have been proud.

She sat down near the window, grateful for a rainy day that didn't interfere with her screen too much, and started her search.

Benmore's tourist website yielded all kinds of information about things to do in a charming Scottish village, but there was certainly no banner running across the screen indicating that there were paranormal deeds going on in the vicinity. She did find a studio run by a guy named Bagley where an interested party could indulge in fencing if desired, but that didn't seem all that unusual. She filed the name away for future reference, then dug a bit deeper.

It took her almost half an hour of following obscure links to random places before she let out her breath and congratulated herself on the fact that she wasn't crazy.

There was a discreet mention of a school specializing in

swordplay run by one Ian MacLeod. There was also a single reference to wilderness survival being taught at that school by someone named Patrick MacLeod.

Bingo.

She knew she was making a bit of a leap by assuming that the school's Patrick MacLeod was the same one she knew, but it was a leap she was willing to make for the moment. She supposed he and Ian could be just business partners, but they also could have been relatives. She supposed in the end it didn't matter. What mattered was what they were doing.

She continued her search, but found absolutely nothing else about the place. She supposed that if it was a school geared toward teaching people how to use swords and survive in the wild, maybe the men and women interested in that sort of thing didn't particularly want to advertise their enthusiasm for the same.

Especially if they were indulging that enthusiasm in a different century—

She stopped herself before she finished that thought. Ian and Patrick MacLeod, if they were the MacLeods who lived around the corner from her, were probably just heavily into history. If they did run a training camp, who was to say they didn't set up the occasional reenactment scenario to go along with their curriculum? Were they like Civil War reenactors, only pretending to fight a different war in a different century and on Scottish soil?

Was that what she'd seen?

And was Nathaniel MacLeod part of that?

She poked around a bit longer, but found only references to the village. From what she could see, it was nothing more than it seemed: a tiny town trying to band together to preserve a fragile economy. She had her own fragile economy she was trying to preserve, so she understood.

Oddly enough, there was nothing on the village calendar that hinted at anything out of the ordinary. No medieval fairs, no buddies getting together midweek for a little battle action, no covens of warlocks dressed in kilts.

She set her phone down and leaned back in her chair to let the details filter through her mind without trying to force them into any sort of pattern. Nathaniel hadn't said anything about hanging out with Patrick or his brother or whoever else might have been family there in the forest. She definitely remembered Patrick having said that he didn't know Nathaniel past his reputation of being the rich but perfectly harmless recluse up the way.

Unless they were all up to something they didn't want anyone, including her, to know about.

She let that thought continue on into the garbage can of ridiculous theories. Maybe Patrick was busy with his family and had a commanding sort of presence because his brother was the laird. Maybe Nathaniel was just a private sort of guy indulging in some serious national pride and he didn't want anyone knowing what he was up to.

Maybe it was just none of her damned business what either of them did with his time.

Go haime, gel.

She rubbed her fingers gingerly over her forehead. If she'd had any sense, she would have hopped on a plane that afternoon and run away from the whole situation.

Unfortunately, her stockpile of good sense had followed her '67 Jag into Lake Washington on that crisp fall day almost four years earlier. She'd tried to replenish that cache with a scoop out of that pile of hidden crazy called Sheldon Cook, but even her mother had very briefly and under her breath agreed that *that* had been a mistake.

All she had was herself to ask for advice, so she pulled herself up by her metaphorical bootstraps and dispassionately considered her options.

She could go back to Seattle, march into the offices of her father's archenemy—or one of them, at least—and promise all sorts of her own family secrets in exchange for their destroying Sheldon in court so he would never bother her again. She could find a job doing something that actually put food on her table. She could go teach art. She could go back to working temp stuff so she could save up enough money to . . .

To come to Scotland.

She laughed a little, because there was nothing else to do. If she had the perfect life and all the money in the world, she would still be exactly where she was. That she was sitting in a lovely little room courtesy of a decent guy who had a fondness for fast cars and junk food—well, maybe what she should do was just be grateful and keep her mouth shut.

Of course, none of that meant she couldn't continue to let odd things show up now and again and sort themselves into the piles they chose.

She grabbed her jacket, shoved her phone in her backpack, and left her room to go downstairs. She made it all the way to the bottom step before she had to pause and look across the lobby at that very lovely, generous man who had offered to share a few of his favorite sights with her, no strings attached.

He was wearing black jeans, boots, and a cabled pullover sweater, topped by a slicker. He looked like he should have been starring in a romantic drama about either a modern Highland laird in a spendy sports car or a gorgeous medieval clansman sitting in the chieftain's chair. She could have seen him in either role.

She examined that thought as it rolled down in front of her like a drop of rain on a windowpane. Was that what he was doing? Prepping for a movie audition?

He turned his head and looked at her.

He smiled.

Well, if that's what he was up to, she completely supported the idea. But until his movie came out, she would take advantage of his relative anonymity and his desire to meander over cobblestone streets. She stepped down the last step and walked across the small lobby.

Nathaniel pushed off from where he'd been leaning against the wall. "Breakfast?"

"Sounds wonderful," she said.

"Do you mind if Brian tags along?"

"Of course not," was what she said, but what she was thinking was, *What a perfect chance to observe you while you're distracted.* Who knew what watching him have a little chat with one of his buddies over breakfast might reveal about him?

She soon found herself sitting with him and his friend Brian in a charming little coffee shop just up the way from their hotel. Breakfast was interesting, but watching Nathaniel talk to Brian about football was better. Apparently Brian had been born in Glasgow, but gone off to Oxford for school. She learned that those two disparate events warred within him and disqualified him in Nathaniel's book from being allowed to have a definitive opinion on the sport in question.

"And what do you think, Emma?"

She realized Brian was talking to her. She smiled and shrugged. "No idea," she said honestly. "I'm just here for the heather."

"Nat, tell me you're not going to leave the poor girl to tromp about the hills herself. At least take her to dinner now and then."

Emma listened to them argue in a friendly fashion about the places she really should see if she intended to form a proper opinion of Scotland's true glory. She couldn't bring herself to protest, not that Nathaniel would have listened if she had. She would have to pull cash at some point, and maybe it was best to do it from Edinburgh. At least that way, if Sheldon had somehow managed to get access to her accounts, he would think she was traveling south.

She shook her head in spite of herself. There was no possible way he'd known anything about her plans unless he'd gotten it from her father, who she knew had gotten it from her mother. It also wouldn't have surprised her at all to know her father had put the screws to one of his buddies from her bank—that was something she would be changing when she went home—and gotten more information from him than she would have wanted. Illegal, but her father didn't let anything as trivial as either the law or good taste stop him from getting what he wanted. He'd been furious when she'd dumped Sheldon, so he'd more than likely decided this was a good way to bring her to her senses.

She could disappear if she had to. Bertie had given her several pointers over the years that would serve her quite well.

She shoved that thought aside as perhaps too extreme for the moment and allowed herself the pleasure of thinking about the previous evening. She'd enjoyed a lovely dinner courtesy of a certain St. Andrews alumnus, then dragged that same man on a ghost walk. She'd been fairly sure she'd seen absolutely everything of a paranormal nature the tour guide had suggested they would. Nathaniel had only shaken his head and smiled wryly.

"Cynic," she'd whispered.

"Hopeless romantic," he'd returned.

But he'd jumped right along with her when someone had leaped out of the shadows at a particularly spooky spot, then laughed at himself.

She had decided that if the women who hunted him could see him for who he really was, they wouldn't give up on hunting him down. He was too handsome for his own good, but seemed absolutely unaware of it. Or maybe he knew and he just didn't care. His friend Brian was one of the, ah, least handsome men she had ever seen, but that didn't seem to make any difference to either of them.

"She's comparing us," Brian said in a stage whisper. "Finding lots to loathe about you, no doubt."

Nathaniel snorted. "You're no prize, either. Perhaps she's deciding how best to run before she's forced to spend any more time with either of us."

"I will do the noble thing, then, and bow out first." Brian smiled at her. "I'm sorry to leave you with him, but unlike your friend here, I've work to get to. Be kind to him. He has a good heart behind that pretty face."

"I was up at five working my arse off," Nathaniel said sourly, "so keep your whingeing to yourself."

"Still not too late to run, Emma," Brian said cheerfully. "I know I would."

She smiled at Brian. "I think I'll survive, thanks."

He shook his head sadly, clapped Nathaniel on the shoulder, then paid for their meal on the way out the door. Emma looked at Nathaniel.

"You're two of a kind, aren't you?"

He smiled and toyed with his espresso spoon. "He's generous."

"So are you."

"Can't take it with you, can you?"

She leaned her elbows on the table and studied him. He stared back at her, then laughed a little.

"You're making me nervous."

"You're a mystery."

"Not worth solving, I guarantee it." He rubbed his hands together. "Where to first, Miss Baxter? I assume you have a list."

"I really think you'll be bored."

" 'Tis Scotland," he said, "which is the most interesting place on the planet. I promise you I didn't see anything important whilst I was at school. Too busy studying."

"Do you mind going to Holyrood, then?" she asked. "I've always wanted to see the inside of it."

"I've never been inside, either," he confessed. "Her Maj always seemed to be camping out whenever I had time for a tour. I don't think she's in residence now, so perhaps we might venture down and see what's to be seen. The walk there is interesting, if nothing else."

She left the restaurant with him and decided it was probably best not to mention that he seemed awfully familiar with using back alleys and side streets as shortcuts. That was no doubt from all the seeing of sights he claimed not to have done during college.

They didn't get anywhere very quickly, mostly because she couldn't convince herself to hurry. The ghost walk the night before had been extremely informative, though she thought she might be tempted to take another tour during the daytime when she might have a different view of things.

"Oh, look," she said, after a quick duck inside a church, "there's something down that side street."

He looked faintly hopeful. "Lunch?"

"We just had breakfast."

"Brian always kills my appetite."

She smiled at him. "How do you know him?"

"We spent our last year at Eton down at the pub, actually, though we'll both deny it." He shrugged. "Two Scots trying to blend in. When he needed funds for a business venture, I invested. And here we are. Handsome, eligible, and rich." He smiled. "That's obviously why neither of us is wed."

"You two are just too much man for your average girl, I guess. And before you think about that too much, what about that place over there? It looks like a museum."

"A small one," he agreed. "Might as well give them some business. Maybe they'll have ideas about lunch."

She rolled her eyes and walked with him along cobblestones that were less treacherous than she might have thought, given how rainy it was. At least she wasn't riding over them on the back of a horse. She wondered how anyone had managed that in the past.

The door opened for them as they approached, which she thought might have been a bit spooky, but she was quickly coming to the conclusion that spooky was going to be her lot for at least the next few weeks.

"Come in out of the wet, you two," an older gentleman said, holding the door open for them. "Nice and dry here inside. I'm thinking you'll want to see my collection of swords."

Emma agreed with him that shelter was very desirable and refrained from comment about swords. She didn't dare look at Nathaniel to see if his opinion on the matter showed on his face. She simply followed their host into his lair and happily listened to him introduce himself as Thomas Campbell, describe for them what they might expect to see, and begin the tour. Metalsmithing was metalsmithing, perhaps, regardless of what one was forging.

"It must have been a very hot business during the summer," she remarked at one point.

"You mean for a day or two in June?" Mr. Campbell asked with a laugh. He looked at Nathaniel. "Ye ken what I mean, aye?"

"Och, aye," Nathaniel said.

She feigned a sudden interest in a glass case full of daggers as curator and Highlander launched into a hearty bit of what she assumed was Gaelic. She decided right then that if she had the chance she would find some sort of crash course in it. Maybe she could bargain for some lessons from her nearest neighbor, though she wasn't sure he would want either earrings or portraits of his very handsome self.

She definitely wasn't going to show him the sketch she'd done of him in Inverness.

She memorized the contents of three glass cases before Mr. Campbell looked at them both, his eyes bright with excitement. "I don't usually make this offer, but would you care to see my dearest treasure?"

"Definitely," she said, realizing as she said it that Nathaniel had expressed basically the same sentiment. She looked at her traveling companion, shrugged with a smile, then followed the collector of treasure to the back of his place.

Mr. Campbell stopped in front of a glass case that was as tall as he was. Oddly enough, it held only a single, foot-long dagger. She wasn't sure how the blade was suspended to make it look as if it were simply hanging there in the air, but she had to admit it was well done.

"We've done a bit of investigating about this piece," Mr. Campbell said, "though I've drawn the line at testing the metal. I believe, based on my own experience and expertise, that the dagger was made in the fourteenth century— Oh, lad, you don't look well all of the sudden. Need something to drink?"

"Water," Nathaniel croaked.

Emma turned and grabbed his arm as he swayed. She suppressed the urge to pepper him with questions about his tendency to swoon over historical items and instead put her arms around him to keep him up. "Bad eggs?" she asked.

"I don't want to think about eggs," he said with a bit of a groan. "I'm not sure I want to think about anything."

She wished she could say the same thing, but she had too many questions that needed answers. Apparently the odd things that seemed to seek Nathaniel MacLeod out weren't limited to Inverness and all points to the north and west of it, and she wanted to know why.

He sat, under protest, in the chair Mr. Campbell provided and leaned his head back carefully against the wall. She supposed it would be impolite to study him like a science project, so she offered her best nursemaiding instead. If she simultaneously and quite furiously filed away details to think about later, well, who could blame her?

Mr. Campbell returned again with water, then accepted an invitation from Nathaniel to distract everyone with a bit more information about that dagger there in the case. She watched Nathaniel out of the corner of her eye, partly to make sure he wasn't going to faint and partly because she wanted to see what the depths of his reactions to a medieval blade were. He had some water, but that didn't seem to help much.

What was going on with him?

Nathaniel was staring at that dagger with an expression she could only identify as horror, as if he'd just seen Death peeking at him from around a curtain, scythe in hand. She decided the kindest thing she could do was get him some peace and quiet, so she drew the curator aside and asked for his views on metalsmithing in the Middle Ages.

It was fascinating, she had to admit. She supposed the forge might have been a decent place to be in the Highlands, especially in the winter, but it seemed like dangerous work. She had scars enough from her own modest forays into silversmithing, so she could only speculate on the potential for injury working on a much larger scale.

In time, Mr. Campbell excused himself to attend to other patrons. Emma glanced at Nathaniel, but he was only continuing to stare at that blade as if he expected it to leap out of the case and bury itself to the hilt in his chest. That was a different sort of horror than his previous expression, though she wasn't sure how to qualify either. She decided after a minute or two that he looked like he'd just seen a ghost.

He started to speak, then his phone rang. He pulled it out, then looked faintly relieved.

"My own business for a change," he said hoarsely. "Sorry, I need to see to this."

"Don't worry about it," she said. "I understand."

"And you're pitying me for it, I can see," he said, heaving himself to his feet. "Brian has another phone waiting for you at the hotel, so don't think you'll be free of this sort of thing forever. Do you mind if we step outside?"

"Not at all." She didn't bother to protest a new phone for herself. She'd already tried and been politely ignored. She did follow him out of the museum, though, thanking Mr. Campbell on her way out.

She leaned back against the stone of the building and wondered about that dagger. She didn't suppose she would have a chance to look at it herself without Nathaniel in tow, but it was tempting to find a way. She watched him pace in front of her, content to let the cadence of his words wash over her like a soothing wave. He seemed to have a different accent for different sorts of business, which would have made an interesting study all on its own. She wondered if he realized it himself.

He hung up, then looked at her. "Again, sorry. Hard to keep up with things at home with no signal."

She understood that. She also suspected she was beginning to understand other things as well. "I couldn't help but eavesdrop on that conversation," she said mildly. "I heard several terms the average guy doesn't generally use while simply hanging out on a freezing November morning. Any brushes with law school you'd like to come clean about?"

He looked like he was near to hedging, then he sighed heavily. "I have my degree from Columbia and I passed the bar in New York. I would rather starve than work for a firm, though."

She was unsurprised. "And your undergrad?"

"I read Medieval Literature." He shrugged and smiled faintly. "I like old things."

She imagined he did, regardless of how they seemed to affect him. She smiled. "I think your path to this spot is just as convoluted as mine."

"I think you might be right," he agreed. He looked up the street, then back at her. "I think I definitely want lunch, but perhaps a bit of a walk first. I'm restless. Would a little ramble toward the castle suit?"

"Absolutely. Especially if we can visit a couple of those shops that sell tartans on the way."

"I'll splash out for a shawl for you," he said gallantly.

"Fergusson colors?"

He shot her a look. "I'm not going to dignify that with a response, never mind that my mother was a Fergusson." He shut his phone off and put it in his pocket. "I'll do whatever you like as long as I can pretend I dropped my phone down a storm drain. I need some distance from—well, just some distance."

She made a noncommittal sort of noise, then walked with him back to their hotel. She understood wanting to get some distance from life. It was, after all, the main reason she'd flown halfway around the world. She wondered what Nathaniel was trying to escape from.

She also wondered why antiques, from dead trees to worn blades, left him so unsettled. There was something going on in his life that seemed very odd indeed.

It was none of her business, of course, but the man had made her breakfast when she'd needed it and was currently gifting her a couple of days in a beautiful medieval city. Nosing about in his private affairs with good intentions seemed like the least she could do in return. That dagger was a very tangible clue, and she wondered how she could ditch him long enough to go have another look at it.

She had the feeling she would regret it if she didn't.

Chapter 12

Nathaniel leaned against the wall outside the hotel, considered the gray sky above him, and wondered if the present moment was perhaps one of those times when a man simply had to cross the border and get himself out of Scotland.

That wasn't something he considered lightly. He had, of course, lived in England whilst at school, and he continued to keep a flat in London simply because he did so much business on that end of the island, but he much preferred to keep himself safely north of Hadrian's Wall. That he was even entertaining the idea of heading south in an effort to escape his life spoke volumes about the sort of day he'd had so far.

Seeing a dagger in the present that he had lost in the past—a dagger that bore a mark he had no trouble identifying—and seeing it in a place where it definitely shouldn't have been had come close to leaving him in a swoon.

There were strange things afoot in the world.

Those things were, he had to admit, almost enough to leave him convinced that perhaps Edinburgh was simply not far enough to escape his doom. He might have to take his life in his hands and cross the border. Perhaps if he didn't move too quickly, he wouldn't startle the natives unduly. Heaven knew he could sympathize with being unsettled by strange things, having had his own brush with things that shouldn't have belonged to his safe, sensible life.

He jumped a little when he realized Emma was standing next to him.

"Sorry," he managed. "Distracted. Lunch now?"

"We probably should," she said. "I think you had a serious case of low blood sugar back there in that museum."

He nodded, because he wasn't about to tell her that his near collapse in the shop had been less from lack of sustenance than it had been a full dose of shock over seeing that blade.

His blade, as it happened. The one he'd had made by Malcolm's blacksmith half a year ago. It had been made to suit his hand, obviously, and he'd reached for it scores of times in the past. There was just one problem with seeing it, seasoned as it seemed to have been by hundreds of years of time, in that man Campbell's most treasured case.

That blade was also currently sitting in the back of his closet, bright and relatively new.

He supposed the answer could be as simple as someone having made off with it in the *future* in the past. It was possible the thief had died of shame shortly thereafter and the blade had gone missing for several centuries. No doubt someone in the present day had found the old thing lying beneath the rubble in an inherited shed and *voilà*, in no time it had been handed off to a man in Edinburgh whose business antique blades was.

"Nathaniel?"

He dragged himself away from his uncomfortable speculations. "Aye?"

"There's a guy fifty feet to your right who's looking at you as if he's seen a ghost."

Nathaniel was frankly rather grateful he was accustomed enough to surprise that he didn't immediately turn and gape at the man in question. "You noticed?"

"I always notice. You?"

"Hadn't a clue," he said honestly. "But my father didn't have an under-chauffeur with interesting skills."

She smiled. "You're distracted."

"Hungry, rather, and I'll likely pay for that someday," he said grimly. "Recognize him?"

"Nope," she said. "Want me to stand on your other side so you can have a look?"

"Very sporting of you."

She looked at him and smiled a very small smile. "This is very odd."

"You, darling, have spent too much time watching spy programs on telly. I'm just trying to avoid having my pockets picked. But you can come stand over here if you like. I'll be—"

He stopped speaking, mostly because he had gotten a robust view of the man who was looking at him, aye, as if he had indeed just seen a ghost.

Actually, ghosts were what they reputedly had in that great whacking castle that found itself residing a ways down the coast. That man now walking toward them would know, given that he was lord of that particular fortress.

Nathaniel bid a fond farewell to any hopes of avoiding anything untoward for the rest of the day.

"Who is that?" Emma murmured.

"The owner of Artane, actually."

She looked at him in shock. "He's nobility?"

"He puts his trousers on one leg at a time, just like the rest of us," Nathaniel muttered, "but aye, he is." He took a deep breath, then found himself preparing to nod deferentially to the earl of Artane as surely as if he'd spent the past five years dealing with all kinds of medieval nobility.

Lord Stephen came to a rather ungainly halt in front of them, gaped for a moment or two, then seemed to get hold of himself. "So sorry," he said with a posh bit of something he'd likely picked up at Cambridge, "I thought you were someone else."

"I get that a lot," Nathaniel said, striving for Brooklyn and settling for Eton. He was too off balance to come up with anything better. "My lord."

Lord Stephen held out his hand. "Stephen de Piaget."

"A pleasure, my lord."

To his credit, the man only laughed a little. "Ah, deference. Delightful. And you are?"

"Nathaniel MacLeod, my lord. Just a humble Scot taking in the sights."

"Again, you look a great deal like someone I know," Lord Stephen said politely, "though it would be a startling coincidence to discover that you know him as well."

Nathaniel suppressed the urge to sigh. "Patrick MacLeod?"

"As a matter of fact," Lord Stephen said, not looking all that startled, "yes."

Nathaniel suppressed the urge to bolt before Stephen started asking questions he wasn't going to want to answer.

"Related, are you?" Lord Stephen continued, studying him.

"Not that I know about," Nathaniel said. "I've only encountered the man once in passing. Just a couple of words, but no time to investigate our genealogies." No sense in spewing out that what he'd encountered had been the driver's door of Patrick MacLeod's car, where he'd more than likely left a dent.

His ability to keep his mouth shut was truly something to be envied.

"I imagine there's some common ancestor somewhere," Lord Stephen said. He smiled, then turned to Emma and held out his hand. "Stephen de Piaget."

"You're the earl of Artane?" she asked, looking absolutely starstruck.

"Or so they tell me," Stephen said with a smile. "And you are . . . ?"

"Just a peasant from across the Pond," she said. "Emma Baxter."

Stephen laughed a little. "You should make a visit and meet my wife. She's from Seattle, you know."

"So am I," Emma said breathlessly. "What a coincidence."

Nathaniel wasn't much of a believer in coincidence, especially when those sorts of things seemed to be piling up in increasingly large piles around him. He wasn't about to credit Stephen de Piaget with anything nefarious, but he was more than happy to look narrowly at Fate and her favorite henchman, Father Time.

Barbados. Surely time couldn't find him in Barbados.

"That would be wonderful," Emma said. "Wouldn't it, Nathaniel?"

He focused on the conversation and realized that whilst he'd been about the necessary work of wondering how long it might take to get himself to some tropical destination, Lord Stephen and His Lordship's newest fan had been making plans to amble around the corner to Stephen's favorite chippy.

"Ah, brilliant," he said. "Thank you, my lord."

"It's Stephen," the earl said, nodding up the street and starting off with them. He shot Nathaniel a look. "I should be honest and tell you that I've heard about you."

Nathaniel ignored the chill that went down his spine, then he realized what Stephen was talking about. "Benmore's a small village," he conceded. "Hard to be a recluse there with much success. You do business with James MacLeod's brother-in-law, Zachary Smith, don't you?"

Stephen laughed a little. "And so I do. I'm not sure Robert Cameron has cornered you at any parties in London to invite you to give him funds for the preservation trust, but I imagine that's just an oversight."

"I've thought about investing," Nathaniel admitted. "Just haven't had the time to do anything about it yet."

"We're always here," Lord Stephen said with a smile, "and always looking for a few quid to pour into some tatty old national treasure."

Nathaniel nodded, then listened to Stephen and Emma discuss just how old and tatty those treasures could be. He wanted to be involved in the conversation, truly he did, but it was all he could do to choke down food he didn't taste and drink whatever it was Emma had shoved across the table at him.

He had never been without that dirk in the past. It had saved his life countless times.

What in the hell had happened to him to leave the past without it?

It was quite possibly the oddest sensation he'd ever felt— and he wasn't unaccustomed to things that were out of the ordinary. To know that at some point in the future that had already happened, he had lost the dagger that, along with his sword, had kept him alive—or, rather, *would* keep him alive, because if it didn't do what it was supposed to, he wouldn't be breathing at the moment.

He realized with a start that he was still sitting at a little bistro table, Emma was missing, and Stephen de Piaget was watching him thoughtfully. He blinked.

"Where's Emma?"

"Off to powder her nose, or so she said," Stephen said easily. "Good of you to bring her south and show her the sights. She seems to have a fondness for history. I understand that you read medieval literature at university."

"Aye, I did—"

Nathaniel felt the words drop off into the silence of the room, mostly because *university* wasn't something that translated into medieval Gaelic, which led him to realize abruptly that *that* was what the good lord of Artane was speaking.

"Ah," he attempted, then he looked at the man sitting next to him. "Hell."

"Hmmm," Stephen noted.

Nathaniel took a deep breath. "Lovely Gaelic you have there."

"Not learned at home, I assure you," Stephen said easily.

Good hell, the man's accent was flawless. Nathaniel wasn't sure what the protocol was for the moment when one's luncheon companion was speaking with an accent last used several hundred years in the past, but he decided there was no reason to add offense by not continuing in the native tongue. His native tongue, that was, not Stephen's.

Though at the moment, he wasn't sure whose native tongue it was.

"I'm not entirely sure how to comment on that," Nathaniel managed.

"I suspect there are several things you might hesitate to comment on," Stephen said.

Nathaniel felt the need for a little lie-down, but he didn't imagine the present was the right time to beg for one. He was in a medieval city with a modern earl speaking an antique version of a Scottish tongue.

His life was, as he would have readily admitted to anyone with stomach enough to listen, very strange.

"My great-grandfather, Rhys de Piaget, built my hall, you know," Stephen said, toying with whatever it was he was drinking.

Nathaniel wondered if it would be rude to send one of the employees over to the nearest pub to procure him a whisky.

"I never had the chance to meet him," Stephen continued.

"His living eight hundred years ago likely gets a bit in the way," Nathaniel observed politely.

Stephen met his eyes. "I know his son, Robin. And his son, Phillip, as it happens. I'm surprised by the men I know."

Nathaniel felt his mouth go dry. "Read a lot of histories, do you?"

"No more than you, likely."

"I'm not sure I know what you're getting at," Nathaniel said evenly. "My lord."

Stephen was unflappable. That could have come from all the years he'd spent with students at Cambridge. It also could have come from any number of other experiences Nathaniel didn't want to attempt to investigate.

"You know what the secret of the MacLeod forest is, don't you?" Stephen asked mildly.

"Haven't a clue," Nathaniel said promptly.

"You and Patrick MacLeod could be twins, you know," Stephen said.

"I hadn't known that, either," Nathaniel said, "before I encountered him a few days ago." He suspected that, given the look he had seen on the good lord of Benmore's face, neither had Patrick MacLeod.

"I'm at Ian's now and again," Stephen said. "Less than I used to be, but my focus now is on my family and my ancestral seat." He smiled briefly. "Less time for swordplay, as it happens."

"A pity, that."

Stephen smiled, a feral sort of smile that sent chills down Nathaniel's spine—and he was by no means a coward.

"I can keep this up all afternoon, you know," he said pleasantly. "This dancing about what you don't want to discuss."

Nathaniel suppressed the urge to bolt. "I vow I've no idea what you're referring to."

"Don't you?"

Nathaniel gave in. "My lord," he said in a low voice, "even if I knew what you were talking about, which I absolutely do not, I wouldn't admit it. Would you?"

Stephen studied him for a moment or two in silence, then he smiled wearily. "I suppose not. The idea of making a journey to—well, how shall we term it? Off the beaten path? Into the mist? It's completely barking. And to venture into the shadows of the past and encounter one's ancestors? Mental, that, wouldn't you agree?"

"I daresay I would." He paused, then looked at the current earl of Artane. "Do you know Robin of Artane personally?"

"Did I say that?" Stephen asked, apparently stopping just short of scratching his head. "I meant I read a lot. Don't you?"

"You rotter."

Stephen laughed, looking far too amused for his own good. "I know how to use a sword, you realize."

"I think I could as well."

"Finally we begin to get somewhere," Stephen said in satisfaction. He had a final chuckle, no doubt at Nathaniel's expense, then shook his head. "They don't know anything about you past what Patrick's lad Bobby has turned up, if you're curious. They know just enough to know you aren't dangerous."

"How kind."

Stephen looked at him in obvious amusement. "You don't have a bloody clue what—or who, rather—you have living next to you, do you?"

"What, a laird from the early fourteenth century?" Nathaniel said with a snort. "His equally medieval brother? His cousin, who you apparently know, who runs a medieval survival school? I hear the rumors down at the pub and consign them to the bin with the rest of the rubbish, as does every other lad with two wits to rub together."

"I think," Stephen said slowly, "that you might want to pay a little visit to your laird."

"He's not my laird."

Stephen only smiled briefly. "I'd make sure of that before you offend him. And bring a sword."

"I am a modern-day businessman," Nathaniel said, grasping for anything that sounded reasonable. "I drive expensive sports cars, drink expensive wine, and enjoy the company of very rich women—"

"And wide-eyed Americans who get a little breathless at the thought of a perfectly preserved medieval English castle?"

"That as well." He looked at the lord of Artane. "Where did you learn Gaelic?"

"From Ian MacLeod. I believe I might have picked up a bit more from Patrick as he was teaching me to survive in the wild under very adverse conditions."

Nathaniel couldn't help but wish he'd taken that class before his adventures had begun.

Stephen smiled. "You're welcome at Artane any time you like, you know. Bring your girlfriend. And you might ring me in the future, if you need aid."

"Very kind, my lord."

"I once found myself in a place I hadn't intended to go,

doing things I wasn't at all prepared to do, and I survived only thanks to the aid of a few choice souls I fortuitously claim as family. I'm paying it forward." He pushed his cup aside. "Go talk to Jamie, Nathaniel. Ring Robert Cameron as well, about the trust. We're always happy to lighten your purse for a good cause."

Nathaniel wasn't going to argue. His head was swimming with things he had never before considered and wasn't at all sure he cared for. He looked at Stephen.

"Do you know Thomas Campbell, the one with the museum down the way?"

"I do," Stephen said, looking faintly surprised. "He's very passionate about steel. I go to him, actually, for all my carbon-dating needs, simply because he doesn't need to run tests. Why?"

"He has a dagger in his back room," Nathaniel said carefully. "From the fourteenth century, or so he claims."

Stephen studied him. "Yours?"

Nathaniel took a deep breath, then nodded.

"And?"

"That dagger is presently also sitting at home in my closet."

"Under your trainers, no doubt."

"And a jumper or two."

Stephen smiled. "That's a bit of a problem."

"I think so as well."

Stephen stood up suddenly. "Ah, Emma, you've returned." He held out her chair for her. "I think Nathaniel will wither away and perish if he doesn't go up to the castle and hug a few old stones. Since he's robbing you of the opportunity to see a proper castle down the way, you'll have to make do with what you have here. Make sure he pays your entrance fee, won't you?"

Emma slid into her chair and smiled. "I will. I'd like to see Artane at some point."

"Come see us when you have a chance, and plan to stay for a bit. We have plenty of guest rooms, a wide selection of para-normal experiences, and my wife, who will no doubt love to catch up on Seattle gossip."

Nathaniel felt as though he had just taken a step out of his own life and was watching it from outside himself. He listened to Emma and Stephen make small talk while he contributed the occasional grunt, then heard himself thank the earl of Artane for such pleasant conversation.

"I'm off to take in a museum or two," Stephen said with a smile. "Do come south, Emma, and bring your lad here. It would do him good to venture out of his comfort zone now and again."

Nathaniel supposed punching Stephen de Piaget wasn't the proper way to thank the man for lunch. Worse still, he suspected by the smirk on His Lordship's face that he knew exactly what Nathaniel was thinking. Lastly, he had the feeling fists were not the earl's weapon of choice.

He walked out of the shop with Emma and Stephen, bid the earl a fond farewell, then looked at the woman who was wearing an expression that a less cynical lad might have called wonder. She managed to keep her enthusiasm in check until Stephen had rounded the corner, then she looked at him in astonishment.

"We were just invited to Artane," she said, sounding as if she were all of twelve years old and on the verge of jumping up and down. "To spend the night!"

"A sleepover," he said, unable to truly add the proper amount of sourness to the words. "Thrilling."

"I bet they have lots of treasures there," she said. "Don't you think?"

He looked at her standing there, wrapped in what passed in the present day for MacLeod plaid, and thought that his heart might just break if he had to look at her much longer. He was tempted almost past what he could bear to pull her into his arms and keep her there for a bit, say the next few decades.

He chose differently, because he was caught up in something that she needed to stay far away from.

"I'll try to get you there" came out of his mouth before he could think better of it. "But first, let's go examine that pile of stones up the way. Then I might have to resign myself to doing a bit of business, if you wouldn't mind."

"I could take another nap," she said. "You know, to recover from the excitement of being invited to have a sleepover in a real live castle."

He laughed a little in spite of himself, put his arm around her shoulders, then pulled her in the right direction. "That sounds delightful. As does tromping over history right now."

* * *

An hour later, he leaned against a bit of castle wall and knew his peace was over.

His mobile rang at him, a single, delicate bell noise that generally signaled some sort of doom. Legal, personal, paranormal, who knew? It was generally one of the three and always unwelcome. He realized at that moment that he was almost tired of looking at those texts, but he was also too damned curious for his own good. He opened a message he realized was from the earl of Artane.

Blade was found in the Fergusson dungeon by P. MacLeod. Campbell reluctant to say how he came by it. No other details, sorry—SdP

Nathaniel watched Emma standing ten feet away from him with her hands on a piece of castle foundation. He almost couldn't see her for the stars swimming in front of his eyes.

His dagger in the Fergussons' dungeon?

He was never without that blade. If Patrick MacLeod had unearthed it in the present day only after it had been lingering in the mud for hundreds of years, that could only mean that he himself had lost it in the past. The only way he could have lost it in the past in the Fergusson dungeon was if he had been trapped in the Fergusson dungeon in a condition that would have made it impossible for him to hold on to that blade.

What in the bloody hell had he been doing there, and what had he been forced to do to escape?

He looked at Emma, beautiful, fresh-faced Yank that she was, and felt his heart stop for a moment or two. It hit him with the force of a dozen angry fists exactly what he was going to have to do, and that was get Emma as far away from him and the madness that was his life as possible. If he had to buy her a cottage somewhere, *anywhere* besides next to his, he would do it without hesitation.

He couldn't allow her to become entangled in what he had the feeling was coming his way.

And it had everything to do with a dagger that found itself where it absolutely shouldn't have.

Chapter 13

Emma stood at a figurative crossroads and tried to ignore the warning noises going off in her head with all the delicacy of gigantic church bells ringing at noon. That was generally the sort of thing that happened when one knew one was headed in a direction that shouldn't be taken.

If she'd had any sense, she would have turned around, settled the MacLeod plaid beret Nathaniel had bought for her more firmly on her head, and found the closest coffee shop to hide in until Fate or Opportunity or Crazy continued on to find another victim.

But she had to know.

She took a casual look around her for thugs, earls, and neighbors made ill by looking at random historical items, then started off in a direction she couldn't help but go.

What she was supposed to be doing was heading back up to Edinburgh Castle to wander around a bit more in history. She'd agreed with Nathaniel that such was her best option while he dealt with business stuff courtesy of a quick use of one of Brian's offices. She still wasn't sure what he did exactly, which would have left Bertie the Spy shaking his head in disbelief that she'd let that little tidbit go unexamined for so long, but she knew it had to do with investing, and maybe that was enough for the moment. It was going to keep him busy while she went off and did some serious nose-poking into things she knew she should stay out of.

Snooping was such an adrenaline rush.

For all anyone knew, she was heading back to talk shop

with a man who was truly well-versed in metalsmithing and had the scars on his hands to prove it. If she happened to indulge her curiosity about medieval blades languishing in his back room, well, who could blame her?

It took her a couple of trips down streets she realized after the fact were the wrong ones before she found the right street and the right shop. She didn't usually make that sort of mistake, but she had to admit she was a little distracted.

She put her hand on the door just as Mr. Campbell was reaching for his sign to turn it over to closed. He paused, then opened the door and smiled at her.

"'Tis you, lass," he said pleasantly. "I was just going to lock up for an hour and take a late lunch, but you're welcome to join me."

"Oh, I wouldn't want to interrupt," she demurred.

"You wouldn't be, of course." He stepped back and held the door open, then nodded for her to come in. "Where's your lad?"

"Off doing business," she said politely.

"As long as your visit this morning didn't put him in hospital, I suppose I won't worry about him." Mr. Campbell smiled. "Come keep me company whilst I have a wee bite. Care for something yourself?"

"I'm fine, thank you," she said.

Mr. Campbell shut the door behind her, then nodded toward the back of his place. "Look around all you like, unless there's something in particular you want to examine right off?"

She smiled. "I'm that obvious?"

"A fellow metalsmith," he said with an answering smile. "Recognized that in you immediately, if you must know. We can't stay away from the stuff, can we?"

"Oh, I don't think I'd ever make anything of steel," she admitted. "I'm happier with silver and gold."

"Never say never, lass," Mr. Campbell said with a smile. "You never know where the forge's fire will lead you if you let it. Now, shall I just turn you loose, or is there something I can show you?"

She supposed plunging right in was the best plan. "I would like to have another look at that dagger, if you don't mind."

He only smiled. "I would have been surprised by anything else. Come along then, and have your look."

Emma followed him through his collections, realizing how much she'd missed that morning. Not only did he have an enormous collection of museum-quality pieces, he had a substantial number of things for sale. She looked at him in surprise.

"Did you make those?"

"'Tis my passion, lass," he said with a smile. "You'd be surprised how many people want a blade forged in the old-fashioned way."

She imagined she wouldn't be. For all she knew those reenactment guys in the woods were his best customers.

She couldn't bring herself to ask.

"I'll fetch my sandwich, if you don't mind waiting," he said.

"I'm happy to," she said, accepting a seat across from the case that held that remarkable dagger.

It gave her the chills.

It was still giving her the chills fifteen minutes later after her host was finished with his lunch and relaxing with his tea.

"That blade there," he said, shaking his head. "I'm not sure what to think about it."

"Is it not fourteenth century?" she asked.

"Oh, it is," he said. "The style is definitely common to the time. I deal in all manner of blades, as you can see, and most have a history of some sort behind them. That thing there, though . . ." He frowned thoughtfully. "There's something odd about it."

She considered, then decided that nothing ventured, nothing gained. "Would you mind if I touched it?"

"Not at all," he said. "You might have an opinion on it."

She didn't hope as much, but she wasn't about to pass up an opportunity to see what that dagger was really about. She tried to look casually interested as her host unlocked his cabinet and stepped back.

"There you are, lass. Let's see if you notice anything I haven't."

Well, for all she knew about it, the thing just looked like a regular piece of metal. It was pretty, true, but she couldn't imagine why just seeing it would send Nathaniel into such a tailspin.

"The date is interesting," the man said. "1387. Etched right there, isn't it?"

Indeed, it was. She felt the world shift in a very strange way, almost as if she had been looking at it expecting it to be one thing, then a film had been drawn back and she saw it in an entirely different way.

She wondered if she might be losing her mind.

"Would you like to hold it?" the man said. "Not often we see a piece of history this old, aye?" He lifted the dagger off what she could now see were very thin wires suspended from the top of the case, then held it out toward her. "There you are, gel."

Time slowed. That was perhaps an even odder sensation than what she'd experienced before. She reached out toward the dagger, but it seemed to take forever—

"Emma, no—"

She paused, then looked back over her shoulder. She didn't remember Nathaniel having been there. She half wondered how he'd gotten inside, but Mr. Campbell hadn't locked the front door, had he? How had Nathaniel known where to find her?

Maybe he was a better tracker than she'd given him credit for being.

She looked back at that dagger there in front of her. Its current owner was holding it with two hands. It couldn't have been heavy, so it must have been precious—

"Emma!"

She waved Nathaniel off, over her shoulder because she didn't want to bother with the effort of looking at him. She was on a mission and her business was in front of her. No sense in squandering energy that could be put to better use. She stretched out her hand and touched the hilt of the blade.

Her world exploded.

She released the weapon immediately, just so she didn't fall over and somehow land on top of the sharp part. She supposed she should have listened to Nathaniel, but it was too late and she had apparently been too stubborn.

She felt arms go around her and break her fall. She would have thanked her rescuer, but she was too busy trying not to lose her breakfast. It was no wonder Nathaniel looked so green when he encountered something that unsettled him.

1387. What in the hell did that mean?

She had absolutely no idea how long it took for her head to

even begin to clear. When she finally became aware of her surroundings again, she realized she was sitting in Nathaniel's lap, cradled in his arms, as he sat on that chair where he'd sat for so long earlier that morning. He'd looked at the time as if he were on the verge of puking his guts out.

She understood, totally.

"Emma?"

She lifted her head off his shoulder and looked at him blearily. "I'm fine."

"Drink."

She wasn't sure what it was, but it was absolutely disgusting. Whisky, perhaps. Her eyes watered madly and she coughed, but she felt almost instantly better. She pushed the glass away and sat up a bit.

"I'm fine."

"You're such a lightweight," he said dryly.

She found it in her to look at him narrowly. "Don't think that little Brooklyn twang to your words is going to get you anywhere with me," she managed. "That was vile."

He sipped, then laughed a little. "I'd have to agree, but I won't offend our host there by telling him as much. He's worried enough about you that I think he was ready to call for a nurse."

"Oh, let's go before he does."

He didn't move, though, and neither did she. She hesitated, then leaned her head back against his shoulder. He didn't hesitate; he put his arms back around her and then began to run his hand over her hair. She closed her eyes and wondered what he was up to. Whatever it was, she had the feeling it wasn't anything she wanted to get involved in. If she had any sense at all, she would leap up and run like hell.

But she didn't move.

And neither did he.

"How is the wee lass?"

"Fine," Nathaniel said. "Just a bit overwhelmed by the magnificence of your prize there, I suspect. Tourist jitters and all that."

She would have elbowed him, but she couldn't get her elbow where it could do damage. He only tightened his arms around her.

"I would be just as overwhelmed," he said seriously. "A lovely piece of history, that. Where did you come by it again?"

"The journey is long and a wee bit convoluted," Mr. Campbell said slowly. "Let's just say someone thought I might want it."

"You being a connoisseur of all things historical and sharp."

"Exactly," Mr. Campbell said, sounding as if no higher praise could be heaped on his head.

"You have a keen eye and a nose for a good buy," Nathaniel said.

"And you've an obvious appreciation for the same," the man said. "Would you care to hold this?"

Nathaniel made noises of regret. "Don't dare, I'm afraid. I might drop it on my tender toes."

Emma closed her eyes and listened to them go on about things that she soon tuned out. She didn't believe in ghosts, alternative medicine, or things she couldn't pin on a board and look at critically. She steadfastly refused to admit that she did believe in yoga, green drinks, and anything her intuition told her, but that sort of thing seemed very logical and sensible.

What she was dealing with at present didn't.

She wasn't sure if she slept or not. She thought she might have dozed. She understood completely why Nathaniel had done the same thing, if he'd gone through what she just had.

"Here's my card, lad," the man was saying. "Call me if you dig up anything in your backyard. I'll pay you a pretty penny for it."

"I will definitely call you first," Nathaniel assured him. "And thank you for the offer."

"You're certain you don't care to put a hand to this blade here?" Mr. Campbell asked. "Hard to pass up that sort of history, aye?"

"And yet I think I must," Nathaniel said. "Have to get this wee lassie home, don't I?"

Emma supposed that was her cue to get back to reality. She forced herself to sit up, then continued on all the way to her feet. If she swayed a bit, she didn't say anything and neither did Nathaniel. He simply put his arm around her shoulders and held her up. She forgave him for the tourist comment.

That might have been because she realized he was trembling. Just the slightest bit, of course, which she wouldn't have noticed if she hadn't been leaning on him. She put her arm around his waist, didn't look at him, and walked with him outside.

"You all right?" she asked casually as they walked back toward their hotel.

"I just had my grandfather's lead counsel for lunch," he said grimly, "so I'm fine."

"How was he?"

"Delicious."

She smiled in spite of herself. "I can only imagine. Well, now that we've both had our share of excitement, what now?"

He took a deep breath, then pulled away from her. "Daft as this might sound, I think I need to get home today. If you don't mind."

She couldn't say why, but she had the same feeling. "Of course," she said. "Whatever works."

He nodded, but said nothing else. She glanced at him occasionally as they walked back to their hotel, surreptitiously enough that she hoped he wouldn't notice. He didn't look pale, but he kept flexing his fingers as if he were trying to bring the feeling back into them.

That was odd.

She grabbed her stuff out of her room, then went downstairs to find Nathaniel trying to switch the SIM card out of her phone into a new one. She put her hand over his before he dropped everything.

"I could do that while we're driving," she said easily, "and I'll pay you for this."

He shot her a look that made her smile.

"All right, I won't. I'll cook you something, though I'm not sure how that's any more appealing."

He nodded, but didn't say anything. He simply handed her both phones without comment. She thought that was equally odd, but he was a man and they were an inscrutable race. Perhaps that post-lunch snack of attorney hadn't been as tasty as he'd tried to make it out to be. He looked like he had a headache, and she had to admit that she couldn't blame him. All she wanted to do was close her eyes for approximately a week.

Maybe when she woke up, she would have an answer for what had happened to her back in that shop.

It was dark by the time they reached the village. Nathaniel slowed, then pulled over. Emma looked at him in surprise.

"What is it?"

He took a deep breath, then looked at her. "I'm going to buy you a car."

She blinked. "Of course you aren't."

"I think it would be best."

She started to answer, but was interrupted by a text. She looked at Nathaniel. "Do you mind?"

He waved her on, then closed his eyes and leaned his head back against the seat rest. Emma saw it was a message from Patrick, wondering when she was coming back and reminding her that a car was waiting for her. He extended an invitation for dinner if she happened to be in the area.

"Patrick invited us to dinner."

"You, more than likely. He doesn't know me."

She was a little surprised by the brusqueness of his tone. She frowned thoughtfully. She wasn't sure what was going on, but she thought she might want to have a set of wheels while she found out. "Would you mind dropping me there?"

He shook his head, put his car back in gear, and pulled out onto the road. It was only then that she realized he was still driving his red extravagance and wondered if he knew it. She thought it was probably best not to mention it. He looked distracted enough as it was.

Fifteen minutes later, he was pulling into Patrick and Madelyn's courtyard. He turned the car off, put his hands on the wheel, then looked at her.

"I think you should move."

She looked at him in surprise. "Move? You mean right now?"

"I mean from the cottage," he said seriously. "I think you should find another place in Scotland to stay."

She felt as if she'd been slapped. In the past, her first reaction would have been to blink, then maybe tear up. Scotland must have done something to her, because all she wanted to do at the moment was punch him.

"Who," she said as crisply as possible, "the hell do you think you are to tell me what to do?"

He tightened his jaw. "I am someone who doesn't want to see you get hurt and, as such, I think you should be very far away from me—"

Her door opened, making her jump. She looked up to find the good lord of Benmore himself standing there, smiling pleasantly.

"Mistress Emma," he said, holding her door open. "Just in time. And I see you've brought a friend."

"I was just leaving," Nathaniel said grimly.

"And I think you should stay," Patrick said. "Highland hospitality, you know. Wouldn't want to offend the local young Himself, now would you? In you come, laddie, and have a meal with us."

Emma watched Nathaniel peel his fingers off the steering wheel rather reluctantly. He turned off his car and got out. She crawled out as well, not because she cared what he did but because she wanted to make sure he—

She looked from Nathaniel to Patrick and back. She felt her mouth fall open, and she was powerless to do anything about it.

They could have been twins.

Patrick shut her door and nodded toward his house. "I'm cooking tonight, which everyone should appreciate. My lady wife is brilliant at it, of course, but I like the challenge of serving up something edible myself. Emma, after you. Coming, Master Nathaniel?"

Emma looked from one to the other again, only for a different reason. She had no idea how to read Scottish men, but there was something going on. It looked a bit like an eighteenth-century fencing match, only there were no swords involved. She wanted to hold up a finger and ask for a pause in the events swirling out of control around her, but she had the feeling that it wouldn't do a damned bit of good.

There was something extremely strange going on.

But there was dinner in the offing, so she supposed she would let Patrick and Nathaniel have at each other and see if there was something she couldn't do in a different room. If Patrick was cooking and Madelyn was chasing children, maybe a seat in front of the fire in the great room might be just the place for her.

She walked with them to the hall, followed Patrick inside, then handed him her jacket when he asked for it. Before she could escape with him to the coat tree, Nathaniel had caught her by the elbow. She decided the very least she could do was give him a cool look, which she indulged in without hesitation.

He was looking at her with the most serious expression she'd seen on his face to date.

"I don't want you to get hurt."

She smiled politely and eased her arm away. She wasn't going to get hurt, because she wasn't ever going to get herself into something she couldn't get herself out of. She had a misspent youth full of those kinds of lessons, and it was about time she learned them.

"I'll be fine."

And she would be. She would borrow Patrick's car for a couple of days, then she would get the hell out of town, not because Nathaniel MacLeod had told her to, but because she wanted to. Men with ridiculously expensive sports cars, several lawyers at their disposal, and gaggles of gold diggers stalking them were definitely not the sort of men she wanted to get involved with.

Not on her life.

She supposed if she repeated that enough times over the next hour or two, she might manage to convince herself of it.

Chapter 14

Nathaniel was too tired for swordplay, verbal or otherwise. What he wanted to do was go home and sleep for a solid week, and that only after having seen Emma Baxter off to somewhere where he wasn't.

Damn it anyway.

Dinner had been interesting. Patrick's wife, his daughter, and even the wee bairn in the high chair had spent most of the meal looking from him to the lord of the hall and back as if they were seeing double. Emma had ignored him. The roast had been delicious.

He was losing his mind.

At least Emma's fury was something he could wrap what was left of his mind around. He had wanted to send her off pleasantly. He'd made a great hash of it.

He was, as he'd noted before, tired. And perhaps a bit of an arse.

He tried to focus on things he could understand, like memories of supper. It had been very good and Patrick MacLeod was an excellent chef. It might have been a pleasure to chat with him over the chopping of veg if the man hadn't been sizing him up the entire time.

He had returned the favor, studying the good lord of Benmore whilst they were about the labor of ingesting his very fine supper and then coming to the conclusion that Stephen de Piaget was absolutely daft. It simply wasn't possible that the rumors that went round the pub down the way about the man sitting across from him were true. Patrick MacLeod was not a medieval clansman, and neither was his brother James nor his cousin Ian. They were simply men who owned castles and estates and wanted to bring much-needed funds into the village coffers. Good men, obviously, and concerned about their neighbors and friends, but just men.

Surely.

"Need help with the bairns, Maddy?" Patrick asked.

"I can help," Emma volunteered.

The lady Madelyn seemed happy for an extra hand, though Nathaniel had to admit he wished he'd jumped at the opportunity first. Now he was going to be trapped with a man he definitely wanted to keep safely in the *Not Medieval* column of his acquaintance ledger.

"Enjoy your meal?" Patrick asked politely.

"Very much, thank you."

Patrick pushed away from the table and rose. "A whisky in front of the fire?"

"Sounds delightful."

The man only laughed a bit. "Aren't you a pleasant guest."

"Trying to be," Nathaniel said. Actually what he was trying to do was keep the lord of Benmore from thinking about how he'd dented the side of the man's car not a week ago.

Had it only been that long? He could hardly believe it.

It was less than a quarter hour later that he was sitting in Patrick MacLeod's great hall, enjoying both a warm fire and a perfect glass of his admittedly favorite libation. His host seemed content to sip in silence, which he appreciated. He applied himself to his own glass and watched the fire, wondering if perhaps he shouldn't have made a visit sooner. Dinner and conversation. How dangerous could that be?

"So," Patrick began slowly, "what do you do with yourself to earn your bread?"

Nathaniel opened his mouth to answer, then he realized not so much what Patrick had said but how he'd said it. Or, rather, in what vintage Gaelic he'd said it.

Damn it, when was he going to stop running afoul of these men who knew things they shouldn't?

He had the feeling his safe, comfortable life spread across several centuries was in danger of becoming not so safe or comfortable. He looked at Patrick and wondered if he might be able to stick his fingers in his ears and plead ignorance.

"Ah," he began.

Patrick smirked. "There's a decent start there."

"I read medieval literature at St. Andrews," Nathaniel said, hoping that might be enough to satisfy Lord Patrick's curiosity.

"That explains it, of course."

Emma came into the room and Nathaniel stood immediately, partly to show her a bit of respect but mostly because he thought he might manage to turn and bolt more easily that way. Damn it, he should have been more careful. He was going to be outed for what he was—

Which was, as it happened, very similar to that man now resuming his seat.

He sat down heavily, then decided that life as a recluse was definitely the life for him. All the socializing he'd done over the past week had obviously been a mistake. He needed to get back to his usual business of hiding in the hills and trying to survive the madness that was his life.

Though he was getting damned tired of it all, truth be told.

"I'm surprised we haven't had occasion to break bread together before now," Patrick said smoothly. "With you living so close."

"It is a pity," Nathaniel said. "Tonight was lovely, though. Thank you again."

"Perhaps we might do this again," Patrick said.

"Oh, I don't know," Nathaniel hedged. "I'm generally quite busy."

"Doing what?"

"I run."

"What a coincidence," Patrick said. "I run as well."

"I run a lot," Nathaniel said, wishing he could just tell the man across from him to shut the hell up. "Wouldn't want to put you to any trouble."

"What else do you do?" Patrick asked, leaning back in his chair and looking at Nathaniel from half-lidded eyes. "If you aren't uncomfortable indulging my curiosity."

"I write poetry."

To his credit, Patrick didn't laugh. A corner of his mouth went up just the slightest bit, though. Nathaniel couldn't blame him.

"That pay much?" Patrick asked.

"Nothing so far."

"How do you feed yourself? If I'm allowed to ask, of course."

"Business. And you, my lord?"

Patrick smiled. "Business. And I'm writing a series of books on medieval Scottish warfare."

Nathaniel was happy he had swallowed the mouthful of whisky he'd been enjoying, or he would have spit it out all over Patrick MacLeod's lovely tartan carpet. "That must be interesting to research," he managed.

"You don't know the half of it," Patrick said. "Ever use a sword, Nathaniel?"

Good lord, would the evening never end? He was caught firmly between the proverbial rock and that unyielding hard place. He couldn't lie because Emma would know, and he couldn't be honest because Patrick would know.

"I've seen one," Nathaniel said, settling for at least some of the truth.

"My cousin Ian runs a stunt training school," Patrick said. "You should come visit sometime. Never know what'll come in useful up here in the woods, aye?"

When hell froze over and not a moment sooner.

"I'll definitely give that some thought," Nathaniel lied. "I'm not sure I would manage to do anything but embarrass myself."

"Never know till you try."

Nathaniel found he had absolutely nothing useful to say to that, so he nodded and buried the curses he wanted to hurl at his host in his cup instead. He was vastly relieved when Madelyn came into the great hall. It gave him reason to stand up for her, then sit back down and try to sink far enough into the sofa that he might be missed.

Fortunately for his peace of mind, the conversation turned to far less perilous subjects. He found he was even able to offer the occasional comment that didn't leave him feeling as if he'd revealed far more of himself than he cared to.

But the longer he sat there, the more he had to admit that rumors that went around down at the pub generally contained a bit of truth. He was a recluse. Mrs. McCreedy was immortal.

Patrick MacLeod was a medieval clansman.

Even allowing the thought to take shape in his head left him feeling like a complete nutter, but there was nothing to be done about that. The man might have been dressed comfortably in jeans and a jumper, but there was something about him that said very clearly that if anyone even considered threatening his wife or bairns, they would be dead before they lifted a hand.

The longer he thought about that, the more convinced he became that Emma Baxter deserved something, some*one* actually, who could offer her that sort of sword lifted in her defense. He would have quite happily stepped forward to offer himself as that lad, but how could he when he could hardly keep up with his bloody emails to his solicitors? He had eventually taken to paying his bills a year at a time because he never knew when he was going to be home or for how long. He ate at the bloody pub because he'd learned not to keep fresh veg in his house.

His life was, he thought he might like to point out angrily to anyone interested enough to listen, absolute hell.

'Twas a pity the MacLeods didn't keep a witch in that little house to the north of the keep as they had in times past. He might have been tempted to make a visit and see if the crone had a bit of advice for him. It was for damned sure he didn't have any for himself.

He came back to himself to realize a transaction had happened and he hadn't been aware of it.

"Oh, are you sure?" Madelyn was asking in surprise. "You can stay as long as you like, really. Jamie insists that the cottage is yours for as long as you want it."

"Oh, I think I should probably just get back to the States," Emma said.

"The States," Nathaniel said in surprise. "That's a bit far, don't you think?"

The look she sent him should have had him in pieces on the floor, but it was gone so quickly, he wasn't sure he hadn't imagined it.

"Best to throw Sheldon off the scent," she said with a smile, then she turned to Patrick and Madelyn. "I do appreciate the offer, though."

"Keep the car, though, until you're sure," Patrick said. "I

can have it picked up in Inverness if you do decide that heading back to Seattle is what you really want to do."

"Or I can ferry you about," Nathaniel offered. "It's no trouble."

She smiled again. "I know you have things to do, Nathaniel, but I appreciate it. Oh, and look at the time. It's been a long day, and I think I'm still not quite over the jet lag."

Nathaniel was fairly certain she was and that she was simply looking for a polite way to leave. Actually, he felt quite sure that she was less interested in getting away from their hosts than she was him, but that was nothing more than he deserved. He just wasn't sure what other choice he'd had. She needed to be safe, he needed to stop living two lives in two separate centuries. He didn't see how those things could reasonably exist in the same place without eventually colliding in a fairly catastrophic way.

Emma made more polite leave-taking talk, but he doubted he could have repeated any of it upon pain of death. He smiled, nodded, and hung back as the ladies walked ahead in proper Regency fashion.

He was utterly unsurprised when Patrick leaned closer to share a private word with him.

"Here's my number," Patrick said, rattling off a series of digits in that rustic brand of Gaelic he seemed to feel the need to trot out every now and again. "Text me and come for a bit of exercise."

Nathaniel knew when to surrender. "If you like, my lord," he said with a sigh.

"Bring your sword."

"Of course, my lord."

Patrick laughed and switched effortlessly back to modern vernacular. "Knee-deep in it, are you?"

"I'm afraid so."

"You might ask for aid."

"I might," Nathaniel agreed. "Or I might not."

Patrick rolled his eyes, then went on to help Emma with their little runabout. Nathaniel offered a final thanks for a wonderful meal, then hopped in his own car and pulled out onto the wee road that meandered away from the hall. He waited until Emma was behind him before he started for home. It wouldn't have surprised him if she'd decided to drive off in a different direction entirely, but she was as sensible as he'd given her credit for being. Then again, he did have her things in his backseat.

He waited for her to open up her house, then lingered on the front stoop instead of just walking in, because his mother had raised him with decent manners.

Emma took her gear from him. "Thank you for a lovely pair of days."

"Emma—"

She started to shut the door, but he caught it.

"Please."

She looked as unhappy as he felt. "Please, Nathaniel. Please just go."

"I don't want you mixed up in the madness that is my life," he said honestly. "That's all."

"I can take care of myself."

"Then let me buy you a house," he said, "so you can stay in Scotland. Let me make you comfortable."

She looked less unhappy than angry. "You want to buy me a car *and* a house?"

Damn it, what he truly wanted to do was buy her a ring and, aye, an authentic castle to live in whilst she wore it, that's what he wanted.

"It would save you hiring one," he said, trying not to grit his teeth. "A car, that is."

"I'm going home."

"Please don't."

She blew her hair out of her eyes. "Make up your mind. Either you want me or you don't."

"My life is daft—"

She shut the door in his face.

Well, to be honest, he couldn't blame her for that. He nodded to himself and turned away. That way, as the saying went, lay madness, and she couldn't be a part of it. Leaving her angry with him was better than having her want to help him.

Assuming she would have wanted to help him.

He crawled into his car, realizing only then that he hadn't switched it out for his Range Rover, then sighed and drove home.

There was nothing else to do.

* * *

H_e was still trying to convince himself of that the next morning over a cup of ridiculously terrible coffee he had brewed to compensate for the sleepless night he had just spent. It only took three sips before he realized the truth.

He couldn't do it.

He couldn't watch her go and say nothing. At the very least, he had to tell her what was going on in his life and ask her if she could wait for him to sort it. That wasn't unreasonable, was it?

He decided it wasn't. He left his car parked behind his house in the garage, pulled on a jacket and trainers, then decided a bit of a run to her house might give him a few minutes to gather his thoughts. That sort of thing came in handy when one had a case to plead.

It took him half an hour only because he didn't hurry and he stopped to think a time or two. He wasn't sure he'd done himself any favors by any of it, so he continued on and was happy to stop on her porch and take a few restorative breaths.

He knocked.

There was no answer.

He frowned and knocked again. When he still had no answer, he made sure Patrick's little Ford was still on the side of her house, then made a nuisance of himself by peeking in her windows.

The house was empty.

He wasn't one to enter where he wasn't wanted, but he didn't hesitate before he picked the lock on her front door with tools he kept in a discreet pouch in one of his jacket pockets. He knocked one more time just to be polite, then opened the door.

"Emma?"

There was no answer. He walked over to her stove, but it was only lukewarm. It was as if she'd built a fire the night before, then let it burn out over . . .

Overnight.

Panic slammed into him. She had touched his dagger in Campbell's back room, hadn't she? For all he knew, she had been drawn back—

He forced himself to stop before he finished that thought. The past didn't want her, it wanted him. He was the one who had reasons to be there, not her. She was safe. She had perhaps become lost in the forest. Hopefully she'd had the good sense to put on a coat before she'd gone for a stroll. Her gear was still on the table, but he couldn't find her phone or her keys. Those were good signs.

He left the cottage, locking it behind him with the spare key he found hanging by the door, shoved the key through the crack under the door, then turned toward the woods and made use of skills he didn't usually need in the present day.

Her tracks were fortunately not washed away by rain and he followed them without delay. He would definitely be having a word with her about wandering off in the dark. He felt fairly safe in the forest at night, but he had five years of practice avoiding things he didn't want to encounter—

He came to a halt, then looked down. Her phone lay there, along with her keys.

Her footprints simply stopped.

He wasn't sure he hadn't made some sort of sound of distress. He supposed if he'd been a different sort of lad, he might have investigated further, but he was who he was. And because he was who he was, he was acutely familiar with the capricious nature of the MacLeod forest.

Aye, he could guess well enough where she'd gone. What he didn't want to think about was what she'd found on the other side of those trees.

He picked up her phone and her keys, then turned and sprinted for home.

Chapter 15

Emma decided that it was past time she started getting organized. The first thing she was going to do was make a list of things to accomplish, perhaps in a series of cheery notes made to herself. It would feel like she was some sort of 1920s movie star with an assistant whose sole purpose was to remind her to take care of daily tasks. She considered for a moment or two, then decided what would be the first item on her list:

Don't visit any medieval movie sets.

That certainly would have taken care of her current problem. If only she'd made that note before she found herself trapped on one of those sets.

She examined what had led her to her current and quite unfortunate locale and decided that perhaps her first mistake had been thinking a little after-dinner walk in the forest would be a good idea. Obviously nothing good happened in the woods near her temporary house after dark.

Her second mistake had been neglecting to dress for unexpected adventures. She hadn't really paid all that much attention to what she was wearing, but it was obviously not the kind of thing that fit in with half a dozen very burly guys in ratty plaid blankets. She would have complimented them on that truly authentic look they'd had going, but she realized very quickly what her third and potentially fatal mistake had been.

Not learning Gaelic.

She suspected that she wouldn't have had to even learn very much of it. All she needed was to be able to say *I'm not a witch* in the local vernacular. If she ever had a do-over of her life, she would insist that Bertie Wordsworth, chauffeur and international spy, teach her teenage self more than just a few swear words to use in London. Hell, she suspected the man could curse in a dozen languages with absolutely no effort at all. Surely he could have drummed up a few Gaelic slurs for her.

None of that was of any use to her at the moment. All she could do was try to keep up with the guys in kilts who didn't seem to have all that much patience for her. She stumbled to a halt, though, in spite of herself. The sun was coming up over the mountains and it was highlighting the castle that sat in a meadow in front of her.

The men said something, pointing at her as they did so. She was relieved that they hadn't done anything worse to her than shoot her suspicious looks while making what she had to assume were gestures to ward off any evil she might be about to lay on them, but perhaps her good fortune was about to end. Before she could decide which way might provide the best escape route, one of the men had taken her by the arm and—after crossing himself repeatedly—started hauling her toward the meadow.

She thought it wouldn't be inappropriate to indulge in feelings of alarm. The suspicious looks she was getting were turning into something entirely different, something that said she was absolutely not going to be welcomed into the castle with open arms. She only would have been surprised if she hadn't been tied to a stake and surrounded by kindling. She wondered if things could possibly get any worse.

She reminded herself that that was a terrible question to ask.

Her escorts stopped and a pair of them pointed across the meadow. Emma strained to see what they were looking at, then regretted it. She was so tired and frightened and desperate to convince herself that she was trapped in some sort of hideous night terror that all she could do was stare dumbly at the figure sprinting their way. She had no idea where he'd come from, though she wouldn't have been surprised to find that he'd brought a box of matches with him.

He joined the group without delay and was greeted with backslaps and friendly sounding ribbing. That was definitely

a step up from how she'd been received. He was obviously a
popular guy.

He was also none other than Nathaniel MacLeod.

There was absolutely no doubt in her mind that it was him.
He was ignoring her, though she couldn't say she blamed him
for it. She had shut a door in his face, and that after having
given him a very chilly shoulder through dinner and after-
dinner conversation the night before. He'd deserved it, the
jerk. At the moment, though, she decided he deserved a
friendly thank-you before she hightailed it out of Scotland.
She needed to get across the border before she found herself
caught up in another similar nightmare.

But she wasn't sure she was going to have time for that.

She didn't manage to catch her breath before two men had
taken her more securely by the arms and were escorting her
toward the castle. Nathaniel, or the man playing the Nathaniel
MacLeod part in her nightmare, had still not looked at her,
though he was certainly having himself a decent chat with a
man who looked to be the head of a raiding party.

Maybe he was indeed indulging in a little payback by having a little joke at her expense with his buddies. They would
get inside the castle and he would break character. For all she
knew, she had just become an extra in a movie.

She really should have dressed the part.

Unless her part was *woman being dragged into a castle
and summarily dumped into a dungeon*. For that, she was
apparently dressed just fine.

She realized that was the case only after she'd landed in the
castle's dungeon, having gotten there by way of a hall that
definitely wasn't boasting electricity or a good cleaning service. She had to admit that Nathaniel had made a few feeble
protestations as the trapdoor had been opened, but he'd backed
off with surprising alacrity and let her be tossed into that pit.
The floor was squishy, which she didn't want to think about,
and it smelled like a sewer, which she couldn't help but think
about.

She realized she was in shock. Maybe that should have
been clearer to her much sooner, but as she stood in that freezing hole, up to her ankles in muck she didn't want to examine,
she realized she was on the verge of hysterics. If she could
have caught her breath long enough to have hysterics, that was.

All she could do was stand there and hyperventilate.

She did that for a very long time.

In fact, time ceased to have any meaning for her. She thought someone might have tossed food through the bars of the grate above her, but she wasn't sure and she wasn't about to go digging for it. She stood where she'd been dropped, with her arms wrapped around herself, and concentrated all her energies on not screaming.

The sounds of the hall above her were things she learned to identify as time wore on. Laughter, the barking of dogs, the occasional ring of swords. At one point, she began to wonder if she had simply lost her mind. She had been out for a walk, but it had been dark. Maybe she had given herself a lobotomy on a branch and she just hadn't noticed.

Maybe she was hallucinating. After all, she had had dinner in Patrick MacLeod's medieval-looking castle the night before, never mind that it was definitely a smaller place than the one she was in currently. Maybe someone had shot her up with something and she was in a full-blown, drug-induced stupor.

Or maybe she was trapped in some sort of sci-fi time warp where men dressed in medieval clothing, there was no central heating, and gorgeous neighbors wandered in and out of her reality as if they didn't find anything wrong with the same.

She tried to cling to the nightmare explanation, but that became increasingly hard to buy into as the day wore on.

All she knew was that if she ever got back home, she was going to get the hell out of Scotland.

She paused and gave that a bit more thought. Perhaps she needed to get out of the UK entirely. England had Stonehenge, Ireland had leprechauns, and heaven only knew what Wales had going on. She needed to get herself somewhere where nothing unusual happened, like Ohio. Somewhere in the middle, where she would be safely far away from anything but bucolic farmland and maybe a few raw dairies.

Oh, but *Children of the Corn*. Where had that been filmed? If she were going to find herself being sucked into virtual reality movie sets, that was definitely one she didn't want to be visiting. Kansas was out as well, so maybe flyover territory wasn't the place for her. Maybe Hawaii was the place for her. Nothing odd happened in Hawaii, did it?

She realized she was babbling inside her head, but she figured that was better than babbling out loud, though she wasn't sure she wasn't doing that as well. She gritted her teeth to stop that and wondered if she might be losing her mind for real.

Scotland. What in the hell had she been thinking?

She realized that there weren't any more sounds coming from upstairs. That was made substantially easier, she had to admit, by the lack of crazy going on inside her head. She didn't dare hope that maybe the director had called *cut* for the day, because that would mean someone on the crew had forgotten they'd dropped her down into hell.

She could hear something dripping. It might have been her tears. She didn't want to think about whether or not it could have been blood from some dead body she might or might not have been sharing her cell with.

The faintest of lights appeared above her, slowly, as if it had been dawn breaking. She looked up and held her breath as the grate was lifted off silently and carefully. It occurred to her that she probably shouldn't have been looking upward, on the off chance that someone was only lifting the grate to dump something foul on her, but she was honestly too destroyed to care.

A hand was suddenly there in the semidarkness, reaching down toward her.

She didn't have to think twice. She grabbed that hand with both hers and jumped. She hooked her leg over the lip of the pit only to realize that she had been standing in the same place for too long and her feet were asleep. Her rescuer, if that's what he was, grabbed her before she collapsed back into the hole, then held her steady until she nodded.

Her rescuer Nathaniel MacLeod, that was. She would have staked her life on it.

He put his finger to his lips and looked at her pointedly. Well, she wasn't about to argue with that. She nodded and tiptoed with him past snoring guards and through the great hall that was equally full of snoring guys in rustic kilts.

They almost made it.

Someone stepped in front of them right by the door. Emma would have cursed, but she was too busy wondering if there might be a sword she could fall on instead. She listened to Nathaniel banter in a friendly whisper with the man there, listened to a bit of negotiation, then didn't object to the ogling the man did of her before Nathaniel winked at him and pulled her out the front door.

He was silent until they reached the eaves of the forest.

"Can you run?" he said, so quietly she almost missed it. Fortunately for her, he said it in English.

She tried to answer, truly she did. It came out as more of a sob, but she supposed she didn't need to apologize for it. She was damned lucky to just be alive, she suspected.

He was fast, she would give him that, but she was motivated by terror. She ran with him as if every terrifying creature from every decent horror movie ever made was behind her, just waiting for her to slow so they could finish her off.

Someone leaped out in front of them. Nathaniel drew the sword from the scabbard on his back and ran that same blade right through the gut of the man standing there. The man gurgled something, then fell. Nathaniel pulled his sword free, wiped it on the man's clothes, then resheathed it.

Emma turned and threw up. She thought it might have been the most sensible thing she'd done in at least a week.

She was still heaving when Nathaniel took her hand and pulled her back into a stumbling run. She didn't argue, because she suspected that might be what saved her life. She ran with him until she felt something shift as surely as if it had been a barrier she'd run through. She continued to run until she saw her house there in front of her.

Nathaniel slowed, stopped, then leaned over and sucked in air. She was gasping, but she supposed that was less from running than it was from horror. She realized she was also still dry heaving.

She wasn't sure how long they both stood there, breathing and heaving respectively, before she thought that if she didn't get in the shower, she would really lose it.

"Thank you," she managed.

He didn't say anything, but she honestly hadn't expected him to. He walked with her to her door, pulled her keys from under a rock, then opened her door for her. He reached in and turned on the lights.

Her phone was on the table. She didn't remember having

left it there, which meant someone had found it and put it there for her. She suspected she might know who that someone might be.

Nathaniel handed her the keys to her house as he eased past her. He built a fire in her stove, then turned and walked over to the door.

"Lock up," he said without looking at her. Then he left her house and pulled the door shut behind him.

She supposed she deserved that. After all, she'd been the one to shut the door in his face the day before. Or had that been two days before? That she didn't know was more alarming than she wanted to admit.

She stood in her kitchen and shook until she couldn't shake any longer. She stripped, opened her door long enough to throw her clothes outside where she wouldn't have to either look at them or smell them, then went and got in the shower.

It had been a dream. She'd been caught up in a terrible dream that was now made only marginally better by standing in a shower and trying to get rid of the smells that clung to her.

By the time she got out she was warm and pruny, which she thought was a vast improvement over cold and smelly. She dried her hair, put on her pajamas, then went to stand in front of the stove. She considered tea, but decided she wasn't up to it.

She heard her phone beep at her. She turned and looked at it. The number of people who had that number were two—Nathaniel and Patrick—unless she wanted to count that weird local number that ended in 1387.

She laughed a little in spite of herself, then stopped immediately when she realized how unhinged she sounded.

1387. Was that where she'd gone? Was *that* where Nathaniel went? If that was the case, no wonder he didn't like dates.

She took a deep breath, flexed her fingers briefly to bring some feeling back into them, then reached for her phone and checked her messages.

Text me if you like.

She wasn't sure what she liked. She wasn't even sure if she trusted herself to do anything but stand and shake inside a kitchen that belonged to people who had been kind to her for no reason besides their own generosity.

Highland magic?

She looked at her phone and wondered just what in the hell she was supposed to say to Nathaniel MacLeod. Thanks for the rescue? Nice seeing you in native dress?

She laughed. Well, she tried to laugh. It came out as something that sounded not just slightly unhinged, but completely unhinged. It was ridiculous, the past twenty-four hours she'd just experienced. Maybe it had only been twelve. It was daytime outside and she had walked into the forest the evening before. It was sort of hard to pin down the precise length of time spent in hell, but maybe that was something she could work out later. The one thing she knew was that she would never look at a blade the same way again—

She attempted a scoffing noise. Of course she would continue to look at swords and daggers, because she liked the way light danced against metal. What she had been through was a complete hallucination brought on by the experiences of the previous handful of days. She nodded to herself over that, then forced herself to stop nodding before she made herself dizzy.

She had been in a castle for supper and all that history had somehow gotten inside her head and she'd gotten lost in some sort of vivid dream. Sleep paralysis and that sort of thing. Her nighttime troubles were nothing more than mentally wandering around places that felt real but hadn't been.

Unless she had stepped into a kind of crazy that was so far past any reasonable amount of crazy that it found itself in some sort of alternate dimension.

Highland magic . . .

She had to have something normal happen to her. Maybe that normal would happen in Nebraska. She'd been born in Nebraska, or so she understood, though her parents had only been there long enough for her father to settle his grandfather's estate and make off with as many spoils as possible. Maybe she needed to get back to her roots.

She picked up her phone, considered, then made a decision.

I'm packing.

The return text was swift.

Breakfast instead.

The negotiations had begun, apparently, but he had tried to give her a big kiss-off, so she wasn't sure she wanted to concede any ground. Then again, he'd also rescued her from what she suspected was a medieval dungeon, so that might earn him at least a bit of leeway. She considered, then texted him back.

Need normalcy.

The reply was instantaneous.

Understood.

There was a pause, then another one came through.

Shopping at Harrods?

She would have smiled, but she thought she might rather weep. She should have taken him up on his offer, then cost him buckets—only the man had buckets of cash, so she imagined she wouldn't be able to stomach all the shopping it would require to make him wince.

Something closer, she replied. But normal.

Be right there.

She sighed and went to find her coat only to realize that her coat was sitting on her front porch, covered in a layer of goo. She opened her door and looked out at the pile, trying to reconcile what she was seeing with what had happened to her and where she was currently standing.

She thought her brain just might split in two.

She was starting to have some sympathy for the man pulling to a stop in front of her house in his very expensive sports car. The speed of his arrival made her wonder if he'd been lurking just around the corner.

Watching over her.

He got out of his car and walked up the one step to her porch. He came to a stop on the other side of the pile of clothes, looked at them for a moment or two, then looked at her.

"Ready?" he asked pleasantly.

She wrapped her arms around herself. "I don't have a coat." She took a deep breath. "Anymore."

He shrugged out of his jacket and walked around the pile to drape it around her. "We'll sort that right away. Go fetch your keys, lass."

She nodded, because she figured that was probably a good thing to do. It made her feel normal. She watched Nathaniel eventually come inside her kitchen, put her stove to bed, then wash his hands. He looked at her.

"Ready?"

She nodded, wishing she didn't feel so absolutely fractured.

He walked outside with her. She realized the pile was gone, but didn't bother to ask him where he'd put it. On the compost heap, probably.

She didn't protest when he tucked her into his car. It was, after all, what he did. That rescuing thing. She wanted to burst into loud, messy tears, but she forced herself to cling to the idea that maybe she had just had a very bad dream. A terrible, awful, extremely vivid nightmare that had somehow carried on into her waking life.

"Could we go somewhere besides the village?" she asked. Well, she croaked it, actually, but there was no point in trying to justify how she sounded. She was a woman on the verge of losing it.

He nodded. "We can drive up north. We'll at least find something to eat there."

"I should have taken you up on Harrods while I had the chance."

"There's time."

She didn't want to remind him that he'd told her to get lost. She wondered if he now thought it was too late, now that she'd seen the madness that was his—

No. She shook her head, on the off chance her brain hadn't gotten that message. Nathaniel MacLeod's life wasn't crazy, and neither was hers. She had a good imagination, she was still suffering from jet lag, and she'd wandered into the forest while sleepwalking. She had gotten herself back to her house only after no doubt having fallen into a bog. Nothing more, nothing less.

She didn't touch him, though, and he didn't reach for her hand. She thought if she made any sort of contact with him, she just might shatter in truth.

Maybe he felt the same way.

She looked out the window and tried to ground herself in her current reality.

It was harder than she'd expected it to be.

Chapter 16

*I*t was difficult to decide what to say to a woman you had rescued from a medieval dungeon, killed a man in front of, and subsequently invited out to breakfast as if none of the other events had taken place.

Nathaniel had never had company on his adventures, and he certainly hadn't the company of a woman he'd saved from being drowned in the lake at sunrise only thanks to some very fast talking. He was actually rather glad she didn't speak Gaelic or she likely would have slapped him instead of going off with him after what he'd had to say about her to Iain MacLeod there at the door earlier that morning.

He drove north because he knew where to find a quaint little pub where he imagined he could procure something tasty to eat. The region was also famous for scenic footpaths, which might come in handy as a distraction. He thought he might even be able to find Emma a coat.

He turned on the radio, because whilst he was very fond of piping, he would have preferred to get the medieval version of it out of his head. Piping left him thinking about battle, which left him wondering why the hell that Fergusson clansman he'd slain had been where he shouldn't have been. At least he had done his duty to the MacLeods and spared them an unexpected early-morning assault.

Of course, none of that began to explain why Emma had found herself joining the medieval madness he'd believed was reserved only for him, but perhaps he knew the answer without giving it too much thought. She'd put her hand to his dagger in Thomas Campbell's museum. For all he knew, that had been enough to send her to a place where neither of them belonged.

He would investigate that later. At the moment, all he wanted to do was stop thinking and keep driving. In truth, he had no idea what to say and he was frankly terrified to look at Emma and possibly find her watching him too closely.

"What's that castle there?"

He looked to his left and suppressed a shiver. "An old Fergusson stronghold."

"Is Hamish the policeman related to them?"

"I imagine so."

She was silent for a moment or two. "Mrs. McCreedy doesn't seem to like him very much."

"He's a royal pain in the arse," Nathaniel said with a snort. "She has good reason."

"She said he gave her a speeding ticket."

Nathaniel looked at her then. "Did he? She doesn't drive."

"She was riding her bicycle."

He smiled. "The bloody punter. He'd best be careful. She has a mean swing with a golf club."

"That doesn't surprise me at all."

He felt himself relax just the smallest bit. "Do you play?"

"Play what?"

He looked at her in surprise. "Golf, of course."

"Golf is a ridiculous game that takes up great amounts of time that could be used more sensibly."

He felt his mouth fall open, then he considered. He slid her a brief glance. "Your mother?"

"Word for word," she agreed. "I wish I had a nickel for every time I've heard her say that."

"Yet you still don't play, not even to vex her."

"No time, no money, no desire," she said. "Do you play?"

"Every chance I get." He glanced at her. "Not interested in being my caddy?"

She glared at him. He would have smiled, but he suspected that might be the best it got for him that day. He had convinced her to come to breakfast with him. He might be wise to take that and run with it.

He was happy to leave the Fergusson ruin behind them and continue on. The roads were very good, the weather overcast

and chilly, and he was driving his favorite car. It was an osten-
tatious bastard, but he loved it in a way that he supposed didn't
do him any credit. He was fond of his Vanquish, but it felt a
little too tame to him. What he had under his hands at the
moment . . .

He shook his head. His life was full of too many good
things.

If only he could have convinced the woman sitting next to
him that perhaps she might like to share a few of those things
with him, he might have enjoyed them more.

He would have held her hand, but he supposed she might
sooner want to clout him on the nose than touch him, so he
forbore and concentrated on not driving them off into a ditch.

It took an hour and a bit to get where he wanted to go, but
he was relieved to see the pub was open even so late in the
year. He supposed there were even a few intrepid hikers brav-
ing the chill to venture out for the view. He couldn't blame
them. He loved the forest near his house, true, but there was
nothing quite like Scotland's coastline to truly restore something elemental to the soul.

He pulled into the car park, then turned off his car and
looked at his companion.

"Normalcy," he said, then almost wished he hadn't spoken.
She looked as though she might just weep if pushed any
further.

He got out, walked around and opened her door, then
locked it behind her. She looked up at him and he almost
pulled her into his arms. The poor lass looked haunted. Sheldon the louse might have annoyed her, but the night before . . .
that had done something entirely more devastating to her.

He reached for her hand against his better judgment. She
didn't pull away, though, which he appreciated. Her fingers
were icy cold, which bothered him, but he wasn't sure what to
do for her save look for a pair of gloves after he'd fed her.

There was a hot fire inside, something for which he was
enormously grateful. He saw Emma seated next to it before he
went and ordered breakfast for them. He returned with two
steaming cups of coffee and sat down across from her. She
was looking at a tourist brochure and he left her to it. He
hardly knew what to say, if anything, and he wasn't going to
force her to process anything she wasn't ready to.

It had taken him a solid fortnight after his first foray into the past before he'd managed to put two words together in any useful fashion. If Mrs. McCreedy hadn't sent a lad out to his house with groceries, he likely would have starved to death.

He pulled out his phone and went shopping. It didn't matter what Emma chose to do; she would need a way to get around. And whilst it was very good of Patrick MacLeod to lend her a car, that wouldn't do over the long term.

Assuming there was a long term.

His tastes ran to things that were fast and expensive, but he didn't imagine either of those things would appeal to Emma presently. He supposed the best he could do was get what he felt was safe and reliable and hope she would accept it. He looked up to find her watching him. He smiled faintly.

"What's your favorite color?"

"Blue, why?"

"Dark or powder?"

She frowned. "Why?"

"Because I'm buying you a car and I want you to like it."

She looked at him evenly. "I thought you wanted me to move."

He felt any smile he might have been wearing fade. "I wanted you to be safe. I still do."

She took a deep breath. "I had a bad dream that I don't want to talk about and you can't buy me a car."

"What color?" he asked politely.

"Black," she said shortly, "and don't put it in my name or I won't drive it."

"Then I'll purchase it and you drive it as long as you want it," he said.

She rolled her eyes and reached for her cup. Her hand was trembling, so she curled her fingers into her palm and put her hands in her lap. He would have winced, indeed he suspected he had, but he didn't know what he could do about it outside of putting her on a plane to a different country himself.

He didn't think he could manage that.

They ate in silence and he finalized a car inquiry over the phone with a dealer in Inverness. Short of either sending her away or locking her in her house, he had provided what safety and security he could for the next pair of days.

After that, he just didn't know.

* * *

S_{everal} hours later, he was standing with her on her front porch, waiting for her to let herself inside. It had been a pleasant day as days out went, full of nothing but the sea and sky and a decent afternoon tea on the way home. He hardly knew what to say and he wasn't going to force her to talk about anything she didn't want to.

She let herself into her house, flicked on the lights, then paused.

"Shall I light your fire for you?" he asked.

She nodded, looking as if not even that could warm her. He'd driven home only after having wrapped her in a blanket he'd bought in the same store where he'd found a warm coat for her, but neither had seemed to be of any use to her.

He lit the fire, brushed off his hands, then turned and looked at her. She was standing by the kitchen table, looking exhausted. And why not? She'd likely been standing in that dungeon the whole time. He understood. He'd spent his own share of time in that pit, and he hadn't dared sit, either.

"I could make you tea before I go—"

"Stay."

He looked at her in surprise. "Sorry?"

She gestured inelegantly toward the little lounge. "Surely you have crap TV here in the UK. Why don't you stay and watch some with me." She looked at him. "You know. Normal stuff."

He let out the breath he realized he'd been holding all day. "Happily."

She moved to take the kettle to fill it. He supposed he wouldn't have managed to catch it before she dropped it if he hadn't been expecting the like.

"Why don't you sit," he suggested. "I'll bring the tea."

"We don't have anything stronger."

"I would imagine there's whisky in the cupboard," he assured her.

"I was hoping for chocolate."

He smiled. "I'll see what I can find."

She nodded, but she didn't move. He put the kettle on around her, then led her out of the kitchen and installed her on the sofa. He turned on the telly, found the least objectionable

bit of satellite rubbish he could—some sappy period piece he
was sure would put them both to sleep within moments—then
retreated to the kitchen to catch his breath and fix what would
have to pass for supper.

Twenty minutes later, he was looking for somewhere to set
his burdens down. Emma moved a sketchbook off the coffee
table, then watched him pour tea with a liberal splash of something strengthening. He pretended not to watch as she struggled to even get the damned cup to her mouth without spilling
its contents.

"You've been sketching," he noted.

"Not today, but before," she agreed. "Yes."

"Might I look?"

"If you like."

He took the sketchbook from her and opened the cover. He
froze. It was him, leaning against his Range Rover. He suspected it was the day when they'd gone to Inverness to drop
off her car. Her talent was absolutely staggering, but that
wasn't what left him feeling completely winded.

He was standing there in medieval dress.

He flipped through the rest of the pages slowly, then shut
the book and looked at her. "You're very good," he said finally.

"You're a good model."

"I'm stunned at my own handsomeness, truly."

He looked at her to find her smiling slightly. It was the first
true expression of anything but panic he'd had from her all
day. She looked at him and her smile faded.

"I don't want to talk about anything that absolutely couldn't
possibly have happened yesterday."

He considered what he should say for several minutes
before he attempted to speak. "You have to be where I'm not,"
he said finally.

"I had a very bad dream. Nothing more. I'm fine."

He looked at her seriously. "You need to be where I am
not," he repeated.

She lifted her chin and glared at him. "I might not want
anything to do with you."

"Well, I suggested you be choosy. I didn't imply that you
should be daft."

She blinked.

Then she burst into tears.

He rescued her cup and put it on the table with her sketch-book, then sat back and gathered her into his arms. He held her and had to admit he got a bit misty-eyed himself. He'd been in her shoes exactly, save that he hadn't been a woman and he'd spoken Gaelic—at least the modern-day incarnation of the same. He had at least been able to understand the lads about him as they'd been trying to decide how best to put him to death whilst inflicting the most amount of pain possible beforehand.

He eventually found tissues for her—nothing more elegant than half a loo roll—and made as many soothing noises as he dared. In time, she was merely breathing raggedly as she pressed her face against his neck and held on to him. She finally stopped shaking and simply breathed, a bit unevenly but without the shudders.

"The program wasn't that terrible," he said finally. "You wanted crap telly."

Her hand twitched as it lay on his chest. "Shut up, you horrible man."

He laughed a little and settled her more comfortably. "Your tea is cold, darling."

"You put a little Scottish flag cozy over the pot. Besides, I wasn't losing it for that long."

He smiled. "I meant what's in your cup. Let me fetch you more, though it grieves me deeply to toss even a splash of that extremely expensive whisky James MacLeod had locked up in his liquor cabinet."

She lifted her head and looked at him. "Did you pick that lock?"

He considered. "Might have."

"Some day you and I will play Truth or Dare," she said hoarsely. "It won't go well for you, I'm sure."

He took her cup and stood up. "I'll think about it. Don't move."

She only watched him go, which he supposed should have made him very nervous indeed. But she didn't move and her hand was much steadier on her next attempt at throwing back whisky-infused tea. He should have been appalled at the waste of the first batch of it, but he couldn't say he hadn't done the same thing himself, and more than once.

He spent the rest of the evening curled up with her on the

sofa with her head on his shoulder and his hands to himself. He was fairly sure he'd slept, because he snorted himself awake. She was indiscreet enough to refuse to ignore that.

"Welcome back, Sleeping Beauty."

He grunted. "You could have refrained from comment."

"You tried to talk me into caddying for you, probably in the snow."

"I bought you a car."

"And forced me to drink whisky-laden tea."

He smiled and suppressed the urge to tip her face up and kiss her. He thought that perhaps it would behoove him to keep his hands and his mouth to himself.

"Nathaniel?"

"Call me Nat."

She laughed, the barest huff of a laugh. "Do I know you well enough to call you Nat?"

"You drooled on my shoulder and you've tempted me to hand you the keys to my car. I think that entitles you to quite a few liberties at my expense."

She sighed deeply. "Thank you. It was a very lovely day."

"My pleasure."

"How do you say *I'm not a demon* in Gaelic?"

He froze. He sat up and shifted to look at her. "What?"

She looked at him, clear-eyed. "You heard me."

"I heard you, but I don't want to answer you."

She took a very careful breath. "Please."

Damn it to hell, what was he supposed to do besides answer her? He cursed a bit, then spat out the words as quickly as possible.

"Chan eil mi a deomhan."

"Don't suppose you know a more vintage rendition of that."

"Don't suppose I would tell you if I did."

She leaned over and kissed his cheek. "Go home, Nathaniel."

"Emma—"

She stood and held down her hand for him. "I'm tired."

He let her pull him to his feet, walked to the door with her, then paused on the threshold. He looked at her seriously.

"Emma, don't."

"I'm not going to do anything," she said seriously. "Are you crazy? I'm going to stay right here and watch as many versions of *Pride and Prejudice* as I can find. Come back for breakfast."

"Emma—"

"Here's your coat, lad," she said, shoving the same into his hands.

She all but shut the door on his arse, which he supposed he deserved. He found himself standing outside her door, in the cold, with his coat in his hands. He frowned, waited until he'd heard the lock click shut, then slowly made his way to his car. That woman was up to something. He couldn't believe that she would actually go back to the past now that she'd seen what it had to offer, but what did he know?

He decided the only reasonable course of action would be to go home and get a decent night's sleep, then find himself a decent spot in the morning from which to watch her house.

He didn't dare do anything else.

Chapter 17

Emma listened to the sound of Nathaniel's car fade into the distance. She washed up the tea things not because she was interested in a clean kitchen, but because she needed to be doing something that felt like it belonged in the current day. She dried her hands off, then turned around and leaned back against the sink.

There were strange things going on in the forest.

She suspected that if she'd had any sense at all, she would have gone to bed and hoped to wake up to a different reality. Or, actually, her regular reality. A reality that didn't now include the knowledge of how to say *I'm not a demon* in Gaelic.

She made a last stab at pretending nothing had changed. Her recent experiences had been a bad dream. Sleepwalking. A crisis brought on by a lack of American junk food. After all, she had been under an enormous amount of stress in Seattle before she'd even gotten on a plane to escape to an entirely different country. It was possible that all that pressure had taken its toll, leaving her vulnerable to something small and insignificant pushing her over the edge.

The truth was, her life was complicated. She was being stalked by a grown man who was actually a ten-year-old boy with keys and a checkbook. She didn't imagine Sheldon had the courage to actually get on a plane and confront her in person, but she'd been surprised by his actions before.

Then there was what she'd experienced so far in Scotland. Hadn't she spent that first day listening to those old-timers down at the pub really hitting their stride with their stories about strange things happening in the woods? Hadn't those stories included time travel, ghosts, bogles, and recluses with fancy cars and gigantic bank accounts?

Well, she knew that last item was actually just an accurate description of her very handsome neighbor who had killed someone dressed in a filthy kilt, apparently to save her life—

She forced herself to take a series of deep, even breaths before she went to find a piece of paper to make a list. Lists made her feel better, even if she only scribbled them in left-over spaces in her sketchbooks, then ignored them. She grabbed her book, sat down at the kitchen table, then started with a fresh page on the off chance good sense returned and she decided to chuck it in the fire before anyone saw it.

She began with everything she'd heard from those grand-pas down at the pub: time travel, creatures from nightmare, guys hiding in the woods, lairds not born in the right century. She added Mrs. McCreedy's bit about Highland magic, but she couldn't remember if the woman had said anything else.

On the other side of the page, she put down everything she knew about Nathaniel MacLeod and his handsome, secretive self. She had to add a little something about his ability to cook, his fondness for golf, and his willingness to offer comfort apparently without expecting anything in return. Oh, and he made her laugh.

There was a big space between those two columns that she filled in with her experience, which consisted of seeing some-one who looked exactly like Nathaniel MacLeod darting in and out of a medieval battle scene, her own raging hallucina-tions about being in a medieval dungeon, and the fact that she had a third of her wardrobe apparently either stashed in a gar-bage can or hiding behind a shrubbery, thanks to its state of ruination.

She studied each column again, adding doodles that con-tained several poisonous substance symbols, a zombie in a straitjacket, and Bigfoot peeking out from behind a tree.

She looked off thoughtfully into her little sitting room and considered what she'd laid out. She didn't want to believe the picture it was painting, mostly because it was just too fantasti-cal to be believed. Men didn't travel through time, the forest near her home wasn't a portal into a different century, and she wasn't caught up in what felt like the middle of both.

If she'd had any sense, she would have forgotten everything she'd seen right along with all the tall tales she'd heard and gone straight to bed. She could have gotten up in the morning, texted Nathaniel, and invited herself over for tea and conversation as if nothing unusual was going on.

Or she could do a bit of very careful investigating.

The thought left her feeling as if she didn't quite have enough of herself to fill her body and what she had left was absolutely terrified. Unfortunately, she just didn't see any other way to put the doubting of her sanity to rest once and for all. For all she knew, she might be of some help to someone.

Nathaniel MacLeod, perhaps.

She banked her fire, because it gave her a reason to stall for a bit, then stood in her kitchen and dithered. Real spies didn't dither, or so she'd always heard Bertie say, and she was beginning to understand why. Too much time spent thinking was not at all good for the nerves.

She walked into her bedroom, changed into black leggings, a black sweater, and a black slicker, slipped tools for the picking of locks into a passport belt she had converted into something entirely different, then left her house. It was black as pitch outside, but she supposed her eyes would adjust in time. She stashed a key under the tire of the car Patrick had loaned her, then made her way toward the forest.

It was odd how normal everything felt. The longer she walked, the more she realized that things felt different from the other night. She paused by the tree where she'd first leaned while watching who she now knew to be Nathaniel fighting for his life against medieval clansmen, and she felt . . . nothing. No tingle, no unsettling vision, no feeling of the world splitting down its center.

She considered that until she realized she was cold, then she turned and retraced her steps to her house. She picked the lock to get inside, just for practice's sake, considered the fact that hiding a key under a tire was overkill, then went inside to give things a bit more thought.

Whatever had been going on before was definitely not going on at present. She thought back over the events of the past several days, looking for something that seemed off. The only thing that came to mind was their experience with that dagger in Edinburgh. Well, that and his reaction at—

At Cawdor Castle. She looked around herself frantically for her guidebook only to remember that she'd set it down on a side table and never picked it back up. Then again, she'd been concentrating on getting Nathaniel to his car, not stockpiling items for use in future time traveling. It was too bad she hadn't managed to slip Mr. Campbell's dagger into her backpack.

She wandered through the sitting room, wondering if there might be something closer to home she could use for the same purpose, then stopped when she noticed a little bookcase tucked into a corner of the room. She walked over to it and scanned the titles there.

A Pictorial History of Medieval Scotland.

She pulled the book free of the bookcase without the world falling to pieces around her. She perched on the edge of the coffee table because sitting on the couch felt like too much of a commitment and she wasn't sure when she would need to get up and run.

She opened the cover of the book, paused for a reaction from any stray Highland magic hiding in her house, then cautiously flipped through the pages. She had no idea who had come up with that title or acquired the photographs as evidence, but she soon realized that the author had obviously spent years collecting pictures of paintings and sketches. She looked to see if things were organized by date or region, then realized they were mostly organized by clan. She took a leap of faith and looked up the MacLeods of Assynt.

And there, in all its glory, was the castle she'd seen in the flesh. She looked at the illustration credits.

The MacLeod Keep, ca. 1387—

That was as far as she got before she realized she wasn't holding that book while sitting on a low table, she was sprawled on the floor, and it hadn't been a comfortable trip there. She crawled to her feet, took the book over to the kitchen table, then set it down.

1387. What the hell was it with that date?

She stood at the table, looking down at that illustration for what felt like hours, until she couldn't ignore the inexorable pull of something that was far, far bigger than what her simple life was able to contain.

Was *that* what Nathaniel felt whenever he heard that date?

There was only one way to know for certain. She ruthlessly squelched the first squeaks of alarm from her common sense, ripped out the page in question, then folded it up and stuck it in her bra. She would ask James MacLeod later to forgive her for what she'd done to his book.

She left the house, locked it, then started for the forest. She would only go as far as she was comfortable with, which she suspected wouldn't be all that far. Perhaps she would see something Nathaniel hadn't. Perhaps she would actually see some sort of doorway through time and have the presence of mind to make a note of its location so Nathaniel could avoid it in the future.

She took a deep breath, reminded herself of all the survival skills Bertie had taught her, then continued on into the forest.

Things were different. Perhaps not so much in the forest by her house, but definitely as she continued on. Something had shifted in a way that was absolutely unmistakable—

She realized too late that she wasn't going to be able to control the gate she was now firmly convinced had to exist between centuries. She was on the other side of it before she realized she'd entered it and it had shut behind her with an almost audible click.

Damn it anyway.

She had as little control over subsequent events as she'd had over her arrival into the midst of them. The one thing she could say with certainty was that informing the lads who arrived as if they'd been following a director's cue that she wasn't a demon didn't improve things in the slightest.

What was surprising, though, was the overwhelming sense of déjà vu she had. It was as if her dream were replaying itself, but with an exactness that was less reassuring than it was extremely unsettling. She found herself escorted through the forest at exactly the same pace, waited with the boys at the edge of the meadow for exactly the same amount of time, watched Nathaniel race across the meadow at exactly the same speed he'd used the time before.

She wasn't surprised when he ignored her. She was actually even less surprised to find herself yet again up to her ankles in the muck of the dungeon, but surely Nathaniel would rescue her.

Unless he didn't.

She thought she had the presence of mind to have things handled, but she realized, as she stood there and fought very unsuccessfully another bout of shock, that she didn't have anything handled at all.

She had only intended to investigate the entrance to, well, wherever she was. She hadn't intended to become embroiled in the nightmare all over again. For all she knew, she had just plunged herself into a situation from which she would never escape. She would die in a medieval dungeon and no one would be the wiser. Sheldon would find some way to completely drain her bank accounts, her father would be happy to be rid of any possibility of her showing up for family gatherings, and her siblings would gleefully rub their hands together over the thought of splitting four ways the inheritance her mother had set aside for her out of her pocket money.

She, on the other hand, would die cold, terrified, and likely as a result of the things she could feel crawling up her shins. Thank heavens she was wearing leggings tucked into boots instead of just regular old pants that might have let things crawl directly on her skin.

She heard the hall settle down for the night and realized after what had to have been an hour that she was holding her breath. She forced herself to breathe evenly and fight off panic. What if he didn't come? What if he was furious that she'd put him in a similar situation two nights in a row?

What if he'd clunked his head on something upstairs and forgotten all about her?

The grate moved. She closed her eyes briefly in thanks, then waited for the hand to be extended. She was better prepared that time and of more help to her rescuer. She held on to Nathaniel's arm once she was free, then nodded.

"Ready," she whispered.

"I am going to yell at you later," he muttered. "Loudly."

She would have smiled, but she didn't dare. She was too busy hoping nothing would stop them from getting out of the hall itself.

They made it to the front door when they were stopped.

Emma honestly couldn't remember if it was the same guy as before or not. The truth was, she'd been so flipped out the night before, she hadn't noticed anything past how badly she smelled and how desperately she wanted not to be where she was.

But within moments they were outside walking toward the forest. Once they were there, Nathaniel looked at her.

"Can you run?"

"Yes."

He glared at her. She shrugged helplessly but didn't bother to explain herself. Hopefully there would be time enough for that later. She simply ran with him across the meadow and into the trees.

She was almost unsurprised when that stray clansman jumped out at them, only this time she noticed the dagger in his hand and how close to her chest it was before Nathaniel skewered him on the end of his sword.

She threw up anyway.

She had to admit that half an hour later when she was stumbling out from the edge of the forest and could see the lights from her house in the distance, she did the most sensible thing she'd done all night.

She burst into tears.

Nathaniel pulled her back into a walk and slung his arm around her shoulders. "We're almost home."

"I never cry."

"You will once I'm done shouting at you."

But he stopped, turned her to him, and held her until she was simply shaking so hard that her teeth were chattering. He finally half carried her to her house. He didn't yell, not even when they were standing on her porch.

"Key?" he asked wearily.

"Under the front tire of Patrick's car," she managed. "I'll go get it."

"Stay here."

She didn't even dare lean against the doorframe. She was just as disgustingly filthy as she had been the first time. If she didn't get hold of her nocturnal activities, she was going to be completely out of clothes before the week was out.

Nathaniel opened her door for her, turned on the lights, then handed her the key. He folded his arms over his chest and looked her up and down.

"Demon garb?" he asked sourly.

"Not anymore," she said. She attempted a smile, but failed. "I was just trying to investigate the gate." She took a deep breath. "I thought I could help you."

"Darling, what you need is a keeper. I would offer myself for the job, but my life is complicated. What I want you to do is take that damned Audi I just bought you and get the hell over to the other side of the country."

She lifted her chin. "No, you don't."

He swore at her. She supposed that was Gaelic. She imagined it hadn't been complimentary.

"Where'd you learn that?" she asked.

His mouth worked for a moment or two, as if he simply couldn't find the words he was looking for. "Where in the hell do you *think* I learned it?" he asked incredulously.

"You're cranky."

"What I am is fighting the almost irresistible impulse to wring your neck!"

She did smile then. "No, you definitely aren't." Then she noticed the stain on the front of his plaid, which was tossed over what looked to be a linen shirt of some kind.

That was blood from the man who had tried to kill her.

She pushed past him before she threw up on him. She leaned over the railing, dry heaving, until she was simply standing there, gasping for breath. It was quite a while before she regained enough control of herself to notice that he was standing next to her with his hand resting lightly on her back.

"I'm sorry," she managed finally. "I'm so sorry."

He took her by the arms, turned her to him, and looked at her seriously. "I am going to go home now, take a shower, and go to bed. I want your word that you'll do exactly the same thing."

"I'm not sure what my alternative is," she managed. "I'm running out of clothes to ruin."

"Which is why we should go shopping very soon, perhaps at Harrods, where you'll be comfortably far away from anything that will get you in trouble." He stepped back. "I want your promise that you'll stay home. Promise me. I'm fully prepared to babysit you if I have to."

"I'm going to strip, take a shower, then go to bed myself. It wouldn't be very interesting."

He smiled faintly. "That is a matter of opinion, I assure you, and almost more temptation than I can bear to walk away from." He nodded toward her door. "Inside, woman. Don't make me prod you there with my sword."

She had no doubts that he would if pressed, and she'd already forced him to—

She couldn't think about that, and she didn't want to ask him if he'd done that sort of thing before because she had the feeling he had. She took a deep breath, then nodded and walked to her door.

"Emma?"

She turned and looked at him. "Yes?"

He seemed to be wrestling with what he wanted to say, but she didn't think she should help him. The truth was, she didn't want to talk about anything more serious than what might be good for breakfast later.

"I'm curious," he said finally and apparently quite unwillingly. He stopped, then simply looked at her in silence.

She understood what he was getting at. She dug around in her shirt and came up with her page. She held it up. "I ripped this out of a book."

"What is it?"

"It says it's a drawing of the MacLeod keep in 13 . . . well, you know."

He was in denial, that man there. He only looked at her and shook his head. "You can't do this, Emma."

"Rip pages out of books?"

He looked at her evenly. "You cannot do this, Emma."

"All right."

He dragged his hand through his hair and swore. He looked at her. "I'm not going to discuss this."

"And you think I want to?"

He scowled at her, but came inside and lit the fire in her stove just the same. He walked past her back outside without looking at her. "Lock up."

"I always do."

"I'll be back later." He looked at her over his shoulder. "You had best be here or there'll be hell to pay."

And not from me was what he didn't add, but she suspected he was thinking it just as seriously as she was.

She nodded, then shut herself inside her house. She stripped right there in the kitchen, showered, then took her clothes outside and tossed them in a garbage can she was sure didn't get emptied all that often. She didn't want to think about what anyone might think of what she'd contributed.

She went to bed because she couldn't remember the last time she'd slept in one. She was going to have to figure things out—

No. No, she wasn't. She was going to pull herself together, thank Patrick for the loan of his car and Nathaniel for the offer of his, then pack her stuff and go. She didn't like to think she had things handled only to find she didn't have anything handled at all.

Maybe that was exactly how Nathaniel felt.

She stared up at the ceiling for a few minutes, grateful for the soft light from the lamp she'd left on in the living room, and wondered how exactly Nathaniel dealt with . . . well, whatever it was he was dealing with, which couldn't possibly be anything she had unthinkably been sucked into.

That was, she decided, something she could avoid thinking about until later.

She closed her eyes and shook until she finally fell into an uneasy sleep.

Chapter 18

Nathaniel thought he just might have reached the end of his tether. Considering how many times he had clutched what he'd thought was the end of that rope, that was indeed saying something. Perhaps what he needed was more than three hours' sleep at a stretch, more than twenty-four hours between trips to the past, and a few answers. A vacation would have served as well, but he didn't see that happening any time soon.

All he knew was that he never again wanted to watch a man leap out of the shadows and manage to get his dagger that close to Emma Baxter's chest before he could be stopped.

Some of it might have had to do with how little he cared to think about that element of his life in the past. He fought to defend his clan, such as it was, and he had now fought the same man twice to defend his woman. He did both knowing that the damage he inflicted on his attackers was permanent and generally fatal. He did it because he had to.

He shook his head. He was starting to sound like a medieval clansman in his head. It was only a matter of time before he started spouting that kind of rubbish aloud and to men in the current day. That was something he could deal with, he supposed. Reliving what felt like the same day in the past more than once was something he was still trying to digest.

It had been the same day, hadn't it?

He didn't know, but he'd already texted the man he thought might be able to help him determine that. He'd been granted an audience, in just those words. He'd been reminded to bring along the appropriate gear. He hadn't had to ask what that gear might be, because he'd already had it clarified for him several days earlier. He suspected a morning facing Patrick MacLeod over blades wasn't going to be very pleasant, but he was backed into a corner and needed answers.

The same day repeating. As if time traveling itself wasn't gobsmacking enough on its own . . .

He steadfastly refused to think about the fact that if he'd tried to sort things a year earlier with Patrick's help, perhaps even a pair of months earlier, he wouldn't have had to save Emma's life twice, nor watch her fall apart in front of him the same number of times.

He would have shaken his head over the state of affairs in his life, but he'd done that so much that he'd gotten a crackle in his neck that took noisy flight every time he turned to look at something.

He pulled to a stop in front of Emma's cottage, then simply sat there and thought about her for a moment or two. The woman owned spy clothes. How extensive that wardrobe might have been was definitely something to investigate before he took her shopping. Depending on what he found, he would no doubt have an opinion on what she purchased. He suspected she would pay as much heed to that as she'd paid to anything else he'd said to that point, which was exactly none.

Damn her to hell, he thought he might never get her out of his heart or his head.

He crawled out of his car, stood on her porch, and gave one last thought to the wisdom of what he was planning. He didn't want to talk to her about what had become a shared experience in a different lifetime, he just wanted it to stop. Unfortunately, he was afraid if he just left her alone, she would go off and do something again that he might have considered ill-advised.

And he might not be able to reach her in time.

He sighed and lifted his hand to knock, then jumped a bit when the door opened before he could. Mistress Emmaline Baxter stood there, dressed in jeans and holding a pair of high-heeled shoes in one hand and plaid muck boots in the other. He blinked, then smiled. She did not smile in return.

"I'm out of clothes," she said with a scowl.

"There's a mercy there."

"And shoes."

"So I see," he noted. "We'll go to Inverness tomorrow and see what can be found. I don't think I'll be buying you any useful shoes, though. Don't want you scampering off."

"You won't need to worry about that, because you're not going to be buying me anything, buster," she said. "I was planning on running into the village this morning to buy my own footwear."

"Why don't you opt for boots and come with me for a morning of adventure at Patrick MacLeod's hall?"

She hesitated. "It sounds better than what I had planned."

"And what was that?"

"I was considering driving to that old Fergusson castle—"

"Don't," he interrupted before he thought better of it.

She studied him. "Any reason why not?"

The list was very long and he imagined she could supply at least a handful of items for it. He looked at her, but couldn't bring himself to say anything. Damn it to hell, he was *not* going to concede to anything as barking as time travel. He simply refused.

She sighed. She put her shoes inside, put her boots on, then pulled the door closed behind her. She locked it, then looked at him. He didn't want to feel any undue pleasure that she was wearing the jacket he'd bought her—she likely didn't have anything else—but there it was.

He was lost.

"So, where is it you're going again?" she asked.

"I was planning on paying a visit to the young Himself, as the locals call him," Nathaniel said. "I think you should come with me so I can keep an eye on you."

She frowned at him. "I thought you wanted me to go away."

"I wanted and still want you to be safe. I have madness to solve." He supposed he didn't need to elaborate on that. "Until it's solved, I want you safe. But apparently that now means I must keep you near me for great stretches of time."

"Well," she said with a shrug, "if you have to."

He wasn't sure if the thought was appealing or repulsive to her, but she wasn't losing her breakfast over the railing, so he decided to reserve judgment. He walked with her over to his car, then opened the door for her. She looked inside, then froze. She simply stood there for a moment or two, breathing lightly, before she looked up at him.

"What's that?"

"I think you know."

"I don't think I want to talk about it."

He smiled wearily. "Welcome to my life."

She looked at him for so long, he began to feel a little uneasy. She said nothing else, but simply slid into her seat, shifting his sword a bit so they both would fit. He walked around his car, got in, then drove them to the village for a quick croissant and something warm to drink. Thus fortified, he made for Patrick MacLeod's house and hoped he would manage to get away from the place with equal ease.

He realized once he'd stopped in Patrick's courtyard that Emma hadn't said anything since they'd left the village. He looked at her to find her looking at the castle.

"Why again are we here?"

He sighed. "I have some questions for him."

"And you thought you would get better answers from him if you had your sword?"

"That's the price of admission."

"There are rumors about him down at the pub," she said slowly, "but I dismissed them." She glanced at him. "What do you think?"

"I'm not sure you want to know," he said, "but I might have a better opinion in an hour or two if you're really curious." He got out of the car, walked around to open her door for her, then retrieved his sword after she'd gotten out. He took a deep breath and looked at her. "Assuming I survive the morning."

"I'll rush to your defense if you need it."

He propped his sword up against his shoulder and shut the door, then smiled. "Could you?"

"My brothers would probably have an opinion on it."

"I think I would like to meet them in a darkened alley sometime."

"My hero," she said seriously.

"You might think differently when you're carrying me back to the car and tucking me into bed tonight, but I'll claim that title for as long as I can."

She glanced at his sword, then met his eyes. "I don't want to talk about the past few days."

"I understand."

She looked at him gravely. "Thank you."

He attempted a smile. "You're welcome."

"I'm sorry I put you in that position."

He reached out with his free arm and pulled her close, mostly so she wouldn't see his eyes growing red. "Dinnae fash yerself, lass," he murmured. "We're likely just imagining it all anyway."

She patted his back. "I'm sure you're right."

He nodded, then stepped away. He could hardly believe he was contemplating his current madness, but he supposed he'd marched into worse. He locked his car, then walked with Emma across the courtyard to the front door.

Patrick opened the door at his knock, looked him up and down, and smiled. "I see you came prepared."

"You said I should," Nathaniel said pointedly.

Patrick stood back and held the door open. "And so I did. You find me in reduced circumstances, I'm afraid. Maddy took the bairns and went with Sunny and my sister-in-law, Elizabeth, to London to escape the chill for a bit."

"A big city, London," Nathaniel noted.

Patrick lifted an eyebrow. "You don't think I sent them off alone, do you? Nay, my friend, we've an entire collection of terrifying lads to accompany our priceless treasures wherever they go." He shrugged lightly. "Old habits die hard, I suppose."

Nathaniel had no intention of asking him what he meant by that, mostly because he imagined he didn't need to. He stood to the side as Patrick asked Emma where she might most comfortably pass a few hours whilst he and Nathaniel took a bit of healthful air and exercise. Nathaniel didn't even consider protesting the length of time. If he managed to get himself out of Patrick's backyard before dark, he would be fortunate indeed.

"I'll watch you two at your work, if it's all the same to you," she said quietly.

Nathaniel caught the look Patrick threw him, but didn't respond. What was he going to say? That Emma had gotten lost in the past, he'd gone back to rescue her from the MacLeod dungeon, and he'd slain the same man twice in a row to get himself and Emma back to the present day safely?

He imagined His Lordship would have all those answers and more anyway whilst he was down on his knees begging for mercy, so he thought it might be best to simply leave them for then.

"You don't mind if we speak in the native tongue, do you?" Patrick asked politely. "I don't want to be rude, of course."

"Feel free," Emma said, waving him on. "Wouldn't want to stand in the way of keeping it alive."

Patrick looked at him and nodded. "Let's go, laddie. No sense in leaving my field untrampled."

"Do you have a field, my lord?"

"I do. I generally wreak havoc at my cousin Ian's, but I'm too lazy to walk there this morning. If you don't mind a bit of rough ground, I think we can find room enough beyond the garden."

Nathaniel wasn't sure what he minded. He was just suddenly beginning to wonder if bringing Emma along had been a grave mistake. He hadn't wanted to leave her unsupervised, but he was also not exactly sure he wanted her to see what he could do. She had already seen too much.

He chewed on that as he followed Patrick outside, saw Emma settled on a bit of low garden wall, then paused and looked at her. She was a grown woman, which he supposed meant that she could make up her own mind about what she wanted to see and what she wanted to look away from. The cold steel in his hand, though, brought him back to reality in a way that nothing had that morning.

"You know," he said to her carefully, "I didn't give you much choice about coming with me."

Her expression was very serious. "You didn't force me into the car with you, Nathaniel."

"But I didn't ask you what you wanted to do—"

"I wouldn't have come with you if I hadn't wanted to, no matter what you're holding in your hand right now." She gave him a half smile. "Besides, you bought me breakfast and offered to buy me clothes in the future. Hard to argue with either of those things."

He wanted to point out that they were completely avoiding what the subject at hand truly was, but she'd already told him that she didn't want to discuss it. That made it difficult to decide how facing off with Patrick MacLeod over medieval broadswords could improve anything.

She nodded toward their host. "Go hack away. I don't think I'll swoon."

He lifted his eyebrows briefly. "I can be pretty spectacular on the field, so you might want to leave the possibility open."

She laughed faintly. "Get lost, show-off. I'll go sit by the fire if I get bored. Patrick's already offered that escape route."

He took a deep breath, nodded, then walked off to follow Patrick out to what indeed proved to be a decent-sized bit of flat ground. As Patrick turned, he realized that the man had left the scabbard of his sword behind, likely against the garden wall, and he wondered why he hadn't thought to do the same.

Because he was completely ill-at-ease, that's why.

The sound of pipes starting up almost had him jumping out of his skin. He scarce had time to fling the scabbard of his sword far enough away that he thought he might stand a fair chance of not tripping over it before the ruthless lord of Benmore was coming at him, looking as though he had every intention of killing him.

That was the last coherent thought he had for quite some time.

When Patrick allowed him to breathe approximately an hour later—in all honesty, he had no idea how much time had gone by, but it felt as if a small slice of eternity had passed— he managed to latch on to at least one thought and that was that he could safely say that Patrick MacLeod was the best swordsman he had ever encountered. Given the number of medieval clansmen he'd faced off against, he thought he might be a respectable judge of the same.

He rested his hands on his sword, which was point-down against the ground, dragged frigid air into his desperate lungs, then managed to look at the man who had provided them with such delightful music to try to kill each other by. His mouth fell open as the piper walked over to them.

"Ah," Nathaniel said, wondering if he would look thoroughly weak if he simply sat down in the mud, "Robert."

Robert MacLeod laughed a little. "Nathaniel, my friend. How do you fare?"

Nathaniel looked quickly at Patrick, but the man was only standing there with his sword against his shoulder, watching him with the slightest of smiles. Obviously, there was no point in trying to avoid anything any longer. He looked at a man he had known several hundred years in the past.

"You're a ghost."

Robert shrugged. "Patty needs a piper now and again and I'm happy to oblige him."

"Nice to see all your fingers straight for a change."

"The beauties of the afterlife, my friend." He looked at Nathaniel. "Will your lady mind if I go visit with her?"

"I have absolutely no idea, but you can try."

Robert smiled and walked away. Nathaniel glanced Emma's way, but she was only watching him with a grave expression. She didn't even flinch when Robert introduced himself to her, which Nathaniel supposed should have concerned him. Then again, perhaps a ghostly piper wasn't the worst thing she'd seen in the past few days.

He took a deep breath, then looked at his host. He wondered if he had displayed enough skill with the sword to earn a few answers or if he was facing a man who would look at him as if he were daft if he asked any of the questions that burned in his mouth. More alarming still was the thought that perhaps he, as Emma continued to insist, had just imagined the past several years of his life.

"Are you ready to tell me anything interesting yet?" Patrick asked mildly.

Nathaniel dragged himself back from the edge of what felt like madness. "I'd rather ask you a few questions, if you don't mind."

"And you think I'll answer them after that feeble showing?"

"I could have a nap, then try again."

Patrick smiled, a quick little smile that Nathaniel imagined had earned him more than one wench willing to warm his bed.

He knew that because he had used that same smile more than once himself.

"I'll show mercy and allow you to pose the odd question, then decide if they're interesting enough to answer." Patrick looked at Nathaniel with a faint bit of alarm. "I sound just like my brother."

"Not a good thing?"

Patrick drew his sleeve across his eyes. "Nay, not at all," he said. "I think a whisky might put me to rights, but 'tis early yet." He nodded toward a section of stone wall. "Let's take our ease there for a moment or two and see if I can't recover on my own first."

Nathaniel nodded and followed Patrick over to sit down on the wall. He tried not to groan as he did so, though he had to admit his first inclination was to weep with relief that he wasn't trying to keep himself alive against the madman leaning casually against the rock and humming a cheerful battle tune.

"I don't suppose," Nathaniel said, when he thought he could voice a question without wheezing, "that you'll tell me your birth year."

"I don't suppose you can cut it from me, can you?"

"Not at the moment. I could try later, when I can move again."

Patrick smiled faintly. "Where'd you learn your sword-play?"

"On the job."

"It was well done." He seemed to consider his words for a moment or two. "I would suggest, however, that you have a care for that gel of yours. Those times are no place for a modern woman."

Nathaniel thought he could agree with that readily enough. "I hesitate to ask how you know that. In fact, I'm not sure, now that we've come right to it, that I'm ready to admit to any of this."

"Ye wee fool, you've been at this for five years," Patrick said, shaking his head in disbelief. "When are you going to be ready to discuss it?"

Nathaniel felt his mouth fall open. "How do you know that?"

Patrick looked at him evenly.

He shut his mouth and groped for something to say, some sort of excuse or explanation or lie to get himself out of the land of crazy and back to the reality where he belonged. Unfortunately, nothing useful came to mind, so he conceded the battle.

"And here I thought I was being so discreet," he managed.

"If it eases you any, 'twas my brother to poke his nose in your affairs and his purpose was to save you pain if he could."

He shrugged. "Once a laird of the clan MacLeod, always a laird of the same, I daresay."

Nathaniel would have asked what Patrick meant by that, but he imagined he didn't need to. He supposed he could pull up any genealogy of the lairds of that MacLeod castle up the way and find out just who was who. It wouldn't take long. He looked at Patrick carefully.

"And you don't worry about being discovered?"

"As what?" Patrick asked blandly. "I'm a simple writer, enjoying my lovely home, my stunning wife, and my sweet bairns." He looked at Nathaniel. "I have no idea what you're getting at."

Nathaniel nodded. "I deserve that."

"Indeed you do, lad. A bit more work?" Patrick asked politely. "Do you want to see if your lady cares to go inside first? She looks cold."

"I will go ask." Nathaniel pushed himself back to his feet. He started to limp away, then stopped. He turned and looked at Patrick MacLeod. Any sensible soul would have labeled him a modern man with a passion for medieval things. If he'd had any sense himself, he would have left it at that and escaped inside with Emma to seek out a hot fire.

But he apparently didn't have any sense.

"1300," he guessed.

Patrick pursed his lips. "1285."

"Impossible," Nathaniel said, with one last, desperate grasp at denial.

Patrick smiled, then nodded toward Emma. "See to your lady. I'm not going anywhere."

Nathaniel nodded, then walked away. He thought Emma looked less cold than gobsmacked, but then again, perhaps not after the things she'd already seen. Those were things she would never see again if he had anything to say about it. The sooner he convinced her to find a different place in Scotland to stay, the happier he would be.

He supposed it would take many, many times of repeating that before he believed it.

Chapter 19

Emma sat on a rock wall and watched Nathaniel MacLeod coming toward her from the far end of Patrick MacLeod's garden. The garden was lovely. The man walking over it was . . . well, he was beautiful in a way that she wasn't quite sure how to describe.

Very easy on the eyes.

Extremely hard on her heart.

She pulled the coat he'd bought her more closely around herself not so much to ward off the mist or to save herself against the breeze, but because he had given it to her. He had wrapped a blanket around her as well, which she appreciated. She closed her eyes briefly. She was cold and she suspected it had less to do with the weather than it did the things she had seen that morning.

Ghosts were certainly one of those things. She'd been a bit startled by conversing outside with a piper whose plaid seemed to swirl thanks to a wind she couldn't feel, but she'd managed to deal with that fairly well. Finding another pipe-smoking, geriatric geezer in front of Patrick's fire when she'd ducked inside earlier for a trip to the bathroom had been equally unusual. Having him instruct her to simply call him *The Glum* had certainly taken things to a new level of odd, but she'd been okay with it. She supposed that if things really got out of hand, she could simply pretend that she was losing her marbles again.

But seeing Nathaniel MacLeod with a sword in his hands, facing a swordsman of Patrick MacLeod's obvious mettle? She wasn't sure she was going to be able to consign that to any-thing but hard truth any time soon.

Nathaniel stopped and looked at her. She had a hard time reconciling the man she was looking at with the man who dressed in a plaid and used a sword, but it was hard to deny. Not now.

He shoved his sword into the ground with an unthinking-ness that, to her surprise, was quite possibly the worst thing she'd seen to date. She had tried to ignore what she'd seen. She'd gone only once to see the clothes Nathaniel had appar-ently dumped in the compost heap behind her house. She'd come so close to chalking everything up to a massive bout of delusory dreaming.

That sword jammed into the ground ten feet away from her, though—that was too real to relegate to nightmares.

She pushed herself off the wall, then walked unsteadily over to where Nathaniel had stopped next to his sword. She reached for his hand and turned it over to look at the calluses there. She ran her finger over them on the off chance her eyes were deceiving her.

He shivered.

She looked up at him, but couldn't bring herself to speak. She simply closed her eyes and stepped into his embrace.

"I'm so sorry," he said quietly.

She held on to him and shook right along with him for a bit until his warmth became hers in spite of the air that was bor-dering on bitter. She turned her head and rested it against his shoulder, where she could look out over the garden, then jumped in spite of herself. That might have been because Rob-ert the Piper, who had never quite left her side, had suddenly been joined by several other medieval-looking guys who had collected themselves in a loose group around him.

"Are you seeing this?" she whispered to Nathaniel.

"'Tis the Highlands, lass," he said, sounding resigned. "I've seen more things than I want to admit to."

She imagined he wasn't talking about the scenery. She would have pursued that a bit, but his phone sitting on the wall was ringing with an insistence that made her want to go answer it.

"I'll be back," he said, stepping away and smiling faintly at her. "The lads will see to you, I'm sure."

She was sure, too. She looked at the half dozen men who were in various states of sword-drawing and squeaked a little in spite of herself. The leader, a tall man who had a wicked scar down one cheek, looked at his companions.

"'Tis just the mobile, lads. Stand down."

Discussion ensued but Emma didn't understand a word of it because it was apparently being conducted in the Mother Tongue. She felt her way back to the wall and sat on it before she fell down. She didn't protest when Robert leaned against the wall next to her. She hardly had to remind herself to ignore the fact that while her teeth were chattering, his were definitely not.

"They're showing off," he said dryly. "They know what a mobile is. They're trying to impress you, I imagine."

"I can't imagine why," she managed.

"Jamie's forbid them going to Nat's house of their own accord, so I think they're trying to get around the laird's edict by making enough of an impression that they'll be invited. I suspect they're trying to enlist your aid." He shrugged with a smile. "Hard to say with ghosts, aye?"

She wasn't sure how to begin to respond to that, so she smiled sickly and looked around for Nathaniel. His sword was still stabbed into the dirt nearby, reminding her of how proficient he was with it in a pair of centuries.

"Mistress Emma," Robert said suddenly, "are you unwell?"

"Fine," she said hoarsely. "Bad eggs. I think I might want to lie down—"

Half a dozen Highland ghosts rushed forward to spread their plaids out on the top of the rocks while their leader folded his quickly and plumped it into a pillow.

She didn't have the heart to comment on the less-than-substantive nature of their clothing. It was bad enough to see them all standing there huddled in a little group, their long, cream-colored shirts not quite reaching their knees. She stretched out because she thought that might be better than falling off backward into what would no doubt turn out to be a patch of nettles.

She looked up at the sky until Nathaniel leaning over her blocked her view. She smiled gamely.

"Chivalry."

"I'd say so. How would you feel about a quick trip to Manhattan?"

"Now?"

"As soon as you can pack."

"I don't think I can move," she said, trying not to pop back up with enthusiasm. Nathaniel out of the country would mean she could do a little investigating in a safe place, maybe in a library that didn't find itself anywhere near the forest. "You go on. I'll be fine."

He gave her his hand and pulled her up into a sitting position. "You're coming with me."

She watched a pair of Highlanders frown, retrieve their plaids, and hop over the rock wall to stand behind her. She looked over her shoulder and was faintly relieved to find they weren't glaring at anyone but Nathaniel.

Thus empowered, she lifted her chin and looked at him.

"Don't boss me."

"I'm saving you."

One of the Highlanders behind her leaned up. "Hate to say as much, but he has a point there."

She looked up at that, er, ghost and felt a little faint. He was really rather handsome in a rugged sort of way, his less-than-corporeal nature aside. "He's telling me what to do."

"He's a man, yer a gel."

"Do you know what year this is?" She blinked, then looked at Nathaniel. "Okay, this is too far down the rabbit hole."

"Which is why you need to come to New York with me," he said firmly. "You can be my assistant."

"Guard his back and all," one of the Highlanders behind him agreed. "Handy with a dirk is she, Master Nathaniel?"

For once, Nathaniel looked as startled as she felt.

"Ah, I'm not sure," he managed. "I think I'm afraid to ask."

"We'll train her whilst ye finish up with Lord Patrick," a different ghost said. "Nae worries."

Nathaniel considered, then pulled his sword free of the ground. He smiled at Emma. "I'll be off then."

"But," she began, not quite sure how to call him a coward for ditching her.

"Ten minutes," he called over his shoulder, "then we'll go home to pack."

Emma wondered if it would be rude to learn to use a dirk on *him*. She looked at Robert for support only to find him smiling in amusement.

"I think you lost that battle," he offered.

"But not the war," she said. "Who wants to help me learn to stab him?"

There was some argument over whether or not that would be a good idea, but the possibility of retribution from Nathaniel was apparently less dire than her inability to protect his back in a tight spot. A tangible knife was produced by a ghost who then collapsed in exhaustion—she was going to have to ask someone about the details of that at some point—and she was given the basics in what she supposed passed for street fighting several centuries ago.

She thought it might properly be termed the longest half hour of her life.

B_y the time she was sitting in Nathaniel's very expensive sports car, heading toward Inverness to switch it for something less ding-worthy, she had decided that maybe normal was just going to continue to be out of reach for a while.

"I think I have a blister," she said at one point.

He smiled at her briefly. "I don't doubt it."

"That was really weird."

"That's one way to put it," he agreed. "I still don't think I believe in ghosts."

"But you believe in other kinds of paranormal activity," she said slowly. "Or am I wrong?"

He drove in silence for a moment or two, then looked at her.

"Are we having this conversation?" he asked.

"I was fully prepared not to," she admitted.

"And then you saw ghosts."

"I saw ghosts," she agreed. She watched the scenery for another couple of miles, then looked at him. "How long has it been going on?" She supposed she didn't need to clarify what she was talking about.

He sighed deeply. "Five years."

She blinked. "You've been going back and forth for *five years*?"

"Aye."

"What, once a week? Several times a month?"

"I haven't kept track—" He trailed off, passed several cars without so much as a pucker marring his perfect brow, then pulled back into his lane. He glanced at her. "I suppose I could tell you exactly when and where I've been probably for every week of those past several years. Trying to balance two lives has been difficult."

She imagined that was an understatement. She thought back over the course of her acquaintance with him. She had suspected there was something going on with him, obviously, having seen who she thought was either him or his twin popping in and out of the mist. But she never in a million years would have guessed this was what that something was.

He might have been exhausted, but he looked a bit like a man who had just unburdened himself of a terrible secret.

"Want to tell me more?" she asked.

"I find I do," he said seriously. He took a deep breath, then began. "My mother had passed suddenly and I thought it would take my father's mind off it—and mine as well, to be honest—to play a few rounds of golf on her native soil."

"Were you living in Scotland at the time?"

He shook his head. "I'd moved to London by then. My father had gone back to New York, I think in an effort to have a change of scenery to ease his grief."

"Wait," she said, "back up a little. Where were you before London?"

He shot her a brief look. "New York, slaving away in my grandfather's firm."

"After having graduated from Columbia," she said.

"Aye, guilty as charged," he said. "The rest is boring, but I'll tell you to keep you awake, if you like."

"I like. Start with Granddad. He sounds fabulous."

Nathaniel laughed a little. "He's less fabulous than he is a miser with delusions of landing himself a title, but he certainly has the money to buy one if he weren't so cheap. I'll admit with a fair amount of shame that I made him buckets of money to add to his enormous piles during my tenure at his firm. I had money enough of my own, though, thanks to my father having given me my inheritance early. I had already been working for myself, living in London, when my mother died."

"Is yours a good business?"

"Extremely."

She smiled. "Hence the Aston Martin?"

"Exactly." He shook his head. "My parents had been here in Scotland, in a little cottage on the shore, for the last few years she was alive. After her passing, as I said, my father returned to New York." He sighed. "He had intended, before she fell ill, to retire and take her on a tour of the world. Events caught them both up before he could."

"What does your grandfather do exactly?" she asked.

"He invests," Nathaniel said. "Or I should say, rather, that he sits in his den, counting his money, whilst others do the investing for him. He limits himself to finding ways either to get back what he's loaned out—which happens very rarely—or to make trouble for his posterity—which he does constantly. He amuses himself by arguing about inheritances until he can see the corpse for himself and make sure it's not going to rise like a damned zombie. Old money and vats of it, I'm afraid." He shot her a look. "I have the feeling you understand that."

"Don't remind me," she said grimly. "My father's Seattle roots extend back to the first timber company."

He smiled briefly. "I understand *that*, believe me." He shook his head. "So, I had rented that wee cottage that is now my house because my father had sold the place he'd lived with my mother and I didn't think I should try to buy it back. We had had ourselves a proper breakfast, then set off to play a bit of golf. A storm came up suddenly, and my uncle and I—my uncle had come along with us to add to the distraction and because he is a very keen golfer—ran with my father to find shelter in the forest." He glanced at her. "I suppose I needn't tell you what happened next."

She shook her head because she honestly couldn't help herself. "If it hadn't happened to me, I would think you had hallucinated it. So, did the three of you travel . . . well, you know."

"My uncle and I wound up in the past whilst my father, quite fortuitously, remained in our current day."

She looked at him gravely. "That must have been terrifying."

"It was," he agreed. He dragged his hand through his hair. "I don't like to think about that next few weeks, to be honest. I was able to come home, but my uncle remained in the past."

"Is he still there?" she asked in surprise.

"Aye, and willingly."

She watched him as he passed another car or two and wondered if he might have unburdened himself enough for the day. "You don't have to tell me anything else," she said. "We could just drive in silence."

He smiled briefly. "Nay, I'm well enough if you can stand to listen. I'm just not a fan of medieval dungeons, so the memory of Malcolm MacLeod's leaves me wanting to go for a bit of a run." He smiled. "Not many I can share that with, are there?"

She had her own thoughts on that, but she supposed the present moment wasn't the time to offer them. Highland magic? She thought she just might punch the next MacLeod who said those words with a straight face.

"No," she said finally. "Not many. So, what happened then?"

"I managed to get home—dumb luck, I suppose—only to find that my father had suffered a heart attack and was in hospital. I saw him before he died." He paused. "I think he was waiting for me."

"Do you have siblings—oh, you do, don't you?"

"Older brother, younger sister. Gavin is not one to linger in any one place for long, but Sorcha lives in London. She has too much money and a bit of a death wish, but I can't tell her that. Gavin has a fondness for extremes, so he's likely presently hanging from some bloody rock face by his pinky fingers alone." He shook his head. "He did manage to show up for the funeral, though, and there we were, a happy little group of three gathered to present a united front on Long Island. That's when the true torture began."

"A fight over an inheritance?"

"A fight being pursued to this day," Nathaniel said. "My father had made me trustee of his portion of the old bastard's largesse. My grandfather objected."

"But your father had a good attorney, right?"

"The best," Nathaniel said solemnly, "and no, it wasn't me. The trust is set in stone, I have control, and my siblings don't care as long as their checks continue to arrive on time. My father fought Poindexter off for years." He smiled at her grimly. "My grandfather believes I don't have the stomach for the same sort of fight."

"He should see you with a sword in your hands."

"I've considered it, believe me."

"Do you care?"

He winced. "I know it's only money, but he offends my sense of fair play."

"That and your mother probably told you to give him hell."

Nathaniel laughed a little. "My father, actually. My mother was the only one who could manage the old fool. The truth is, my grandfather doesn't need the money. I think he fights because he's bored. Add that to the usual assortment of greedy cousins, daft aunties, and, again, my grandfather who refuses to listen to his very expensive attorneys, and you have a family drama made for telly."

"And all the while there you are, taking these day trips to another time zone," she said. "Exhausting."

"Very," he agreed. "I will say it tends to put things into perspective in a way I don't think I could manage on my own. When one begins to dream in medieval Gaelic . . . well, haggling over hundreds of millions in my grandfather's boardroom seems rather pedestrian by comparison."

She considered that until they had garaged his car and were setting off in his Range Rover. She waited until they were back on the road south before she looked at him.

"Do you ever wonder why you continue to go back? To, well, you know when."

"Every day," he said with a sigh. He considered, then shook his head. "There always seems to be something I need to do, but I can't imagine why I'm the one who needs to see to it. I can't do anything the MacLeods aren't already trained to do, and far better than I."

"What about your uncle?" she asked. "Is it possible you're supposed to rescue him?"

"He doesn't want to be rescued," Nathaniel said. He looked at her. "The truth is, my uncle is drunk most of the time and hopelessly in love with the laird's daughter the rest. He almost became a Jesuit priest, so his command of Latin is impressive. He's the local vicar, in a manner of speaking. They love him, and he has his own designated spot by the fire. I can see why he wouldn't want to come home and face my grandfather."

"Maybe there's someone else you're supposed to rescue."

"I can't imagine who," he said with a sigh.

She didn't think she had enough information to speculate. "Do you ever wonder if you're related to those MacLeods in the past?"

"I haven't had the stomach to investigate. If Uncle John actually manages to marry the laird's daughter it would mean that my uncle is my uncle and potentially my medieval grandfather at the same time."

"Eeww," she said. "That's disgusting."

He laughed a little, then reached for her hand. He looked at it briefly before he put it on his leg and covered it with his own. "You have blacksmith marks on the back of your hand."

"I know," she said. "I should wear gloves to avoid the sparks, but I don't." She looked at the little round scars there, then smiled at him. "It would have been a good profession to have, I suppose, back in the day. Warm in the winter, don't you think?"

"What I think is that you'll never know the truth of it because all you'll do from here on out is speculate," he said, shooting her a look.

"I learned how to use a dirk this morning, you know," she said. "I'd be worried if I were you."

"Emma," he said with a sigh.

"I won't go anywhere without you," she said.

"I saw you cross your fingers just now."

She smiled, partly because he was charming and partly because he was stroking the back of her hand and that was enough to distract her from subversive thoughts. For the moment.

She thought that might not last.

Chapter 20

Nathaniel realized the taxi had stopped only because Emma elbowed him awake. He supposed he should have been counting how many times she'd already done that, but he was so damned tired he didn't think he could manage it. How he was going to face off with his grandfather, he surely didn't know.

He tossed the driver money, crawled out of the cab behind Emma, and suppressed the urge to look for somewhere to sit down.

"More coffee?"

"Whisky would be better."

Emma smiled at him. "Didn't you sleep on the plane?"

He shook his head slightly but supposed there was no useful reason to tell her why not. The truth was, he'd sat in a lovely first-class seat next to that beautiful woman who had stolen his heart, and he'd spent eight hours watching her sleep. He supposed she knew he'd been doing it because every time she woke, she would remind him that watching her while she drooled was impolite. He'd promised her every time never to use that against her at an inopportune moment, held her hand, and wondered how it was he had been fortunate enough to encounter her on the edge of an enchanted forest.

Fate's make-up call, he supposed.

At the moment, she looked as if she'd just stepped out of an issue of *Gorgeous Lawyers Quarterly*. He would have signed whatever she put in front of him just to buy himself more time to look at her.

He realized with a start that she was studying him a bit more closely than he was comfortable with.

"What?" he asked, wondering if he'd forgotten something important, like his trousers.

"I'm still confused as to why you bought me this great court outfit yesterday so you can take me along to your meeting."

"I wanted company."

She pursed her lips.

"I wanted to supervise you."

"Better, but not perfect."

He considered her a bit longer. "I wanted your company and I wanted to keep an eye on you. How's that for honesty?"

"*That* I believe," she said. She looked over her shoulder at the building there, then back at him. "What now?"

"We march into the fray. Stay behind me."

She laughed a little at him, but walked with him inside just the same. He forced himself to stay grounded in the present moment—an alarming thought, to be sure—and not remember the countless number of times when he'd stood in front of that bank of elevators and waited for a posh box to take him up to his grandfather's offices. He'd worked for his grandfather for only five years, but he thought he could bring to mind a piece of misery for each one of those days with hardly any effort.

"You okay?"

He smiled briefly at Emma. "Fine."

She lifted her eyebrows briefly, then turned to the elevator doors as they opened. Nathaniel held the door open and looked at her only to find her looking in astonishment at someone inside.

"Dad," she managed.

Nathaniel had thought he was past surprise, but obviously he was not. He stepped back from the man striding out of the elevator, and he never stepped back from anything.

"Emma, what are you doing here in Manhattan?" the man demanded. "You're supposed to be in Scotland."

"Ah—"

Nathaniel rubbed the back of his neck on the off chance someone had mistaken his unthinking motion for what it was—reaching for a nonexistent sword strapped to his back—then held that hand out toward Emma's father.

"Nathaniel MacLeod," he said briskly. "And you must be Emma's father."

"Frank," Emma managed. "Frank Baxter. My father. Dad, this is Nathaniel MacLeod."

"A pleasure," Nathaniel said smoothly.

Frank Baxter sized him up with a brutality that Nathaniel couldn't help but admire. If he'd been a lesser man or perhaps encountered Emma's father at a different point in his life, he might have been pleased to have that sort of adversary to take on. At the moment, he was simply satisfied to let the man have his look and not give any ground.

He was, however, happy he'd bothered to comb his hair and do a decent job on the knot of his tie.

Emma's father grunted, dismissed him without comment, then turned back to his daughter.

"What are you doing here," he repeated, "and not in Scotland where you're supposed to be?"

Nathaniel looked at Emma and winced. She looked as if she'd just walked into a clutch of medieval Highlanders who had decided she might make a good addition to the fire they already had going. He supposed he'd spent too much time in an environment where split-second decisions, made without regret, were the order of the day, but apologies could be made later. He stepped between Emma and her father, put his hand on her back and guided her into the elevator, then stepped inside himself. He turned and favored her father with his chilliest smile.

The man had, after all, destroyed a '67 Jag. Unforgivable, really.

"Wait one min—"

The doors closed. Nathaniel supposed he was fortunate Frank Baxter hadn't shoved his hand between them to keep them from closing, but perhaps things were looking up. He looked at Emma.

"Sorry," he said, not meaning it in the slightest.

"He'll be waiting," she warned.

"One could hope," he said cheerfully. "I'll watch you have him for lunch later. We've got breakfast to face first."

"Thank you." She smiled, but it wasn't a very good smile. "He does business here quite often, but I never would have expected to see him here this morning." She took a deep breath. "Thanks for the rescue."

"I'm quite sure you'll return the favor at some point."

"Well, I have been well-trained in the art of the dirk."

"See?" he said pleasantly. "You're just waiting for the right opportunity to exercise your prodigious skills." He smoothed his tie down and buttoned his suit coat. "I will be your second, of course, standing just behind you whilst offering helpful suggestions in my best Windsor-approved poshness that I use when I want to intimidate. Your father will be bleeding from the crispness of my consonants alone."

Her smile was a bit better that time. "What do you use with the gold diggers who hunt you?"

"Cockney, lass. Throws them off."

She smiled. "And with Grandfather?"

"A bit o' the old Gordie," he said. "I learnt it from Brian, of course, who cut his teeth on the same from his da in Glasgow. Drives Lord Poindexter absolutely to drink. Watch and see if he doesn't have a decanter at his elbow just in case."

She looked at him and shook her head. "You don't look at all nervous."

He sighed in spite of himself. "I've done this too many times to be nervous any longer. Now, 'tis just an extremely tedious business to endure so I can get on to more pleasant things. Feel like a show later?"

"Anything but a variation on the Scottish play."

He blinked, then laughed a little. "After our brush with Cawdor, I couldn't agree more."

The elevator doors opened, and Nathaniel walked out first to make certain they weren't going to be mowed down either by a gaggle of his grandfather's lawyers, who would want to assault him, or any number of relatives, who might want to trample him to death before he could get to his own lawyer. To his relief, there was only Peter diSalvio there, slouching negligently against a wallpapered wall, yawning hugely.

Nathaniel sympathized. If he had to do too many more of these, he would simply lie down and die from boredom.

It was all a completely useless exercise, of course. His father, Archibald Poindexter MacLeod III, had come into his inheritance at thirty, then managed his money quite capably on his own for many years. When he had grown tired of it, Archie had looked over his own posterity, rightly judged his eldest, Gavin, to be a complete loss at maths, identified his youngest, Sorcha, as too distracted with other things to pay attention to anything that didn't have to do with sticking arrows into targets from ridiculous distances, then turned his gentle eye on his middle child.

Nathaniel had accepted his fate, signed the damned papers at twenty-six, and taken over the trust.

He supposed the enormous amounts he'd added to the funds didn't interest his grandfather. He had already pulled his personal share out, so what was left he simply managed for his siblings, which his grandfather damned well knew. If Dexter had had any sense, he would have walked away. If he himself had possessed any sense, he would have let his grandfather win.

But he kept at it for his own father's memory, and for Gavin, who didn't like numbers, and for Sorcha, who came to lunch with him in London on occasion when she wasn't off training for this competition or that. He kept at it because his grandfather was bored, had too much money, and needed to be told no on occasion. It was expensive, but the alternative was worse.

He stopped in front of his attorney and smiled. "You rang?"

Peter rolled his eyes. "Nice of you to make time for this." He looked at Emma and straightened. "Hello, who do we have here?"

"My assistant—"

"Of course she isn't. Why would she want to spend any time with a loser like you?"

Emma laughed a little. "I'm here as moral support."

Peter blinked. "You're American."

"She is," Nathaniel said with a warning look. "She's also done the slog through law school, so I wouldn't push her too far. She'll sue."

Peter smiled and shook Emma's hand. "I annoy him because I can." He turned to Nathaniel. "Lord P. is already in a temper. He had a meeting with some venture cap guy from Seattle who really rubbed him the wrong way."

"Frank Baxter?"

Peter looked surprised, which Nathaniel supposed was a new sensation for him. "Actually, yes. Know him?"

"My father," Emma said with a sigh. "We ran away from him downstairs."

Peter studied them both. "This is a story I would like to hear, but maybe later. We might as well get in there and get this over with. Nat, just so you know, Gavin's here."

"Why the hell for?" Nathaniel asked, wondering if it just might be the day for surprises.

Peter shrugged. "He's got on a suit, no doubt in deference to your grandfather, but he looks gloomy. He's glaring at Gerald, if that makes you feel any better."

What would make him feel better would be dropping his cousin off on a deserted island with a handful of other annoying cousins, but he didn't suppose that was going to happen any time soon. He nodded, then followed Peter inside the boardroom.

All the players were already there, which he expected. Poindexter MacLeod liked to have the battlefield set before the enemy arrived. He realized he tended to prefer things that way himself, but decided that wasn't a very useful realization to linger over at the moment.

"Who is that with you?" a posh, upper-crusty sort of voice asked.

Nathaniel looked at his grandfather mildly. "My new assistant."

His grandfather frowned. "I don't like employees at my negotiations who haven't been vetted by my staff."

"Given that she's not your employee, Grandfather, I think we can proceed."

He made sure Emma was seated, sat down himself, then let loose the Peter of War. His attorney, he had to admit, was the sort of paragon all good attorneys should wish to emulate. His ability to slip daggers between ribs whilst smiling pleasantly was something Nathaniel had never failed to admire. There was also Peter's willingness to slap his hands on the table and shout furiously in a way that left everyone in the room shrinking back into their chairs. Heartwarming, truly, and money well spent.

He sat back and studied the playing field. His grandfather's clutch of lawyers was large but not necessarily impressive given that it was headed up by his own cousin, Gerald. That Gerald happened to be his uncle John's eldest son was something Nathaniel didn't let himself think about very often.

After John's disappearance and subsequent funeral—something Nathaniel had nudged along behind the scenes per his uncle's request—Gerald had rolled over and let Lord Poindexter take over John's trust because he had very stupidly believed that getting along was the way to go. Nathaniel supposed his cousin might never see all his money until Poindexter died.

He wondered if his grandfather slept with one eye open. He knew he would have in his shoes.

He looked at his brother and raised an eyebrow. Gavin pulled out his cell phone and typed. Nathaniel felt the text hit his phone but he waited what he thought was an acceptable amount of time before he pulled up what he'd gotten.

Moral support only.

He smiled, glanced at his brother, then decided that perhaps having family about wasn't such a bad thing. His older brother might just have earned a dinner invitation.

He looked up at the ceiling and thought fondly of lochs and forests and the pleasures of no mobile phone signals. He realized that when he began to consider the beauties of a medieval battlefield with a piper piping in the distance, he had perhaps gone too far—

"Nathaniel!"

Nathaniel dragged himself back to the matter at hand and realized his grandfather was shouting at him. "Aye?"

His grandfather looked as if he were going to have a stroke. "*Yes* is the proper response, quickly followed by, *Forgive me, Grandfather, I was distracted by all the money my never being available has cost you.*"

Nathaniel didn't bother to answer. He simply let Peter step in front of him, figuratively, and take over. He suppressed a yawn, then went back to ignoring what was going on. In fact, he was doing a damned fine job ignoring most everything that had gone on for . . . He looked at his watch. Good lord, it had already been two hours and he couldn't remember a damned thing that had been said. He glanced at Emma.

She met his eyes, then shifted aside the file folder she'd been using to shield her notepad from prying eyes.

His grandfather had been rendered there, wearing a duck costume.

He had to rub his face to stop himself from belly laughing. He gave her a stern look on principle, then reached over and wrote on the edge of her pad.

You're marvelous.

She considered, then answered in the same spot.

I know.

He almost asked her to marry him there on the spot, but he supposed there might be a more romantic time and place. Perhaps after he'd gotten them out of quite possibly the most boring meeting ever held and made certain they both would remain in their proper place in time.

The only thing he could say was even mildly interesting was watching Peter and knowing the man was fighting the urge to leap over the table and plunge a pen into Poindexter MacLeod's eye. It was almost a pity 1387 wasn't calling at the moment. Nathaniel suspected Peter would have had a delightful time there.

Emma passed him a note. He found that curious given that her file folder had seemingly been guarantee of enough privacy before. He unfolded it, then frowned thoughtfully at what was written there.

That's your brother, right?

He didn't look up. Gavin was sitting next to Gerald, who was sitting, rather uncomfortably it had to be acknowledged, next to the old duck himself. He only slid her a slight nod.

She wrote something else, then passed it to him.

Next to him?

He supposed she might want to know so she could label her drawings properly.

Cousin Gerald.

Her hand shook as she wrote.

I've seen him before.

He felt a hush fall over the room, and it wasn't because Gerald had stopped bloviating long enough to take a drink. He doodled a little sword on Emma's note, then wrote down a single word.

Where?

She only looked at him. The truth was, she didn't have to say anything. He didn't even bother to ask her if she was sure or not.

Emma had seen Gerald in the *past*?

He reread the note, then saw the letters begin to swim before his eyes. He'd never felt anything like it before. If she reached over and clutched his knee hard enough to make him wince, well, he supposed that was better than a sharp slap. He reached for water, managed to get some of it down without pouring most of it on himself, then set the bottle aside.

He looked at Emma and made a production of smiling at her as if they'd just shared a private joke, then he turned back to studying his grandfather's minions sitting around the table. He looked at his grandfather for a bit, watching his mouth move but hearing nothing, then he glanced at his cousin Gerald.

Gerald was staring at him with soulless eyes.

"Grandfather," Gerald said suddenly, "perhaps a bit of a break. I want to talk to Nathaniel for a minute or two. Help him see sense."

Dexter MacLeod drew himself up. "An excellent idea. Mirna, where's my coffee? Straight up, black. None of that dessert garbage kids drink these days."

"Right away, Mr. MacLeod."

Nathaniel looked at his cousin. "I'll pass, thanks."

"It wasn't a request."

Nathaniel supposed it was a good thing he didn't have a sword handy, because he would have drawn it and used it on the fool sitting across from him. He looked at Peter. "I'm finished here," he said. "Let's wrap this up with what you brought."

"But billable hours," Peter protested.

Nathaniel mouthed a suggestion about what Peter DiSalvio could do with his billable hours. Peter and his brother Tony had made enough over the years never to need to work another day in their lives, something Nathaniel had contributed to handsomely. They would both survive.

Peter sighed the sigh of a martyr who was going to have to work an extra hour to manage the mortgage payment on his second home in the Hamptons, then slid a folder across the table not to Dexter, who was looking highly displeased that things were continuing on without him, but to Gerald. Nathaniel smiled at his cousin.

"Don't know that you've seen this lately."

"What is that?" Dexter demanded.

"Just a second, Grandfather," Gerald said soothingly. "Nothing to worry about, I'm sure."

"I'm sure," Nathaniel agreed. He looked at his grandfather and wondered how it was possible they were related. "I wouldn't have a clue what it is, not having your cracking legal team to tell me what I'm reading, of course."

"I gave you a job," Dexter spat.

"And I worked hundred-hour weeks for you for years," Nathaniel said sharply. "I made you more profit and took away far less than the cadre of leeches sitting on your side of the table has."

"You mean *lawyers*," Emma murmured.

He looked at her. "Why, thank you, Miss Baxter. Indeed, I did. I must have misspoken."

She looked at his grandfather's henchmen, then back at him. "I can let that stand in the notes, if you like."

"You decide," he said. He turned back to watch as Gerald read what he'd been given.

His cousin rolled his eyes. "It's Archie's will. Nothing we haven't seen before."

"You've seen it, but perhaps you haven't read it carefully enough," Nathaniel said pointedly. "There is specific language in there that states that the trust does *not* revert to Grandfather upon my father's death." He pushed back from the conference table and looked at his grandfather. "I have humored you, Grandfather, because I knew it was your grief over your son that drove you, but I am finished. I have made the trust substantial sums of money, so trying to oust me because of mismanagement will go nowhere. I will tell you here and now that if you come after me again, I will crush you."

"He threatened me," Dexter said, looking around for potential witnesses. "Someone write that down!"

Nathaniel held out Emma's chair for her, then put his hand on Peter's shoulder briefly before he walked around the table. He leaned in close to his grandfather.

"I know where all the bodies are buried," he murmured, "and if you think I won't go to the press, think again."

Poindexter MacLeod felt his way down into a chair and looked up at him. "You wouldn't," he blustered. "I mean, there are no bodies—"

"Metaphorically speaking," Nathaniel said smoothly.

He straightened and left his grandfather to wheeze, his cousin to swear, and his brother to watch him with a half smile on his face. Then again, that one there knew which side his bread was buttered on, as the saying went. Nathaniel looked at his brother.

"Dinner later?" he mouthed.

Gavin gave him a little salute, then leaned back and propped his feet up against the edge of the conference table.

"Gavin, get your feet off the furniture!" Dexter shouted.

Nathaniel smiled and looked at his attorney. "They're all yours, Pete."

"This might take a while," Peter said, frowning thoughtfully. "A long while."

Nathaniel imagined it would, and that it would be damned expensive, but if he didn't have to deal with it, he didn't care how much it cost. He escorted Emma from the conference room, then pulled the door shut behind them. It was only then that he allowed himself to give thought to what she'd said. He leaned against the wall, because he wasn't sure he could stand up much longer.

"Are you sure?" he managed.

She nodded slowly. "I'm afraid so."

He rubbed his hands over his face briefly, then shook his head and looked at her. "I think it's time to go home."

"I'll be interested to see who follows us there."

"Hopefully just my cousin and not your father."

She smiled briefly. "I suppose things could be worse."

They could indeed, which he didn't think he needed to say. He pushed away from the wall and walked away. There wasn't anything else to do.

He had seen to one piece of madness.

It was past time to see to the other.

Chapter 21

E^{mma} knew she should have felt safe and grounded where she was. After all, she was far from anywhere with paranormal elements like ghosts, she was fairly sure she wasn't going to run into any medieval Highlanders lingering in Times Square, and she thought she was fairly well acquainted with any modern-day guys who might or might not have visited the past while masquerading as medieval Highlanders.

Or she had been until she'd looked across that very elegant conference table at Nathaniel's cousin.

It had been yet another thing to add to her list of odd things that had happened to her in the past couple of weeks. She had looked at Gerald and seen him not as he was, dressed in a very nice suit and holding on to a pen, but as she'd seen him, dressed in a ratty kilt with a sword in his hand.

Or at least she thought she'd seen him. To be honest, she wasn't entirely sure, because if he was the one she'd seen, he'd been hiding behind a tree near the other man who had leaped out at her and wound up on the end of Nathaniel's sword. She would be the first to admit that the situation hadn't exactly been conducive to keen observation. All the more reason to perhaps consider a brief trip back to 1387 where she did less participating and more spying. Now that she had some idea of what to expect, she might manage to slip in and out without being noticed.

She came back to herself to find that she was in the elevator and Nathaniel was watching her. She attempted a smile. "Hi."

"Oh, nay," he said, "none of that. And you can stop with the subversive thoughts as well."

"I wasn't thinking subversive thoughts."

"You were thinking investigative thoughts," he said pointedly. "Those are worse, I'm sure, though they might be an improvement on mine at the moment."

She leaned back against the wall and looked at him. "What does your grandfather ever accomplish with all that drama?"

"Absolutely nothing," he said. "Nothing changes because there's nothing to change. He'll never manage to throw me off the trust because I'm just so damned responsible and ethical."

"He must hate that about you."

He smiled a quick little smile at her. "You have no idea, love."

She felt some of the tension ease out of her. "So what now?"

He shrugged. "A day of liberty and an enormous apple to enjoy. What do you want to do? See a show later? Have dinner with my brother, the vexer of dodgy cousins and grandsires?"

"I'd like that. As for anything else, why don't you take me to your favorite place? Somewhere besides the service entrance to your grandfather's building."

He laughed a little. "I think I'll avoid that for both of us. Here's our stop. Perhaps I'll take you touring and you can draw my grandfather for me again in various states of duck."

She exited the elevator in front of him, then came to a halt so suddenly that he ran into the back of her. He steadied them both with his hands on her shoulders, which she appreciated, then he stepped beside her and drew her hand into the crook of his elbow. Emma decided it was too late to yank him back into the elevator and pick a different exit besides the ground floor.

She looked at the men standing there. "Dad," she said politely. She looked at the man standing next to him and decided perhaps Sheldon Cook didn't need any greeting.

Her father was looking at Nathaniel. "You're Poindexter MacLeod's grandson," he said without preamble.

"Bribed his secretary for the information?" Nathaniel asked.

"I had forgotten my newspaper in your grandfather's waiting room," he said stiffly. "She was good enough to tell me who you were when I went back up to get it."

Emma refrained from snorting only because she was so practiced at it. Her father read his phone, not the newspaper, and he was almost as compulsive a snoop as she was. For all she knew, he had originally hired Bertie the Spy to get inside places he couldn't and scout out sordid details to use in his negotiations. She and Nathaniel had been the only ones in the elevator; he'd likely made note of where the elevator had stopped, then he'd hassled secretaries until he'd found the right one to divulge the details. Standard fare for him.

"Odd that we find you here," she said, wishing she'd had a Highlander or two behind her egging her on to ever greater heights of surliness. Then again, she had one right next to her, so maybe that was good enough for the moment.

"I don't know why you would find it odd," her father said. "I'm here to do business with Dexter MacLeod."

"I was making conversation, Dad."

"Too much time in menial jobs hasn't done you any favors, Emma," her father said shortly. He dismissed her with a look and turned to Nathaniel. "I understand you're the MacLeod in MacLeod and Perkins in London. A fairly exclusive little boutique investment group, aren't you?"

"We are," Nathaniel agreed.

"Perhaps you'd be interested in discussing a little business over lunch?"

Emma looked at Nathaniel and wondered how his grandfather even thought that crossing him was ever going to end well. She'd seen him with a sword in his hands, which had been intimidating, but she'd never seen him wear that look that said he came from extremely old East Coast money and just who the hell did Frank Baxter think he was to pester him?

It was tempting to swoon.

She was tempted to make a hasty exit to the ladies' so she didn't have to watch the bloodshed, but Nathaniel put his hand over hers before she could. He didn't, however, take his eyes off her father.

"We are *extremely* choosy about our clients," Nathaniel said with frigid politeness, "and even more choosy about our partners. I'm not sure we're looking for any joint ventures at the moment, especially with those who don't have, shall we say, the pocket depth we're accustomed to."

Emma almost gasped. She had never in her life heard anyone insult her father that way, and she had heard all kinds of things said about him, behind his back and to his face.

Her father lifted his eyebrows briefly, then nodded. "Of course."

Well, if there was one positive thing that could be said about her father, it was that he knew when he was beaten. It was unfortunate that the guy standing next to him practically hopping up and down with the need to be noticed didn't possess even a hint of that same talent.

Emma looked at Sheldon, ignored whatever he was babbling about, then looked at her father. "Why did you bring Sheldon?"

"I didn't bring him," Frank said with something that might have been mistaken for disgust. "He was on my flight and talked the poor girl at the counter to death until she upgraded him out of a robust sense of self-preservation. I believe he's here for his cousin's wedding."

"Then why is he standing here with you now?" Emma asked.

Her father frowned. "He followed me. I would say that showed initiative, but I'm finding it a bit unpleasant at the moment."

Emma thought she might have a different word for it. She started to ask her father why in the world, then, he had been so thrilled to have her date that guy standing next to him, but decided there was no point. Her father's motives were strange and inscrutable and she honestly didn't care about them any longer.

"A pity we can't linger for more of this fascinating chit-chat," Nathaniel said. "Must dash, sorry."

Never let it be said she didn't know when to bolt for the nearest exit. She ignored Sheldon, shot her father a cool look, then walked quickly with Nathaniel in a direction that didn't seem to be leading to the front door. She supposed if anyone would know where he was going, it would be him.

"Back entrance?" she asked.

"Side exit," he said, then he shot her a quick smile. "Sorry if that was rude."

"It was perfect," she said, feeling a little breathless. "That lesser-royal accent really leaves me feeling a little weak in the knees."

He stopped suddenly and looked at her in surprise. "Does it?"

"A little."

He drew her out of the main current of businesspeople. She leaned quite happily back against the wall to catch her breath. He put his hand on the wall next to her head.

"If that makes you a little weak in the knees, what does the native Scottish business do for you?"

"I generally need to find somewhere to sit down at that point."

He considered. "What would happen, do you suppose, if I dispensed with accents and went straight for a discreet kiss?"

"Here?" she squeaked.

"It's a nice hallway."

She was beginning to wonder if the day could become any more filled with ridiculous things.

"I could hold you up," he offered. "In deference to your knees."

She attempted a scowl, but it was difficult in the face of all that charm. Well, and that accent. "I think you are far too convinced of your own impossibly irresistible appeal," she said, grasping for the only reasonable thing she could think of.

He leaned closer. "It's all an act," he whispered. "I'm trying to make up for how off-balance you've left me from the first moment I sat down at your breakfast table."

"That's because of Lord Patrick's excellent eggs."

"Nay, darling, it's because of your excellent self."

She looked up at him standing there with his mouth approximately three inches from hers and tried not to swoon. "I should remind you that you quite recently wanted to get rid of me."

"I wanted to keep you *safe*," he said. "Different thing entirely."

"Are you telling me you don't want to keep me safe any longer?"

"I want to keep you safe, kiss you, and hopefully do both for an extended period of time, in that order—"

"Emmaline!"

She closed her eyes briefly, then looked at Nathaniel. "Can you kill both of them and make it look like they fell and bludgeoned themselves on the drinking fountain?"

"'Tis a bit crowded for that sort of thing, but I'm willing to try. As long as it doesn't interfere with my plan to kiss you."

She laughed a little, because she wasn't quite sure if he was serious or not. Unfortunately, she realized she wasn't going to have the chance to figure out which it was before their escape was thwarted. She wouldn't have argued if Nathaniel had taken her hand and run, but apparently he was trying to be polite. He leaned his shoulder against the wall and looked at Sheldon, who had blocked his way and was currently babbling about what was probably one of his current investment projects. Nathaniel wore a slightly perplexed frown. She understood. That was the look most people generally got within three minutes of meeting the man.

Her father, though, was a different story entirely. She looked his way to find that he wasn't watching Sheldon, nor was he looking Nathaniel over for weaknesses.

He was watching her.

She wanted to lay into him for possibly helping Sheldon find her in Scotland, then decided that when it came right down to it, she just didn't care. She suppressed a yawn, then looked at her escort, who had been buttonholed by her former boyfriend.

"Do you *ever* shut up?" Nathaniel asked in exasperation.

Sheldon looked horribly offended. "Everything I say is of great interest to those around me."

Nathaniel shook his head in disgust, then looked at her father. "If you'll excuse us, we're still late for an appointment."

"Just one minute," Frank said. "What is it you're doing with my daughter?"

Emma was so surprised by the question that she was still trying to come up with something cutting to say as Nathaniel pushed off from against the wall and looked at her father. On the whole, it was a fairly respectful look, which was probably more than her father deserved.

"I've commissioned several paintings from her for the castle I'm restoring," Nathaniel said. "After that? I thought I would date your daughter for a bit and see if she is open to the idea of anything more permanent."

Her father's mouth fell open. "You want to marry her?"

"I believe that's our private business."

"But I'm her father!"

"And you pushed my Jag into the lake," Emma put in. "I'll let Mom know what I'm doing and you can try to get it out of her."

Nathaniel took her hand. "Apparently she'll let her mother know what she's doing. Cheers."

Emma walked with him out of the building, ignoring the squawking going on behind her until it faded into the blissful sounds of normal city life. She didn't dare look at him until they were several blocks away.

"Are you restoring a castle?" she asked seriously.

"It's on my list, right after taking care of my most pressing problem."

"Hmmm," she said, studying him. "Did you just ask me out on a date back there?"

"I believe I asked you out on a date earlier in the day. I asked you to marry me back there."

"That was a proposal?" she asked faintly.

"A poor one," he said. "I'll try a better one in a more romantic spot."

She stopped and looked at him. "You don't have to do this, you know."

He pulled her out of the press of people and under the shelter of an awning. "Is it the fact that I tried to get you to move that leaves me looking less than appealing," he asked slowly, "or is it my second job?"

She would have smiled if her heart hadn't hurt so much. "Neither," she said. "I just don't think you know me very well. I might snore."

"Well, I wasn't suggesting we pop into the jeweler's right off," he said carefully. "A few dates, perhaps. I'll let you drive the Lamborghini and see what I think about that." He flashed her a brief smile. "I'll trot out whatever accent you like best whenever you like."

"That is tempting," she agreed.

His smile faded. "I'll solve the other, Emma. I'll make it so you can stay in Scotland as long as you like. You can see if you can bear the sight of me for more than a few days at a time, then we can discuss other things."

She looked at his hand holding hers, then met his gaze. "I'm assuming that deal includes a little test spin in your Vanquish."

He smiled, a more genuine smile that time, then leaned over and softly kissed her cheek. "We'll see."

"Deal's off, then."

He laughed, then took her hand in both his own. "Well, if you're going to play hardball, then I'll reconsider. Let's go back to the hotel and look for a show. Would you mind if my brother came to dinner? He'll make a list of all my failings for you, I'm sure. Important to know those before you get too much further into this, I imagine."

"We could invite Sheldon as well," she offered. "He can make a list of mine for you."

Nathaniel snorted. "The only list I want from him is all the ways he can say *I'm boring the hell out of you, aren't I?*"

"That could take a while."

"We'll leave him making it whilst we're off for a lovely evening."

She couldn't imagine anything more useful for him to do than that.

A handful of hours later, she was starting to really get behind that plan.

Nathaniel had taken a suite for them in a very nice hotel, she'd had a lovely nap, then she had dressed for an evening that seemed more like afternoon given the time change. She was beginning to wonder, though, if she would exit any elevator in present-day Manhattan without running into someone she didn't like.

Sheldon was skulking around in the lobby, obviously waiting for someone.

"Does he do this often?" Nathaniel asked mildly.

"Stalk?" she asked wearily. "Yes."

"Perhaps it's time you told him to stop."

She looked at him. "And he's going to listen to me?"

"Give it a try," he said with a shrug. "I'll be your second, as I promised. You might point out that you knew he was in the cab behind us the entire way to the hotel."

She supposed it wasn't attractive to gape at him. "Was he? How did you know?"

Nathaniel shrugged. "Sixth sense honed by time spent in other places. That and he seems like a very predictable sort of bloke. I assumed first, then verified next." He smiled. "Keeps me head atop me shoulders, aye?"

She looked at him in his quite lovely suit and shook her head. It was far too easy to forget what else he did with his days besides show up to boardrooms. She put her shoulders back and walked across the lobby, her second hard on her heels. Sheldon caught sight of her and drew himself up.

"Get lost," she said, before he could gather enough wind to spew anything out.

"You have my *White Album*," he snarled.

She took a deep breath. "No I don't."

"I want it back! Besides, you damaged the cover."

"Prove it," she said, realizing at that moment exactly how close she could be to never having to talk to him again.

"I'll sue—wait, who's your attorney?"

Emma gestured elegantly to Nathaniel. He cleared his throat and stepped up beside her.

"I say, old bean," he drawled, reaching out to pluck a bit of nothing from Sheldon's suit coat, "I believe you've become somewhat trying to my client. I suggest you withdraw before I'm forced to alert the authorities."

Emma couldn't help but gape at Nathaniel. The only thing that surprised her was that he wasn't wearing a tweed tam on his head and sporting a shotgun folded over his shoulder. She looked back at Sheldon.

"What he said," she agreed.

Sheldon glared at her. "I have no intention of walking away from this. You have things of mine that are mine!"

Emma watched Nathaniel pull out his phone and dial. He smiled briefly at her, then fixed Sheldon with a polite but somewhat steely gaze.

"Alex?" he said. "Aye, I know what time it is. I need your particular services—aye, the usual business of digging into all kinds of things that were never intended to see the light of day, of course."

"I won't tell you my name," Sheldon said, starting to become a little red in the face.

"Sheldon Jedediah Cook," Nathaniel said. "He's vexing my girlfriend and it's beginning to annoy me. See what you can find, won't you?"

"You won't find anything," Sheldon spluttered as Nathaniel ended the call. He shifted. "Nothing interesting."

"Then you have nothing to worry about, do you?" Nathaniel asked smoothly. "Come along, Emma, and let's leave Master Sheldon to his ruminations and the quick call to his attorney I'm certain he's going to make."

Emma looked at Sheldon and shrugged. "What he said."

Sheldon began to yell, but she felt absolutely no compulsion to stay and listen. She walked away with Nathaniel toward the front doors. She looked at him.

"Who's Alex?"

"Former client of my attorney's brother. He does some discreet investigating in the UK these days." He shot her a look. "He's a terrible snoop. You'd like him."

She smiled. "I imagine I would." She walked with him outside, then looked at him as they waited for a cab. "Girlfriend?"

"I thought it might terrify you less than fiancée, though we could just skip right over that part and go straight to wife." He took her hand. "You know, you could handfast with me. You'd have a year and a day to decide if you want to keep me or kick me to the curb."

"What would be my relationship to the Lamborghini if I agreed to that?"

He shot her a look. "You have an unhealthy fascination with my cars."

"I'm deflecting."

"So I imagined." He opened the back door of a taxi, then piled in after her and gave the driver an address. He sat back and looked at her. "Did you really trash his *White Album*?"

"Of course not," she said with a snort. "He left it out in his office and spilled coffee on it. I had nothing to do with it."

"Is there anything else you feel you need to confess?"

She laughed a little in spite of herself. "*I* didn't do anything to him," she said. "Someone else might have gone through his mint-in-box Hot Wheels collection, unsealed each one in turn, removed a single wheel, then engaged in a little-known technique used by terrible people everywhere to stick the backs of the packages on again."

He smiled. "And the thug?"

"My brother, Arnie." She looked at him solemnly. "He owed me."

"Arnie?"

"Arnold," she clarified. "My other brother's name is Jack."

Nathaniel flexed his fingers. "I'm starting to feel an unwholesome affinity with your father, seeing as how he has so wisely chosen golf legends for reference in naming his sons." He smiled. "You didn't really do all that to Sheldon's cars, did you?"

She sighed. "To be perfectly honest, we only defaced the '67 Jag, but the package was already opened because he used to roll it across the counter to bug me."

"What a prat."

She added that to the mental list of insults she was going to have to memorize at her earliest convenience, but nodded just the same because he'd said it with disgust.

She realized he was studying her and it made her a little uneasy. "What?"

"I don't think you'd put up with that now."

"I don't think I'd do anything but take the handle of my dirk and flatten his toy," she said, feeling extremely fierce. She looked at him. "I have friends in Scotland who taught me all about that."

"I have the feeling I'd best tread lightly," he said. "I don't think I particularly want to tangle with your lads."

She smiled because the thought was so ridiculous. "I can't believe I have lads. And while they might have caused some soiling of that fancy suit Sheldon was wearing, I think you did enough damage all on your own."

"The phone is a powerful thing."

"So is snooping—"

"Which you won't do any more of," he finished pointedly. He paused and considered. "Feel like a trip to London on the way home?"

"What's in London besides your Vanquish?"

He smiled wryly. "My office. I thought you might want to see how my ill-gotten gains are earned." He paused. "You know. For future reference."

She nodded, trying not to put any more weight on the moment than she should. She watched him pull up flights on his phone, then freeze. She watched his face, but his expression gave nothing away. He finally let out his breath slowly, then turned the screen toward her.

"What do you think?"

She was starting to gain an appreciation for the weirdness of his life. "Flight 1387," she managed. "Well, I think I'm glad it doesn't leave until tomorrow."

He shivered. "Agreed. Well, we'll take it and let time wait a bit for us. How do you feel about sushi for tonight?"

"Disgusting."

"Good," he said, sounding relieved. "I'll tell Gavin you're insisting on steak. He tends to roll right over me when it comes to choosing places for supper."

"I'll protect you."

"I have the feeling you just might, lass."

She hoped her duties in that regard would never be more difficult than nixing a restaurant in a city full of them.

She had the feeling time might have a different opinion entirely.

Chapter 22

Nathaniel stood at the window of his office with a choice view of the Tower and stared out at the street below him. It was a view he quite liked, actually, but he had always appreciated the endless movement of humanity in a big city. London had always felt less like a large city than a small one that had sprawled over enough acreage to give it a formidable place on the map. He enjoyed his little corner of it, loved his little flat in Notting Hill, was happy to step outside his door and encounter coffee and shops instead of medieval lads and swords.

That wasn't to say he didn't consider his home to be the Highlands, though, for he did. He craved the heather and the sea and the endless sky. He loved the fact that he could go walking for hours and not see another soul. That was made slightly more complicated by his having continual brushes with a more unvarnished Highland experience, but what was there to do about that? He couldn't seem to solve it on his own, Patrick MacLeod seemed perfectly content to wait for him to come to terms with his double life and ask for aid, and he honestly wanted nothing more than to exchange his sword for a much smaller piece of metal to go around a certain gel's finger.

He leaned back against the wall and looked at the woman in question. She was sitting at his desk, flipping through binders full of projects that he had funded. He'd considered the idea as he'd been sitting in that expensive conference room of MacLeod Surety Company, wishing his grandfather had something else to do to keep himself busy, and wondering why Gerald was finding himself lurking in places he shouldn't have been.

He'd put off thinking about Gerald on their last day in New York in favor of simply enjoying a life that felt normal. He'd had a lovely dinner with a brother he realized he spent far too little time with, watched that brother and a woman he fell harder for every moment he was with her get along as if they'd known each other for years, then slept through some show about witches and the rehabilitation of the same.

He hadn't wanted to admit to being nervous about anything at all, never mind how Emma might truly feel about him, but he couldn't deny that he had been. He still was. He'd listened to Emma tell Gavin a few of her father's more noteworthy escapades as a corporate raider and he'd been very clear on how she viewed the same. That was not a woman who cared for destruction.

He supposed Patrick MacLeod had a point: medieval Scotland was likely not the place for Emma Baxter.

They'd landed at dawn and he'd happily caught a cab to his flat and made her breakfast before he'd given her his bed for a nap.

Lunch had been something off the street before they'd caught the Tube to his office. She'd been quiet on the way there, which he understood. It felt as if a monumental hurdle was there in front of them both.

He'd turned her loose in his office and let her choose what she wanted to look at without trying to influence her in any way. It was probably best she form her own opinions about his work. Given her background with her father and her recent experience with the less noble members of his own family, he thought it might be all that would give him any hope with her.

He'd hijacked his partner's office and done a bit of business, occasionally leaned into his office to see if Emma was still there, then left her to her own devices.

He'd finally given up pretending to work and taken to pacing, though that hadn't taken up as much time as he would have liked considering the modest nature of his office. His partner's office was enormous, which suited him, but Nathaniel didn't particularly care for sitting behind a desk. He preferred to meet with clients in coffee shops or in the park.

Well, that and he spent so much time on the road, as it were. A fancy office seemed like a waste of money when he was rarely there—

He realized suddenly that Emma had paused in her perusing and was looking at him.

Tears were streaming down her face.

He looked at her carefully. "Good?" he asked.

She pushed back from his desk and stood up. He leaned back against the wall because he realized that, beyond any reason, he felt as if he'd known that woman forever and forever wasn't going to be long enough to keep knowing her. If she pitched him now—

He stopped thinking when she walked to him and stopped in front of him.

She leaned up and kissed him softly.

"Well," he managed as she smiled briefly at him, then walked back over and sat down on his chair. "Well."

She ran her fingers over the last page of that particular binder. Those were his micro loans, little bits of money that no one else would have cared about but changed lives in places where people didn't often go. It was his favorite book, as it happened.

"You," she said, looking up at him, "are not my father."

He sat down across the desk from her in the client's chair that was also hardly ever used. "I don't think so."

She leaned her elbows on his desk. "I hereby give you permission to destroy him in a round of golf."

"Only one?"

"You're one of those, aren't you?" she asked in disgust. "I bet you're hiding an entire closet full of saddle shoes and Izod golf shirts."

"The game was invented by my people," he said archly. "I am only celebrating my heritage."

"Rubbish."

He smiled and relaxed for the first time in hours. "So," he said carefully, "what do you really think?"

She looked at the binder in front of her, flipped back through the pages with a reverence that moved him more than he thought he might want to admit, then gently closed the book. "I think you're a dreamer."

"And you approve?"

"Very much," she said. She smiled. "I want to hammer my dreams into metal. You want to give people the chance to breathe their dreams into life. That's pretty heady stuff there."

He was fairly sure he swore. He knew he blustered about and tried to draw attention away from the fact that his eyes were stinging with the same enthusiasm they might have if he'd just plunged his face into a patch of nettles.

She leaned back in his chair and simply stared at him.

"You're lusting after me in this ridiculously expensive, hand-tailored Italian suit, aren't you?" he managed.

"You were wearing that to your grandfather's offices in New York," she said. "You're in jeans now."

He supposed he was fortunate he wasn't trotting around without his trousers, something he found himself worrying about more often than not. Too much time in a saffron shirt with the only need for a plaid being clan pride and a bit of warmth on a chilly day.

"Don't become too attached to that suit," he said, latching on to a less tender topic gladly. "I only own three of them and I'm not buying any more."

"Not even for a wedding?"

He considered. "Perhaps for a wedding. If it's mine."

"What would you wear for slumming in Paris?"

"Are we slumming in Paris soon?"

"I've never been, but I think there's ample scope for an artist's imagination there."

"If you get me to Paris, I'm donning poet's clothes and never getting out of them again."

"What sorts of things do poets wear?"

"If we're Scottish, we wear the plaid," he said, "in our clan's colors, and all around us admire and wish they were Scottish as well."

She smiled. "You and your national pride," she said. "Very attractive. It worked for those half a dozen flight attendants fluttering around you all the way back over here."

He sighed, but couldn't help a bit of a smile. "If they only knew the extent of the madness that is my life. You, darling, have a very strong stomach to even stand to the side and watch it."

She looked at him seriously. "Do we need to go back to Scotland?"

"I think perhaps we should," he said. "We could take a sleeper to Inverness, then pick up your car." He looked at her sternly. "I will be following you all the way home, so you can set aside any thoughts of slipping off to do any investigating on your own."

"Where would I go besides that cottage next to yours you keep trying to kick me out of?"

He pursed his lips. "I'm never going to live that down, am I?"

"We'll see how the rest of the winter goes."

He supposed they would, though if he had anything to say about it, he would have his problem solved far sooner than the full arrival of a hard winter.

"Feeling pulled?" she asked.

He had to get up and pace a bit. "I might be."

"I'm ready whenever you are."

"Let's go find some dinner, then we'll catch a late train." He didn't add that he was almost tempted to try to sleep for a change. He wasn't going to be worth anything to anyone if he didn't and he was finding that he had a very good reason to want to stay alive.

He helped Emma put books back in their proper places, let his secretary know he was on his way out of town for a few days—grateful he didn't have to explain the same yet again to his business partner—and didn't waste any time getting to the station with Emma.

There was something he loved about being on a train. It was the perfect combination of the opportunity to sleep along with the chance to think. He sat in a comfortable seat, held Emma's hand, and watched the moonlight spilling down on the countryside they passed through. He glanced at Emma to find her watching not the countryside but him instead. He smiled.

"Enjoying the view?"

"If I thought you were really that conceited, I would tease you about it."

"I've no doubt you would," he said. He shifted to look at her. "I texted Patrick earlier to come get his little runabout you've been using."

"Thinking of stranding me in my cottage now, are you?"

"We'll pick your car up on our way home," he said. "And

just so you don't think I'll be turning my back on you any time soon, I booked us all the way through to Inverness. I'll have Brian pay one of his flunkies to go fetch mine from the airport in Edinburgh."

"You're in a hurry."

"I've never been in less of a hurry for anything, if you know what I'm getting at," he admitted. "But I can't deny that I feel like I'm late for an appointment."

"I won't go with you this time," she said quietly.

"You're damned right you won't. You'll sit by the fire like a proper medieval clanswoman and wait for your man to do his duty. This time and every other time until I solve this."

"If you like."

He wasn't sure how that acquiescence, if that's what it was, made him feel, but he was fairly sure it didn't make him feel any better.

She had seen Gerald and potentially not in the current day. He wasn't sure where to even begin with that. The last thing he wanted was to scour the MacLeod forest in *any* century looking for his daft cousin who likely wanted him dead.

He closed his eyes and enjoyed the feeling of Emma's hand in his. He liked the idea of her having a car parked in front of the cottage down the road from his. It felt permanent, which he liked, but it left her near him, which he liked but didn't like at the same time.

He was starting to feel torn in two in a way he never had before.

He had the feeling that the sooner he had his answers, the better.

Chapter 23

E^{mma} stood in her small living room and looked at the wall in front of her. She still had things to add to what was already taped there, but it was a start.

She was looking for a pattern.

She contemplated what was there a bit longer, then forced herself to walk into the kitchen and get something to drink. She'd been staring at the same things all morning without anything new coming to her. Sometimes letting her mind work on the problem while she was doing something else was the way her best breakthroughs were made. The trouble was, she wasn't sure what she could be doing. Walks were out, she couldn't even check her email, and pacing in her house was about to drive her crazy.

She finally took her life in her hands and walked out onto her little porch. It was cold, very true, but she had the coat Nathaniel had bought her, as well as clothes she hadn't needed but he'd insisted on purchasing for her anyway while they'd been in New York.

She had to admit dinner with his brother and a decent show that had had nothing to do with anything but someone else's reality had been a welcome relief as well. She'd felt like they were just a normal couple out on an enjoyable date. She'd actually slept on the plane back to London, confident that she would wake up in the same century.

Those few hours spent in Nathaniel's office, looking at his life's work, had been something she hadn't expected. He might have been as rich as a more charitable, friendlier version of

Scrooge McDuck, but the things he did with his money were truly life changing for those he helped.

If she hadn't been crazy for him before, she would have fallen in love with him right then.

It had been unsettling in the extreme, though, to come back to her little cottage, park that beautiful black Audi in front, then watch her, ah, friend who wanted to be much more than that tell her good-bye before some mystical time gate sucked him back where she definitely didn't want him to go.

He'd exacted a promise from her before he left that she would, yes, stay inside, then pulled her door shut from the outside and rushed off presumably to do what he did. She hadn't watched because, again, she'd promised not to open the door.

Well, not open the door very often, but she had supposed at the time that she was better off not to say as much.

She'd slept, but not much. The jet lag wasn't as bad, but she supposed that had been because she'd never adjusted to the time change in Manhattan anyway. She'd been up before dawn, taken a little trip into town for groceries, then locked herself in her house to do what she could with what she had to hand. If she'd paced a bit on her porch, well, who could blame her? She had firmly ignored the impulse to go off on a little exploration, which left her feeling very virtuous and trustworthy. She would have preferred sneaky and informed, but things were what they were.

What she had decided, though, was that it was past time to stop tap-dancing around the issue at hand. She needed answers and she knew how to begin to get them. She had found tape in a drawer and started to put together a storyboard.

She'd made illustrations of everything she personally knew about her journey into the past and put those up on the wall in the right order. She'd moved on to Nathaniel's part in the craziness but quickly realized she only had a very cursory idea of what went on with him. He heard a certain set of numbers, he grabbed his sword and put on a plaid, then he went to do what he had to do.

She did make a note of how long he'd been doing it and she added way off to the right the new fact that 1372 seemed to have affected him adversely.

She also added in the fact that touching that dagger in Edinburgh had somehow subsequently allowed her to pop through a gate in the forest she definitely hadn't been able to see in any kind of normal way.

That had been a couple of hours ago. She knew she should have been noticing things beyond what was just there, but in her defense, being tossed in a medieval dungeon had colored her perception of things a bit more than she was comfortable with. Subsequently spending time with her rescuer while he was in a very lovely suit, facing off with her own intimidating father, then having to listen to her former boyfriend blather on about things she couldn't remember hadn't helped anything, either.

She jumped a little at the knock on the door, even though she'd heard the car pulling to a stop on the gravel in front of her house. It was a Range Rover, though it could just as easily have been Patrick's as Nathaniel's. She'd heard Nathaniel's be delivered to his house earlier that morning and knew she should have memorized the sound. That she hadn't was undeniable proof that she was definitely off her game.

She was, however, very happy when she opened the door to find one extremely handsome time traveler standing there in jeans and a black leather jacket.

"Dangerous," she noted.

"Sleepy," he said wearily. "Feel like lunch?"

"I'm thinking. I can't eat while I'm thinking."

"Well," he said slowly, "I didn't mean to put you off your food."

"I wasn't thinking about you," she said, then she paused. "Well, I *was* thinking about you, but not in the way you're thinking I was thinking."

"You make me dizzy."

She didn't want to comment on what he did to her, so she simply stood back and invited him inside.

"What mischief are you combining?" he asked.

She shot him a look before she could stop herself. "What an interesting way of putting that."

He opened his mouth, then shut it. "Long night in a different language. Never mind anything else," he added, not quite under his breath.

That man there needed a change. She shut the door behind him. "I imagine so. And I'm just doodling. Want to come and look?"

"Love to," he said.

"I can make you a sandwich," she offered. "I ran to Mrs. McCreedy's this morning and she said you never buy bread but you like it, so she sold me what you'll eat."

He stopped in mid-step. "It molds."

She winced. "I'm sorry. I should have known that."

He smiled briefly. "I'm tired and talking too much. A sandwich sounds brilliant." He shrugged out of his coat, draped it over the back of a chair, then walked into her living room.

She followed him. She thought it might be interesting to get his perspective on things given that he likely knew more of the players in the drama than she did.

He stopped in front of the wall, looked at it for several very long minutes in silence, then looked at her in astonishment.

"What are you doing?" he asked.

"Doodling."

He backed up and sat down hard on her couch. "Sorry?"

She sat down next to him. "I like to make storyboards," she said. "It puts things I can't wrap my mind around in perspective."

"Does it now," he said hoarsely. "I don't like where this is going."

"Take a nap, then. I'll make you lunch. You'll like it all much better after lunch." She started to get up, then noticed the look he was sending her. "It's hard to ruin a sandwich," she said pointedly.

"But possible."

He was laughing at her silently, damn him. She glared at him. "What did you eat last?"

He put his hand over his stomach. "Must I say?"

"I think you'd feel better about my sandwich if you did."

He took a deep breath. "Haggis, but it was not fresh and there were things in it I didn't want to identify."

"And you thought ham and cheese wasn't going to be a big step up," she said archly as she went into the kitchen.

She made him lunch, then carried it back in with a glass of juice. He was, unexpectedly, sound asleep, tipped over on her couch. She left him there, set his sandwich down on the coffee table, then considered her wall. It didn't take her very long to realize that her drawings were much less interesting than the man sprawled on her couch. She sat down in one of the comfy chairs nearby and watched him for a bit.

She supposed his hair was disreputably long for a business-man, but she could see why he kept it that way to fit in with the other half of his life. She wouldn't have guessed there was anything unusual about him based on anything else past his being unsettlingly handsome.

Or she thought that until she watched him wake up, freeze, and figure out exactly where he was before he moved.

He opened his eyes and looked at her. She held up her hands slowly.

"Friend, not foe."

"I'll pass judgment after your sandwich," he said, his voice rough from what was probably very little sleep the night before.

She smiled to herself and watched him sit up and rub his hands over his face. He looked at the plate on the coffee table, then at her.

"Thank you," he said quietly. "Very kind."

"It's just lunch, Nathaniel."

"I bet it would taste better if you'd come sit next to me."

"But then I can't ogle you."

He pursed his lips as if he was trying not to smile. "Well, wouldn't want to rob you of this fine view, so stay where you are."

She did, then simply watched him as he ate. She supposed she had Mrs. McCreedy to thank for his lunch being tolerable, which she imagined he appreciated. She continued to watch him for little tells that he wasn't what he seemed to be. They were subtle, but she was used to looking for subtle.

That was a man there who didn't spend all his time in a boardroom.

He had a long drink, set his glass down with a hand that wasn't terribly steady, then looked at her. "Thank you. Delicious."

"I had nothing to do with the taste, but it was made with great affection."

He smiled. "Someone's been driving her Audi."

"You said you put it in your name, but yes, it is a lovely car."

"I did put it in my name," he said, "temporarily, and I'm happy you're enjoying it, hopefully for longer than temporarily." He looked at her wall. "Come over here and tell me about this madness there, Emma."

She supposed there was no reason not to join him on the couch, so she did, then nodded at her drawings. "I thought if we could see it on paper, we could identify the patterns."

"The only pattern involved is madness," he said grimly, then he looked at her reluctantly. "I'm tired, sorry. Say on."

"The world moves in patterns," she said. "People move in patterns, unless they don't, but even when they don't, there's generally a pattern to what they do."

He looked at her as if he'd never seen her before. "Do you think so?"

"When you go back to the past, what do you do?"

"I check my modern sensibilities at the door and take care of business," he said without hesitation.

"And you don't do the same here?"

He opened his mouth, probably to deny it, then he frowned at her. "I don't think I like this. Still."

She imagined he didn't, but she had to help and she couldn't think of any other way to do so at the moment. "When you go to battle with your grandfather, what do you do?"

He took a deep breath. "I take care of business."

"And how do you do that? In a metaphorical sense."

"Brutally and to the point."

She smiled. "See?"

He rubbed his hands over his face, then looked at her wearily. "Doesn't this idea turn people into robots? Slaves to instincts they can't control?"

"I'm not saying people don't change or that they *can't* change, but it's been my experience that unless there's a compelling reason to do things differently, people tend to act in patterns. They protect themselves and they protect what's most important to them, but they generally do it in ways they've done it before simply because it's comfortable and safe."

"And what does that have to do with anything we're embroiled in?"

"I think we're trapped in some kind of something."

"Time travel," he said in resignation.

"Yes," she said. "Time travel. But I think it's more than just a random thing." She shrugged helplessly. "I think there's a pattern to it. Maybe even a purpose to it."

He shook his head slowly. "You realize this sounds absolutely barking. We could be imagining it all."

"I have a pile of clothes in a garbage can in the back that says we're not." She looked at him seriously. "Patrick MacLeod isn't crazy."

He looked at her for a moment or two in silence. "I have something you might want to see," he said finally.

"It better not be clothes or another car."

He smiled and heaved himself to his feet. "I wish it were, but unfortunately it isn't."

She decided he was a man who looked like he needed something else to settle his nerves, perhaps tea. She had fortunately become adept at not flooding the house with smoke, but that was about as far as she'd gotten with that damned Aga. She retreated to her kitchen, filled a kettle, then looked at her nemesis. She wasn't sure if the thing needed more wood or if it would magically know just how hot it needed to be in order to cook what she wanted it to.

"Very domestic."

She looked at Nathaniel, who was closing the door behind himself and taking off his boots.

"Yeah, well, you weren't just transported back to the 1950s, so don't get too excited about it." She looked at him as he straightened. "I'm a terrible cook."

He set a manila envelope down on the table, then took the kettle away from her. "You make excellent sandwiches. As for the rest, I'm a very keen chef, so why don't you sit and read whilst I make us some tea." He slid her a look. "What have you eaten your whole life?"

"Whatever the local coffee shop shoved across the counter at me. When I was feeling particularly ambitious, I hit the nearest juice bar." She smiled briefly. "I eat lots of peanut butter and jelly."

He made a noise of horror, then started fiddling with her stove. She left him to it and opened the envelope he'd put on her table. She slid a folder out and opened it.

She felt a silence descend.

She only realized that, actually, because Nathaniel wasn't moving any longer. She looked up to find him watching her. He lifted an eyebrow.

"Worthy of your wall?"

"This is a copy of a parish register."

"And so it is," he agreed. He paused. "It was a gift from Alexander Smith, if you're curious. He thought since he was providing me with so many juicy details about Sheldon, he would tuck in a few other things I might find interesting."

"He is a first-class snoop, isn't he?"

Nathaniel leaned back against her counter. "Absolutely. I hesitate to introduce the two of you for fear you would set your sights on tumbling superpowers. But let me distract you with a little interesting tidbit I didn't realize until this morning: my favorite investigator Alexander Smith has a connection to our little enchanted forest in the person of his sister Elizabeth."

"Is she Scottish?" Emma asked in surprise.

"By marriage," Nathaniel said slowly. "She's married to James MacLeod."

"Patrick's brother."

"The very same."

Emma frowned. "You know, Patrick said something to me about his family marrying Americans in droves, but I thought nothing of it at the time."

"I guess you could call it a pattern," he said solemnly.

She scowled at him. "You just wait until I really get going here."

"I'm half afraid of what you'll find," he admitted.

"You probably should be. So, why does it matter that Elizabeth is married to James MacLeod?"

"Dig through those papers and see what you think." He smiled, then turned around to deal with the kettle.

She watched him gather things for tea, then looked at what was on the table in front of her. She flipped to the first page and realized quickly that she was looking at a genealogy of the Clan MacLeod that stretched back into the early Middle Ages. Nothing was highlighted, though, which gave her the opportunity to draw her own conclusions about what she thought was important.

She frowned thoughtfully over the players operating at the turn of the fourteenth century. There was a laird, James, born in 1279. While that in itself wasn't particularly noteworthy, it was interesting that he had a brother named Patrick. She was also quite interested to learn that those MacLeod boys had had a cousin named Ian, who had died in a Fergusson dungeon on a date she couldn't quite read. Then again, she couldn't really read the death dates for either James or Patrick.

That *was* interesting.

She looked at Nathaniel as he set a cup in front of her and put a cozy over the teapot.

"We have some smudges here," she noted.

"This is a private parish register," he said easily. "The more public one puts death dates somewhere around 1320 for all three of those lads."

"So young," she murmured.

"And yet still so alive," he said sourly. "I know this because our good Lord Patrick said as much, though I was doing my damnedest not to believe him at the time. Apparently he was born six years after his brother James, way back in 1285, and he somehow trotted through that bloody forest and set up shop in the current day."

"Then those pub rumors are true," she said.

"It would seem so." He poured tea, then sat back and looked at her. "Hard to deny that business there, especially given who sent it to me. If anyone would know family secrets, you would think it might be Alexander Smith, James MacLeod's brother-in-law. I'm guessing that Alex probably has a sword in the back of his closet."

"Is that where you sword-wielding types keep them?"

"Behind the hand-tailored Italian suits," he said. "As it happens."

She sighed deeply. "What do you want to do?"

"Run away with you to Paris and live in a little garret where I will write poetry and you will sketch or hammer or whatever it is you decide you want to do, though your drawing is breathtaking."

She smiled. "Really?"

"Really what?" he asked. "Do I want to run away with you? Aye. Do I want to write poetry? Nay, I'd rather just lie in the sun, drink expensive wine, and look at you whilst you're art-ing. And aye, your art is glorious. Do I think you'd agree to any of it? I'm afraid to ask."

She wondered if he would notice if she took her napkin and fanned herself a bit. She was fairly sure she was blushing.

He set his cup down, leaned over, and looked at her. "May I?"

"May you what?"

"If you need to ask, lass, I have obviously not been living up to my reputation as a desirable and rakish recluse."

She looked up at him. "I'm not interested in your reputation."

"You just want me because I have a terrible habit of pulling you out of medieval dungeons—"

He stopped speaking. That was likely because she had leaned over and kissed him.

And she'd thought seeing the numbers 1387 had rocked her world.

If he pulled her to her feet and made, as he might have said, a proper job of the business, she didn't argue. She didn't have the energy to and, truthfully, she didn't want to.

The girls from London had no idea what they were missing.

She decided quite a while later that she was absolutely not going to rush down to the pub to tell any of them who might be setting up camp there. She also didn't take it personally when Nathaniel asked her very politely if he could indulge in a bit of a swoon on her couch. She tucked him in, then watched him fall asleep almost instantly. She wasn't offended, because as lovely as it was to have him awake, she had business that he didn't need to be a part of.

She watched him for a moment or two and came to a decision. He was exhausted, but that wasn't the worst part about it. He was so enmeshed in what was happening to him, so completely at its mercy, she was half afraid he would never have the luxury of stepping back far enough to see what was really going on.

She, however, did.

She made a decision, left him a note, then dressed as sensibly as she could. If she'd gone to the local charity shop that morning after Mrs. McCreedy's and found herself something that might have passed in a different day for normal women's clothing, well, she did like to be prepared.

She looked at the copies on her kitchen table, traced the MacLeod line until she found the appropriate number, then felt something shift as surely as if she'd opened a door. She looked quickly at Nathaniel, but he was still sleeping peacefully.

She was going to leave him there without telling him what she was planning because she had no other choice. She needed to find out what was going on without involving Nathaniel in it, and not just out of a desire to save him trouble. If she alerted him to what she was thinking, he might do things differently from his normal pattern, then change things in a way neither of them could predict.

There was something odd going on. Once was unusual. The same series of events happening exactly the same way twice in a row was a startling coincidence. But having them potentially happen a third time?

That was a pattern.

She let herself silently out the front door, unearthed the very small go bag she'd put there earlier, and wished she had even a fraction of Bertie Wordsworth's skills.

Well, what she had was enough.

She would make do.

Chapter 24

Nathaniel washed up the dishes partly because he'd made a habit of it after the first time he'd been unexpectedly gone and come home to things rotting in his sink but mostly because it gave him something to do with his hands besides wring the neck of the woman sitting out on his deck.

He looked around for something else to do, then decided on making coffee. He did it slowly because he needed some time to think. It was one thing for his life to affect just himself, to be looking over his shoulder to protect nothing but his own sweet neck, to have no one to think about but himself in a place where survival depended solely on his own skills. It was another thing entirely to be responsible for someone else.

As Patrick had said, the past wasn't a place for a modern woman.

The problem was, his woman wasn't listening to any of that.

She hadn't even bothered to wake him to tell him she was going anywhere, though he supposed he hadn't needed her to. He'd known the moment he'd woken and realized he was on her couch and not in his bed and the only lamp lit was a very small one geared not to waken sleeping idiots. He'd cursed himself thoroughly as he'd rolled to his feet.

Damn her to hell, she was going to shatter his heart long before a lifetime of loving her managed to do the same thing.

He'd found Alex's notes laid out very carefully. It hadn't taken any special powers of observation to mark how the handle of Emma's spoon was pointing to some event in the MacLeod annals that had occurred in 1387.

He should have known, even in his sleep. He'd felt the gate between centuries open, but the truth was, he'd thought he was having a nightmare and he'd gone right back to sleep.

He'd thought he might be tempted to shout at her when he saw her, but once he'd been trailing her in the past—again—he found that all he could do was continually try to put himself between her and danger. In the end, she had pushed past him and tried to do the honors herself of taking out that Fergusson clansman who had come at them. Nathaniel had watched her sweep that man's feet out from him, then leap toward him.

Unfortunately, she hadn't counted on a clansman's ability to never lose his dagger. It had been nothing but dumb luck that he'd managed to pull her aside and send her attacker speedily into the afterlife.

The only other notable difference had been that instead of losing her previous meal, she'd concentrated on looking around herself, as if she was looking for someone in particular.

He understood. He'd been looking for Gerald as well.

He hadn't thought he could speak without shouting and she hadn't seemed particularly interested in conversation either, so they'd made the journey back to their proper place in time in silence. It occurred to him as he'd seen her house there, hiding behind a bit of a mist, that they were damned fortunate they always came back to their proper place in time. He didn't fancy a trip back to eighteenth-century Scotland, or any time other than his own, for that matter.

He was beginning to wonder if there might be a purpose to all the madness in truth.

He had then sat in her kitchen as she'd showered, then insisted that she come with him to his house so he could remove the medieval grime from himself. All of that had left him exhausted, with too much to think about. He suspected Emma was in the same condition.

He wasn't sure what to do with her short of handcuffing her to him and keeping her with him at all times, but that would mean that if he were forced into the past, she would have to go as well, without it being her choice.

There was in truth no good solution.

He poured two mugs of coffee, then walked out onto his deck. He set the mugs down on the table in front of the chairs, then collapsed into his own place. He looked at the woman next to him, wrapped in blankets, staring out over the water. She sighed, then looked at him.

"Hi," she croaked.

He supposed there was no reason not to be blunt. "I thought you weren't going to do that again."

"Did I say that?"

He wasn't sure what tempted him more: bursting into tears or brandishing his sword and threatening to . . . well, he never would have been able to do damage to her and she knew it as well as he did. He sighed and opened his arms.

"Do you want me to stab you or come sit with you?" she asked hoarsely.

"The latter, assuredly, for then I won't have to make so much of an effort to shout at you."

She sighed, got up, then moved to sit with him. She unwrapped her blanket as she did, then pulled it over the two of them. He closed his eyes as she put her head on his shoulder and wrapped her arm over his ribs.

"You're trembling," she said quietly.

"I'm tired," he said.

She only nodded. He suspected she knew it wasn't just weariness and he imagined she felt the same way.

Something had to change. Soon.

"You can't follow me into the past again," he said finally.

"I didn't *follow* you into the past," she said. "I went first."

"Emma—"

She lifted her head and looked at him from haunted eyes. "I was trying to save you, Nathaniel."

He wasn't going to weep. He considered swearing, stomping about, cursing her thoroughly, but he absolutely wasn't going to weep.

She leaned over and brushed something from his cheeks. He caught her hand, kissed her palm, then shifted so he could put his arms more fully around her. If he didn't protest when she rested her chin on his shoulder, well, who could blame him? That way at least she wouldn't be looking at him as he indulged in a stray tear or two.

"Sentiment makes me uneasy," he admitted.

"Which is why you long to be a poet, obviously."

"My poems are epic rants full of bloodshed and mayhem," he said. "Too violent for a woman's delicate sensibilities, to be sure."

She laughed a little. He would have elaborated on just how gory and bloodshed-filled his yet-to-be-written poetry could be, but his text alert interrupted them both. He looked at his phone sitting there so innocently on a footstool near the edge of his deck, then looked at her.

"I don't want to look," he said.

"I'll look."

"I don't want you to look, either."

She rolled her eyes at him, then unwrapped herself and got up to fetch his phone for him.

"Password?" she asked.

He took a deep breath, then gave her the appropriate numbers. She entered them, then checked his text message. He thought he was being thoroughly discreet by not mentioning how relieved she looked. She handed him his phone.

"Car dealer. They want to make sure you're happy with your purchase."

"I'm thrilled," he said with a grimace. "I'll be even more thrilled if you don't use the damned thing to run me over so you can be off and doing things you shouldn't." He pulled her back onto his lap, set his phone on the deck, then leaned his head back against the chair. "We could take a little drive this afternoon."

"How far away do you want to go?"

He understood what she was getting at. "Farther than Inverness, apparently. I would say moving back across the Pond would do it, but that doesn't seem to have been far enough, does it?"

"It doesn't," she agreed. "Edinburgh doesn't seem to do it, either."

He had to agree, though he did so reluctantly.

"That dagger we saw," she added. "I won't say the date. That was a bit odd, wasn't it?"

"Very," he agreed, then he wrestled with whether or not to keep his mouth shut. He decided that perhaps it was best she heard things from him before she decided she needed to don her deerstalker and be off on yet another hunt for clues. "The dagger is mine."

She leaned up so quickly, her head clipped the edge of his jaw. She stared at him in shock. "It isn't."

"It is," he said carefully, "and yet it isn't." He paused. "It's sitting in my closet at the moment."

She frowned. "While also sitting in Mr. Campbell's glass case in Edinburgh, only that one is hundreds of years old."

He supposed it might not be useful at the moment to enlighten her about Stephen de Piaget's texting him to tell him that the dagger had been found in the dungeon of the old Fergusson keep.

Truth be told, that was something he was trying to forget.

"It's almost like time is folding back on itself," she mused.

"That's one way to look at it," he agreed.

"Have you noticed anything odd about it? You know, apart from the obvious."

He opened his mouth, then shut it. He had to pull himself together for a moment or two before he thought he might be able to speak. "I must confess I haven't."

"You're sounding very Etonian today."

"Those crisp British consonants make me feel more in control."

"I'll just bet they do." She stared out over the loch for a bit, then looked at him again. "What if that's really what's happening? Time folding over itself, I mean."

"I don't follow."

"Well, it seems to be the same experience every time, doesn't it?" she asked slowly.

He considered, then shook his head. "I've been there for five years. It's never repeated for me."

"No pattern at all?"

He shifted uncomfortably. "Good lord, woman, you should get a job with those spies over here."

"What I should do is call my father's under-chauffeur, but he would go back to the past and render everyone there unable to make any more trouble. I think we'll have to make do with just us."

He didn't want her to think she was going to be making do with anything, particularly anything to do with his madness, but he supposed she wasn't going to take kindly to being told what to do.

But the thought of her lost in the past . . .

"Do you always go back to 1387?" she asked.

"Nay I started in 1382, why—" He shook his head. "It hasn't always been 13 . . . well, you know. It started five years ago, but that was five years ago then as well."

"So time has been passing at the same rate in both places?"

He started to say that that was definitely the case, then realized he honestly couldn't say for certain. He looked at her and frowned. "I haven't marked the dates on a calendar," he said, "but I would say aye."

"This entire time?"

"Aye," he said. "Until . . ."

He stopped speaking. She was only watching him carefully, which he might have appreciated if he hadn't been so busy trying not to ignore what she was implying.

That things had changed when she'd come to the village— nay, that wasn't exactly true. He had continued to go back to his accustomed time and place. Things had changed when he'd gone to Cawdor and heard the date of 1372.

But the truth was, he never would have gone to Cawdor if Emma hadn't been there with him. He wasn't sure he wanted to face the possibility of her having been the catalyst for something, but he was beginning to think he didn't have a choice.

"Let's go for a drive," he said, helping her off his lap and pushing himself to his feet. "I'll take you shopping."

"I don't want to go shopping."

"Then you can take me shopping. I love to spend hours admiring myself in the mirror."

She smiled. "You don't."

"I don't," he agreed, "which is why my wardrobe is limited to three business suits and a handful of moth-ridden jumpers. We'll take your car." He looked at her seriously. "I need a bit of distance."

She took a deep breath. "I understand."

He imagined she did, but he couldn't bring himself to discuss it in any more depth than that. There was something almost comforting in knowing he wasn't carrying his secret by himself, but that was balanced out very nicely by wishing that the person he shared that secret with wasn't the woman he was currently following into his house.

All he knew for certain was that he had no intention of seeing her back in the past ever again. Not unless he was dead, which he thought he might want to make sure Fate didn't think was an invitation.

H_e walked along the shore with her at sunset after a lovely, leisurely drive up the coast. It was such a normal thing to do, to stare out over the sea washing up endlessly against the shore, but it gave him a sense of timelessness that he wasn't altogether sure he cared for.

"Think it looked this way before?"

He looked at her. "I would guess so, but I've never been this far north whilst . . . well, you know."

"I know."

He stopped and turned to her. "I have to solve this."

"We," she said firmly. "We have to solve this." She looked at him seriously. "What you're not saying is that things were rolling along as usual until that afternoon I saw you in the middle of a battle."

He nodded, but he wasn't sure he could give voice to any of the facts. The truth was, whilst her arrival in Benmore had changed his heart, their journey to Cawdor had changed things in a way he honestly couldn't put his finger on.

He was beginning to wonder what encountering his dagger in Thomas Campbell's shop in Edinburgh had set in motion.

"Nathaniel?"

"I will solve this," he said, dragging himself back to the conversation at hand, "whilst you stay in your lovely cottage and look at your board for clues. Paris calls for us to visit it in the future, and if you're not with me, I won't go." He looked at her seriously. "What if I lose you somewhere in the weeds of the fourteenth century?"

"Well, I wouldn't want to rob the world of its freshest poetic voice," she said thoughtfully.

He had the feeling she had no intention of doing anything but exactly what she wanted to do, which he knew should have alarmed him very much indeed.

"Very sensible," he said. "Speaking of sensible, I called James MacLeod and made an appointment for tomorrow."

"I wondered what you were doing," she said with a frown.

"Likely marching into a battle I haven't the skill to fight," he said grimly. "I've been instructed to bring my sword."

"Do these guys do anything else?"

"I suspect not, and I imagine they assault life with the same sort of enthusiasm they pour into their swordplay. What was it you called that sort of rubbish?"

"Patterns," she began, then she pursed her lips. "Mock me all you like, but you have to admit there's truth to it."

"There's more truth to it than I want to acknowledge," he said honestly. "I have the feeling our good Laird Jamie conducts his life now just as he did hundreds of years ago. He doesn't seem to have given up using a sword to make his point, as it were."

She smiled faintly. "He's in the right place for it, I guess." She walked with him a bit longer, then looked at him. "Can he help, do you think?"

"There's only one way to find out."

She nodded, but said nothing else. He understood, for there was nothing else to say. Either James MacLeod would have answers for him or he wouldn't.

He could only hope when he heard those answers, they would be ones he could stomach.

Chapter 25

E*mma* supposed, thinking about it as the sun was dropping toward the west the next afternoon, that whether or not James MacLeod could help them or not wasn't the only thing they'd found out.

She sat on a bench pushed up against a castle wall with a blanket as a cushion and a water bottle keeping her warm under another blanket and watched absolute madness going on there in front of her. Patrick MacLeod was a civilized gentleman compared to his brother when it came to swords. James MacLeod was . . . well, she didn't know what to call him. Ruthless, maybe. Dangerous, possibly.

Medieval, definitely.

If she hadn't seen his birth date, she might not have believed it—well, actually she would have believed it without hesitation. The man was as intimidating as any other medieval clansman she'd encountered so far, only he took it to a level she almost couldn't believe.

Chief of the clan, and rightly so.

She had to admit that Nathaniel wasn't doing poorly with the business of swords. Jamie probably could have had him for lunch, but it wouldn't have been an easy meal to choke down. Nathaniel was tall, strong, and fast. That, and he seemed to have an extensive vocabulary of medieval insults that left Jamie grinning ferally every time Nathaniel pulled one out and flung it at the laird of the hall.

She was in trouble. Very big trouble.

By the time the sun had set, those two crazies had put up their swords and were chatting amicably about things she didn't pay attention to. She was too busy looking at a medieval laird and his new friend.

She was starting to think her life was as weird as Nathaniel's.

Jamie tucked his sword up against his shoulder as if he'd done the same thing thousands of times—which she suspected he had—and held out his hand.

"Mistress Emma," he said. "I hope your afternoon was passed most pleasantly."

"I'm still trying to recover."

Jamie laughed and reached out to clap Nathaniel on the shoulder. If Nathaniel winced, she couldn't blame him. He didn't look much worse for the wear, but she supposed that might have been because he'd been putting off meeting the laird of the hall up the way for five years, and getting that out of the way at present had to have been a relief.

"He showed well," Jamie said. "I'm not saying I couldn't wrench a bit more finesse out of him with the proper time and attention, but he's done well all on his own."

"He's saved my life," Emma said honestly.

"And that, lass, is something we should talk about. My wife and bairns have deserted me to make mischief in Her Majesty's little village down south, so I've nothing but time on my hands. We'll have supper tonight, then investigate this situation at our leisure."

Emma slipped her hand into Nathaniel's as they walked and didn't meet his eyes. There was nothing to be said about their situation and there was absolutely nothing to be said about the way his hand was trembling. She didn't blame him a bit. If she'd had to face that maniac James MacLeod over swords, she wouldn't have been trembling slightly, she would have been in hysterics.

She squeezed her friend's hand and walked with him back to the great hall, very glad she was going to be keeping to the upper floors of the MacLeod keep for a change.

Supper was very good mostly because Nathaniel cooked it. She sat at a worn table in the kitchen with Jamie, enjoying a very lovely glass of wine, and pretended to watch Nathaniel when the truth was, she was watching Jamie.

How was it a man had hopped over so many centuries yet managed to carve out such a perfect life for himself? He didn't mention anything specific about his past or his transition to the present, though it was obvious he assumed both she and Nathaniel knew. Actually, she suspected he hadn't assumed anything. If there was one thing she thought she might guess with a fair degree of confidence, it was that James MacLeod found himself caught by surprise very rarely.

She wished she could say the same for herself.

She found it somewhat interesting that he didn't seem to be hiding behind a façade. He was who he was without apology or embarrassment. Then again, if he had been the laird of the clan MacLeod at the turn of the fourteenth century, he supposed he had faced much sterner tests than a couple of modern-day gawkers.

"Mistress Emma, perhaps you would care to wander around the castle?"

She came back to herself to find Jamie watching her. She attempted a smile. "I'd love to see the upstairs."

Jamie lifted an eyebrow. "Upstairs?"

She needed to get a better grip on herself, she decided abruptly. "Oh, you know, the whole keep, I mean."

He looked at her in a way that left her with absolutely no doubt that anyone had pulled anything over on him, ever.

"Have you seen other parts of my keep, Mistress Emma?" he asked politely.

"The dungeon," she admitted, feeling as if she were all of ten getting caught in a whopper of a lie. "In 1387."

Jamie sighed gustily. "I want it noted that I filled that pit in to please my wife, many years earlier. I can't control what anyone who came after me did." He looked at Nathaniel. "I believe 'tis time, lad, that you and I had speech together. Your lady may certainly stay if she cares to."

"Or I could just go wait in the car," Emma offered.

"No," Nathaniel said, shooting her a look. "You'll drive off without me."

"I might need a nap."

"You might need a keeper," Jamie said wisely. He smiled. "You could go investigate upstairs, if you like. There is a chamber down the passageway from my thinking chamber you might enjoy. 'Tis full of steel."

"Can I borrow anything—"

"No," Nathaniel said, sounding horrified.

Jamie looked equally horrified, so she supposed they were in agreement there. She dropped a casual little laugh.

"Just kidding, of course. Why would I need a dagger or anything?"

She excused herself before anyone stopped her or gave her looks she was going to have to acknowledge. She had to stop and stand in the middle of the great hall for a moment or two, simply to appreciate the fact that she wasn't catching a quick glimpse of it on her way to being tossed down into Malcolm MacLeod's dungeon.

She supposed she might go a very long time without having that be a part of her reality without missing it one bit.

She hoped Jamie meant what he said by making herself at home, took a deep breath, then headed toward the stairs. It was odd to think about how many people had gone up and down those stairs over the years, which led her to wondering what James MacLeod thought about the same. Maybe he never thought about it. Maybe he was too busy making a dash for his armory, such as it was, in order to fight off any stray time travelers who might show up at his door.

His life must have been very odd.

She understood that, unfortunately, as she took her time getting to that room, then spent more time in there than she probably should have. There was actually a great deal to be impressed by. His collection of things that didn't look brand-new was extensive. She decided abruptly that she absolutely wasn't going to ask how many of those things he had used himself over the years.

She wandered back down the hallway, then paused by another open door. He had told her to make herself at home, so she took a deep breath and peeked inside. A study, by the look of it. She ignored her unease and went inside, then paused in shock at the sight of the map hanging over his desk.

It was Mrs. McCreedy's map.

Actually, on closer inspection she realized that while it was in the same style as Mrs. McCreedy's, this one was far more extensive. It was the ultimate pirate map. She stared at it for several minutes without making any judgments about it, just letting it tell her what it would. It was very well drawn, she conceded. It was also covered with those painfully familiar Xs. She leaned up a bit to have a closer look and realized that next to those Xs were labels.

Barbados. Salem. Victorian England with *Don't go there again* in parentheses next to it.

Medieval Scotland.

She lost count of the marks that indicated something of a medieval vintage. She frowned thoughtfully as she looked for Nathaniel's cottage.

There was an X penciled there, but no tag—

She moved as the sound of voices coming her way reached her. By the time Jamie and Nathaniel entered the study, she was wedged behind a sofa and wondering what the hell she was doing.

Nothing good ever comes of eavesdropping was what her father always said. *But everything interesting does* was what Bertie Wordsworth had always added under his breath as her father had been walking away. She knew that because that was the lecture her father had always given his under-chauffeur and she had always been privy to that conversation because she'd always been eavesdropping. Just for the practice, of course, not because her father had ever said anything interesting.

She'd had an interesting childhood.

She had the feeling her life was about to become substantially more interesting if she could just keep from wheezing long enough to listen to those two settling into chairs.

Chapter 26

Nathaniel was extremely happy for a chance to sit down, have a glass of extremely lovely whisky, and not feel like he needed to have his sword within reach. It was, he could safely say, the first time he'd ever been in the MacLeod familial hall where that had been the case.

Dinner had been very edible, but he'd cooked it. He supposed Jamie had done that on purpose so he could keep an eye on the field of battle, as it were. Emma had done a fine job of avoiding anything controversial, but Nathaniel had the feeling his comfortable evening was about to end.

"So," Jamie said, studying him carefully, "Mistress Emma has gone back how many times?"

"Three, my laird," Nathaniel said respectfully.

"And she encounters the same thing every time?"

Nathaniel nodded. "It doesn't seem to matter what either of us does," he said carefully. "She winds up in the dungeon every time."

"Weel," Jamie said, shifting uncomfortably, "I'll admit we do have a rich tradition of tossing bodies in that pit, but please don't bring that up with my wife."

"You don't mean she found herself there," Nathaniel said, feeling slightly aghast.

"I refuse to admit to anything," Jamie said, "but please don't bring it up at any family gatherings. I filled in the pit, but obviously someone decided that was unwise. I'm sorry your lady has seen the inside of it." He shivered. "'Tis full of vermin and filth."

"I know," Nathaniel said dryly, "having had my own stay there. I would prefer that Emma not see the inside of it again, which is one of the reasons I wanted to see you." He thought it might be prudent not to add that he was thrilled to be discussing things with the laird of the hall over a whisky and not over blades.

Jamie snorted. "I imagine you have several reasons for coming to see me, not the least of which is to see for yourself who lived over the hill from you."

Nathaniel shifted. "Well, I wasn't entirely sure about you—"

"You couldn't do a bit of investigating?"

Nathaniel looked at him seriously. "I didn't want to."

"Now, there's a piece of truth," Jamie said. He set his glass aside and looked at Nathaniel seriously. "Tell me the tale whilst your lady is out of earshot, and spare no details. I've all night to listen."

Nathaniel wasn't sure if he should fall to his knees and kiss Jamie's ring or simply burst into tears. Since he couldn't decide, he took a deep breath and spewed out everything.

It sounded daft, even though he'd lived it. The round of golf, his own time in the MacLeod dungeon, the fact that his uncle was now—or had been in the fourteenth century—masquerading as the laird's most trusted priest.

"He will have had a house," Jamie said, "and enough to eat. Can't say I blame him."

Nathaniel conceded the point. "He does seem happy. I believe he's even learned to use a sword."

"You've done well enough with that yourself," Jamie said. "Who taught you?"

"Malcolm himself."

"Well," Jamie said carefully, "I can see how he might want to do that."

Nathaniel frowned. "Why?"

Jamie waved him on. "Not important at the moment. Keep on with your tale."

Nathaniel had another strengthening sip of whisky, then made quick work of describing trying to keep himself alive and the terror of never knowing if he would get back to his proper place in time.

When he was finished with that, he gave Jamie a brief summary of his life in the present, the madness with his grandfather, and his never having any idea how long he would have to take care of his business.

"And then Emma Baxter walked into your life."

Nathaniel nodded. "She stepped into the past as easily as you would step into another room. I thought I was losing my mind. Or, rather, she saw me step into the future. I'm not sure which it was."

"At the edge of the forest," Jamie finished for him.

"Aye. She was standing there, I was in the middle of a skirmish with the Fergussons, and I almost ran into her bodily. She definitely saw me. That seems to be what started the whole madness for her."

Jamie sat back and pressed the tips of his fingers together. "And then?"

"She's been back to the same place in time, the exact same situation, three times now."

"And you let her go?" Jamie asked in surprise.

"I didn't know she was going."

Jamie shook his head. "Have you thought about locking her in your house?"

Nathaniel supposed telling the man sitting across from him that such would be considered kidnapping in the current day was unnecessary.

"I would prefer she stay because she wants to," Nathaniel said firmly.

"Then woo her to your bed, ye wee fool," Jamie said, throwing up his hands. "Lads these days."

Nathaniel smiled in spite of himself. "She's got a mind of her own."

"They generally do," Jamie said with a snort. He considered for a moment or two, then frowned. "I do have a thought or two for you."

"That's why I came, my laird."

"As well as for my superior swordplay."

"That, too," Nathaniel agreed.

Jamie only laughed. Nathaniel spared a wish that he had known Jamie in the past. He wasn't unfond of Malcolm MacLeod—heaven knew he had slain enough Fergusson clansmen to satisfy the man—but there was something about Jamie that he supposed might never be repeated. He had certainly been legend enough in 13 . . .

Well, whatever date that was. He didn't dare even think it lest it decide to call for him.

"More whisky," Jamie said, rising. "You'll need it."

Nathaniel imagined he would. He took the opportunity to look about the chamber where he currently sat. It was Malcolm's private chamber, but he supposed that shouldn't have surprised him. What did surprise him, however, was that he hadn't noticed what was over Jamie's desk.

It was a map.

Jamie was standing at that desk, filling glasses. "Come have a look."

Nathaniel didn't mind if he did. He rose and walked over to join his host. He studied the map for a moment or two, noting all the Xs scattered over what he was assuming were Jamie's lands. He considered, then looked at the lord of the hall.

"And?"

"Gates," Jamie said succinctly.

"To the past?" Nathaniel asked in surprise.

"Some are," Jamie conceded. "Some are to other places."

Nathaniel smiled until he realized Jamie was serious. "Other places?"

"Let's just say that Elizabeth has forbidden any more trips to Barbados, not that I can find anyone willing to go with me after what my brother-in-law Zachary revealed about our last journey there." He considered his own map. "It was startling at first, of course, to realize what my land contained."

"Can anyone use these?" Nathaniel ventured. "Or are they your domain exclusively?"

Jamie looked at him and shrugged. "It depends, I suppose. Others have used them with a fair amount of success, but there has always been a need. I suppose the odd tourist who trespasses on my lands runs the risk of having more holiday than they bargained for, but that isn't my worry, is it?"

"I don't suppose it is."

Jamie studied him. "Is your gate in the same place every time?"

Nathaniel frowned thoughtfully. "I hadn't plotted it out exactly, but I know the general location of two of them. There's one in front of my cottage door. The one Emma seems to use is near your cottage, in the forest there."

"Do you ever think about going to the past when those gates are open?"

Nathaniel looked at the man standing next to him and could hardly believe they were having their current conversation. If he hadn't been up to his eyeballs in the madness himself, he would have thought it absolute rubbish. Unfortunately, he knew better.

"I don't think about anything in particular," he said, shrugging. "They seem to be out of my control. I see a certain date, I feel the world shift, and I know that I'm being called to a different time."

"A certain date we won't voice aloud."

"That might be best." He looked at Jamie seriously. "How long will this go on, do you think?"

"Until your task is done, I'd imagine," Jamie said. "I have no experience with your present business."

"But these wee Xs all over that damned map of yours," Nathaniel said, feeling faintly exasperated, "those were just things you had to go back to the past to put right? Did you make that decision or was the decision made for you?"

Jamie sighed deeply. "I'm afraid that might be the one thing I can't answer properly." He handed Nathaniel his refilled glass, then considered for a moment or two. "I'm going to tell you something, but I'll slay you if you noise this about."

Nathaniel didn't doubt he would and leave it looking like a horrible kitchen accident. He resumed his seat because he thought that might be wise. He sipped on his whisky to keep himself busy as Jamie took his seat again as well.

"In the beginning," Jamie began, " 'twas simply a bit of sport. Seeking out gates and using them, that is. There was a fair bit of purpose behind it, I'll admit that, for I had no mind to have my wife or bairns wandering out in the garden and disappearing." He shot Nathaniel a look. "You might understand that now, I daresay."

"I daresay," Nathaniel murmured.

"Caught you by surprise, did it?"

"What?"

Jamie leveled a look at him that would have had Nathaniel smiling if he hadn't felt so ill all of the sudden.

"Love?" Nathaniel asked unnecessarily. "Aye, it did."

"Love does that," Jamie said philosophically. "And so you now understand what drove me to my investigations at first." He considered for another long moment, then shook his head. "I began to understand that there were indeed things I had to do in these places and times, that these steppings between centuries weren't merely random or even under my control. But I daresay you've come to understand that as well, haven't you?"

Nathaniel held up his hand in surrender. "I haven't done anything but lend a hand in battle," he said. "I think that could have been done by anyone with a sword."

"I imagine there is more to it than that, but perhaps we'll discover the truth of it as time goes on." He frowned thoughtfully, then looked at Nathaniel. "Can you let her go?"

Nathaniel looked at him in surprise. "What do you mean?"

"Can you let Emma go," Jamie repeated slowly. "Could you travel back in time to repeat the first encounter you had with her, then step back instead of stepping forward? Avoid meeting her and allow her to go on past you without seeing you?" He shrugged. "Let her go."

Nathaniel felt as if Jamie had punched him in the gut. "Why would I want to do that?" he rasped.

"Because I fear you'll never escape these endless circles until she stops following you."

"Or going ahead of me."

"Even worse," Jamie agreed. "Until she is no longer part of your life, I daresay nothing will change."

Nathaniel rubbed his hand over his face, finding it almost impossible to even face that thought. "How do you know she isn't just stumbling on the gates all on her own?"

Jamie shot him a look. "Because she's using those gates to aid you, isn't she? Poor gel, I believe she fancies you, though I haven't a clue why. I don't think you're all that much to look at."

"I could be your brother's twin."

"As I said."

Nathaniel attempted a smile, but failed. "It could have been worse. I could have been *your* twin."

"You could only hope to resemble my extremely handsome self," Jamie said with a snort, "but since that's far beyond your abilities, my lad, be content with your lack."

Nathaniel sighed and imagined he should be. He considered, then looked at his host. "Have you ever gone back where you shouldn't have? Or back to the same time period to change something you did before?"

Jamie looked green, if such a thing were possible. "Aye."

Nathaniel waited, but apparently details were not going to be offered freely. "Perhaps I shouldn't ask."

"I wouldn't answer," Jamie said. "At least not willingly. Besides, I'm not certain those tales would serve you in your present business." He leaned back in his chair. "I think you, my lad, have been given the very great gift of going back and redoing the same experience over and over again until you get it right."

"Do you think so?"

"I'm trying to look on the positive side of things," Jamie said dryly. "In truth, I haven't a clue what time is doing with you. That is my best guess."

"But what could it possibly matter?" Nathaniel asked. "My going back to the same time, I mean. Worse still, why is Emma caught up in all this?"

"Perhaps she was never meant to go," Jamie offered.

"Or perhaps she was, because she sees things I'm missing—"

He stopped speaking. He thought that was better than gasping as if someone had just shoved a sword into his gut.

She had seen Gerald in New York and recognized him from the past. That was something Nathaniel imagined he never would have managed on his own. It wasn't something he wanted to think on, but if his cousin were truly loitering in the past, how had he figured out how to get there?

Nathaniel realized with a horrifying moment of clarity that he hadn't been nearly as careful with his popping through time gates as he should have been. Heaven only knew what Gerald had seen that he shouldn't have.

"Does Emma remember all the times she's gone back?"

Nathaniel dragged himself away from those unsettling thoughts. "Aye."

"Can you wrench the gates to your own purposes? Change your destination or arrival time?"

Nathaniel looked at him in surprise. "It never occurred to me that I might, so I haven't tried. What damage would I cause?"

Jamie chewed on his words for so long, Nathaniel began to worry that he'd forgotten what he wanted to say. When he finally spoke, Nathaniel wished he hadn't.

"I can't say for certain," Jamie said slowly, "and I haven't had your experience of having my destination out of my control. But given what you've told me and seeing how your lady has been dragged into something that quite possibly might prove fatal for her, my advice is that you try to go back before she first sees you and close the gate."

Nathaniel blinked. "What do you mean?"

"Close the gate," Jamie repeated. "Decide when and where it is that she first sees you, then close that gate before she does. Then you should, as I said before, let her go."

Nathaniel knew his mouth had fallen open, but he couldn't do anything to remedy that.

"And how the hell would I do that?" Nathaniel said, doing his damndest not to curse the man sitting across from him. "If I wanted to, mind you, which I don't."

"I can't tell you how," Jamie said seriously, "just that I think you need to. Name the alternative, Nathaniel. She chooses to go back endlessly—presumably in an effort to somehow save your sorry arse—you go back endlessly to rescue her, you're endlessly living these half lives in two places."

"Which I've been doing—"

"Alone," Jamie interrupted pointedly. "You've been doing it alone. Now you're drawing a woman into the circle with you."

"I didn't—"

"Not intentionally," Jamie said stubbornly, "but she is there because of you. You are the only one who can stop this cycle."

Nathaniel wished he could do something else besides grit his teeth.

"Do you love her?"

Nathaniel decided his response was best made in Gaelic and not very politely.

Jamie only smiled gravely. "When you tell her the same, I would phrase it differently."

"And how would I tell her that?" Nathaniel asked grimly. "When my whole purpose, if I take your advice, is to avoid meeting her?"

"I'm talking in circles," Jamie said wearily. "All I can say is that I think you need to allow her to live her life free of yours. The alternative is an endless loop you cannot control."

Nathaniel set his glass aside and rubbed his hands over his face, not because he was sleepy but because he needed to buy himself time. Jamie had a point, damn him. He either had to save Emma or he had to save himself—

Unless he could do both.

He breathed carefully, unwilling to disturb the thought that suddenly occurred to him lest it rush away from him and he lose it. What if he could solve time's mystery and keep Emma safe in the future?

If he could do that, then he could solve it all.

He nodded, then looked at Jamie. "I'll see to it."

Jamie studied him for a moment or two in silence, then rose. He nodded toward the door. "Let us retreat downstairs. It's best your lady have no idea what we've discussed. For her own sake."

Nathaniel couldn't have agreed more with that. He left Jamie's study with him and walked back downstairs. He studiously ignored how odd it was to be walking through a medieval keep in the current day with a man who had ruled over that keep hundreds of years earlier. He wished he had time to press James MacLeod for more answers to things that puzzled him, but perhaps that would have been only a distraction. He already knew what he needed to do.

He would go back and he would solve things himself.

He had no other choice.

Chapter 27

Emma stood with Nathaniel while they took their leave of James MacLeod and tried not to think about the fact that she'd just spent an evening in the castle of a medieval laird.

Or, perhaps more to the point, crammed behind a sofa in a medieval laird's private study.

Getting herself downstairs after Nathaniel and Jamie had decamped had been something of a trick, but she wasn't beyond thinking on her feet. She'd waited until she'd heard male voices fade, then quickly slipped out into the hallway and made it sound as if she'd just hurried out from the laird's room of swords. It was simply amazing, she had told them breathlessly, how quickly time had passed while she'd been lingering over that incredible collection of historic weapons.

If Jamie had reached out and casually plucked a dust bunny from off her shoulder, she'd pretended not to notice.

Never admit anything had been Bertie's favorite axiom, and she clung to it with both hands. She had been cheerfully polite, thanked Jamie profusely for his hospitality, and waved as she and Nathaniel had left the hall and walked to her car.

She didn't comment when Nathaniel put his sword in the car, wedging it between their seats. If he took her hand and put it on his leg as they were driving so he could cover it with his own except when he was shifting gears, she didn't argue with it. When he came inside her house and built up her fire, she only thanked him. But when he headed toward her door, she stopped him.

He wasn't going to get away that easily.

"It's early," she said before he reached for the doorknob. "Interested in some of our usual fare of crap telly?"

He stopped with his back half to her and his head bowed. He sighed, then turned and pulled her into his arms. He held her in silence until she half wondered if he ever intended to let her go. Perhaps he would simply stand there forever, unmoving and unspeaking.

"You could stay," she whispered.

He cursed. She thought that she might want to make a list of those Gaelic curses at some point, though she had to admit she was starting to recognize a few things she'd heard before. She held on to him tightly.

"How do you say *I love you* in Gaelic?"

"*Tha gaol*— Wait, why?"

"No reason."

He sighed deeply. "*Tha gaol agam ort.* And it sounds nothing like 'tis spelled."

"How did you learn all this?"

"My mother, for the most part. The rest? On the job, darling. On the job."

She pulled back. "Stay. At least for a while."

He sighed, released her, and took her face in his hands. He shook his head, then kissed her.

"Telly," he said, "then I'm locking you in your house." He looked at her seriously. "Don't go anywhere without me, Emma."

She nodded, though she had absolutely no intention of paying any attention to that.

She'd obviously heard what he and Jamie had discussed and she had the feeling he'd come to a serious decision in James MacLeod's hall. Given what she knew of Nathaniel MacLeod, she had no doubt what that decision was. If he followed through, he would never encounter her across time's boundary, then he would likely simply keep out of her sights until she unthinkingly left Benmore behind to pursue her original reason for coming to Scotland.

To turn dreams into reality.

She didn't want to think about the cosmic ramifications of that.

She considered several ways to get around Nathaniel's likely plan. She could write herself a note to remind herself that she was terribly in love with the man holding her in his arms, or send herself something to an email account she could bury under other accounts, or, as a last resort, she could text Bertie a secret code that would lead her down a trail to a certain recluse in the Benmore forest.

She put her jammies on because she thought it might throw him off guard to see some MacLeod plaid on display, then sat down on the couch with him and the cups of tea he'd made. She put her head on his shoulder, her arm around his waist, and closed her eyes.

She hadn't wanted to agree with Jamie that Nathaniel should try to fix things by making sure she never met him, though she had to admit that it was the most straightforward and sensible solution of all those available. It was hard, unyielding chivalry.

Very medieval chivalry.

She struggled to keep her eyes open, but Nathaniel wasn't wearing his boots, and a quick look proved that his eyes were closed. She snuggled closer to him, feeling warm and safe with not a set of medieval numbers in sight.

She drifted off and couldn't bring herself to fight it.

She woke to darkness and panicked until she realized she was lying on her couch covered in a blanket, not sprawled in the MacLeod dungeon covered in goo. She sat up, her head spinning, and it occurred to her that maybe that tea hadn't been just tea.

She considered, then dragged her hand through her hair. She could credit Nathaniel MacLeod with quite a few things, but knocking her out was not one of them. She had been exhausted, and she suspected he'd felt the same way. What he was probably doing was snoozing peacefully in his bed.

She pushed herself to her feet and walked unsteadily over to the window to pull the curtain back. Damn it, it had to be at least nine. She checked her phone and realized it was almost ten.

She walked over to open her front door. Well, her car was still there, which she supposed boded well. It definitely wasn't too early to head to Nathaniel's and make sure he hadn't done anything she wasn't going to like.

She threw on clothes, made sure her stove wasn't going to burn the place down, then grabbed her gear and left her house.

She drove to Nathaniel's house, pulled to a stop behind his Range Rover, then got out. She paused as she shut the door to her car. She was hardly a professional at sensing changes in anything, but she couldn't deny that she felt something . . . off.

She wondered if she were being watched or, worse still, if something had happened to Nathaniel thanks to someone else's nefarious intentions. His cousin Gerald came immediately to mind, which left her running up to his porch to bang on his front door.

There was no answer.

She forced herself to breathe normally and not jump to conclusions. He could have been in the shower, or deeply asleep, or off on a walk. Then again, if any of those had been the case, she probably wouldn't have turned his doorknob and found it unlocked.

She pushed the door open carefully, then reached inside and flipped down the light. Light switches going the wrong way, cars driving on the wrong side of the road, innocent people walking through the forest and finding themselves in a different century—she was starting to wonder if she would ever get used to how things were done in Scotland. The first two were rather charming.

The last one, not so much.

She eased inside Nathaniel's house carefully, because she never walked into a place without knowing exactly what lay in store for her. She had a look around, very carefully, then realized that what she'd suspected was definitely the truth. Nathaniel wasn't there.

She would have bet good money on where he'd gone.

She walked into his kitchen and saw something on the table. She picked it up, then swore.

There was a man who loved a woman he couldn't have
and he did what he had to do . . .
Tha gaol agam ort

Damn him to hell, he was right. Gaelic didn't look on paper at all like what it sounded. For all she knew, he'd just told her to get lost.

She went back through his house and looked for medieval gear. There was nothing hiding in his closet, which only stacked the odds against his having dashed up the coast for a bit of hiking. She cursed him as she locked up his house and got back in her car.

It didn't take her long to consider then discard half a dozen possibilities for what to do next. She could go after him, true, but she had no idea where to look for him or if she would even be in the right time. What if he had gone back a week in time, or two weeks, or however long it had been since she'd been in Scotland, and he had landed in one place while she might land in another and they would never cross paths and she would die in the MacLeod dungeon—

She forced herself to take deep, even breaths and let that thought continue on its way. It didn't do her any good to allow herself to entertain anything but success.

She considered different alternatives. She could just run into the forest and take her chances, of course, but that was something else to discard immediately. Just running without a plan would very likely do nothing but leave her repeating the same loop she'd already experienced a handful of times.

She considered going back inside Nathaniel's house to hack into his computer, but given how unwilling he was to even talk about his journeys back in time, she imagined he wasn't about to keep notes on his computer. His phone was a possibility, but she set that aside as something to perhaps be contemplated later. She would probably have to rifle through his entire house to find it.

Her only other option was to go to James MacLeod's house and beat some details out of him. She had the feeling that if anyone would know what had happened to Nathaniel MacLeod, it would be that fourteenth-century laird up the way.

She put her car in gear, backed out, then headed down to the village. She supposed she should have eaten something, but she was too wound up to consider breakfast. James MacLeod might have been a medieval laird, but she was the protégé of an MI6 expat. She thought she might be able to do a few things he might not expect.

There was a black Range Rover sitting in front of his castle when she got there, along with a red Porsche. The Range Rover was Patrick's, but she had no idea who owned that other thing. Perhaps it was a meeting of medieval guys who routinely gave out bad advice to men who weren't from their time period and should have been taking care of business in the present day.

She got out of her car, ran up the steps, and banged on the front door. It was answered fairly quickly, all things considered, and a man stood there who she didn't know. He looked quite a bit like Jamie, though, so she supposed he was a relative. Ian MacLeod, perhaps.

"I need to see Jamie."

The man lifted an eyebrow. "And who are you, lass?"

"I know who she is," Jamie said, coming to stand next to the man. "Mistress Emma, this is my cousin, Ian. Ian, Mistress Emma is here, I suspect, to kill me."

Emma glared at him. She hoped that might earn her a few points as well as give her courage, because that man there was intimidating as hell. She looked at Ian MacLeod and nodded shortly.

"I am," she said crisply. "You'd best move."

Ian looked at her thoughtfully. "Bare hands or steel?"

"Bare hands," she said without hesitation.

"Pat," he called over his shoulder. "Have a live one for you here."

She threw herself at Jamie. She supposed, in hindsight, that it hadn't been very well thought-out, but she was furious and he was definitely deserving of her ire. The thing was, she'd forgotten that he was a medieval sort of guy with a powerful instinct for self-preservation. She stopped her hands just short of his neck because she would have run into a pair of daggers.

Well, she wouldn't have really, because she would have landed face-first on his floor and missed that steel entirely, as he had stepped back before she could get to him and Ian MacLeod had caught her as she fell. Ian set her very carefully back on her feet, then very deliberately took his hands off her and stepped back a pace. She looked at Jamie, then at Ian, then she did the most sensible thing she'd done all morning.

She pulled herself up by her bootstraps and got hold of herself.

"Well," Ian said, sounding nonplussed. "I thought a batch of tears was coming our way."

"By the saints, move," Patrick MacLeod said, shoving his cousin aside. "Emma is not a weeper." He looked at his brother. "Put up your steel, you fool."

Jamie looked rather horrified. "I have never in my life drawn a blade against a woman."

"I'm terrifying," Emma croaked.

Patrick smiled. "That you are, lass."

Jamie tossed his knives to Ian, then held out his hand to her. "I don't apologize often—"

"Ever," Patrick said dryly.

Jamie glared at his brother, then took her hand. "You startled me."

"I'm angry," she said. She shook his hand because she was certainly happy to move right past their recent encounter, then she wrapped her arms around herself not because she needed the comfort, but because she was freezing. "I know what you told him. I didn't mean to eavesdrop, but I got caught behind your sofa when you two were talking."

"I know."

She wasn't at all surprised. "And yet you said nothing."

"Why?" Jamie asked with a shrug. "I knew you knew I knew—" He paused, frowned, then shrugged again. "I thought it best we keep it between ourselves lest we influence Nathaniel unduly. There are things going on in that forest that I've never seen before and I offered the best advice I could."

"I didn't like your advice."

Ian let out a low whistle and leaned his shoulder against Patrick. "Well, she *is* something, isn't she?"

She didn't feel like something; she felt cold and tired and not at all happy with the turn of events.

"I imagine you didn't, lass," Jamie said. "Why don't you take your ire out on my brother here, or my cousin. I'd like to see what you can do."

She blinked. "Why?"

He blew out his breath. "How are you going to go get that poor fool if you can't protect yourself?"

She didn't weep, but she began to have some trouble breathing. And when three medieval guys gathered around her and tried to offer her suggestions on how to regain her breath, she knew they were doing their best in spite of the way they were suffocating her. She didn't have the heart to tell James MacLeod that patting her on the back with his hands the size of dinner plates wasn't helping at all.

Again, medieval chivalry was rather tough stuff.

"Food first," Jamie announced, "then you'll work with Patty this morning whilst Ian and I decide on a plan. What can you do?"

"Besides kill men with my bare hands?" she asked, dragging her sleeve—the sleeve of the coat Nathaniel MacLeod had given her—across her eyes. "Pick locks, hot-wire cars, and curse in six languages."

"That won't help you against steel, lass," Jamie said with a faint smile, "but we'll solve that in time. Can you spin? Cook? Tend sheep?"

"I draw and I can drive fast cars." She paused. "I spent a summer working with a blacksmith at a medieval faire."

Jamie lifted an eyebrow. "In a true forge?"

"Yes."

He looked at Patrick. "Feed her, train her, then let's send her off after him. I don't like the feeling of the world this morning."

"That's because you made your own breakfast," Ian said with a snort. "How you manage to toddle from one end of the day to the other without aid, I just don't know. *I'll* go cook you something, Mistress Emma."

Emma thought that might be best. She walked with Ian away from the door.

"Now, tell me a little about your friend," he continued. "I understand he's filthy rich and looks a bit like a Sasquatch. Or Nessie. Never can keep it straight."

"He looks like me," Patrick said, falling in on her other side, "which makes him very braw indeed."

"The saints preserve the unfortunate lad if that's what he faces in the mirror every morning," Ian said. "What's your pleasure, Emma? Do you mind if we call you Emma?"

She shook her head. "I'm fine and I'm not really hungry—"

"You will be once Pat has finished with you," Ian said cheerfully, "and you'll want to ask me all kinds of things about the Fergusson dungeon—"

"Shut up, Ian," Patrick said.

But it was too late.

She came to an ungainly halt and looked at them both, each one in turn. "What?"

Patrick rolled his eyes. "Ian, is it possible for you to ever think before you open your mouth?"

Ian sighed deeply. "Apparently not." He looked at Emma. "He's in the Fergussons' dungeon."

"How can you possibly know that?" she asked in astonishment.

Ian shifted. "I had a feeling."

Patrick sighed gustily. "You can blame that on *your* cooking, not Jamie having called us to come over for a parley."

"About Nathaniel?" Emma managed.

Patrick nodded. "I rang Stephen de Piaget this morning and asked him to find out if Nat's dagger was still in Edinburgh. He made a call, then rang me back to tell me aye." He looked at her seriously. "If Nat wasn't currently loitering in that dungeon, his dagger wouldn't have been found there hundreds of years later by my loose-tongued cousin standing to your left and given by me to that collector of ancient weapons you met recently in the old city."

"That's all you have to go on?" she asked. Her mouth was suddenly so dry, she could hardly get words out.

"It's enough," Patrick said quietly.

She stopped still and looked at him. "Is he dead?"

Patrick lifted his eyebrows briefly. "Hard to say. Any opinions, Ian?"

"Don't remind me of that dungeon," Ian said, "lest I say things no one will want to hear." He patted her on the shoulder. "He's canny, that lad of yours, or so I hear. Pat didn't slice him to ribbons and Jamie left him still breathing. That bodes well. I'll make some hearty porritch and we'll decide on our options."

She watched him go, then looked at Patrick. She glanced behind her to find Jamie standing by his fire with his back to them.

"Is he worried?" she asked.

"Shaking off the terror of a woman almost strangling him, rather," Patrick said with a smile. "Actually, I imagine he's thinking. 'Tis a very great effort for him, so we'd best leave him to it."

She swallowed, hard. "Will Nathaniel die?"

"Can you pick a medieval lock?"

"That, I don't know."

"We'd best find out then, hadn't we?" He paused, then looked at her seriously. "Could you kill a man if it meant Nathaniel's life in trade?"

She shivered. "I don't know that, either."

"We'll start there." He paused. "I don't know what you'll need to go through to get to him, but if you can free him, he can do what needs to be done. He's more dangerous than he looks in those pricey suits he wears. But you'll have to work fast. You've been in our dungeon here and know what it does to you."

"Is that Fergusson dungeon worse?"

"Much."

She followed him into Jamie's very modern kitchen, which should have seemed incongruous. Somehow, given everything she'd seen over the past few days, it wasn't nearly as weird as it should have been.

She ate, because she had to. She gave Patrick an unflinching list of her less savory skills, because he needed to know where her weaknesses were so he could remedy them. She apologized to Jamie and had a most abject and lairdly apology in return and a cementing of eternal friendship on her way out the door to see what Patrick could make of her before they burned through all their daylight.

She didn't like to think about the fact that Nathaniel probably couldn't even see any daylight.

She supposed she would eventually figure out exactly where he'd gone and just what he thought was going to do once he got there.

Change history? Let her walk past him?

She could hardly bear the thought, so she put that thought behind her and went to work.

Chapter 28

There were certain events in a man's life that caused him serious reflection. Birth. Death. Threats from enemy clansmen.

Rats nesting in his hair.

Nathaniel considered his situation and wondered just how in the hell he'd managed to get himself where he was at present.

He hadn't meant to find himself in the Fergussons' dungeon. He supposed, looking back on it now, that he was damned fortunate he was alive to enjoy his luxurious accommodations. If that was an improvement over taking a chance with death whilst roaming free through rugged forests and beautiful meadows, he wasn't sure how.

The truth was, given where he was, he just wasn't sure how long his life would be. The decaying corpse sitting against the wall across from him might have had an opinion if he'd had the ability to spew out any details.

Nathaniel leaned his head back against the wall, reminded himself that he'd been in his current locale for only a handful of days, then decided to distract himself by bringing to mind how he'd come to be where he was. With any luck, examining those details might lead him to a solution he might not see otherwise.

He had, however many days ago it had been, refused to wait for time to call him and instead had forced the time gate to do his bidding. Jamie had advised him that such a thing was possible, if not perhaps a less-than-desirable thing to succeed at. Nathaniel had felt he hadn't had a choice, so when the gate had opened, he'd plunged ahead, knowing that he had to do what was necessary regardless of his personal feelings on the matter.

Leaving Emma sleeping on her couch had been the single hardest thing he'd ever had to do.

He turned away from that thought and concentrated on retracing his steps. He had been accustomed to walking into battle; he hadn't been accustomed to interrupting the laird of the clan Fergusson stirring himself to do a little scouting to see if his men were reporting things accurately.

He'd been welcomed with open arms by a handful of men he had definitely been less than pleasant to in the past, then escorted with all due haste and diligence to their keep. He'd seen that keep before, of course, in both the past and the future, and he could say without hesitation that the place was disgusting no matter in which century it found itself.

He would admit, grudgingly, that whilst the Fergussons never had much imagination on the battlefield, they made up for it in their dungeon. His dagger had been taken from him, of course, but now it sat five paces away, jammed artistically into the floor. Too far for him to reach but just far enough away to give him a clear view of it.

No wonder Patrick MacLeod was going to find it hundreds of years in the future.

Nathaniel didn't want to entertain the thought that perhaps Patrick might be digging up his bones as well in that same distant future.

He considered the condition of his potential final resting place and decided he just didn't care for it. A pity he hadn't wound up in the MacLeod dungeon. It was definitely a step up, as far as dungeons went, and he would certainly know. He'd spent a day or two in that place whilst Malcolm decided if it was possible to have sired such a handsome bastard as he himself was. Blessing his own mother for having instilled a love of Gaelic in him from birth, he had spent that time fine-tuning his accent and trying to accept where he'd found himself.

He had also, at the time, been congratulating himself on having listened fairly well to those rumors that went round down the pub about those MacLeod men up the way.

Time travel. What bollocks.

Of course, it had been a bit dodgy here and there and he'd lied his bloody arse off at the time to convince his new MacLeod friends that he was neither a demon nor a witch of any stripe, but a man did what he had to do to survive.

He wasn't sure any of that was going to serve him at present.

It didn't seem exactly fair, he mused, that he should have been attempting to come to an understanding with Father Time about a certain dark-haired Yank only to have his good intentions land him in a pit. He supposed it could have been worse. He could have been a Fergusson clansman and doomed to live out his days with the lot upstairs.

He continued to hold out hope that he might manage to get himself free. He had done his best to continue to exercise his muscles as much as his shackles would allow. He'd eaten what he'd been given, though he'd considered the very real possibility of plague infesting those meals. There hadn't been anything to do about that, because he hadn't had a plague vaccine, and it was a bit difficult to get to the local surgery for the same at the moment.

He should have taken Emma and fled to Paris.

He shifted against the wall and contemplated his life, mostly because he had nothing else to do. He tried to count the days he'd been sitting where he was and decided that perhaps he had misjudged them. It must have been at least a week. During that time, he had learned the voices of the guards upstairs, timed the changes of those guards, and learned more than he cared to about the plans the Fergussons had for the MacLeods to the south of their keep.

That last bit was nothing he wasn't familiar with, though, and he'd heard nothing new, so he'd basically dismissed it. Then again, they never came up with anything new. He was just surprised by how many lads they always seemed to have ready to sacrifice for whatever madness they contemplated. He wondered if they ever tired of it.

He thought he just might be tiring of it, which was reason enough to put a stop to the whole madness of his visits to the past.

He supposed if he'd had any sense before, he would have taken a few days and grilled Jamie about his experiences with popping into different centuries. The man certainly had more than his share of experience with the same. He'd been planning on it, actually, in the back of his mind as they'd been sitting in Jamie's study, talking about things that shouldn't have existed outside the realm of nightmare. Then Emma had asked him to stay and he'd spent the rest of the evening trying to keep his hands off her, because he knew he would have to let her go.

Of all the things he'd experienced since his time-traveling madness had begun, short of losing his parents, the thought of losing her had been the worst.

And so he'd made a decision. He had planned to simply wrench time to his own purposes. Jamie had obviously been back and forth to various centuries more than once and apparently each time managed to keep what he wanted.

Why not him?

Well, apparently because he was a stupid arse, but perhaps that could be debated later, after someone dug up his bones several centuries in the future and did a little DNA testing to make sure it was him.

He would have dragged his hands through his hair, but his hands were shackled to the wall and he couldn't bring them to his hair. Hence the new home for his rodentish friends.

The problem, he decided in a leisurely fashion, given that all he had to hand was a leisurely amount of time in which to decide such things, was that he wanted it all. Especially if *all* included himself, Emma Baxter, and his Lamborghini, all in the same century.

That wasn't too much to ask, was it?

He hadn't thought so, which had left him deciding at the last minute that he would march off not to his front door but to Emma's gate into the past, present himself at its gaping maw, and demand that it take him where he wanted to go. And where he wanted to go was not to the point in time where he'd first seen Emma so he could do the sensible thing and avoid her.

That, he supposed, had been the problem. He hadn't wanted to go to the spot where he'd first seen Emma, he'd simply wanted to go back and somehow break the loop time seemed to be putting him through. He hadn't even been all that clear about exactly what that place looked like or when it found itself, which had resulted in his current locale.

That had obviously been badly done.

And now he was definitely in a place where he was going to be of no use to anyone. Not himself, not Emma. His grandfather would have him declared dead and confiscate all his assets. The thought of that crotchety old bastard driving either of his cars was almost more than he could think about without gritting his teeth.

He listened to the hall begin to settle down for the night, but that somehow wasn't as comforting as it should have been, because he heard booted feet coming his way. The grate was pulled back and two men jumped down into the hole with him. The torchlight almost blinded him, truth be told. When he could open his eyes again and squint at the two men facing him, he could hardly mask his surprise.

Well, at least his surprise over the identity of one of his visitors. The man on his left was Simon Fergusson, currently the laird of the clan Fergusson, a man as ruthless as he was unpleasantly determined. And the man on Simon's left?

Gerald MacLeod.

His cousin.

He supposed he could have outed his cousin right then, but he supposed that such a declaration would only result in unpleasant things for himself. Either Gerald would deny it and tell Simon to put the prisoner to death before his madness infected the entire keep, or Simon would turn on Gerald and slay him, then decide that Nathaniel should be slain as well before *his* madness infected the entire keep.

Either way, he would be facing death.

He listened to Simon and Gerald discuss things as if they were standing in a pleasant garden, not a sewer. Gerald's accent wasn't terribly good, but his Gaelic was adequate and he freely admitted that he was a MacLeod turncoat. Nathaniel could see why that would send shivers of delight down Simon's spine.

"Then we don't really need *him*, do we?" Simon was saying.

"Don't slay him yet," Gerald said, with surprising deference. "I'll wring things out of him first. Family things."

Simon frowned, then shrugged. "As you will. If you can bear being down here for as long as that takes."

"I live to aid you, my laird."

Nathaniel had to admit that if there was anything in this world or the next that Gerald MacLeod excelled at, it was sucking up. Nathaniel thought that deference bordered on sycophancy, but what did he know? He was the one, after all, sitting in the muck in chains while Gerald was free and now holding on to *his* dagger. Perhaps he should have taken a few cues from his cousin.

A ladder was provided, Simon clambered up it, then Gerald put his hand on the wood to steady himself. Actually, Nathaniel supposed Gerald didn't fancy finding himself locked below and that was simply a bit of security against the same, but in that he couldn't blame his cousin. He would have done the same thing in his place.

"Interesting place you have here," Gerald drawled.

Nathaniel yawned, though that cost him quite a bit. "Thought I would spend a week or so slumming. Local flavor and all that."

"Oh, I think you'll be here longer than that."

Nathaniel looked at him evenly. "What do you want, Ger?"

"That should be obvious, even for an idiot like you. I want everything you have."

"Don't you have enough of your own?" Nathaniel asked wearily.

"I want yours."

"Your father has been dead for years," Nathaniel said, supposing he would be doing his uncle John a favor by keeping a few details about the man's whereabouts to himself. "You have all his—"

"Grandfather has all his money," Gerald spat. "He made my sister trustee."

"Then you'll have all Grandfather's—"

"He made *you* his heir, you stupid bastard!"

Nathaniel shifted to settle the rat atop his head more carefully, then paused to wonder if his buddy might be willing to venture south and clean out his ear for him because he was just certain he'd heard that incorrectly. "He what?"

"He changed his will! Two bloody years ago. Weren't you paying attention?"

"Nay, not really—"

Incoherent spewing of curses and slanders and other inarticulate sounds ensued. Nathaniel would have enjoyed the sight of his cousin coming completely undone—Gerald was a first-class prat, to be sure—but things were what they were at the moment. When one found oneself chained to a wall, helpless, whilst facing a madman not likewise fettered, one tended to want to keep one's damned mouth shut. He supposed telling his cousin that he tried never to open any letters from his attorneys might be a less-than-wise thing to say at the moment.

It made him wonder just why his grandfather continued to try to sue him over his own trust, but he suspected that was less Dexter's doing and more Gerald's.

"I don't want his money," Nathaniel managed when Gerald paused for breath.

"He won't care!" Gerald wailed.

Nathaniel had to admit his cousin had a point there. Poindexter MacLeod was a man firmly committed to his own vision. Nathaniel wasn't sure he had ever known his grandfather to take anyone's advice but his own, to the endless frustration of his accountants, bankers, and attorneys.

He had to admit, rather grudgingly, that he liked that about the feisty old fellow.

Dexter was also, Nathaniel had to admit as well, a very shrewd judge of character. Gerald was not only a prat; he was an idiot with absolutely no imagination. If he'd been in charge of MacLeod Surety's billions, he would have made a small fortune out of a very large fortune in no time.

"How did you get here?" Nathaniel asked.

Gerald looked as if he'd been slapped. "I followed you, of course. How stupid do you think I am?"

"How long ago?" Nathaniel asked.

"A couple of years ago," Gerald said, drawing himself up and puffing out his chest. "It wasn't hard. Neither was learning the language, but I went to Yale, not Columbia."

"So you did," Nathaniel agreed. "Well done, you."

Gerald wasn't finished, apparently. "I befriended the laird, promised him details, got him details, and waited for when I could put you where you are now."

"Where you'll let me rot."

"That's the plan." He smirked, then dropped Nathaniel's dagger again into the muck. "Grandfather will have no choice but to make me his heir once he resigns himself to your being dead. Let that thought keep you warm on your way to hell."

Nathaniel would have shrugged negligently, but he was too tired to. He watched his cousin crawl up the ladder, watched the ladder be pulled out of the pit, then didn't bother to watch the grate be put back in place.

He hadn't thought his life would end with such little fanfare, but perhaps it was what he deserved. Recluse in life, anonymous in death.

He stared at his dagger glinting faintly across the dungeon from him, then closed his eyes. He would die surrounded not by those he loved but by cold, damp, and vermin.

The only thing he could hope for was that Gerald would be satisfied with all that money and forget about other things. He couldn't bear to think about what the man might do if he found Emma in a darkened alley—

Nay, that wouldn't happen. She would be safe. The MacLeod men would understand what had happened to him, someone would nose out Gerald as having been responsible, and they would take care of her.

He wasn't sure he could contemplate anything else.

Chapter 29

Emma stood in front of the wall in her cottage, almost blind with weariness, and tried to make sense of what she was seeing. She'd been looking at the same thing off and on for almost a week with no appreciable change in her thinking. She rubbed her eyes, then looked again, because she had to find something that made sense while she still could.

Nathaniel had been gone a week.

A week in a dungeon, if that's where he was, was too long.

She rubbed her eyes and looked again at what was in front of her. She'd been doing the same thing whenever she'd had a chance, mostly after an interminable day spent with Patrick MacLeod, learning how to be a medieval ghost.

That's what they'd eventually taken to calling what she was going to have to be, because no other persona had a hope of getting her in and out of 1387 with herself and Nathaniel both alive and moving. Her plan was to sneak in, find him, and get them out with as little damage as possible. If she got into trouble, she was going to pose as a journeyman blacksmith and try to buy herself time that way.

It was too bad Patrick MacLeod wasn't in a position to go back and take care of things for her. He and Nathaniel looked so much alike, that fact alone probably would have scared Simon Fergusson into coughing up the guy in his dungeon.

She knew exactly how Patrick MacLeod looked, because she'd spent a week working with him on those medieval ghost skills that Bertie Wordsworth would have salivated to call his own. It had come to the point where she'd asked him to stop being so careful. Jamie and Ian had turned their backs and put their fingers in their ears. She'd earned a bruise or two, but unfortunately that medieval chivalry had been too much for Patrick to get past. She had the feeling he definitely wasn't so gentle with the men he trained.

She envied their wives, she had to admit, if those were the sort of men they had guarding their doors and their children, not to mention their own selves.

She had the feeling her life might look a bit like that, if she could get Nathaniel out of the dungeon and leave him free to possibly ask her for some sort of permanent arrangement.

It wasn't that she hadn't tried to get back to 1387. She had, every day. She was almost tired of basing her dinner takeout orders down at the pub on whatever would add up to that amount so she would get either a bill for it or change back from it. That Keith MacLeod had just looked at her blandly when she'd been standing at his bar every night, calculating furiously, was a mixed blessing. He was helpful, but she suspected he thought she was crazy. She couldn't blame him.

She was beginning to wonder about that herself.

Or she would have, if she hadn't had the wall in front of her to keep her company every night after she'd failed to get back to where she needed to go.

But today was going to be different. She'd begun early that morning simply because she hadn't slept well the night before. Dreams of haggis and change and a nagging feeling that she was missing something had woken her at dawn and left her pacing, unable to find any relief. She was scheduled to go foraging with Patrick at noon, so she'd taken the opportunity to spend some time with her board. She had added several pages to what was there, but all she could see was how much Nathaniel looked like Patrick.

It occurred to her with a startling flash of something that felt like Fate clunking her over the head . . . What if Nathaniel was actually related to Patrick, and not with eight hundred years separating them?

Was it possible Nathaniel was one of Malcolm's bastard sons in truth?

She leaned over her coffee table and sorted through papers

there until she found the things Alex Smith had sent Nathaniel. She wasn't so much concerned with Malcolm's genealogy as she was—

She realized there was something written on the back of the copy of the parish registry. She felt her way down onto the table and looked at the rather lengthy list there.

Malcolm's bastards, apparently.

She read each name, noting the birth dates next to them, then felt time slow to a crawl.

Ceana, b. 1372.

She felt the world shudder. If she hadn't been sitting down, she would have fallen down. It wasn't so much the name as it was the date . . .

Or maybe it was the name.

She dug under papers until she came up with Nathaniel's cell phone. She'd charged it, which she supposed might have been the smartest thing she'd done all week. She unlocked it, then scrolled through his contacts. She didn't hesitate before she made good use of that little telephone icon next to Gavin MacLeod's name.

The phone rang several times before it was answered.

"If this is my ugly brother," a voice said sleepily, "instead of a gorgeous woman wanting me only for my body, I'm hanging up right now."

"Gavin, this is Emma."

There was the sound of a phone taking a tumble past a nightstand onto a hardwood floor, then some fumbling, then a less sleepy voice on the other end.

"Is he hurt?"

She would have smiled, but she couldn't. "He's fine," she lied, "just a little out of touch. It's a long story."

"I'll be on a plane this morning."

"That'd be great," she said, wondering if that would be a good thing or she was bringing someone into the mix who should really stay home, "but that's not why I called. This is going to sound like a crazy question, but what was your mother's name?"

"Ceana," Gavin said without hesitation. "Why?"

Emma picked her phone—well, Nathaniel's phone, actually—up off the floor. "No reason," she said breathlessly.

"But while I have you on the phone, I have another question. How old was she when she married your father?"

"Eighteen, I think."

Emma frowned. "That's interesting." Interesting, but not very useful. If she wanted to fit Ceana into her storyboard—

"But my dad met her when she was fifteen," Gavin added, "if that makes any difference to you."

"Oh," Emma said, feeling her breath be stolen by some unseen force. Curiosity, no doubt. "Do you know where they met?"

"In Scotland," he said. "Actually, in Benmore." He paused. "That's a little ironic, isn't it, that Nat should end up there."

"Oh, yes," she wheezed. "Very ironic. I'd love to hear the rest of the story."

"Well, it's more romance than I'm comfortable with," he said with a bit of a laugh, "but I'll humor you if you like. My father was in Scotland for a gap year of sorts. He had money enough, but he was a bit of a do-gooder, so he liked to look for ways to make a difference."

"Sounds like your brother."

"Nat is my father, only mouthier," Gavin said dryly. "Anyway, apparently my dad was doing some odd jobs in the area, and he happened to meet my mum while she was doing the same. It was a love match from the start, though she was obviously too young for anything serious. My mother was an orphan, so Dad asked one of the local couples to foster her."

"Very chivalrous," Emma murmured. "Do you know who they were?"

"Ryan Fergusson and his wife, Flora. My father paid for all her expenses as well as contributing heavily to village coffers, in spite of the Fergussons' protests. My mum always used to say Ryan and Flora were the only Fergussons she ever liked."

"I think I'd have to agree with her at least in principle."

"I haven't been there enough to know, so I'll take your word for it." He paused. "You know, if he wasn't such a jerk, you would probably get along with our cousin Gerald. He's into genealogy, too."

Emma was starting to think Gerald might be a little too involved in that sort of thing, but she didn't think that was something Nathaniel's brother needed to know.

"The other thing is, my mum always talked about someone named Moraig," Gavin said thoughtfully. "She was a MacLeod woman who lived in a little house near Benmore castle. Everyone always claimed she was a witch."

"I don't believe in witches," Emma said without hesitation.

"Neither do I," Gavin said wryly, "but don't tell my brother the dreamer. I'm sure Moraig was nothing more than a woman who liked to keep all that rubbish about Highland magic being in the forests alive. It's just tourist stuff, don't you think?"

"Why would I think anything else?" Emma asked with a light laugh. "Got to keep them coming somehow, right?"

"Absolutely." He was silent for a moment or two. "Have you talked to Nat lately?"

"He's out of range," Emma said, hoping she wasn't interfering where she shouldn't. "I'm sure he'll get back in touch with you the moment he can. He's talked about you a lot."

"It was good to reconnect," Gavin said. "I don't want to lose that. You only have one set of siblings, I guess."

Fortunately was what almost came out of her mouth, but she stopped the word just in time. Her siblings were who they were and they did what they had to, but that didn't mean she had to like them.

"On second thought, I don't think I'll fly over unless you need me," Gavin said slowly. "Nat won't like to have me nanny him. But you'll let me know, right?"

"I will," she said. "Thank you, Gavin."

"No problem. Keep my brother honest."

She was more concerned about keeping him alive, but she agreed that she would before she hung up and came to terms with the things she'd just learned.

A girl named Ceana was listed as one of Malcolm MacLeod's bastards. She had been born in 1372. Nathaniel's mother was named Ceana and she had apparently been an orphan in the Benmore village at age fifteen.

Coincidence?

There was only one way to find out.

An hour later, she was past frustrated with things she couldn't seem to control.

She looked for the dozenth time at the page from Jamie's book that she'd ripped out. It was full of holes, but that might have been because she'd spent the past hour first looking at it pointedly, then repeating the numbers 1387 out loud until she'd been tempted to shout them, then taking a pen she'd been using to make notes with and stabbing it through those numbers with more enthusiasm than she likely should have used.

A knock sounded on her door, almost sending her pitching forward onto the floor. She set her pen aside very carefully and deliberately, then went to open the door.

Mr. Campbell stood there.

She was so surprised to see him, she hardly knew what to say. "Um, hello" was the best she could manage.

He took off his cap and smiled. "Sorry to startle you, Miss Baxter," he said, with a nod. "I went to see the young Himself and he sent me here. Said you'd be interested in what I have."

"Patrick sent you?" she asked blankly.

He nodded. "Said you'd be interested."

"Given your extensive collection of wonderful things and your knowledge of blacksmithing," she said without hesitation, "I am definitely interested in anything you have." She stepped back. "Please come in."

"Oh, I wouldn't want to intrude," he said. He bent and pulled something out of a leather satchel at his feet. He handed it to her haft first.

It was the dagger from his collection.

Nathaniel's dagger.

"I know you admired this and so did the young Master Nathaniel," Mr. Campbell said with a smile. "I thought perhaps you both would like to tend it for me for a fortnight or so. I'm off to see cousins in Florida, you see, and don't particularly want to leave it in my shop."

Emma took the dagger and felt the world shift. She could almost hear the gate opening. She suppressed the urge to throw her arms around the man standing in front of her.

"I would *love* to," she managed. "I mean, Nathaniel would love to, I'm sure. I'll get it to him right away."

Mr. Campbell beamed at her. He picked up his satchel, then looked at her. "I've been doing some research on blacksmithing."

"Have you?" she asked, wondering if it would be rude to just shove him off her porch.

"Guild secrets and all," he said. "I read the other day that there was a particular guild here in the Highlands, smiths of course, who were mightily fierce at protecting their own."

"Sounds plausible," she said, trying not to hop up and down in her frustration.

"Passwords and all," he continued. "Funny thing, that, isn't it? Today we have them for our mobiles and back then, they had them for their business. *Siubhail* was a word I stumbled upon. Means *traveler*. Interesting that, aye?"

"Very," she said. "And thank you."

"Godspeed, lass," Mr. Campbell said, smiled again, then turned and walked away.

Emma didn't wait for him to even leave the front of her house. She went inside, shut the door, and changed into her preferred outfit for ghosting. She shoved Nathaniel's dagger down the back of her belt, then looked at herself in the bathroom mirror. She took a deep breath, took her hair in her hand, and cut it off up to her chin. If nothing else, she would look like a boy. A bit of dirt smudged on her cheeks and she would be set.

She grabbed her go bag, locked up, and hid her key. She would have run right off her porch, but she found that her way was blocked by one Patrick MacLeod. She pulled the dagger from the back of her belt.

"I have the key," she said succinctly—then it occurred to her what had happened. "You called Mr. Campbell."

"Actually, I didn't," Patrick said slowly. He looked at the dagger in her hand, then met her eyes. "If he came on his own, it begs the question why, doesn't it?"

"I'll let you know when I find out."

He nodded, then tilted his head toward the forest. "I'll walk with you to the trees."

She had to admit she was happy for his company, as strange as that sounded. They didn't speak, but there was nothing left to say. They had talked about all the contingencies they could think of already. She had a backstory ready if she were found by Fergussons and she had a password to give to the MacLeods . . .

She slowed, then stopped. She considered, then looked at Patrick, then thought a bit more.

Funny things, those passwords.

"Emma?"

She shook her head. "I'm fine. Just thinking too much, but I'm done. Can't afford it now."

"Sometimes that is best," Patrick agreed.

She stopped at the gate as confidently as if she could see it, which she wasn't entirely sure she couldn't. She made sure her small bag was strapped securely to her back, looked at Patrick, then attempted a smile.

"See you on the other side."

"Back on this side, preferably," he said dryly, "but aye. Good hunting."

She drew Nathaniel's dagger, took a deep breath, then leaned over and shoved it into the ground.

And the world felt as if it had cracked in two.

She crossed through the gate before she could make a different choice, looked over her shoulder to see Patrick very briefly before both he and Nathaniel's steel disappeared. That was something, she supposed.

She stuck to the trees, keeping to as much shadow as she could manage. By the time she'd hid to avoid what looked like a scouting party going toward the MacLeod keep, checked her mind to make sure she hadn't lost it, and paused to catch her breath and calm her nerves, it was twilight and she was closer to the Fergusson keep than she'd ever wanted to be. She ran bodily into someone before she saw him, which she knew should have alarmed her. She was fully prepared to find it was Gerald MacLeod come to kill her, only to find it was Mr. Campbell.

Only about thirty years younger.

Her Gaelic was awful, she was the first to admit that. She wasn't sure telling him she loved him was going to fly, so she trotted out the second thing that came to mind.

She held out her hand. *"Siubhail,"* she said easily.

He looked as if someone had dropped a boulder on his head, but he took her hand just the same.

"I need work," she said, because Patrick had thought that might serve her well.

Mr. Campbell, or his ancestor who looked just like him, nodded. "Thomas," he managed. "Apprentice blacksmith."

Of course he was. Emma decided abruptly that she didn't need to know more than that. She gave her little speech about being a journeyman blacksmith escaping a terrible master, all the while trusting that what she'd memorized thanks to Ian shouting it at her while Patrick was trying to kill her would do what it was supposed to.

Thomas the blacksmith only nodded, wide-eyed, no doubt having been in those exact straits himself. When he invited her to come with him back to his master's shop—at least that was what she hoped he'd been inviting her to do—she thanked him most kindly and followed him.

It was fully dark before she reached the forge. She was happy to see that the village was mostly asnooze, as it were, and all she had to do was stand behind Thomas and let him negotiate for her. The head blacksmith, a man with absolutely enormous muscles in his arms, looked her over, then nodded shortly to a spot in the corner. She thanked him briskly, then decamped for her spot without further comment. She sat, then looked at the girl who was stirring something in a pot over a small fire.

"Orphan," Thomas said, coming to squat down next to her. He nodded at the dark-haired girl. "She's a bastard, but we don't care. She's a good gel, so don't vex her."

The girl looked up. Emma supposed it was years of pretending to yawn while being absolutely caught off guard that saved her at the moment. That girl looked almost exactly like a photo she'd seen of Nathaniel's sister . . .

"Ceana," Thomas said, "give the lad dinner. He'll begin work in the morning."

Emma ate what she was given and listened to the blacksmith discuss with Thomas and another of his lads the fact that they had a prize in the dungeon that pleased the laird enough to keep him off their backs for a bit.

Or words to that effect.

And all the while, that beautiful, dark-haired teenager watched her carefully, as if she didn't dare hope for anything that might look like a rescue. Emma hadn't anticipated having to help two people, but she didn't think that would matter. There was no way she was going to leave that girl, a girl she would have bet her father's fortune was Nathaniel's mother, behind in Fergusson clutches.

She made herself more comfortable on her scrap of dirt floor and tried not to sigh in relief, on the off chance that someone found that odd. She had arrived where she was supposed to, found shelter where she hadn't dared hope for it, and still had all her gear with her.

The first hurdles were behind her.

That was enough for the day.

Chapter 30

Nathaniel wondered if it would be ungrateful to wish that the first thing to truly fail in his generally useful mortal frame would have been his ears, not his legs. He couldn't feel his feet any longer, but he could damned well hear far too much.

He wasn't quite sure who was sitting right above him blethering on endlessly, but he had been privy to their discussions for what felt like at least a week. Their conversation seemed to lurch between discussing how many years it might take for them to rid themselves of all the MacLeod and Cameron clansmen in the area and how long they could starve the MacLeod bastard they had in their pit before he simply gave up and died.

Fascinating stuff, truly.

The only thing that brightened up yet another interminable day had been realizing that the keep seemed to be quieting down a bit sooner than usual. He had stopped trying to keep track of time in any fashion, but he had learned to at least differentiate between meals being served above. He was fairly sure he'd heard dinner making the rounds upstairs, but unfortunately his had been overturned and fallen through the grate. He could only stare at the heap of slop that resided a foot beyond his feet, which he could no longer feel, and mourn its loss.

There came a time in a man's life when even rat stew began to have a certain appeal.

The hall above seemed to fall silent more quickly than usual, or perhaps he himself had slept and not realized it. The truth was, he was just too damned tired to care any longer. He was going to die. He was resigned to it. He just wanted to have it over with quickly so he wouldn't have to listen to those punters above him speculate on how long his journey to the afterlife might be.

In time, there was absolute silence. Well, there might have been the occasional snort from the guards above, but the conversation had mercifully come to a stop. He closed his eyes and wondered if he could dream himself into the next life. His mortal coil was apparently too tenacious for a mere shuffling. He was going to have to use a pry bar if something didn't change very soon.

Such as, perhaps, the grate above him being moved.

He would have winced at the scraping noise it made, but maybe they were sending lads to do men's work because all the men were asleep. He watched numbly as a figure dropped down into the muck in front of him.

Ah, demons now. That demon there, it was a slender thing and moved with a grace that Nathaniel had the energy only to envy. He watched without comment as the demon unlocked his chains, then shook him.

"Let's go, sport."

He was just sure he was either hallucinating or he had finally crossed over and landed not in Heaven but no doubt where he deserved to be.

"Damn," he rasped. "Hell?"

"Escape," the demon said. "You have to help."

He would have pointed out that there was no escape from the underworld even if his legs had been working properly, but the fiend from hell wasn't listening. He thought he might have wept as his tormenter pounded on his legs, perhaps to bring feeling back to them. Odd that his disembodied spirit was so, er, corporeal. Was that how things were going to be, then?

He supposed he should have discussed a bit more theology with his uncle when he'd had the chance.

"Come on, Nathaniel, *stand up*."

Well, at least they knew him in hell. He supposed he should have been flattered. He saw the ladder come down and rest in the muck, which he supposed was a promising development. Perhaps they wanted him to climb to a different spot in the afterlife.

He accepted help to his feet, then fell onto the ladder because it was right there in front of him. He clung to it until he thought he had stopped shaking enough to even attempt to lift his foot to the bottom rung.

"Hurry, damn it, before we're caught."

Ah, his rescuer didn't want to live out eternity in a pit, either. He agreed that it was time to go and steeled himself for a last attempt to save himself.

He climbed up the ladder even though the price was more than he thought was possible to pay.

He fell onto the floor above, but there was apparently no rest for the weary. It had never occurred to him that in hell a man might be forced to continually stumble forward in something of a run. It had seemed more like a place where one sat down whilst being tortured. The endless need to keep moving was absolute torment.

He realized one demon had turned into two. They wouldn't let him stop, those two demons who kept harping at him with their soft voices and endless demands. He refrained from cursing them, because even in hell he was a gentleman, but he damned well thought many, many vile things.

He wasn't sure how long it was before they let him stop. He was fairly sure he wasn't in the Fergussons' keep any longer, because when he fell to his hands and knees, he landed on hard earth, not slime or stone.

A flask was put to his mouth and he was commanded to drink. The whisky burned all the way down his throat to set up a bonfire in his gut, but he didn't complain. It was truly the best thing he had ever tasted. He filed the incongruity of that away for contemplation later, then simply sat there for several minutes with his insides on fire, trying to keep that whisky down in his belly where it might do him some good.

He realized eventually that his head was beginning to clear. He wasn't sure if that was an improvement or not, but it was at least something different. He lifted his head and looked at his rescuers.

It was Emma.

And his mother.

Nay, not his mother. The girl there looked like his sister as a teenager, but if that were the case, what the hell was she doing in medieval Scotland? He rubbed his eyes with the backs of his hands, but that accomplished nothing but getting slime in them. Someone did him the favor of wiping his face so he could again see his two rescuers. He would have fallen over from shock, but his abused body was apparently just too damned robust to put up with that sort of weak display.

"This is Ceana," Emma said carefully. "She's been a servant in the Fergussons' hall for ten years now."

Nathaniel looked from Emma to his—well, that had to be his mother. He gaped at her, then looked at Emma, trying to wrap what was left of his mind around the improbability of what he was facing.

"I thought she should be rescued," Emma said, looking at him pointedly. "You know. So she can get on with her life."

He would have nodded wisely, but he suspected that would lead him to planting his face on the ground in front of him, so he forbore.

"Where was she?" he rasped as he slowly stood.

"With the blacksmith," Emma said. "The blacksmith has an apprentice whose name is Thomas. I think you would recognize him as one who has a long-standing fondness of blades."

He landed on his arse. He wasn't quite sure how he'd managed to do it so gracefully—something to determine and admire later—then looked up at his two saviors. Emma was, well, Emma. His mother was, still, a teenager.

"We should go," Emma said in Gaelic. "Ceana, ready?"

Ceana nodded, then looked at Emma. "I'm a MacLeod, you know," she said quietly. She lifted her chin. "Not that I could admit as much before." She paused. "I'm not sure I should admit it in the future either."

"Bastard of Malcolm?" Nathaniel asked hoarsely.

Ceana nodded carefully. "And you?"

Nathaniel nodded, because it was the best he could do at the moment. Ceana smiled and he thought he might want to weep. He had no idea how his mother had come to be in the past, much less how she had ever gotten to the future, but he was beginning to think there were quite a few things about life that he just didn't understand.

"Can you run?" Emma asked.

"Do you have more whisky?"

She nodded, then helped him drink the rest. He gulped it

down, half surprised it didn't immediately come back up, then took a deep breath. He accepted help to his feet, then waited until his head stopped spinning. "Ready."

"I couldn't find your dagger," Emma said quietly.

"Best to leave it behind," he said.

"I have my own," Emma said. She pointed to the blade shoved down the side of her boot. "If that'll do."

He looked at her, that ragged-looking urchin with her shorn hair and filthy face, and thought he had never in his life seen anything more beautiful.

"Marry me," he said.

"You're under duress."

"All the more reason to have what I want whilst I can," he said. He looked at Ceana. "I want her to wed with me. Should she?"

Ceana smiled. "Aye, definitely."

"Well, there you go," Nathaniel said. He looked at Emma in surprise. "Gaelic?"

"Boot camp," she said in English. She smiled. "Thank Ian MacLeod later."

"I will," he said faintly. He took a deep breath and looked at his mother. "We'll get you to Laird Malcolm. You'll be safe there."

"And where will you go?"

"Ah, back to our home," Nathaniel said, half afraid that anything he said would result in his never being born. Why his mother had married his father, and in the future no less . . .

And he'd thought his life was strange.

"We need to go," Ceana said. "They won't sleep forever."

Nathaniel nodded and concentrated on moving as quickly as he could. The whisky helped. The thought of possibly standing in a shower at some point in the future helped even more. He would never again turn his nose up at anything left on his counter, especially moldy bread. At the moment, he would have been thrilled with just the green bits.

He had no idea how quickly time was passing. It was the middle of the night, he was out of his head with exhaustion, and it was all he could do to keep moving. That was no doubt why they ran bodily into a small group of clansmen before he realized how little heed he'd been paying to his surroundings.

He patted himself for a dagger, wanted to argue when Emma moved to stand in front of him with her blade in her hand, then realized there was no need for any of it. He could hardly believe his eyes, but the clansmen were MacLeods and they were led by none other than his uncle John MacLeod himself.

"Ah," he managed.

John looked at Lachlan, a man Nathaniel had fought alongside for the past five years. "I need a moment with this one here. Keep us safe, if you will."

"Anything for a priest," Lachlan said. He walked up to Nathaniel and put his hand on his shoulder. "We heard you were in the Fergussons' dungeon. They'll pay."

Nathaniel shook his head. "Not worth the trouble, my friend."

Lachlan looked at him. "If it soothes you any, we were on our way to rescue you, but looks as if there was no need."

"Nay, I had angels on my side this time."

Lachlan nodded wisely. "Off on another adventure, are ye?"

Nathaniel nodded to Emma. "My woman has come for me. I'll make my home with her clan from now on."

"More room there?"

Nathaniel smiled. "Enough," he said. "I'll never have these hills far from my heart, though."

"If ye weep on me, Nat, I'll stick ye."

Nathaniel smiled, then watched the man who had saved his neck too many times to count walk off and melt into the forest. He took a deep breath, then looked at his uncle. John had introduced himself to Emma, advised her to run away from his nephew as quickly as possible, then looked at Ceana and shook his head. He looked at Nathaniel and said absolutely nothing.

Nathaniel lifted his eyebrows briefly, then introduced his mother to her future brother-in-law.

"Ceana, this is John MacLeod. He's the laird's priest."

Ceana bobbed a curtsey, which Nathaniel imagined had been the first thing in years to almost bring his uncle to his knees. John cursed a bit in an extremely non-priest-like fashion, then blew out his breath.

"I see. Well, perhaps it's a good thing I'm where I am."

"No point in asking you one last time if you'll come with me?" Nathaniel asked.

John shook his head. "Don't want to, lad. I've almost talked Grudach into marrying me."

"You're old enough to be her father," Nathaniel wheezed.

"It's a May-December kind of thing," John said with a shrug. "Besides, Malcolm is begging me to take her. Since Angus is wed and his wife is already pregnant, the line will continue. Grudach can do as she pleases. And she likes my little vicarage there near the hall."

Nathaniel wondered if he could blame the feeling of faintness over that particular thought on something other than the mental picture of his uncle being married to a girl half his age. Stranger things had happened, he supposed.

"Besides, I'm very well preserved," John said. "They think I have supernatural powers."

Nathaniel looked at his uncle and realized the man was staring at him with a clarity that belied his reputation for being endlessly drunk. "I'll just bet they do." He glanced at his mother, then at Emma. "Any words of advice for him? Or for Ceana?"

"She'll want to go see the MacLeod witch," Emma said very quietly. "I don't know exactly when, but I imagine it's soon."

"I'll see that she is free to do as she likes," John said. "Fate balances everything out in the end, you know. One soul dropped here, another dropped there." He smiled. "Balance."

"Well, wouldn't want to clutter up the current day with one too many," Nathaniel said slowly. He looked at his uncle. "Are you as surprised as I am?"

"Every bit," John said.

"Grandfather would soil himself."

John grinned. "Which makes it all the better, doesn't it? That my father should be so involved in things that would terrify him? I would love even a single day with him here."

"It wouldn't be worth it."

"Nay, but thinking about this will be." John rattled off three account numbers along with passwords, then looked at Nathaniel. "Get all that?"

"Absolutely." Nathaniel looked at Emma. "You?"

"Yes."

John smiled. "Swiss, of course. It's all siphoned off the main trust, which has likely escaped the notice of anyone who cares. Go drain them, laddie, and do something good with the money. I'm not going to need it. I'm assuming the old miser had me declared dead."

"Two years ago."

"What about Gerald? Did he demand my inheritance?"

Nathaniel spared a moment to wish he'd talked to his uncle about that sooner. "He's fighting Grandfather, but I can't bring the exact details to mind at the moment."

"He's my son," John said with a sigh, "but he's not all that clever."

"He's also here," Nathaniel said, because he had no choice. "I don't think he should stay, but I'm not in any condition to do anything about it at the moment."

John looked at him seriously. "He's responsible for your being where you were?"

Nathaniel didn't dare nod for fear it would send him back to his knees, so he merely looked at his uncle.

John pursed his lips. "Then definitely drain those accounts and give it all away so he doesn't get his hands on it. Everyone else has more than they need. You have enough for your legal bills?"

"Aye."

John smiled, embraced him briefly, then pulled back quickly and wrinkled his nose. "Forgot where you've been, laddie. Don't particularly care to wear any of that." He turned to Ceana and smiled. "Come along, lass, and come home. We'll take care of you."

Tears were streaming down her face. "Thank you." She looked at Nathaniel. "And where will you go?"

"We're going home," Nathaniel said, not arguing as Emma drew his arm over her shoulders. "Time to marry this lass here before she gets away."

"She's very pretty," Ceana said with a faint smile. "Good fortune to you both."

Nathaniel smiled. "John will take care of you," he said. He looked at his uncle. "Do what you have to, aye?"

"You know I will, Nathaniel." John looked at Emma. "Lovely to meet you, lass. Grind this one under your heel as often as possible after you wed him. I'll see that he's born, which is likely the least I can do for him. Now, off with you both before Nat falls on his arse. Be safe, children."

Nathaniel nodded to his uncle, refrained from putting his arms around his mother and bawling like a bairn, then decided that perhaps it was best they get on with getting home.

Assuming they could.

He turned away before he couldn't make himself turn away, then stumbled along with Emma toward where he knew the gate lay.

"Is Gerald still following us?" he asked very quietly.

"I can't hear him any longer," she said. "He's not very careful, but I would have to leave you and go have a look to know for sure."

"Nay," he managed, "let's just keep going. If we can get home, we might find some help there. And to keep my mind off the fact that I wish I were dead, tell me where you learned to do all that."

"Do what?"

He was truly unhappy with how hard he was leaning on her, but he couldn't do anything else. "Steal keys and liberate half-dead Highlanders from medieval dungeons."

She shouldered more of his weight. "Well, it was more theory than practice, if you want the whole truth. Patrick sharpened up my fighting skills while Ian was teaching me Gaelic. Jamie watched with a lairdly frown. They weren't happy about my going, but I didn't give them any choice."

She fell silent and he didn't have the strength to press her for a reason why. It took him almost all the way to the gate to be able to have the energy to speak again.

"And the lock picking?"

"Bertie, of course," she said with a faint smile. "I had to have something to do to fill my rebellious teenage days, and he had to have something to do besides polish cars. My father had four drivers, in case you were curious."

"I was," he wheezed.

"My parents had to keep up appearances, you know," she continued. "They live in an enclave within yachting distance of Seattle and routinely use words like *exclusive* and *elite* to describe the guest lists created for intimate, extremely important dinner parties."

"You bluestocking, you," he managed.

She laughed a little. "You wish I were," she said. "Unfortunately you know the reality is I'm the dorky middle child who learned to pick locks so I could get out of anything my brothers could lock me into, namely the attic."

"Cinderella practices unsavory skills, is that it?"

She nodded. "Exactly."

He found that he couldn't speak anymore. It was slightly unnerving to him that he had to concentrate so fully on just continuing to walk quickly, but he supposed perhaps he couldn't have reasonably expected anything else. He managed to take one last decent breath for speaking.

"Thank you, Emma."

She smiled up at him, then squeezed his arm that was slung over her shoulder. "Almost safe home."

He almost didn't dare hope for it.

Chapter 31

Emma had never in her life been so grateful for the sight of a house that didn't belong to her as she was for the sight of James MacLeod's little cottage on the edge of the woods. She would have thought she had dreamed the past few days, but the fact that she was filthy suggested otherwise. The fact that she was holding on to a man who looked as if he'd spent almost two weeks in a medieval dungeon was conclusive proof.

She paused, because she wasn't sure Nathaniel could move much more. He was shaking badly. She didn't know why the gate had swung open for them so easily and at the moment, she honestly didn't care. For all she knew, James MacLeod had been standing there in the shadows, key in one hand and treatise on *How to Matchmake Like a Pro* in the other, and he'd been responsible. She suspected she would only have the answer over blades.

"Can you make my house?" she asked.

"The saints preserve me if I can't."

She smiled at him. "My Gaelic isn't that good, Nathaniel."

"I think your Gaelic is amazing," he managed, in English. "At the moment, I think all I can speak is *moan*."

She smiled. "My house or yours?"

"Mine, but let me rest on your porch for a minute or two—actually, nay. We'd best keep going. If I sit, I'll never get back up."

"I'll drive you," she said.

"Are you mad?" he asked. "I'm not getting in your Audi in my current state."

"You can sit on the hood."

He laughed uneasily, then had to stop and cough. He straightened and shook his head. "I need to walk. Just prop me up against that tree there for a minute or two whilst I catch my breath."

She did, then looked him over. He was filthy and his plaid was disgusting, but he looked more like himself than he had before. She wished she had pockets to put her hands in, but all she could do was hug herself.

They had made it.

She wished she felt more at peace.

"How did you know?" he asked. "Where I was, I mean."

"Patrick said as much."

He leaned his head back against the tree and looked up at the sky for a moment or two before he looked at her. "I wonder if you would be open to another brief but fond embrace?"

She nodded. She supposed it would be indiscreet to say anything about how hard he was shaking, or the fact that she'd had to help him put his arms around her, so she simply held on to him and was grateful for it.

He sighed and rested his cheek against her head. "Did you hear my conversation with Jamie?"

"Yes."

"You wanted to call me a foul name just then, didn't you?"

"I did," she agreed. "It's a testament to how happy I am to see you that I refrained."

"I wanted to keep you safe."

"I know."

"You realize we can't carry on like this, don't you?"

She didn't dare move. "Traveling back and forth in time?"

"Nay, with your chasing me all through the centuries because you simply can't resist my charming self."

She laughed a little. "You're a jerk."

"Aye, I daresay." He paused. "You are going to have to marry me, you know."

She pulled back and looked at his filthy, too-thin face. "Am I?"

"I think you'll go mad without me, actually."

"That is the single most unromantic proposal I have ever

heard," she said, fighting her smile, "following hard on the heels of your other proposal, which wasn't all that great, either. Actually, I think you've brought it up more times than that, but obviously your speeches need some work."

He wheezed out a laugh, but that seemingly cost him. "Lass," he managed, "if I offer anything more romantic after what we've just been through, I'll weep." He took a deep, unsteady breath. "I think I need to go home."

"I'll drive you."

He shook his head. "You truly do not want me in your car, and I'm not being fastidious. I can make it home. You'll have to stay and tend me round the clock for the saints only know how long, but you're too altruistic to leave me on my own."

"Especially after I ventured across centuries to rescue you?"

His smile faded. "Exactly that." He pushed away from the tree, swayed, then nodded. "Let's hurry."

She put her arm around him again, drew his arm across her shoulders while ignoring his grunt of pain, and walked with him past her house and down the road toward his. She looked up at him.

"Shall I distract you with mindless chatter?"

"Please," he said seriously. "Anything to keep me awake."

"Then I'll tell you about the visit on the morning I went back to get you." She looked at him to make sure he was still conscious and not just sleepwalking, then pressed on. "I had made the connection with your mother and 1372—"

"Is that her birth year?"

"Apparently so," Emma said, "which is why I think it got to you at Cawdor. Anyway, there I was getting ready to come rescue you and who should show up at my door but Thomas Campbell, collector of all things sharp, with your dagger in his hand. He's off to Florida, you see, and wanted you to babysit it for him. Imagine my surprise to find a substantially younger version of our good curator acting as an apprentice to the Fergusson clan's blacksmith."

He paused, breathed raggedly for a moment or two, then shook his head and walked on. "Storyboard material, that."

She smiled. "I think I might have a few things to add, definitely. So, I dressed in black, grabbed my go bag, and left the house, only to run straight into Patrick MacLeod. He was good enough to walk me to the forest, then watch me shove your dagger into the, well, I guess *door* is the only thing to call it. The door opened, I hopped through, then turned around to find both Patrick and the dagger gone. Maybe there's only one of those blades now, which will make Jamie and his plaid of time happy."

"Sorry?"

"Jamie has a theory about pulling threads out of the fabric of time," she said. "He says it's bad. Messes up the pattern."

He nodded, but his breathing was very ragged. She understood, actually. They walked in silence almost all the way to his house before he stopped, breathed for a moment or two, then looked at her.

"I wonder if the gate is closed."

She started to answer, then realized that she should have been paying attention to their surroundings, not trying to distract Nathaniel with conversation. She looked at him, then ducked under his arm and drew the dagger from her boot at the same time.

Gerald MacLeod stood there in a worn, medieval plaid, a sword bare in his hand. He looked at her, then laughed shortly.

"You can't be serious," he said contemptuously. "*You*? You think you're going to fight *me*? With that pitiful little dagger?"

"Emma."

Emma looked to her right to find Patrick MacLeod standing there. He flipped a long dirk toward her. She caught it, flung off the sheath, then realized what she was holding.

Nathaniel's medieval dagger. Well, the incarnation of it that resided most of the time in Thomas Campbell's glass case. She didn't feel ill, which she thought might be a good sign.

She glanced at Nathaniel to see if he had a different opinion, only to find him leaning back against the railing of his porch. *Leaning* was probably the wrong word for it. He was swaying so badly, she thought he might be on the verge of passing out, but he was looking at Patrick MacLeod sternly.

"I need a sword," he wheezed.

"Of course you don't," Patrick said with a snort. He walked over and did Nathaniel the favor of pushing him back upright. He looked at the grime now on his hand, then at Nathaniel. "Don't expect any more help than that and leave your woman to her work. She'll see to it well enough."

She supposed that was enough of a vote of confidence for her. She smiled at Nathaniel, then turned to face his cousin.

"Is this any better," she asked politely, "or would you like to rest before we end this?"

Gerald looked at her in astonishment. "I can't believe you expect me—"

That was the last thing he said for quite some time. She supposed all that dirty fighting Patrick MacLeod had taught her wasn't exactly what Gerald was expecting, but her, er, boyfriend had spent almost two weeks in a medieval dungeon thanks to the idiot standing there, which she supposed disqualified him from any mercy she might have been willing to show. Considering that amount was exactly zero, she supposed he wasn't going to have a very good morning.

His sword was sharp, though, and he grazed her arm before she decided that any Marquess of Queensbury rules were definitely off the table. She didn't think it would go very well for her to just stab him, so she spent most of her time just nicking him and verbally getting under his skin. It was almost too easy to set him off, which left her thinking that maybe Poindexter MacLeod was smart not to let Gerald have control over any of his assets. She also was beginning to understand why John wasn't terribly sad over not getting to see his son on holidays and long weekends.

"This is ridiculous!" Gerald shouted finally. "I don't want her, I want a real swordsman—"

She took the hilt of Nathaniel's dirk and smashed it into Gerald's nose.

Gerald dropped his sword and clutched his face. "She broke my nose!"

Emma kicked him as hard as she could in the gut, sending him sprawling. She flipped his sword up with her foot, then tossed it to Patrick, who reached out and casually caught it by the hilt. She paused for a moment to appreciate that medieval nonchalance, then looked back at her fallen foe, who was rolling around on the ground, howling.

"You tried to kill my—" Emma paused, which was annoying because she quite suddenly lost the rhythm of the diatribe she had been getting ready to let loose.

"Future husband," Nathaniel called.

Emma looked at Gerald. "My future husband," she said. "Now, get up and stop being such a baby. It's no wonder your grandfather doesn't want you having any of his stuff when you act like this."

Gerald actually kicked his heels and pounded his hands against the ground. She had never seen anything like it before. She checked him over for other weapons, saw none, then decided she had done all she could do. It was going to be up to Nathaniel to make some decisions—

Or maybe Archibald Poindexter MacLeod, Jr., could jump right in and offer an opinion.

She shifted so she could still see Gerald out of the corner of her eye and looked at the little collection of men who were leaning against the railing of Nathaniel's porch. She spared a brief thought that if three of the four leaned any harder, the railing would simply give up, then took a moment or two to identify the players now involved in the current drama.

Patrick MacLeod was farthest to the left. He had shoved Gerald's sword into the ground next to him and was currently standing there—not leaning—with his arms folded over his chest, smiling faintly. She supposed that was a smile of approval.

Nathaniel was next to him, wheezing. She didn't expect anything else from him, but she thought he might be thinking kind thoughts about her.

She wasn't so sure what Poindexter MacLeod and Franklin Baxter were thinking. They were both gaping at her as if they'd just witnessed a horror movie come to life. Emma retrieved the sheath of Nathaniel's dagger, then walked over to hand it back to him. She shoved her own blade down the side of her boot, then looked at Nathaniel's grandfather.

"Mr. MacLeod," she said politely.

"Ahhh," was all he managed.

She left him to his grappling with whatever he was thinking and turned to her father. "Dad."

Her father's mouth was working, but no sound was coming out.

She thought it might have been the most delicious moment of her life to date.

Dexter MacLeod looked at her father. "My grandson has wine inside. Perhaps we should go pour glasses all around."

"Whisky instead," Frank said. "Please."

They felt their way into Nathaniel's house. She watched them go, then looked at Nathaniel.

"They'll drink your good stuff."

"It's locked."

"Well, that'll buy us ten minutes," she said. She walked over to put her arms around him and tried not to think too hard about what he was covered in. She looked at Patrick. "Well?"

"A good job," he said, nodding.

"He nicked me."

"It happens," Patrick said. He looked at Nathaniel, then shifted a bit farther away from him. "Sorry, lad, but you smell. I'll take care of the refuse and leave you free to bathe. What shall I see to first?"

Nathaniel nodded gingerly toward where Gerald was now sitting up and looking around for his sword. "That."

"Done." Patrick walked over, hauled Gerald to his feet, then said something that had him very silent very quickly.

"Wonder what that was?" Nathaniel murmured. "I wish I'd known it several years ago."

Emma watched Gerald walk over to them with Patrick at his side. She felt Nathaniel tense, which she couldn't blame him for. If she pulled her knife free of her boot, well, who could blame her? She liked to be prepared.

"What shall we do with him?" Patrick asked politely.

"Do?" Gerald spat. "Who are y—" He squeaked and fell silent.

Emma supposed it might be impolite to look too closely at Patrick's thumb on a pressure point in his new friend's neck. Patrick pulled his phone out of his pocket and handed it to Nathaniel.

"A text from my brother," he said with a shrug. "It says, *I've closed your cousin's gate.*" He looked at Nathaniel blandly. "I wonder what that means."

"You sent it to yourself," Gerald scoffed.

"No, I don't think so," Nathaniel said slowly. "The text is from James MacLeod."

"Who?"

Nathaniel sighed. "If you don't know, I'm not going to help you." He leveled a look at his cousin. "You can do what you want to, of course, but don't come to me for help when you're trapped where you don't want to be."

"You're bluffing," Gerald snarled. "I can still get back there!"

"You might," Nathaniel agreed, "but I'd be more worried if I were you about getting back *here*." He took a ragged breath. "I have to go sit down. Do what you like, Gerald."

"I'll tell anyone who'll listen what you've been doing!"

"No one will believe you," Nathaniel said wearily.

"Then I'll make a name for myself in antiquities. I've already sold one sword to a guy in Scotland for plenty of money."

Emma suspected Gerald didn't have the patience or the social skills for that sort of thing, but she didn't bother to say as much. He had launched into a diatribe full of slurs first in English, then in Gaelic. She wondered how so much unhappiness could find itself in one person. She had the feeling no amount of money could possibly fix that for him.

She looked over Nathaniel's shoulder to find his grandfather and her father coming outside, highball glasses in their hands. Poindexter offered Nathaniel what he was holding, but Nathaniel shook his head.

"Another time, Grandfather, thank you."

Emma took what her father held out, tossed it back, then wished she hadn't. She wasn't about to show any weakness in that crowd, though, so she blinked rapidly and tried not to vomit her drink back up on Nathaniel, not that he would have noticed in his current state.

Poindexter looked at Gerald and his eyebrows went up so far, they almost touched his perfectly coiffed white pompadour.

"Gerald," he said crisply, "what in the hell are you playing at?"

Gerald was silent. Emma suspected that was because Patrick seemed to have grown suddenly weary, which required him to lean on his thumb pressing against Gerald's neck.

"Nathaniel, what is this madness here?"

Nathaniel looked at his grandfather. "A bit of reenactment

business, Grandfather," he managed. "Sharpens the senses for battle in other arenas. I suggested it to Gerald a year or two ago and he took to it like a duck to water."

Emma supposed that was as good a cover story as any. If Nathaniel shot his granddaddy a look that said Gerald had taken to it a bit *too* well, she wasn't about to correct the record.

"So, Nathaniel, you're dating your assistants now?" Poindexter asked tartly.

Emma didn't have a chance to even take in a breath before her father had leaped into the fray.

"She is *not* his assistant," Frank said, his voice dripping with newer old money, "she's a successful businesswoman in the middle of launching a fine jewelry business. All her own creations, of course. Her client list already is extremely exclusive."

Emma looked at Nathaniel and shrugged. That much was true. Her client list consisted of her mother's bridge partners, and they were indeed filthy rich and very exclusive.

Her father looked down his nose at Nathaniel. "What I want to know is what you intend to do with that thing there who assaulted my daughter."

"Why don't I offer my refuse removal services?" Patrick put in pleasantly. "I'll see to him, these two can clean up from their recent adventures, and we'll all meet up later at my brother's. He's the chief of the clan MacLeod, though perhaps Lord Poindexter is already familiar with that?"

Emma leaned back gingerly against the railing with Nathaniel. "If he attaches a title to my father's name," she murmured, "I'll know we will have definitely come back to an alternate reality."

"If that reality has a shower and a bed, I don't care how alternate it is," he said.

She drew his arm carefully over her shoulders and helped him up the step to the porch and into his house. "Want me to get Patrick to come back? I think he knows some medieval sorts of herbal remedies."

"Aye, if you would."

"Do you need help with anything else?" she asked. He didn't look at all good, which made her wonder why the hell she hadn't stopped the madness outside a bit sooner.

"You just cannae keep yer hands off me, lass, can ye?" He

smoothed his hand down the front of his disgusting plaid. "I can understand why."

"Do you ever stop talking?"

"When I'm dead, darling, and even then I imagine I'll have aught to say. I think I can manage a shower on my own, though I'm not opposed to company."

She pointed toward his bathroom. "Go."

"If you hear a crashing noise, that would be yours truly, taking a header out of the tub. Come rescue me and don't linger over the view."

She laughed, and hoped it didn't sound as forced as it felt. She was accustomed to Nathaniel being larger than life. He looked presently as if most of the life had been sucked from him. She helped him over to the bathroom, then turned him loose.

"Be a love and text Patrick, would you?" he said. "I have to admit—and deny it loudly later—that I feel particularly awful at the moment. I would prefer not to alert the rest of the rabble to my condition." He clutched the doorframe of the bathroom and looked at her blearily. "I may go right to bed after I wash up, which doesn't do anything for you. My apologies. Can you find my mobile?"

"Since I'm the one who used the password you gave me to get into it last, probably," she said cheerfully. She watched him shut himself into the bathroom, waited to listen for the shower to start without any loud crashes, then went to go find his phone.

She texted Patrick for help, then set Nathaniel's phone down with hands that weren't at all steady. She sat down on a kitchen stool, cold and tired and hungry, but relieved.

If she patted Nathaniel's dagger that was sitting on the table, no doubt waiting for a certain collector to come back from Florida to claim it, well, who could blame her?

She sincerely hoped she would never have to see it again outside its Plexiglas case.

Chapter 32

Nathaniel woke, froze, then realized several things in no particular order.

He could stretch out his legs, which was less comfortable than he would have expected it to be. He could feel his hands, which was also less comfortable than he would have expected it to be. He wasn't, however, sitting in slime any longer, he didn't smell any longer, and there was someone in his kitchen humming a medieval drinking song.

Ah, the future. What a place.

He looked up at the ceiling and wondered how long he'd slept. There was sunlight leaking in through the curtains, so he supposed it was daytime. Whether one day or many days had passed since he'd stumbled out of the shower and into bed, he couldn't say. He remembered with uncomfortable clarity the things that Patrick MacLeod had forced him to drink. He also remembered quite well all the things he'd called the young Himself, which he supposed Patrick was used to.

He sat up, clutched his head for a moment or two until the world stopped spinning so wildly, then swung his feet to the floor. The stone was bloody chilly, but at least it was a chill he knew he could mitigate with a pair of slippers. He looked for clothes, managed to cover the bottom half of himself without falling over, then stumbled over into his kitchen to examine the lay of the land, as it were.

The good lord of Benmore was sitting with his feet toasting quite well against his Aga. Patrick looked over at him.

"Breakfast?"

"Please—" Nathaniel cleared his throat. "Please. Where's Emma?"

"She went to Mrs. McCreedy's for more eggs. She promised to return."

"And why not?" Nathaniel croaked. "When she has this to come back to?"

Patrick smiled dryly. "She said almost the same thing. I think you two have a glorious future ahead of you."

"Congratulations on seeing the truth as well." He sat down next to his, er, cousin, and looked at him. "Thank you—and I apologize for all the names I called you over the last several hours."

"Days, rather," Patrick noted mildly. "You're welcome, and don't fash yourself. Trust me, I've heard much worse, and that from both my wife and sister-in-law." He handed Nathaniel a mug of something steaming. "Lovely of your lady to rescue your sorry arse."

"Indeed it was." He had a drink, then came damned near choking. "If that's coffee, I would hate to taste what you use in your driveway."

"Gravel, which that is not," Patrick said. He helped himself to a hearty sip of his own brew, then cradled his mug in his hands. "Emma said you found your mother, but left the details for you to relate. Was she one of the Fergussons' gels?"

"Actually, she's one of Malcolm MacLeod's bastards."

Patrick choked. Nathaniel would have taken a bit of pleasure in that, but he found he couldn't. He waited whilst his guest got hold of himself, then looked at him seriously.

"You didn't know?"

"Hadn't a bloody clue," Patrick said, looking at him with wide eyes. "I thought she was a Fergusson."

"So did we."

Patrick shook his head slowly. "Genealogy is a dodgy business." He leaned back in his chair. "Feel up to giving me the entire tale?"

Nathaniel supposed there was no reason not to. He had another sip of truly awful coffee, then told Patrick in as few words as possible about his initial journey to the past, the impossibility of convincing his uncle to come forward with him, and the absolute improbability of finding that his mother had been helping Emma get him away from the Fergusson keep.

"It was Emma to realize who my mother was, of course, thanks to her own brilliance and a quick look at some notes Alexander Smith sent me."

Patrick lifted his eyebrows briefly. "Alex does love a good mystery."

"I won't ask for a list of things he's already solved," Nathaniel said. "But a mystery it definitely was. We encountered my uncle—my father's brother—in the forest, he offered to take my mother back to the MacLeod keep, and I'm supposing the tale ended well since I'm still breathing."

"Balance is restored, I suppose."

"I think my uncle said exactly that."

"A wise man, your uncle." Patrick shrugged. "He eventually sends her forward, he stays in the past, there are no stray threads in the plaid of time."

"Save that my mother bore three children where she wouldn't have if she'd stayed in medieval Scotland."

"Well," Patrick said with a small smile, "I didn't say 'twas a perfect system now, did I? Just don't tell Jamie."

Nathaniel snorted. "There isn't a damned thing I can do about it now, is there? And before I forget to ask, was I having a nightmare, or did I see my grandfather here yesterday?"

"Day before yesterday, and aye, that's who you saw."

"And Emma's father?"

"Can't vouch for the spot he takes up in your dreams," Patrick said with a smirk, "but aye to that as well."

"Where are they now?"

"Jamie's."

"Good lord."

Patrick laughed. "With Elizabeth still on holiday in London, you should be offering a few more substantial prayers than that. I nipped over earlier to see what they'd done with your cousin, but trotted right off before I could be forced to stay."

"In the hall?"

"In the lists. My brother was overseeing a bit of swordplay with his guests."

Nathaniel put his face in his hands, then laughed. "Tell me that's the only thing that's gone on whilst I've been asleep."

"Your cousin Gerald has been seasoning down in one of Hamish Fergusson's cells until you decide what to do with him."

"Poetic justice, that," Nathaniel noted.

"It is," Patrick agreed. "I suggested that perhaps the matter should be settled on the field. If Gerald can best Jamie with the sword, he earns himself another chance with Lord Poindexter."

"Tell me they haven't started yet."

"I made them promise to wait for you."

Nathaniel studied him. "How long do you think Gerald will last against your brother?"

"Your lady destroyed him with a pair of daggers," Patrick said, his eyes twinkling. "How long do you think he'll last? A better question is, how long do you want it to last? Your cousin is the reason you found yourself in that dungeon for almost a fortnight."

Nathaniel considered, then looked at him. "Is that gate closed?"

Patrick nodded.

Nathaniel shifted, trying not to wince. "So my choice is to either kill my cousin and end all possibility that he would ever come after me, or let him live and look over my shoulder for the rest of my life."

"You could push him through the nettle patch in my garden," Patrick said with a shrug. "I did that with an enemy once."

"A modern-day enemy?"

Patrick looked at him. "A medieval enemy who had found his way to the modern day. 'Tis a bit complicated and perhaps something to be saved for an evening when we're both well into our cups and our ladies have given us up for lost and gone to look for more interesting conversation."

Nathaniel supposed he shouldn't have felt pleased at the thought of being so included, but he couldn't help but admit he was.

"Bastard relative that you are," Patrick added.

Nathaniel leveled a look at him. "Careful," he warned. "That's my ma you're talking about."

Patrick only laughed. "I meant to insult you, not her, which I'm sure you knew. As for the nettle patch, 'tis your choice. Send him off to wreak havoc elsewhere or show him mercy and see if it changes him."

"The thought of James MacLeod keeping an eye on him for the rest of his life might inspire Gerald to make some changes."

"It did me," Patrick admitted with a smile. "My brother can be impossible, but he is intimidating. I would never admit to having said that, though, so don't bother quoting me."

"Wouldn't think of it."

Nathaniel heard a car pull up outside and started to get up, but Patrick stopped him.

"I'll see to it."

Nathaniel nodded, listened to Patrick open the door, then heard Emma gasp.

"Is he all right?"

"The patient is alive and complaining," Patrick said, "which should tell you all you need to know. Here, let me take those and you can go see for yourself."

Nathaniel stood up, came close to falling onto his stove, then managed to catch himself on his counter. He almost immediately found Emma ducking under his arm and pulling it over her shoulders.

He looked at her. "I think I might feel faint."

"Let me help you."

"This may last several months."

She rolled her eyes, then looked at him critically. "You look better. At least you're not drooling any longer."

"Blame his wee lordship there for anything untoward I've done in the past twenty-four—"

"Forty-eight," she corrected.

He had to take a deep breath, then he shot Patrick a look of promise over her head. "Whatever he gave me over the past *forty-eight* hours almost finished off what Simon Fergusson began."

Patrick looked thoroughly unimpressed. "I'll cook something for you," he said, "and put the rest in the fridge."

"Mrs. McCreedy sent along soup," Emma said. "She said it was very helpful for those recovering from a shock."

"That woman," Patrick said with a smile. "She knows more than she lets on."

"I don't want to think about what she knows," Nathaniel said with a sigh. "I think I need some fresh air. Emma, if you'll excuse me?"

"Notice he doesn't ask my leave," Patrick said sadly. "The lack of respect is truly a comment on the state of affairs these days, isn't it? Emma, did Nathaniel tell you that he thinks we might be cousins, bastard though he is—"

Nathaniel thought it best to leave the kitchen before he killed Patrick MacLeod. He shot him a murderous look before he put on a coat and went outside to breathe in the air of freedom.

It was glorious.

The afternoon was waning as he woke from yet another in a series of naps he couldn't seem to stop himself from taking and saw Emma standing near his stove, putting on the kettle for tea.

"Ah, a proper Scottish lass you are," he said with a smile. "Tea for her man. Now, when you begin to forgo the tea and go straight for the appropriate liquid, I'll know something has truly changed."

She turned to look at him. "You don't drink very often, do you?"

"Not anymore," he said lightly. "I had my brush with too much drink after my mother died. But I'm surprised to find that an abrupt trip to the past has an immediate effect on one's alcohol consumption." He pushed himself to his feet, swayed, then walked over to her. He put his arms around her and sighed deeply. "Have I thanked you properly for the rescue?"

"I don't think so."

He smiled. "You cut your hair and braved a medieval forge. I'm not sure there are adequate thanks."

"The forge was a cakewalk. It was that dungeon that was really disgusting."

He smiled, because they'd already discussed that more than he supposed either of them wanted to during the parts of the afternoon during which he'd actually managed to stay awake. Staying on his feet with any success was a bit more difficult, so he didn't argue when Emma pushed him over to the couch and told him to sit down.

He accepted tea, drank, then leaned back against the sofa. He waited until she'd joined him before he spoke. "I have an invitation to extend," he said slowly.

She curled her feet up under her and turned toward him. "What?"

"I had a phone call with your father today."

"Did you?" she asked. "Before or after Jamie almost drove him to a heart attack in the lists?"

"After," he said pleasantly.

She smiled grimly. "I haven't had a chance to talk to him yet."

"Well, I did and we worked a few things out. You may not like them."

Her mouth fell open. "I think what I'm not going to like is how much my hand is going to hurt after I punch you. And stop looking for blades in my hands," she snapped. "I left mine in my house, but I can certainly go get it if necessary."

He decided the present time was likely not the proper time to point out to her that she was discussing stabbing him with a dirk as easily as she might discuss slapping his face. Truly, their lives were very strange.

She looked at him in shock. "I can't believe you called him."

"I didn't call him," Nathaniel said slowly. "He called me while you ran home for pen and sketch pad. I think he doesn't quite know how to apologize to you, so I agreed to be the messenger. Never hurts to butter up the in-laws."

"Still not a romantic proposal in sight, is there?"

He smiled and laced his fingers with hers. "Your mother apparently told your father that if he didn't mend fences with you, she was going to leave him, but only after she'd rolled his Bugatti off the end of the pier. She already had burly lads retained for the job."

She let out her breath slowly. "My family has an interesting relationship with the lake."

He smiled. "So I hear. And just so you know, after I buttered your father up, we had a substantially less lovely chat."

"Did you chew him up and spit him out?"

"Thoroughly."

"Hmmm," she said. "Then what?"

"He admitted that he'd been astonished to find out

Sheldon's true character, but even more surprised to receive a bit of intelligence from an unnamed source."

"Intelligence?" she asked skeptically.

"Notes from Alexander Smith, of course. I thought your father might appreciate them. Let's just say that I don't think Sheldon will be bothering with you again."

She looked at him in surprise. "My father is coming to my rescue?"

"He is."

"And you inspired him to."

"I only talked to him on the phone, Emma," he said carefully. "He came to that decision all on his own."

"Jamie might have helped."

"That's a possibility as well." He shifted. It was less uncomfortably done than he'd dared hope, which he supposed was progress.

Her smile faded. "I want to be done with this."

He looked at her for a moment or two in silence, then reached for his phone and handed it to her. "Check the alarm."

She turned his phone on, entered his password whilst ignoring his feigned protest, then looked at the timer he certainly hadn't set for himself. He actually wouldn't have been surprised to learn Patrick MacLeod had done so simply to annoy him.

Emma met his gaze. "1387."

"Feel anything?"

She paused, then shook her head. "But that doesn't mean anything, I don't think. What about you?"

"I think we could try an experiment," he offered. "We could sit here for the evening, watch a little telly, then open my door and see what's there. If we see medieval clansmen, we'll just shut the door right back up. Or we could just lock the windows, bolt the door, and not venture out for a few days."

"I could cook," she offered.

"Or you could watch me cook."

She shot him a disgusted look, but moved closer to him. "I'm not that bad," she muttered.

"I think I should just keep my mouth shut."

"I rescued you from a medieval dungeon."

"And that, darling, has earned you a lifetime of my cooking and occasionally cleaning up after myself."

She smiled and looked at him. "Will I hurt you if I put my head on your shoulder?"

"'Tis a pain I'll gladly bear."

"You talk altogether too much, Nathaniel MacLeod. But while you're talking so much, why don't you tell me how it feels to now be related to the guys up the way?"

"Bastard cousin and all that."

She put her arm over his waist. "Your grandfather no doubt wishes he had such a claim to that lord's chair."

"We'll go find out later, then see if there's anyone still breathing who has a birth date more recent than 1400. With what I hear has been going on in those lists, I'm not sure we'll find anything save James MacLeod cleaning off his sword."

She shivered. "I think I could be done with the past for a while."

He thought he might want to be done with it forever, but he wasn't sure that was going to happen any time soon. He understood that Jamie had a family ring waiting for him to use if he cared to handfast soon with the woman falling asleep in his arms. He also suspected he would be driving either his grandfather or Emma's father or the both of them to a certain curator of blades in Edinburgh to see what could be made specifically for them. That would be made substantially easier given that said blacksmith, who was supposed to be across the Pond, had apparently been putting his feet up for the past few days down at Roddy MacLeod's inn.

Gerald, he supposed, would come to terms with his life or he wouldn't. There was nothing to be done except contemplate that patch of nettles in Patrick's garden, but he supposed he wouldn't be contemplating very long. He'd seen enough death for a lifetime.

All of which could be thought about on the morrow. For the moment, he had numbers on his phone that didn't disturb him, a warm fire in his stove, and the woman he loved in his arms.

That was enough present for him.

Epilogue

E^{mma} sat in a lovely floral chair in a sitting room that overlooked an adorable little street in Notting Hill and stared at the man sitting across from her, reading in the sunshine.

That man happened to be her husband, but perhaps that wasn't anything unexpected.

He was reading, for what she was sure was the thousandth time over the past six months, a letter his mother had written him.

She supposed *thousandth* was an exaggeration. He'd read the letter many times during the few days after he'd retrieved it from the box his mother had locked it in, a box his grandfather had told him about on the day of their wedding.

The combination had been 1387.

Neither of them had been surprised.

The letter was long, written in a rather medieval-looking hand, detailing Ceana's adventures with her natural father Malcolm, who had been very kind to her, and her subsequent desire to test the secret of the MacLeod forest, which had also been very kind to her, if not a bit terrifying.

Emma didn't envy her, having had her own brush with the secret of that forest.

Ceana had written of her struggles to assimilate, her desire never to go back in time, and her very lovely marriage to Nathaniel's father. Her children had been her joy and her former life had seemed like nothing but a dream until she had,

one fine day in the fall of Nathaniel's eighteenth year, looked
at him and noticed something she'd almost forgotten.

He was the lad she had helped rescue from the Fergussons' dungeon who had in turn rescued her from the Fergussons' keep.

Emma watched Nathaniel turn the last page, sigh, then
look at her. He smiled.

"Sorry."

She shook her head. "Don't be. I'm happy she had a good
life with your father who adored her and you and your siblings
who loved her so dearly."

"I imagine she did," he agreed. He smiled, folded the letter
and put it away, then leaned over and kissed her. "I'll go make
tea."

She watched him go, then stared out the window and considered the state of both their lives.

Gerald was, it had to be said, struggling. Their grandfather
had sent him to the Hamptons as a restorative measure, but
that hadn't seemed to help. Emma didn't know that what
would have served him better wouldn't have been a quick trip
back to medieval Scotland, but that wasn't for her to judge, she
supposed.

Nathaniel's sister, Sorcha, had turned out to be a lovely if
not slightly mysterious sort who seemed to love the social
scene but had something else going on inside her that Emma
couldn't seem to pinpoint. Gavin had become a regular visitor
to wherever they were staying at the moment, something she
knew Nathaniel treasured.

She thought he treasured a bit less dealing with the realities
of being his grandfather's heir, but she supposed he would
deal with that as well when he had to. If Poindexter and her
own father had become inseparable golf buddies, well, she
hadn't begrudged Nathaniel and his brother any time spent
with them on the course.

Life was very good.

She had seen her family several times, most notably at
her wedding, where James MacLeod had officiated. If her
father had still been unnerved by the sight of Nathaniel in
proper Scottish dress, he hadn't said anything. Her brothers
had looked terrified, which had made her happy, and her sisters had simply gaped, but she couldn't blame them for it. She

had, after all, married a very desirable, extremely handsome recluse who had been hunted by more skilled girls than her own flesh and blood.

She had seen her mother perhaps most of all, which had been a sweetness added to her life she hadn't expected. Her mother had gone shopping with her in Paris, then made regular trips since to wherever she and Nathaniel were calling home at the moment.

She looked up as the man she loved brought in tea, set it out, then poured her a cup. She accepted, then smiled.

"Thank you."

He only smiled in return. "I was thinking about summer in Paris."

"Can you do business there?"

"Occasionally," he said. "If you don't mind."

She didn't. It wasn't the money. He had too much, she didn't need any, and they lived as simply as they could considering the places they called home.

But investing was in his blood, and his grandfather seemed to feel that his legacy might be salvaged if he funneled money to worthy charitable things. In addition to everything else, Poindexter had hired Nathaniel's company to do just that, and their budget was staggering. Nathaniel turned his own profits into loans for others who were trying to make their dreams come true.

And if there was one thing, among all the things her husband was, he was a dreamer.

Scotland in my dreams.

She looked at that man sitting across from her, the one who turned dreams into reality, and wondered what he would say if she told him that's why she'd gone to Scotland in the first place.

She suspected he would understand.

family lineage in the books of
LynnKurland

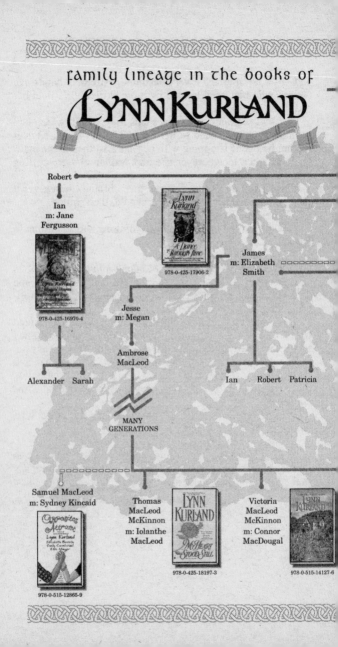

Robert

Ian
m: Jane
Fergusson

978-0-425-16970-4

Alexander   Sarah

Jesse
m: Megan

Ambrose
MacLeod

**MANY
GENERATIONS**

978-0-425-17906-2

James
m: Elizabeth
Smith

Ian   Robert   Patricia

Samuel MacLeod
m: Sydney Kincaid

978-0-515-12865-9

Thomas
MacLeod
McKinnon
m: Iolanthe
MacLeod

978-0-425-18197-3

Victoria
MacLeod
McKinnon
m: Connor
MacDougal

978-0-515-14127-6

MACLEOD

Douglas

Patrick
m: Madelyn Phillips

978-0-425-19202-3

978-0-515-14470-3

978-0-515-15346-0

978-0-515-15616-4

Sunshine
Phillips
m: Robert
Cameron

Derrick
Cameron
m: Samantha
Drummond

Nathaniel
MacLeod
m: Emma
Baxter

Alexander Smith
m: Margaret of
Falconberg

Zachary
Smith
m: Mary
de Piaget

Julianna Nelson
m: William
de Piaget

978-0-425-18237-6

978-0-515-14624-0

978-0-515-13151-2

Frances   Amery

Megan MacLeod
McKinnon
m: Gideon de Piaget

978-0-515-12174-2

Jennifer MacLeod
McKinnon
m: Nicholas
de Piaget

978-0-515-14296-9

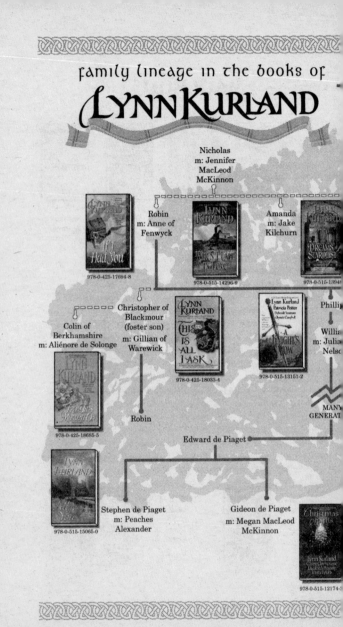

family lineage in the books of
LYNN KURLAND

Nicholas
m: Jennifer
MacLeod
McKinnon

Robin
m: Anne of
Fenwyck

978-0-425-17694-8

978-0-515-14296-9

Amanda
m: Jake
Kilchurn

978-0-515-1394

Colin of
Berkhamshire
m: Aliénore de Solonge

Christopher of
Blackmour
(foster son)
m: Gillian of
Warewick

Phillip

William
m: Julia
Nelson

978-0-425-18685-5

978-0-425-18033-4

978-0-515-13151-2

Robin

MANY
GENERAT

Edward de Piaget

Stephen de Piaget
m: Peaches
Alexander

978-0-515-15065-0

Gideon de Piaget
m: Megan MacLeod
McKinnon

Christmas
Spirits

978-0-515-12174-

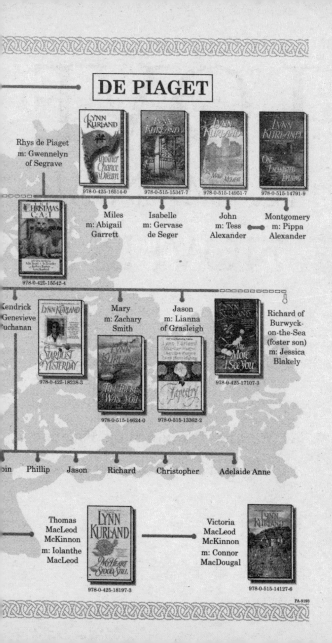

DE PIAGET

Rhys de Piaget
m: Gwennelyn
of Segrave

978-0-425-16514-0

978-0-515-15347-7

978-0-515-14951-7

978-0-515-14791-9

978-0-425-15542-4

Miles
m: Abigail
Garrett

Isabelle
m: Gervase
de Seger

John
m: Tess
Alexander

Montgomery
m: Pippa
Alexander

Kendrick
Genevieve
Buchanan

978-0-425-18238-3

Mary
m: Zachary
Smith

Jason
m: Lianna
of Grasleigh

Richard of
Burwyck-
on-the-Sea
(foster son)
m: Jessica
Blakely

978-0-425-17107-3

978-0-515-14624-0

978-0-515-13362-2

oin   Phillip   Jason   Richard   Christopher   Adelaide Anne

Thomas
MacLeod
McKinnon
m: Iolanthe
MacLeod

978-0-425-18197-3

Victoria
MacLeod
McKinnon
m: Connor
MacDougal

978-0-515-14127-6

PA-9193

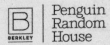